THE BREAKER

THE SECRET OF SPELLSHADOW MANOR

2

BELLA FORREST

NIGHTLIGHT PRESS

First Edition

THE BREAKER

THE SECRET OF SPELLSHADOW MANOR

2

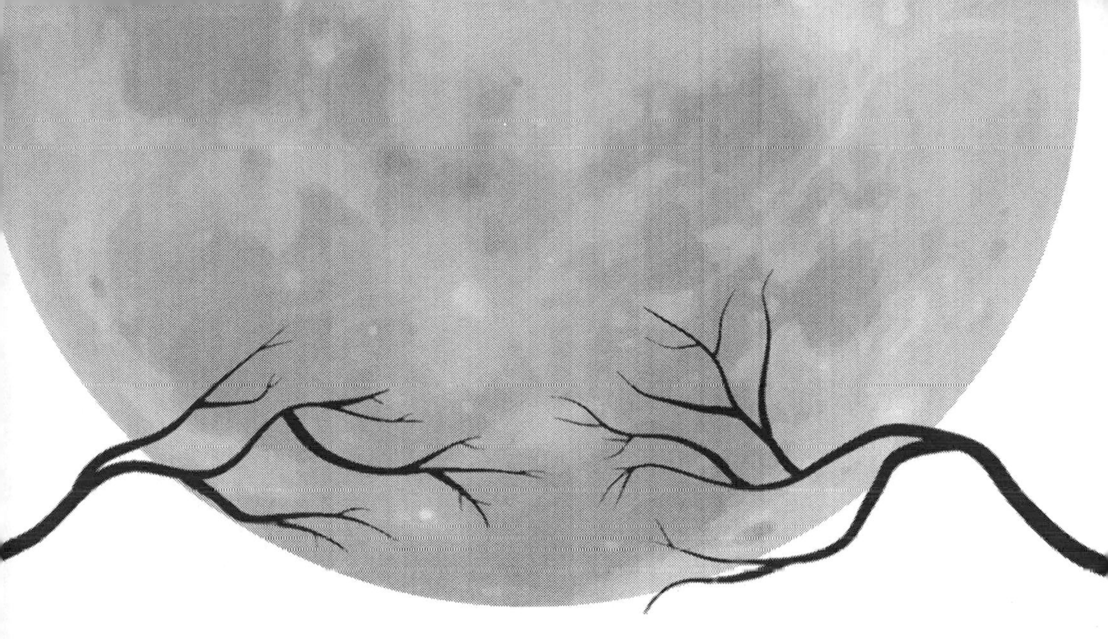

CHAPTER I

ALEX STOOD ON THE SINGED MAIN LAWN, scuffing his shoe against the white line that had been painted around the area where Derhin and Aamir had fought. The line was already fading into the dry ground, soaked up alongside the blood—Derhin's blood, spilled under the impact of Aamir's desperate fist. The battle had taken place barely two weeks ago, yet it felt like a lifetime.

He looked up at the wall, at where the creeping gray ivy had been blown away during the duel, the masonry scorched. Alex walked up to the bare patch of wall and examined it, running his hands over the smooth, rusty-red brickwork for what felt like the hundredth time, hoping to have missed something he could use to escape. He felt a familiar cold ache ripple from his fingertips to his stomach as his body prepared to retaliate against the magic of the manor.

It's going to take a lot more practice before I can destroy it, he thought. He removed his hands from the wall and stared down at them, disappointed by their ineptitude. He wished—not for the first time—that anti-magic were as seemingly simple to use as the golden light that gleamed easily and swiftly from his friends' fingertips, doing as it was told.

Alex sighed, shoving his hands into his pockets, out of sight, as he wandered over to the gates, which were still curtained in ivy. A spark of anger burned in his chest at the memory of the fateful day he had arrived at Spellshadow Manor: slipping in behind the ghostly gray creature and a zombified Natalie, wanting so much to save her that the consequences hadn't seemed so dire.

His mind drifted back to the tomb and Finder's demise, and he found himself wondering silently if they had done the right thing. Finder had seemed to know so much more about everything than everybody else, the Head being the key exception. And Elias, of course, but Elias only seemed to want to tell Alex a censored version of events—just what Elias wanted Alex to know. No more, no less. Alex wondered where the shadowy figure had gone; he hadn't seen him since before Derhin and Aamir's showdown.

With Finder dead, whatever the phantom knew had been taken to his long-overdue grave. All his knowledge about the Spellbreakers and why the school existed as it did, what the Head did behind locked doors, what exactly "graduation" entailed… All gone. All of it. Elias knew some of the answers, Alex had no doubt about that, but he wondered if Elias would prove an even harder nut to crack than Finder might have been. A shiver of uncertainty trailed up his spine as he recalled the ghost's ghastly gray face and tattered rags. What on earth had made Finder agree to let the Head do that to him? Alex had the feeling it must have been a matter of life or death, and that worried him deeply.

Still, Alex wasn't stupid; he knew Finder wouldn't have simply given up all his information. It would've likely taken more magic and anti-magic than Natalie and he had to spare, and they may still have ended up with nothing. At least they had stopped Finder from recruiting more students to the school for a while. That was a decent consolation prize. Regardless, Alex couldn't shake the peculiar feeling that they had made some sort of mistake in getting rid of Finder so quickly. After so many years in phantom slavery, Finder had been fed up with the Head—they had heard him say as much. Maybe they could have broken him; maybe he would have given them some answers.

Now, they'd never know.

Alex's rage toward the manor burned a little brighter, and he kicked the wall in frustration, wincing as a twinge of pain shot through his foot.

"Maybe it's not so wise to kick magic walls," Natalie's familiar voice called out from behind him, with its exotic French undertone.

Alex turned. The color had come back to Natalie's face. Shortly after Derhin had been dragged away, kicking and screaming, to wherever they had taken him, Natalie had brightened up, a rosiness returning to her pale cheeks, a liveliness that hadn't been there for months. Natalie seemed to have come back to life, the curse's chokehold no longer draining her of energy. In the week or so since, she had become healthier than ever—her vitality restored, her black hair shining, her skin glowing, her eyes glittering.

Alex was glad to see her looking better, but it was hard not to remember Ellabell's whispered words from the library: *"Just kill whoever cursed her."*

Derhin must really be dead. Alex shivered at the thought, still hearing the man's terrified pleas ringing in his ears. *"We were going to escape together."* The words could not be shut out as they came back to Alex, spoken so desperately by the doomed professor. Lintz's face haunted Alex too, the resignation as he had said he'd do it—whatever *it* was…

At least it was nice to see Natalie smiling again.

"Yeah, that wasn't the smartest idea I've ever had." Alex grinned, his toe still throbbing.

"You had the same thought as me, huh?" she muttered, nodding toward the bare patch of wall. Strands of silky black hair fell over one eye, and she brushed them back behind her ear in a single sweeping motion.

"Yeah."

"I keep hoping the duel might have caused a weakness in the gate that I just haven't spotted yet," she added, with a nod toward the unharmed metal.

Alex sighed wearily. "Me too."

They stood on the grass in silence for a while, their gazes focused on the top of the wall, their arms folded against the light breeze whispering around them. Overhead, the sky was angry looking, bruised clouds gathering in a dark, metallic gray swarm, rippling out to purplish edges. Between the clouds, the sky was a dusky pink, the day coming to a close. It looked sinister, and the scent of rain was in the air. At least it would wash the blood away, once and for all, Alex thought grimly.

"Alex?" Natalie said quietly.

Alex turned his face toward her.

"Do you think the Head still doesn't know?" she asked, her voice barely a whisper.

It was the very question Alex had been wondering himself, and to hear it out loud made his heart beat faster. He saw the fear on Natalie's face, and hoped she couldn't see it on his own.

"I'm not sure," he replied. "I don't think he knows. I'm pretty sure Finder used to be away for long periods of time anyway, snatching kids for the school." He paused, thinking back. "I remember seeing him leave from the library window once, and he didn't come back again for like two, three weeks… I doubt the Head will have noticed yet. We still have time," he added, trying to reassure Natalie, though he knew very well that Finder could have come back to the manor within that time. It was a hope Alex was clinging to, that his hunch was right.

Neither of them was convinced by the tale, but they both pretended to be for the moment. Natalie didn't continue her line of questioning.

"Any sign of Jari?" Alex asked, wanting to change the subject.

"I saw him on his way to the boys' dormitories," Natalie replied.

"I'll go see what he's up to." Alex tried not to leave Jari alone for too long these days. Since Aamir had returned a few days ago from wherever it was the Head had taken him—he still refused to say—they'd barely seen the older boy, except in two classes.

"Goodnight, Alex." Natalie gave him a smile, though it didn't quite reach her eyes. She was fidgety, and Alex could see that she was still nervous about the Head discovering what had happened to Finder. He was too.

"Goodnight. Try not to worry too much," he said, patting her on the arm.

"Will try," she mumbled, dropping her gaze as Alex tried not to hear the note of dishonesty in her voice.

"When are you coming in?" he asked, pointing toward the gaping mouth of the manor's entrance.

"Not just yet. I would like to stay outside a little longer, see if we have missed any exploded holes," she explained with a wry grin, glancing up at the blasts in the creeping gray ivy. Some of the blows had gouged dents in the brickwork, but nothing even near big enough to escape from.

Alex laughed. "Okay, well… see you soon."

"Yes, mother hen," Natalie teased.

Alex grinned, then headed back to the manor, his shoes crunching the wispy grass beneath as he walked.

The hallways were mostly empty as Alex made his way, his footsteps echoing loudly. The great walls of the corridors cast long shadows, clawing at his feet as he passed. The only light came from the flaming torches that burned brightly in the brackets attached to the stonework, making it difficult to see what lay ahead. Outside the windows was a darkened forest with creepers dangling, snakelike, from the boughs of huge trees, creatures fluttering across every now and then in a burst of movement. Bats, perhaps, with their leathery wings flapping. From another window, Alex saw a long, pebbled beach in chilly daylight, the sky overhead a stony gray as the savage sea charged against the shore time and time again, the waves snapping in tooth-like peaks. It didn't look particularly inviting, and Alex was certain the water would be freezing if one waded in to swim.

He was glad when the dormitories finally came into sight. He crossed over the familiar border to the boys' section and walked down a few more passageways, knowing the route by heart now, until he came to his own room. He didn't bother to knock as he entered.

Jari was sitting on his bed, and turned with a wide smile as Alex stepped into the room. His eyes lit up with excitement as he crawled to the edge of his bed and sat up on his knees.

"Where have you been? Having some alone time with Natalie again?" Jari grinned.

"Just out in the grounds, checking on the ivy situation." Alex couldn't help but smile in return. Jari's cheerfulness, even at the worst of times, was infectious.

"Any luck?" Jari asked.

Alex shrugged. "Not really," he admitted.

"That's a shame… Can you believe Aamir is a teacher now?" Jari asked, flopping back down onto the mattress and staring up at the ceiling. "How cool is that?"

Alex sat down on his own bed, pulling out his pajamas. "It's pretty cool." Jari's fixation on Aamir's "promotion" was starting to get on Alex's nerves; yes, it was a major relief that Aamir had swerved away from graduation, but they had no evidence whatsoever that this promotion was going to turn out to be a good thing for Aamir.

"I mean, the way he took down Derhin like that—I can't get over it!" Jari whooped, punching the air, imitating Aamir's last blow to Derhin's face. "He's a hero."

"I guess so." Alex tried not to picture the blood on the grass, but Derhin's last-ditch attempt at survival replayed over and over in his mind… That golden monster he had summoned, seemingly from the ground. What *was* that thing, anyway? The memory still bothered him.

"What do you mean you 'guess so'? He was amazing! I can't believe he's a teacher." Jari laughed. "I mean, I always knew he was going to go places, but—this is awesome! I bet he'll give us some perks, too," Jari proclaimed, peering around the side of his bed to eye Alex.

"Like what?" Alex asked.

"I don't know… Like, teach us really cool stuff. Some dark magic. Proper, complicated stuff that he might have picked up… I bet he will." Jari lay back again.

"That'd be interesting," Alex humored his friend, though dark magic wouldn't be good for him. The more complex the magic, the harder it was for Alex to cope with.

"We should ask him tonight—ask him what goes on behind that blue line." Jari winked, sitting up again, restlessly shifting around on his mattress with sheer excitement. "Do you reckon he knows where Esmerelda sleeps?

I bet he does... *Oh, Esmerelda, my darling!*" Jari pursed his lips and squeezed his eyes shut, pretending to kiss the air as he wrapped his arms around himself.

Alex snorted. "That's gross, Jari. Aamir does *not* have a thing for Esmerelda...And anyway, I don't think Aamir is ever going to tell us anything like that."

"What do you mean?" Jari replied, the humor fading from his voice.

Alex sighed. "Aamir's golden band."

"So?" Jari snapped.

"*So*, I'm just saying Aamir won't be able to tell us much. Don't expect too much from him," Alex replied, holding his hands up in surrender to Jari's sudden mood swing.

"Aamir is stronger than some stupid golden line," Jari mumbled after a pause. He turned away from Alex to pick at the threads in his sheets.

Alex didn't want to burst Jari's bubble more than he already had. Changing quickly into his pajamas and sitting back on the bed, he wondered if he might be able to break the golden line on Aamir's wrist. Alex presumed it was made from the same magic as the lines in the forbidden hallways and tombs of the manor, and they had proven pretty easy to break so far—a few stray spears of magic to duck and run from, but nothing major. Then again, those lines weren't attached to a living, breathing person. The idea sat uneasily with Alex. He didn't know what might happen if he broke the line and it hurt Aamir in some way; he wasn't sure he could forgive himself for something like that.

He was about to ask Jari for his opinion on the matter when he caught sight of the other boy staring over at the empty bed in the room, still made from the day before the Head had taken Aamir away, when he had last slept there. The absence of Aamir in their dorm still felt wrong, like some important piece was missing.

"Well, I'm going to hit the hay," Alex muttered, trying to distract Jari from the empty bed.

Jari nodded. "I'm just going to… stay up a little longer," he said quietly.

"Okay… goodnight, Jari." Alex sighed as he nestled down beneath the sheets, turning off the light.

"Goodnight," Jari replied faintly.

Alex's eyes were drawn to the empty bed, bathed in moonlight, as he lay beneath the covers. Everything was crisp and neat and in place, the pillows perfectly plumped and the quilt turned over at the top, as if Aamir had never slept there.

Despite Jari still holding out hope that he might return to share their dorm, Alex knew, deep down, that he never would again.

CHAPTER 2

THE MESS HALL WAS ABUZZ WITH ACTIVITY AS morning light filtered in through the windows, some stray beams shining through from the slow sunrise. Alex and Natalie were seated at one of the small circular tables in the far corner, discussing Jari and Aamir. In between snippets of conversation, Natalie was wolfing down a plate of toast with a large glass of orange juice. Her appetite had returned with her new lease of life, now that she was curse-free, and Alex felt a pang of envy as he watched her eat. He wished he could. Alex had lost his appetite somewhat, pushing two squares of limp, buttered toast around on his plate, glancing up at the door every time it swung open, hoping to see Jari emerge.

When Alex and Jari had awoken that morning, to their unease, Aamir's bed had been stripped bare, the bedclothes stacked at the end of the mattress, though neither Jari nor Alex could recall anyone coming in during the night to perform this strange task. An image of a short, peculiar woman jogged Alex's memory—Siren Mave, with her back alleyways and secret passageways around the manor. *Maybe she aids in the removal of students as well as the enrollment of them*, Alex thought as he tore a hole in a corner of his soggy toast. Yet, he didn't remember hearing a soul, not even a tiptoe of feet. Nothing had stirred or woken him the night before. Whatever it had been, it was stealthy.

Jari had simply stared at the deconstructed bed for a good half hour that morning, his face blank. Alex had felt bad leaving Jari alone in the dormitory, but the boy had encouraged him to go on ahead, promising not to be too long. Breakfast was almost at its end, and Jari was still nowhere to be seen.

Finally, just as Alex was about to go look for him, Jari stepped into the mess hall, his face pale, purple bags beneath his eyes. He smiled faintly when he saw his friends in the corner and raised a hand to them before plucking an apple from the silver fruit dish and making his way over.

"Any sign of Aamir?" he asked hopefully, sitting down

in one of the empty seats.

Alex shook his head. "Afraid not."

"You sure?" Jari turned to look around the mess hall, eyes squinting, as if that might make their friend appear. "He didn't come for breakfast?" Jari added, almost to himself, a flash of disappointment crossing his face.

"Not unless he was here really early," Natalie chipped in, swallowing the last of her breakfast.

"That must be it—he always likes to eat early." Jari nodded, as if that made perfect sense. "We'll see him in first period anyway, won't we?" He smiled cheerfully at his two friends before turning to the rosy apple in his hand, lifting it to his lips and biting into it with a loud crunch.

Natalie passed a secret look of concern over to Alex, but Alex could only shrug; there was nothing they could do. Jari was determined to remain optimistic, and who were they to stand in his way?

Jari chattered happily as they left the mess hall and headed to their first lesson, previously Professor Derhin's but now belonging to the rightful victor, Professor Nagi. Outside, they waited with a few of the other students, discussing the texts they had learned the day before, preparing for the session.

After five minutes, Professor Nagi called them in. They bustled into the lesson, ready to see their friend and former classmate. The last time they had seen him, he had been happy to be in their company again, if still stressed out by the line on his wrist and the new information in his head. The three of them had expected to be greeted in much the same way—at least with a smile or a whispered welcome—as they entered the classroom.

However, it did not seem like that was going to be the case. Aamir stood at the front of the class, dressed in his sleek black robes, the sleeves covering the golden line the three of them knew to be there. He addressed them politely, asking them to take their seats, as he turned and began to write on the blackboard. He wrote much quicker than the sluggish Derhin ever had, his lettering curving and curling elegantly, but the words seemed familiar somehow, as if taken from the very same book Derhin had used.

Alex glanced at Natalie, frowning. It didn't look like the lesson's format was going to change at all from Derhin's dry style. Jari, however, could not be swayed from his optimism as he watched his long-time friend with a grin, trying to get his attention at the back of the classroom. He sparked up a small shower of fireworks when Aamir turned back to them with the instruction that his students copy the given information and attempt the spell if they had time. His voice, usually so bright and rich with the flavor of his heritage, was stern and dulled as he ignored the flurry of golden sparks at the back of the classroom.

The other students did not seem surprised by this change in Aamir. There was a quiet murmur of casual gossip, whispered in low voices, before they simply began the work they had been set, their fingers moving quickly across paper, copying out the information. Even Natalie and Alex set to it, but Jari was determined.

"Aamir?" Jari raised his hand.

The room went silent.

Aamir turned in Jari's direction, a look of frustration passing across his face. "Please, stop what you are doing," Aamir said, addressing the whole class. Everyone looked up, pausing in their task as they tried hard not to look at Jari.

"This is a note for all of you," Aamir began calmly. "This class is now taught by me, in replacement of Professor Derhin, and you will all address me as Professor Nagi from now on. I will neither accept nor tolerate any other term of address—I am no longer your classmate. I am your teacher, and you shall speak to me accordingly, with the appropriate level of respect." His gaze focused for a moment on every single student, hammering the message home. His voice was stern and steady, his intention clear, and completely devoid of the warmth his friends were used to. Instead, there was a silent threat, bubbling just beneath the surface.

"Yes, Professor Nagi," every voice in the room chorused. All except one.

"Now, continue," Aamir instructed, turning again to write on the board.

"Aamir?" Jari raised his hand again, his tone bold. The

room froze, everybody's eyes snapping to the blond-haired boy with his hand up and a mischievous smile on his face.

Aamir turned very slowly, his stern gaze resting on his best friend. "Jari, you will address me as Professor Nagi," he insisted. His voice was even, though Alex picked up on a tiny hint of something like regret in the way he said 'Jari.'

Jari frowned. "I just need some help," he said, his cheerful voice tightening. Alex noticed Jari's hand was shaking.

"Very well," Aamir sighed, making his way through the desks toward Jari.

Aamir stopped beside the desk, waiting impatiently for Jari's question. A glance of panic passed from the younger boy to the older, but Aamir only tapped his foot on the stone floor, the noise echoing across the room. "Aamir, I just—" Jari began, but Aamir cut him off sharply.

"You will address me as Professor Nagi. I will not tell you again," Aamir snapped, the students in the room shifting in their seats with discomfort.

"Aamir, I—" Jari tried again.

"You will address me appropriately, Jari," Aamir growled, his voice low.

Jari sat back in his seat, biting back tears as he looked up to his former friend. "I just wanted to ask you a question," he said quietly.

"What is it, Jari?" Aamir said, very impatient now.

Jari shook his head. "I forgot," he answered miserably,

dropping his gaze.

"You forgot?" Aamir sighed heavily. "In future, make sure you *have* a question, Jari." Aamir strode back to his place at the front of the classroom.

The class returned to their work, including Jari, who barely looked up. Alex glanced at Jari, mouthing to him, *You okay?* Jari nodded slowly, his hands balled into tight fists.

"I don't understand," Jari whispered.

"I'm sure he doesn't mean it," Alex whispered back.

"What is wrong with him?" Jari asked, his eyes watery.

"Jari? Is there any particular reason you are talking when you should be working?" Aamir frowned at Jari, who looked up at him, his cheeks hot with embarrassment.

"I just wanted to ask Alex something," Jari said.

"Well, don't. Get back to your work," Aamir said, his eyes warning Jari as he moved to turn away again.

"Sorry, Aamir," Jari muttered.

Aamir's whole body whirled back around, his eyes glittering with annoyance. "You will address me as Professor Nagi! I will *not* warn you again."

"I'm sorry," Jari said, horrified. He hadn't meant to say 'Aamir' that time, Alex could tell; it had simply come out that way.

"I'm sorry… what?" Aamir waited, poised to snap again.

"I'm sorry… Professor Nagi." Jari struggled to say the

unnatural words, choking them out.

"That's better. Now, if you can be quiet and get on with your work, you might actually make it through this lesson." Aamir exhaled, tilting his neck from side to side as if he had a crick there that needed stretching.

Eventually, a sense of calm settled over the room as the students all went about their business. Natalie started to get the spell up on its feet, and Jari joined her. It was a spell to create and maintain two three-dimensional objects, simultaneously, on the table in front of them. Natalie had managed to forge a candlestick on one side of her, but was struggling with a small wisp of golden mist on the other side. Nobody was sure what it was meant to be, and Natalie laughed, explaining it was supposed to be a flower. Alex stood beside Natalie, pretending to conjure with his hands, even though nothing appeared. He didn't dare try too hard, in case he managed to manifest an object made of ice and snow. Aamir ignored him for the most part, understanding why. At least enough friendship remained between them for Aamir to keep Alex's anti-magic a secret.

Jari, meanwhile, had a small, perfectly formed carousel on the right-hand side of him, on the wooden tabletop. The golden horses whirled around in a circle, rising and falling beneath the elegant domed roof. He grinned, pleased with it, holding it there as he conjured a second object. On his left-hand side, he began to form a creature of some sort, bigger than the carousel. He waved his left hand delicately, in a slim figure eight, and pressed his middle finger into his palm, narrowing his eyes in focus. His other hand moved in an almost identical way, and the creature on the table slowly became more detailed. First, Jari added gleaming panels, which looked almost like scales and formed the beginnings of two beady black eyes, peering out from the wispy swirls of golden energy. These were followed by silvery strands that stood up, horn-like, from the creature's rounded head, and by six delicate legs sticking out from beneath the metallic body. He puffed out the rest of the creature's carapace, rounding its back and bringing its head to a point, adding thin lines and swirls of detail onto the magical paneling.

Alex nodded at him, impressed and slightly envious. The beetle was familiar, looking very much like the clockwork one they had almost broken into pieces the year before. Alex smiled sadly at his friend, wondering if he had made the beetle on purpose. Alex wasn't sure; Jari seemed too cheerful to be reminiscing, with no hint of sadness on his grinning face, but it might have been there in his subconscious. Jari held both objects in place on the rough surface of the table.

"A carousel and a beetle!" Jari said with a laugh, the sound drawing Aamir's attention. He eyed Jari stiffly from across the classroom, then warily approached to examine the work.

Clearly pleased by the sudden attention from Aamir,

Jari became bolder… too bold. "Hey, Aamir, remember the one you made out of—" He didn't get to finish. Aamir slammed his fist down on the desk. In fright, Jari's hands jerked upward, the two objects disappearing in a tangled mist of splintered golden magic, the sparks falling to the desk like the last flakes of a snowfall.

"I said I would not warn you again." Aamir glowered. "You will address me appropriately, or you will leave this lesson!"

"But I just wanted to say, about the—" Jari panicked. Alex wanted to help but knew better than to butt in. He had never seen their friend this way.

"Do you understand?" Aamir nearly shouted. The other students had turned to stare again.

"Aamir, why—"

It was the last straw for Aamir.

"Get out," he said, his voice a tight growl, his eyes flashing.

"Aamir?" Jari's voice was unbearably sad, pleading.

"Get *out*!" Aamir yelled, pointing at the door. His billowing sleeve revealed just a sliver of the golden line clasped around his wrist.

Jari opened his mouth as if he was about to say something else, but closed it again, thinking better of it. Slowly, he picked up his things, his head down and his shoulders slumped, and walked the short distance to the door. He opened it and stepped outside, letting it fall closed with a soft click. The whole class watched his walk of shame, including Natalie and Alex, who turned to Aamir with expressions of confusion and disappointment. Alex wanted to confront Aamir for treating Jari that way, for speaking to him like that. But he understood, as Aamir met his gaze, that if he did he would simply be sent out too.

When the lesson was over, the class hurried from the room, passing a now defiant-looking Jari leaning against the hallway wall with his arms crossed. Natalie and Alex hung back until Jari slipped back into the near-empty classroom. Aamir turned to the trio as he sat down in his chair, visibly relaxing, as if a weight had slid from his shoulders. He sighed and lowered his head into his hands. Jari stood beside Natalie and Alex—an accusatory jury, waiting for an explanation.

"I'm sorry, Jari," Aamir said quietly, too ashamed to lift his gaze.

"Why did you do that?" Jari asked, the hurt still clinging to his voice.

Aamir shook his head. "Jari, I'm so sorry. It's this thing," he explained, exposing his wrist. The golden line sputtered and sparked across his copper skin. "I can't be seen showing favoritism. I've been… warned," he said, gritting his teeth. The golden line seemed to thrum and glow brighter, the band apparently stinging him for revealing even that much.

"Did you have to be quite so harsh?" Alex asked.

"I know… I'm sorry," Aamir repeated, his face tired. "I don't know what came over me," he added, a look of panic glimmering for a moment in the depths of his warm brown eyes.

"I forgive you," Jari said softly.

"You do?"

"I do. You're my best friend—of course I do." Jari smiled.

Aamir winced, perhaps at the golden line's bite. "Thank you."

"We're going to go spar tonight in the cellar. Will you come?" Jari asked.

"I'm not sure, Jari." Aamir sighed. "I'll try, but I can't promise."

"We can break out a new wine bottle. I might even let you land a punch." Jari waggled his eyebrows.

Aamir let out a low chuckle. "I promise I'll try."

It was enough for Jari. Aamir stood, and the four of them made their way out into the hallway. Aamir gave them a shy wave as he set off in the opposite direction, walking toward the forbidden corridors hidden behind the sapphire-blue line of the teachers' quarters.

Jari's eyes followed his long-time companion as he walked away from them. Natalie and Alex exchanged a look of concern. There was a lost expression on Jari's face, as if he couldn't quite process what had just happened.

"Aamir is still our friend. He just has to act a bit

differently now," Natalie said, putting her hand on Jari's back in an attempt to steer him away from the sight of Aamir's disappearing figure.

"Yeah, he's still our friend," Alex jumped in. "It's that golden line forcing him to talk like that—it's not him. He said so himself." Alex recalled the wince on Aamir's face when the golden band had sparked against his skin and given him a warning nip.

"I know," Jari muttered, tearing his eyes away from the now-empty corridor.

"It'll all be fine. *He* will be fine," Alex reassured.

"Sorry, guys, I have somewhere I need to be," Jari said suddenly, shaking his head as if trying to shake off his worries. "I'll see you tonight?"

"Seven o'clock."

"See you at seven," Jari said as he disappeared down the corridor and was swallowed up by the darkness.

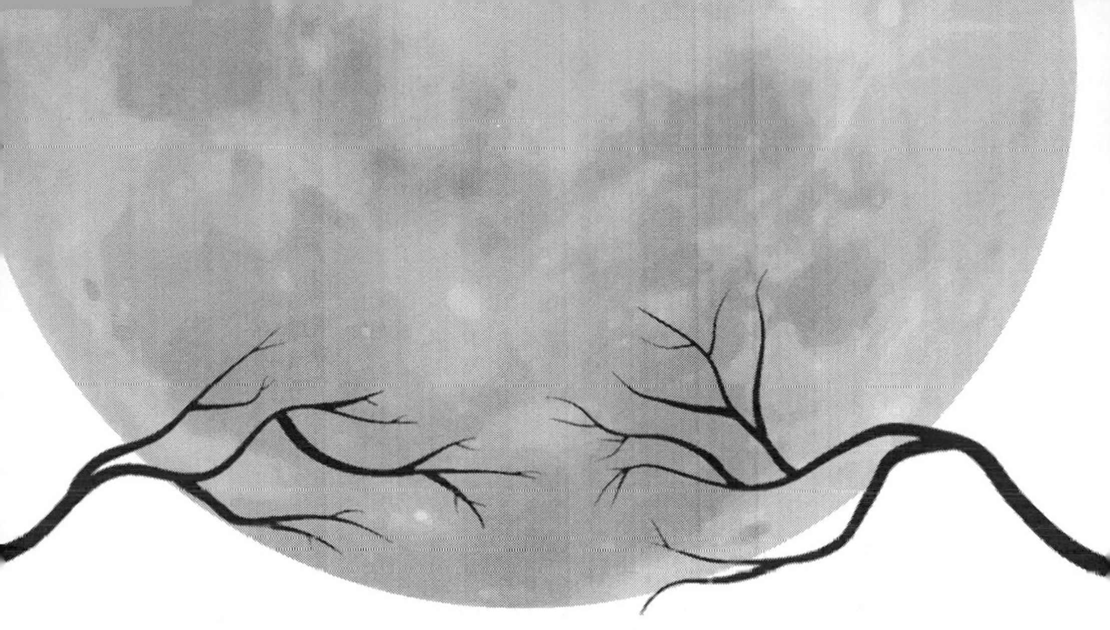

CHAPTER 3

ALEX SAT IN THE LIBRARY, TUCKED AWAY IN ONE corner, with a stack of unread books on the table in front of him. He had asked Natalie to come with him, hoping for some company to distract him and quiet his mind from the confusion of the morning, but she was busy. Professor Renmark, one of the teachers they had so far avoided, had asked her to come along to a private session, wanting to meet her before the start of the academic year.

Renmark taught second year onwards and had a fearsome reputation. Natalie had seemed baffled by the request to meet him, but was excited, too—she was always eager to learn as much as she could, to strengthen her growing powers. They had heard from the hallway gossip of other students that Renmark was a particularly strong wizard. Natalie had told Alex, thrill in her voice, that she was sure Renmark was going to teach her some new, fascinating things from books they had never even seen before—maybe even some dark stuff. Alex had tried to talk her out of venturing too far into the study of darker magic, particularly anything in the realm of life magic, but doubted he was going to change Natalie's mind when new magical knowledge was at stake.

So, he found himself alone in the library, flicking through textbooks in an attempt to look busy. Outside, the sky was unusually bright and cloudless, a clear blue, the sunlight gleaming in through the big window that ran along the far edge. With a groan, he got up and headed toward the great columns that held the stacked shelves of books. Other students flew up effortlessly around him, their feet landing delicately on the level they aimed for. Alex grumbled as he began the long climb. After getting off at the right floor, he shook his hands out, his palms sore from the trek up, and gazed down at the ground, so far below. It was a good thing, really, that he didn't suffer from vertigo. Even so, he quickly stepped away from the railing, not wanting to tempt fate.

The stacks themselves smelled of ancient paper and well-thumbed leather, and he inhaled the musty scent as he wandered through, his fingers brushing along the spines, searching for the book he needed. He stopped midway through a shelf, startled by a figure on the floor, resting her back against the books. Her knees were drawn up almost to her chin, her curly brown hair tied up in a neat bun at the back of her head. Ellabell hadn't noticed him, and he felt torn as to whether to cough or something, to make his presence known, or whether to just leave her to her peace and quiet.

He was about to tiptoe backward, away from her, when he remembered the note in his pocket—the torn piece of paper that had been sandwiched between the pages of the book Elias had given him, the *Historica Magica*. By now, he almost knew the words by heart: *Of our havens, nine remained. Of those nine, we now have four. If you are magical, seek these places. Kingstone Keep. Falleaf House. Stillwater House. Spellshadow Manor.*

Glancing down at Ellabell, Alex wondered whether to ask her about the note and its cryptic wording. She was good at that sort of thing, he recalled. He had just put his hand in his pocket, fingers curling around the little folded square, when she looked up.

"Alex?" she said, a little surprised.

"Sorry, didn't mean to disturb you," he replied.

"Not at all—just catching up on some light reading." She smiled, lifting the hefty cover of her book to show the title *A Comprehensive Guide to Botanical Properties and*

Natural Remedies.

"Any good?" Alex asked.

"Bestseller," Ellabell replied, her blue eyes sparkling with amusement. "What're you up here for?"

Fingers still curled around the small square of paper, Alex found that he really wanted to tell her about the note and see what she had to say. Yet something held him back. He remembered the curious look she had given him the last time they'd spoken, and her observations about secrets. Unfurling his hand, he decided he would keep his own secret a little longer—just until he could be sure he could trust the intelligent young woman who sat on the floor before him.

"I'm just looking for a few books on... mechanics, clockwork, that type of thing," Alex said, after a stilted pause that lasted just a little too long.

Ellabell looked up at him with that same curious expression, one eyebrow slightly raised—a look that told Alex she knew he was keeping secrets still, at least from her. She got to her feet, brushing the front of her skirt. Alex thought she was about to walk past him and leave, but she reached up to one of the taller shelves instead and brought down a slim, leather-bound book, handing it to him with a small smile.

"*Wrexham's Introduction to Clockwork.* A good place to start," she explained as Alex took the book from her.

"Thanks."

"No worries. There are a few other good ones. Worth a read, if that's your cup of tea, anyway," she said, beginning to write a list of titles on a small scrap of paper, torn from one of her notebooks. On it were recommendations for other mechanical books, neatly written in her precise, cursive script, which was elegant and distinctly feminine.

"Thank you. This is great." Alex smiled as he read the titles.

"No problem. Good to see you taking an interest in something," she teased, gathering her books from the floor. There was a mighty stack of them; it looked like Ellabell might topple under the sheer weight, but she held them easily, balancing them like a skilled circus performer.

"Hey, don't let me disrupt you if you want to keep reading," Alex said.

"I needed to get going anyway," she told him.

"Well, can I at least give you a hand?"

"No, I'm good, thank you." Ellabell moved away, toward the edge of the stack. "Happy hunting!" Then she jumped over the banister. Alex knew she was capable of magic, but all the same, he found himself running to the edge, looking down just in time to see her land gracefully, her books still neatly stacked. She flashed a look back up at him, as if to say, *See?*

Seeing that Ellabell was safely on the ground, Alex tucked the tan leather book under his arm and clambered up another floor or two, walking to a small alcove at the end of one stack. In the alcove sat a giant, dusty tome—the library Index. He heaved the gigantic pages to the letters he was looking for, flurries of dust flying up into his face as the rest of the pages came down with an unceremonious slam. First, he looked under 'H,' hoping to see the word 'haven.' An obvious choice, but Alex was optimistic. The word itself was not there. Undeterred, he tried the other three names instead: *Stillwater House, Falleaf House,* and *Kingstone Keep.* Half expecting there to be nothing, Alex was surprised to find two or three books per name, preserved among the stacks. He quickly wrote down the numbers, his heart pounding with excitement, as he raced off through the towers to find the corresponding books.

The first ones should have been up on the very top floor of the second tower. But, as he ran his finger along the numbered spines, his hand stopped short at a small but noticeable gap. Between the numbers, three books were missing—the three books that had appeared under the name *Stillwater House* in the Index. Frustrated, Alex checked the next set of numbers, and climbed back down to the second floor of the tower, walking along until he came to the right section. Again, where *Falleaf House* ought to have been, there was a small but noticeable absence of books. Trying not to lose faith, he walked over to the third tower and climbed to the very top, where the last of the books should have been. He didn't even need to see it as he neared. The gap was obvious; there were no books left on *Kingstone Keep*. They had all been removed. On purpose, Alex knew, clenching his jaw in annoyance as he felt the familiar burn of rage toward the manor and the man—or thing—who ran it.

Defeated, Alex plucked the other square of paper from the pocket of his pants, deciding to scavenge for information on the Spellbreakers instead. Slowly, he clambered back up the endless ladders to the alcove with the Index tucked away, and scanned the 'S' section until he came to the word he was looking for. When he had first come to check for any information on Spellbreakers, after hearing the word for the first time, he had been surprised to even see it listed, but it had been there, clear as day. It still was, although there were limited books on the subject. Only four, to his knowledge, and he had already been through one of them without much success. But there was enough uncharted territory to keep him busy for a while. Three books remained, begging to be read. He scurried up to the correct floor and plucked the further three tomes from the shelf, wishing he didn't have to climb back down one-handed with them tucked under his other arm.

Once safely on solid ground, Alex wandered back over to his spot by the window. The sky had darkened with clouds. He sat down, the armchair swallowing him in a cozy embrace, as he flipped open the first of the books, entitled *The Families of the Old World*. It was as dull as the *Historica Magica*, but Alex forced himself to read. It covered much of the same ground, but seemed to repeat six names over and over—the main bloodlines of the Spellbreaker clans. He picked up the other book, curious. In it, it repeated the same thing. Six names, over and over, the only names of any real importance. Six great houses of the Spellbreakers: *Rorschach, Bessamer, Volstag, Muldoon, Wyvern,* and *Copperfield.*

When he picked up the third book and riffled through it, his anger almost overwhelmed him. He could feel the heat of it in his cheeks, the mist of it in his eyes, as he traced the words from page to page. It was a fiction book—a great, heroic novel marking the myths and tales of the Mages of old and their archnemeses, the Spellbreakers. His people were always the bad guys, and the writer of the fictional story had relished in descriptions of their demise. Bodies ripped apart by golden explosions of *good* magic; warriors bursting into shards of pure light from the pierce of a Mage's spell; Spellbreaker children and women crying to see their fathers and brothers and husbands turned to glittering dust—the fear, knowing they would be next. The writer delighted in the Spellbreakers' misery, and it was almost more than Alex could take. He slammed the book shut, startling a nearby student.

Alex felt a pang of sadness twist at his heart. Six houses, with such a rich and wonderful history in each one. And yet where were they now? The last of them were buried in a watery grave, with nobody to remember their names. Nobody to remember they even existed, except in victorious, vile tales of magical battles, from the very folk who had put them under the lake. Whole families, whole lineages wiped out by Mages, without so much as an apology for their genocide. The bitterness welled up in Alex as he looked around at the clueless students—the very kind of people who had delighted in the deaths of his ancestors, and they didn't even know. They had no idea a different kind of Mage had existed once. His kind. Alex wasn't sure they'd even care.

A chill ran through him. Looking down, he quietly gasped in horror as he saw that wisps of black and silver ice coiled around his hands and across his arms—his anti-magic aura, brimming through his skin. He closed his eyes and focused, trying to rein in the tendrils of anti-magic that threatened to break free. He breathed slowly and deliberately. Though the images of his murdered ancestors broke through in vivid fragments, he managed to regain control of his senses, pushing the imaginings to the back of his mind.

When he opened his eyes again, the coils of anti-magic had disappeared. He breathed a low sigh of relief, hoping nobody had seen his outburst.

He shoved the book of fiction out of the way with the heel of his shoe, and set his copy of *Historica Magica* on the table to join the rest. Seeing those six names had made him curious about his own bloodline. Alex figured he must be in there somewhere. He was a Spellbreaker, after all. He had to belong to one of the bloodlines—a smaller one, or a weaker one, maybe. One that was less important. The two books beside his, one in a red cover, the other in dark blue, only really mentioned the six main houses, but he knew the *Historica Magica* contained every name in Spellbreaker history. Boring, unending lists of names and houses and bloodlines and people long dead. His people, his heritage, had to be in there somewhere.

He flicked to the index at the back of the *Historica* and searched for 'Webber,' but could find no mention of his surname. Dismayed, he glanced out the window, catching sight of a glittering spire and buildings beyond the horizon. Familiar buildings. The ever-shifting scenery beyond the grounds had chosen to show his hometown that day. He couldn't remember the last time it had done that. To think that his house was just through the gate and up a dozen or so streets—so close, and yet…

Unbidden, the memory of a blurry photograph returned to Alex's mind. He had found it in a crumpled old shoebox, years ago, when he was helping his mother with spring cleaning. It had been stuffed at the back of the wardrobe in her room, gathering a blizzard of dust, when he had happened upon it. Lifting the lid, he had rummaged through the small number of belongings within, not expecting to find much. He had come across a faded sonogram from his first scan, his first baby blanket, a bright green pacifier, and a small, cream-colored teddy bear with multi-colored buttons down the front.

Alex remembered reaching in to remove the blanket—baby blue and still soft to the touch—when something fell from within the fleecy layers. A rectangle of card, face down, a small notation on the bottom right corner, written in blue ink that had turned green over time. It read, '*Marianne & Alexei 1995.*' He had bent to pick it up from the carpet. At that moment, the photograph was torn away from him, his mother snatching it from his grasp. He had looked up to see her standing in front of him with her eyes wide, cradling it to her chest as if it were a precious jewel he had unearthed.

The unexpected image of his mother, crystal clear in his mind—healthy and so much younger—made his heart clench.

He recalled asking who it was in the photo, and tears had sprung into his mother's beautiful blue eyes.

"Your father and I," she had said.

"My father?" Alex remembered saying, and seeing his mother nod. He had asked to see the picture, and she had shown it to him with a pull of reluctance. A faded, blurry thing, the photo made it nearly impossible to make out a clear image of the man or the woman. He had only known it to be his mother because she had said it was her. The man, however, was a stranger. Alex could not have pointed him out in a lineup.

But, remembering that moment so vividly, and seeing his history laid out on the library table before him, Alex couldn't help but dwell upon his father. That faded man in the blurry photograph, kept in a shoebox the whole of Alex's life. He knew nothing of the strange man who had created half of him—had never seen him, met him, or heard him mentioned much. His mother hadn't liked to talk about him, so Alex had stopped pushing.

Where else would this power have come from but him? Alex pondered, his eyes on the clouds beginning to trail across the overcast sky. He tried hard to sharpen the detail around the man in the photo, but he couldn't envision his face. Alex looked back at the list of names in the index, a thought niggling at the back of his mind: *Is my father's name among these bloodlines?*

'Webber' came from his mother's family, not his father's. His father's name could well be there, in front of his very eyes, and he wouldn't know it. He had never dared to ask his mother more about his father than she was willing to tell, and she had never been very willing to say much on the subject. Alex knew his father's name was Alexei, but that was all. The mere mention of him always brought sudden tears to his mother's eyes, leaving her silent and mournful for hours after.

Either that, or I'm a mutant, Alex thought dryly as he checked over the names again, seeing if any jumped out at him. None of them did.

Alex's eyes were drawn once more to the glittering lights in the distance. An enchanting, tormenting spectacle. He couldn't help but gaze at it. The pain in his heart increased, his chest tightening, as he thought about his mother, waiting out there for him to come home, sitting by the phone and hoping the next call would be from her son. Watching the door, praying the next knock would be his knuckles on the wood, heralding his return.

He bit back bitter tears as he gazed out to the glimmering horizon, wishing he could run through the glass and not stop until he reached home. He missed her, and hated to think she was in pain because he had never come home that day. He hated to think of her worrying and panicking—or worse, thinking he was dead. In her state, all of this was terrible for her health. Alex gritted his teeth against the twist of loss inside him, hoping desperately that his mother was still out there, alive and awaiting the return that he promised would come one day—however long it took.

A mix of emotions rose up in Alex, surging through his veins, overwhelming him. The frustrations of his dead-end heritage; the irritation of knowing his name might be on the page but unrecognizable; his untrained powers coiling inside with nobody to aid their growth; the blurry image of his deadbeat dad and the secrets of what lay, icy and dark, inside of him. And, most frustrating of all, the keenly felt loss of his mother, of being so seemingly far away and unable to comfort her—the helplessness he felt, locked up behind walls of someone else's design.

The outside called to him, and he knew he had to get out of the stuffy confines of the library before he released an icy fury on the place and everyone in it. Checking the clock, Alex saw it was close to seven. Jari and Natalie would be expecting him soon anyway.

Picking up the books on the table, he hurried to put them back where he had found them until only one remained in his hand. He tucked his *Historica Magica* away again and set off toward the wine cellar. Sparring would be a prime opportunity to let off some pent-up steam from a lifetime of unanswered questions.

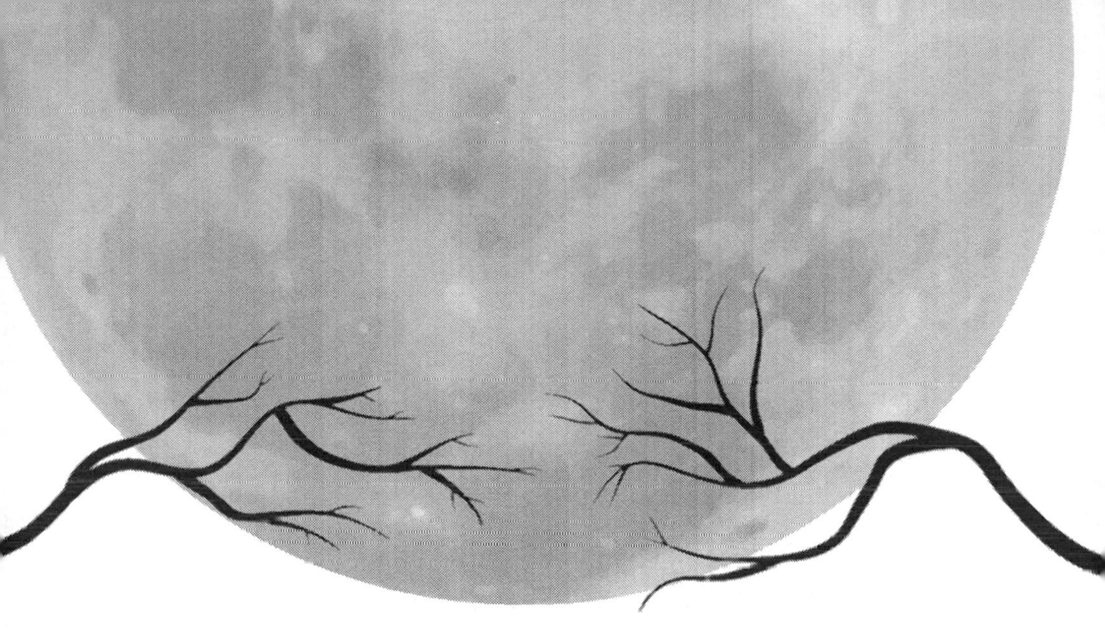

CHAPTER 4

NATALIE AND JARI WERE ALREADY WAITING IN the stagnant warmth of the wine cellar when Alex arrived, breathing heavily from his run. His friends seemed locked in a peculiar standoff, the freckled boy glowering at the onyx-haired girl.

"Did I miss something?" Alex asked as he dropped down the last few rungs of the cellar ladder.

"Jari says we are not permitted to begin until Aamir is also here," Natalie explained, her voice tight with frustration. Jari's glower deepened, his eyes narrowed to almost reptilian slits.

"It's only right that we wait," Jari said, folding his arms

across his chest as he sat down on the ground and leaned against one of the crumbling wine racks, sending spiders skittering in all directions.

"We could wait a few minutes, I guess." Alex shrugged, though he was eager to get started, his muscles wound tight from his library ordeal.

"We are waiting until Aamir gets here," Jari said firmly, his tone brooking no wiggle room for negotiations.

"What if he does not come?" Natalie cut in.

Jari whipped his head toward her. "He *will* come—he promised."

"No, I believe he said that he promised he would *try* to come," Natalie retorted, sighing loudly. "We are wasting time."

"We aren't starting until Aamir gets here," Jari repeated.

Natalie grunted, sinking down onto the floor, against one of the side walls.

Alex followed suit, sitting on the dirt opposite Natalie, so they made up a wonky triangle on the floor. Jari's gaze settled on the hatch to the cellar, unmoving. Natalie rolled her eyes. Alex tilted his head back, staring up at the earthen ceiling, noting silently where the roots were coming through from the trees and plants above, the pale tendrils creeping through like slender, skeletal fingers.

Half an hour passed, and still Aamir had not come.

Alex was sure he had drifted off for a while. Natalie

tapped her foot on the dirt in a vague attempt to amuse herself. Jari stared at the hatch.

"How did your meeting with Renmark go, Natalie?" Alex asked, breaking the silence.

Natalie paused. "It was okay, I suppose. It was nothing so special," she said finally, though Alex had the uncertain feeling that Natalie was being tight-lipped about it. He couldn't say why, but there was a shiftiness in her as she spoke, and she was unwilling to meet his gaze.

"Well, what did you do?" Alex pushed, intrigued by Natalie's coyness.

Natalie shrugged. "Nothing so difficult. It was more of a meeting—I did not learn anything new," she answered stiffly.

"Do you think you will?"

"It is hard to say. Perhaps," she replied, picking up an abandoned cork from the floor and flipping it between her fingers in a distinctly antsy display. "How was your trip to the library?" she countered, leveling her gaze at Alex.

"It was fine," Alex said, trying to push down the bitter feeling that rose up his throat.

"What were you looking for?" she pressed, with a knowing smile.

"Nothing much."

Now it was Alex's turn to feel uncomfortable. He didn't feel as if he could explain the true reason he had gone to the library. He still had not told his friends about the mystery shadow-man Elias and all the secret gifts he had been bestowing upon Alex since his arrival at the manor. There was something about Elias that held Alex back—as if the others might think he was under the influence of some dark magic, like Natalie's curse. Or that Natalie might regret their attack on Finder, if she knew of Elias's involvement in the whole thing. Elias was an odd enough phenomenon to Alex's mind; he had no clue how he would explain him to the others. None of his friends had seen Elias for themselves, and Alex somehow sensed that Elias would not appreciate being talked about or revealed in such a way. A shiver crept up Alex's spine every time he thought about telling the others of Elias and his gifts, like a silent threat. An invisible warning not to say a word.

And so, Alex didn't.

"You must have been looking for something, I think?" Natalie frowned.

Alex thought of his literary dead-ends, and the earlier frustrations of the empty gaps in the shelves, wondering why he felt he should be so secretive about them. It was crazy. If anyone could help, they could. Alex looked across at his friends, and felt the urge to tell them both about the havens. He was just about to open his mouth, to begin the tale of these other schools, when there was a creak at the overhead hatch. The words stopped dead on his tongue as Aamir dropped down into the cellar.

He looked flushed and exhausted, but happy to see them, his weariness falling away as he brushed the dirt from his hands. He ran a hand through his luxurious black curls and sighed, the sound whispering around the room, his lips curving easily into a broad smile. Jari jumped up and ran to him, and the older boy pulled him in for a tight hug. Natalie and Alex couldn't help but smile too at the sight of such pure friendship.

"Right, then, shall we get to it?" Aamir grinned.

They set up the cellar for a sparring session, placing a few ancient bottles in the center and drawing lines in the dust.

"What kept you?" Jari asked lightly as he dragged one of the racks out of the way, searching for more bottles behind it.

Aamir sighed more heavily, and not out of relief. "Things have changed. I can't just be at your beck and call all the time anymore. I have duties, responsibilities, restrictions. I can't get away on a whim, whenever I like." A sudden bitterness tainted his voice. Aamir opened his mouth, his brow furrowed, as if he were about to apologize, but he didn't say the words.

Alex was surprised by Aamir's coldness toward his friend—toward all of them. It had been easier to understand in the classroom, but they weren't in the classroom anymore. There was something unmistakably different about him; he seemed weighed down, his temper quick and the lines around his eyes showing the first telltale signs of unspoken exhaustion. Alex longed to reach out to Aamir, to ask what troubled him, but didn't feel like getting the same snappy response Jari had gotten.

"Then let's just get on with it, shall we, if you're in such a rush?" Jari retorted, returning Aamir's frostiness, as they moved to either end of the cellar, behind the drawn lines.

"Jari, don't be—" Aamir began, but Jari had already sent a spiral of liquid gold searing toward Aamir's face.

Aamir ducked just in time, watching the magic explode into a shower of glittering dust against the far wall of the cellar. Jari fired another, twisting his hand to conjure up a ball of energy that pulsed in his palm before he launched it at the unprepared Aamir.

Aamir quickly sidestepped the magical missile as it sailed past his head. When Jari turned his hand to create a more solid javelin of magical energy, Aamir was ready for him, moving his hand slightly to one side, flicking Jari's magic away. He conjured a shield around his friend, trying to keep Jari's energy hemmed in. Jari raised his palms and twisted both hands counterclockwise, sending a violent pulse out from within the shield, shattering it. There was a flash of fury in the younger boy's eyes.

The pulse knocked everyone in the room backward, Natalie and Alex included, as Jari regained his stance, breathing heavily. Sweat beaded on his forehead, dampening his blond locks. He sent wave after wave of magical artillery at Aamir, who swiped them away, snatching the magic from the air and diffusing it against the walls of the cellar, dirt and dust and splintered wood flying everywhere. Aamir was sweating too, trying to defend himself from the barrage of attacks.

Jari drew streams and spirals of magical energy from within himself. The ripples curled and weaved about his fingertips, golden and powerful, before he hurled them at Aamir.

There was such rage, such anger, behind the blows that Aamir's face had gone pale. The magic was powerful because it was driven by emotion, but it was spiraling out of control. They could all see it, bristling around Jari like static electricity, sparking and pluming from his body as if he were on fire. The entire surface of his smooth skin seemed to be alight with golden flames, rippling through his veins, the glow visible beneath his flesh. His blows were erratic and fearsome, his hands twisting and turning so fast they were barely visible, one after another in quick succession. Each narrowly missed Aamir as he tried desperately to cast them all aside, not wanting to hurt his friend in retaliation.

Suddenly, Alex saw Jari conjure up a solid blade of golden light in one hand, the boy's hands shaking from the strain of molding it. Jari's eyes were ablaze, as if drunk on the power. He raised his hand and sent the golden blade directly toward Aamir's chest, sparking a wispy trail of magical energy as it soared through the air toward its target. It would have hit Aamir, too, had Alex not seen and realized what was going to happen. Thinking quickly, Alex focused his anti-magic on the fast-moving blade of magical matter, and deftly turned his hands, feeling the weight and texture of the magical weapon as he exploded the object from within into a flurry of harmless snow.

Alex stood, stunned, as the fight came to an abrupt halt. He stared down at his hands, still covered in rapidly melting flakes of snow. He had managed to look at an object and a person and form the right anti-magic to defuse the magic, without even having to close his eyes. Natalie gave him a thumbs-up from across the room, though it seemed a peculiar moment to feel pleased about his success. Jari was trembling on his side of the room, his face drained of color. Aamir was much the same on the other side, and seemed to have realized the blade had been intended to inflict actual, savage pain on him.

"Jari, calm down. You need to calm down," Aamir said softly, moving across the room to stand with his friend. He placed a hand on Jari's shoulder, rubbing it gently to try to soothe him. Jari's breaths were labored and rasping in his throat. Sweat dripped from his brow, pooling across his shirt as he tried to regain control, his hands shaking, his knees knocking, his whole body shivering.

Aamir sat Jari down on the floor, beckoning the others to join them in a circle.

"I'm sorry," Aamir began. "I'm sorry that I don't seem like myself. Believe me, I don't feel like myself. You are my friends, and I have been unkind to you all," he continued, his face downcast. "It's this thing—you have to believe me when I tell you, it is all this thing," he confessed, pulling back his sleeve to reveal the golden band, glinting wickedly in the low torchlight of the cellar. A look of pain passed across Aamir's expression, his forehead furrowing.

"What does it do?" Alex asked.

"Hurts, mostly," Aamir said wearily. He looked far older than his nineteen years.

"What sets it off?" Natalie asked, examining the thing cautiously.

Aamir shrugged. "I'm not entirely sure. I don't know exactly how much power it has. All I know is, when I say things, it sends a shock of pain through my body. I don't know how much it can do—whether it hears what is going on around me, whether it monitors me as well as keeps me from saying things it doesn't want me to." Aamir's face screwed up into a grimace, and he winced in pain. "You should be careful of what you say and do around me. Exercise caution. Don't say or do anything that could get you in trouble." He glanced at Alex intently for a moment, conveying a silent message. "I'm not even sure I'm supposed to be doing this, with you." Aamir gestured around the room, his shoulders sagging.

"Do you want me to try and…" Alex trailed off,

remembering not to say anything condemning. He pointed to his wrist instead and waved his hands about in the air, hoping Aamir understood the charade.

Aamir shook his head. "I don't think it's a good idea. Too risky."

"I don't mind," Alex insisted.

"I mean, *they* will notice if it isn't there anymore. They will see," Aamir explained, his eyes wide.

"You could at least try," Jari muttered sullenly, shaking Aamir's hand off his back.

"I'm sorry. It's like I said, things have changed. Everything has changed," Aamir replied. "Even if you could get this thing off, it wouldn't mean I was free. I still wouldn't be able to come here as I pleased, and run about with you guys the way I used to. Even if it was gone, I'd still have to act as if it were there. Do you understand?" Aamir's voice was heavy with sadness as he sat back against the cellar wall, glancing up at the ceiling. He looked so very tired. "The risk is too high, for all of us."

"Aamir?" Alex said.

Aamir tipped his head forward again, leveling his gaze with Alex. "What is it?" he asked.

"Would you mind if I tested the… in case it comes up later on… down the line?" Alex pointed at the band on Aamir's wrist.

Aamir looked down at the line, watching it pulse and fizz and crackle against his skin. He looked to Alex, and nodded slightly. “Just to check—to touch and no more,” Aamir warned.

Alex agreed and moved closer to Aamir until he sat cross-legged in front of the older boy. Slowly, he reached out toward the golden band, and had barely touched a fingertip to the ripple of energy before it began to retaliate against Alex’s anti-magic. The power was immense, sending a pulse of frozen tendrils up Alex’s arm, numbing his fingers. He snatched his hand away and drew a sharp breath. The golden line was more powerful than Alex had imagined. He felt the shiver of it still as it snaked through his veins toward his stomach. Trying to break it would be futile, Alex realized, but he couldn’t bring himself to reveal this to Jari, who watched him with quiet hope.

“It’s not too bad,” Alex managed. “I imagine, with practice, I might be able to come up with something. Maybe a pair of scissors.” He laughed stiffly, the humor not reaching his eyes. Natalie chuckled softly and Jari broke a smile, but Aamir’s face remained stoic.

“Thank you for trying,” Aamir said quietly. He reached out to shake Alex’s hand, drawing him into a hug as he did so. Alex understood. Aamir knew what Alex knew—that it was useless trying to remove the thing.

“I’ll work on it, Aamir. I promise I will,” Alex murmured close to Aamir’s ear. “Somehow, we’ll get you back.”

When they drew apart, Alex could see the misery in Aamir’s eyes, though he covered it swiftly as Jari asked if he wanted another round. A mask of bravado fell across Aamir's face, smothering the vulnerability, as he glanced over to his friend.

"I can't stay," Aamir said apologetically. "And you should all be thinking about heading back."

"Let's call it a night," Alex agreed.

There had been more than enough excitement for one evening.

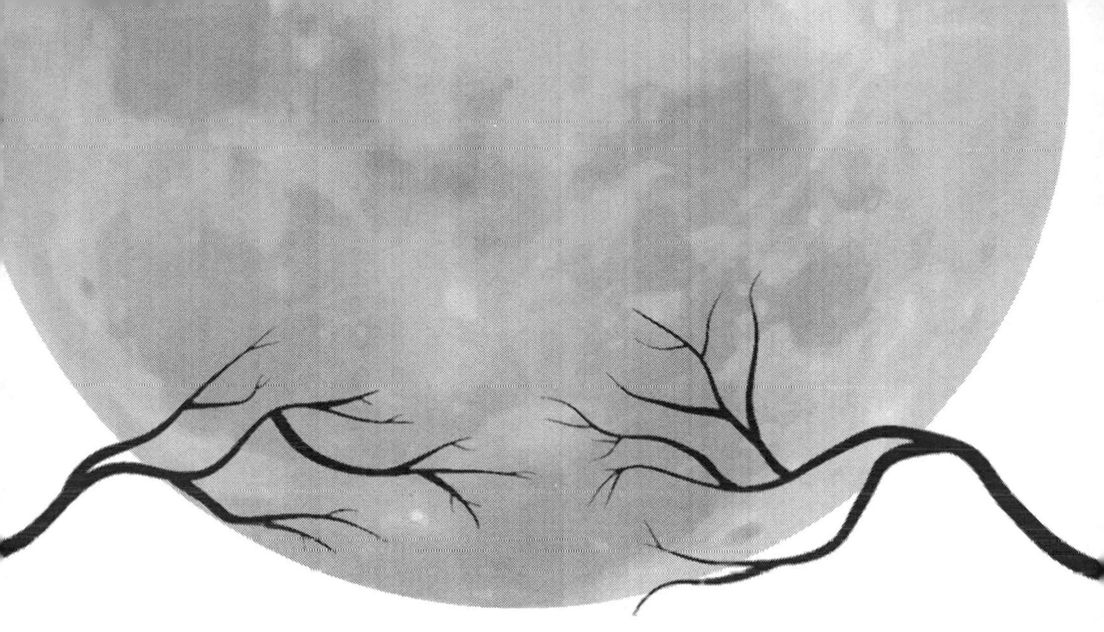

CHAPTER 5

Alex stirred in his sleep, waking suddenly to the darkened room around him, the soft sound of his roommate breathing the only noise. The curtains above him billowed slightly, but that was not what had awoken him. Rubbing his eyes, still scratchy with sleep, he propped himself up onto his elbows and glanced around.

Part of him expected to see Siren Mave, furtively removing the last traces of Aamir from the room—gathering up the folded pile of his bedding from the mattress nearby, stealing away with pillows and duvets and sheets, into the night. But that part of the room was still, the bedding undisturbed, everything neat and in its place. Jari was splayed out in a bizarre position, one leg hanging off the side of his bed, arms stretched out on either side of him, snoring into his pillow.

Something else had woken Alex.

His sleepy eyes caught a glimpse of a shiny blur that darted across the bottom of the bed. It moved quickly, with a quiet whirr. Alex sat up a little higher, squinting to try to make out the object running to and fro across the blanket. Whatever it was ducked and rolled, barreling into one of the wrinkles in the sheets made by Alex's leg. He felt it knock into his knee with an ungainly thud.

Peering around the corner of the wrinkle were two small, beady eyes, glittering black in the darkness of the room. The creature crept out from its burrow, moving stealthily toward Alex, across his stomach and up onto the rise of his chest, the tiny feet barely making an indent. Alex could see that it was a mouse, delicately crafted in silver and gold panels of different shapes and sizes, all working together in perfect unison. The clockwork parts were intricate and beautiful to behold as they powered the small legs forward, one at a time, its impossibly fine tail whipping from side to side as the precise, bronze, half-circular discs of the ears twitched. Even the nose, a painstakingly applied triangle of gold inlay, seemed to sniff the air as the mouse approached, those glittering eyes watching Alex cautiously—the behavior so skillfully lifelike. The creature paused on the upward incline of his ribcage, and Alex saw the glow of pale amber light flowing easily through the mechanisms, keeping the pieces moving.

The mouse twitched its ears at Alex, turning sideways a little. Alex could feel the pad of the mechanical feet on his chest, which brought an awestruck smile to his face. The smile turned to a frown of curiosity as he caught sight of a small scroll, rolled up and tied to the mouse's delicate metal leg with a thin ribbon of silver twine. He reached over gently, expecting the mouse to dart away from him—the creature was so realistic—but the mouse stayed put, allowing Alex to remove the small roll of paper from its hind leg.

He unrolled it slowly. On the minuscule sheet of paper was a message, written in the tiniest hand. Alex had to strain to see it in the darkness as he brought it closer to his eyes, using the sliver of moonlight that strayed in through a gap in the curtains to read. There was a lot written, for such a small scroll.

The note was a warning.

You ought to be more careful with your secrets, Alex. Not everyone can be trusted with them. Think twice before you speak. Your lack of discretion is disturbing—I would have expected more from you. Be careful. You never know who is listening.

Alex turned the paper over for some clue as to who the sender might be, but it wasn't signed.

Frustrated, he read the note again, its vagueness irking him as he tried to make sense of the warning. The tone was definitely threatening. Almost accusatory, Alex thought as he paused on his 'lack of discretion.' What lack of discretion? Racking his brain, he tried to think who might have sent it. Who might want to warn him, or at least chastise him like that? His eyes darted to the shadows that draped from the rafters.

The suggestion in the note annoyed him too. He wasn't quite certain who it was he was supposed to be suspicious of—these non-trustworthy individuals whom he had to keep his secrets from. Natalie and Jari would never breathe a word if he told them. Aamir was a bit of an anomaly, but Alex had been careful not to say too much around the new teacher. Did it mean Ellabell?

Alex scrunched the note up in the palm of his hand. Who did the sender think they were, anyway, telling him whom he could and could not speak to? He knew his own mind, and it had steered him okay so far. Besides, how was he supposed to gather any information on all those glaring gaps in his knowledge if he couldn't speak to anyone? He tossed the note onto the floor, watching as it skidded away under a chest of drawers.

Slowly, he reached toward the clockwork mouse, feeling the resistance of the golden magic within as he closed his hand around the mechanical creature. He felt the icy anti-magic flow eagerly from his palm, encircling the mouse, working its way into the intricate design and dispelling the warm glow from within until the shiny clockwork lay still in his hand, the current of magic gone from its limbs. The glitter dimmed in its eyes, and the moving parts ceased to twitch. Dead, for all intents and purposes. Alex felt a twinge of remorse as he held the mouse up to his eyes, running his thumb gently across the impeccably constructed mechanics, feeling the smooth metal, cold beneath his fingers. Even with the magic sucked out of it, the mouse was beautifully lifelike—a true work of craftsmanship.

He placed the creature on the smooth wooden surface at the top of his bedpost, as if the mouse were standing guard over him.

The note raced through his thoughts as he lay back, knowing sleep wouldn't easily come again. The absent spaces in the shelves of the library still bothered him, and the note's message had only increased his irritation. Who else was he supposed to ask for information? He thought of the still-missing Elias, wondering silently if the shadow-man had sent the clockwork. But it didn't seem like Elias's handiwork. He seemed to prefer paying Alex an actual visit whenever he had some vague message to impart. A secret, unsigned message was too subtle for Elias.

The ghost of Malachi Grey plagued Alex's thoughts. Finder, with all that information tucked away—that fountain of knowledge, now dried up. A low sigh escaped his lips. Jari stirred in his sleep, and Alex froze, not wanting to wake his roommate.

"Who sent you?" Alex asked the mouse, even though he knew it wouldn't answer. Frustration gripped him, and he wished he'd asked that question before he'd sucked out the magic. Not that the clockwork creature had a voice, necessarily, but Alex wondered if magic itself was traceable. If it was, it was too late to investigate now.

A crawling, creeping sensation prickled beneath his skin as he looked beyond the mouse, up to the shadows gathering across the ceiling and snaking down the walls, hunched in corners with an inky mystery that Alex found suddenly disturbing. The darkness seemed to move like something living, shifting liquidly where it pleased, shrouding unseen eyes from view. The hairs on Alex's arms stood on end as he became intensely aware of a familiar feeling—the feeling of being watched. He sat bolt upright, straining into the darkness, and tried to peer into the impenetrable mist of shadows.

"Elias?" Alex hissed, willing the shadowy being to waltz from the dark. "Elias, I know you're there," Alex spoke a little louder, anxiety constricting his throat as he stared into the shadows, utterly unconvinced that the penetrating eyes belonged to Elias. "Elias?" Alex whispered, one last time, a shiver rippling through him.

If Elias was there, he wasn't being forthcoming.

Alex shook his head, telling himself quietly that it was

all in his mind. He forced himself to settle back down beneath the covers. The shadows were just shadows, the feel of eyes on him merely a figment of his overwrought imagination. It was the note that had spooked him, that was all, conjuring up beasties and ghouls where there were none. Either that, or it was Elias playing tricks on him.

Alex turned from the far wall, where the shadows were deepest, and closed his eyes tightly, willing sleep to come as the tingle of something sinister continued to creep through his veins, chilling him to the very core, as if a nightmare had found its way from the safe confines of sleep and crept into the waking world.

CHAPTER 6

HANGING FROM THE STONE WALL OF THE MESS hall, written on a tapestry in great, sprawling black letters, was a message for the first-year students of Spellshadow Manor. Each day at the school was much the same, so any break in the staunch routine was met with a hum of curiosity.

The tapestry informed the students that, over the next week, they would be meeting with their second-year teachers for an introductory session before the next academic year began, which would give them a flavor of what was to come. That day, they were expected to meet with Professor Renmark instead of having their usual first lesson with Professor Nagi, with further instruction to attend an introductory meeting with the elusive Professor Gaze later in the week.

Alex and Jari stared up at the notice, discussing what their new teachers would be like. Natalie didn't seem too worried.

"So, what's Renmark like?" Jari asked in an attempt to pry some information from Natalie.

"He is… different," Natalie replied.

"What do you mean 'different'?" Alex pressed.

Natalie shrugged. "His methods of teaching are not quite the same as many of the other teachers," she explained, making nothing clearer.

"Come on, give us a clue!" Jari cried. "Will we hate him?"

Another shrug. "I honestly could not say. You'll both just have to see for yourselves." She smiled as Alex and Jari rolled their eyes.

"What use is a spy on the inside if you won't tell us anything?" Jari exclaimed, nudging Natalie playfully as they moved out of the mess hall and into the hallways, headed for the mysterious Professor Renmark's office.

"Is he more like Derhin or Lintz?" Alex asked, trying a different tactic.

"He is like neither." Natalie smiled more widely, not falling for the bait.

"Do *you* like him?" Alex asked.

Natalie paused. "He is an excellent teacher, if you are willing to put in the work. I think he is firm but fair," she said thoughtfully.

"Then what am I supposed to do?" Alex asked, his tone hushed.

Natalie's brow furrowed. "I hadn't exactly thought about that," she admitted.

"Are the lessons hard?" Alex asked, more worried now.

Natalie nodded. "A little."

"Am I going to be in trouble?"

"I don't think so—I will do my very best," Natalie promised.

"Thanks," Alex muttered, though a sense of dread fell over him as they neared Professor Renmark's classroom.

His door was painted black, crisscrossed with a complex pattern of red intersecting lines, giving the impression of a labyrinth within the dark wood. Beside it, screwed into the stonework of the hallway walls, was a bronze plaque bearing Renmark's name. It had oxidized in places, the bronze turning green—a sure sign of age. Alex wondered how long it had been mounted there, beside the door.

"Come in!" a gruff voice barked from within the room beyond the latticed black and red.

Natalie led the way, nobody else wanting to be the first. She opened the door, and they stepped into a darkened chamber. The room smelled faintly of cloves and lit matches; a cindery scent, masking a sour, almost metallic undertone.

At the head of the class, awaiting his new students, stood Professor Renmark. With his tall, slim stature, he was more of a wisp than a man. His hair was thin and blond, growing white at the sides, and his steely eyes, a peculiar hazel color, almost yellow, glanced over the group in a curious manner. There was a hawkish look to the rest of his thin, drawn features, reminding Alex of a bird of prey—a kestrel he'd seen as a kid at a county fair. One of the students, a small weasel of a boy named Billy Foer, moved to sit at one of the desks, pushing past Natalie, who was still standing, her eyes resting evenly on Professor Renmark.

"You will *not* sit unless I tell you to sit!" Renmark barked, sending a sharp, thin bolt of golden magic toward the unlucky boy who had taken a seat.

Billy jumped up in shock, the spell hitting him in the arm. Suddenly, his whole body began to convulse. His limbs shook uncontrollably, his mouth frothing as he fell to the ground in a heavy heap, trembling against the stone floor. Ellabell, hidden at the back of the group, rushed forward to help the boy.

"Do *not* touch him!" Renmark shouted.

Ellabell froze. Helpless, the group watched as Billy shook on the floor, the tremors lessening slowly, until finally they ceased, leaving the boy heaving for breath, his limbs splayed out on the ground.

"*Now* you may assist him," Renmark said calmly. Ellabell sank down beside the poor boy, helping him to sit up.

Billy's eyes were wide with panic, his face an ashy gray, his hands shaking violently as Ellabell lifted him to his feet. He didn't dare look at Renmark as he scurried behind the others.

"I am Professor Renmark, and you will not find my lessons easy. I will not ask you to write from textbooks, and you will give me your full attention," Renmark growled, addressing the group. All eyes were fixed firmly on him. "You will leave this room feeling as if you have been at war. If you are not exhausted, you are not working hard enough. I will not treat you as if you were wrapped in cotton-wool. In my class, you will learn, or you will fail. Is that understood?" The students stood in rigid silence. "Are you mutes? Do you understand?" Professor Renmark repeated tersely.

"Yes, Professor," they chorused.

"Good. I will test you, and I will work you hard. I will make you worthy wizards and worthy adversaries—I will challenge you, and most of you will end up on the floor, making fools of yourselves as our young friend just has." Renmark grimaced in what Alex thought was supposed to be a smile as he sought out Billy's sheepish face amongst the group. "Isn't that right?" Professor Renmark addressed Billy directly.

Billy nodded quickly. "Yes, Professor Renmark. Sorry, Professor Renmark," he mumbled.

Renmark looked disgusted by Billy's desperate apology, his thin lips turning upward, his yellow eyes narrowing.

"Despite the obvious lack of talent at Spellshadow, I know there will be a gifted few among you who will offer at least a hint of a challenge for me," Renmark said, glancing at Natalie. His gaze rested for a moment on Jari, too, assessing the blond-haired boy, one eyebrow raised in silent contemplation. When his eyes crossed over Alex, Renmark's brow creased momentarily.

"Now, find an empty space in the room and listen to what I say. If you listen and you work, you will find this easy. If you don't, you will not," Renmark warned. The class dispersed, each student finding an empty space on the floor, in between the desks.

Standing at the front of the room, his black robes swamping his meager frame, Renmark began to instruct them on a series of patterns and movements that would enable them to use the same spell he had just inflicted upon Billy. A spell to incapacitate one's enemies, making their bodies convulse and spasm, rendering them defenseless. It involved both intense focus and complex hand gestures. Alex bent his wrist around with the rest of them until he thought it might snap, even though he knew he could not conjure up the spell Renmark desired. Jari bristled with energy as he created a thin filament of magic between his fingers, and looked to Renmark. The professor seemed impressed, asking Jari to send the spell toward him. Jari obeyed, flicking the thin stream of magic toward Renmark, who snatched it from the air and held the conjuration in front of him, inspecting it closely before clapping it between his hands, the golden wire of energy dissipating into the air.

"A good first attempt," Renmark commented. "Now do better." He turned to prowl around the room, inspecting the other students' work.

As Renmark neared Alex, Alex looked over to Natalie with mounting concern. She stood far enough away from the professor, whose back was now turned. Alex watched as she moved her hands delicately, the twist of her wrists a natural one, unlike Alex's haphazard attempts to copy the movements. Before his hands, she conjured a stream of magic, thin and wire-like, just as Renmark reached Alex's position in the classroom. It was all Alex could do to keep his anti-magic from manifesting as the professor bent to inspect the conjuration. He pursed his lips in confusion, looking from the manifestation to Alex and back again.

"Not bad. Not good, but not bad," Renmark said, finally, as he stood to his full height, his eyes narrowing in suspicion before he turned sharply away. The spell disappeared as soon as Natalie stopped her wrist movements, and Alex breathed out in relief.

The lesson seemed to go on forever, the spells getting gradually harder as Renmark challenged them more and more. After the incapacitation spell, he taught them how to freeze an enemy, followed by instructions on how to create a magical spear that would cause intense pain to the inflicted, and, finally, a method for laying a weak curse within somebody—a temporary one, intended only to affect the cursed for a day or two.

Prowling around the room, his eyes ever watching, Renmark observed sourly as the students attempted to follow his instructions, to varying degrees of success. Whenever he passed Alex, Natalie would hurry to create the spell again in front of Alex's hands, but it proved more difficult than either of them had suspected; the spells were complex and took a great deal of energy to conjure. Each time Natalie stepped in to help Alex, the task grew harder. The shimmering golden glow of Alex's apparent magic emerged, a faded, feeble echo of Natalie's original conjuration. It seemed that creating such an advanced spell, even at that short a distance, was a tricky thing to execute. Renmark grew less and less impressed by Alex with each lap around the classroom as Alex's 'magic' dimmed. Natalie cast a worried glance at Alex, mouthing an apology, after Renmark moved away for the fourth time, tutting under his breath at Alex's clear lack of talent.

With each spell, Renmark would bring a student up to the front of the class to fire a newly acquired conjuration at him, only to fling it away with ease, a smirk lifting the corners of his grim-set mouth. It was clear to everyone that Renmark was a truly remarkable wizard. Even under Natalie and Jari's artillery of strengthened power and self-taught spells, Renmark brushed off every attack as if it were little more than a fly.

It was only when Renmark retaliated that things became interesting. It was obvious to Alex that the professor liked to duel with his students, that he relished exerting his power over them. Ellabell had managed to dodge a series of magical spears, out of sheer luck rather than any attempt to defend herself. Even with her talent for shielding, there hadn't been time to utilize shields in the face of Renmark's swift, savage delivery. She was only given a second to panic before she had to slide one way, then the other, ducking and weaving between the glinting shafts of the thrown spears.

Jari hadn't fared much better, only narrowly missing the thin stream of magic intended to make his body seize up into convulsions. When Renmark sent another, Jari had thrown up a frantic shield, the dome crackling, and made from a weaker veil of magic than usual, barely able to keep the slender bolt at bay. The two stood at an impasse, the sliver of magic trembling in the air. The tip of Renmark's bolt buzzed and sparked against Jari's hastily made shield, unable to get fully through as Jari strained against his opponent's strength. Only when Renmark flicked his wrist, removing the stream of magic, did Jari breathe a sigh of relief, bringing down the shield around him.

Natalie put up a good fight, deflecting the first two attacks without much trouble. Renmark used some spells none of the students had seen before. Alex saw sweat beading on Natalie's forehead, her brow corrugated under the pressure as she raised shields and twisted her hands. Her fingers danced delicately in the air as she sent Renmark's barrage of spells crashing into the walls as she cast them aside. One spell slipped through, and she lost control of her powers. The spell hit her square in the shoulder, and Alex nearly stood from his chair. Natalie winced on impact, letting out a gasp of pain. A burn mark had appeared in the black material of her top, singeing the skin beneath.

While Natalie was busy clutching her injury, Renmark shot a fast-moving stream of light toward her head. Incredibly, Natalie grasped Renmark's magic from the air and redirected it toward the far wall of the classroom. The blast skimmed past the shoulder of poor, trembling Billy Foer before disintegrating into nothingness.

Renmark smirked. "A nice trick," he commended, not waiting for her to recover as he fired several more in her direction.

The strain was evident on Natalie's face, but Alex was left in awe of how much more powerful she had become over such a short time. Seeing her snatch Renmark's blows from the air sent a jolt of envy through him. That was the missing gateway between his potential and his ability. If he had a tutor like Renmark, anti-magic would probably come just as effortlessly to him as magic did to Natalie.

A stray blast caught Natalie on the side of the leg, freezing the limb. She toppled, hitting the ground with a thud, raising her hands in the motion of surrender he had taught them. Renmark stared down at her with a victorious grin. She had tried her best, but it hadn't been enough against Renmark's strength and ferocity. He barely looked fazed; there was no sweat on *his* brow, no discomfort on *his* face. He looked as fresh as the moment they had stepped into the classroom.

Jari rushed forward and helped Natalie onto her one good leg. Her other would need time to loosen.

Suddenly, Renmark's attentions shifted. "You." Renmark pointed in Alex's direction.

Alex glanced quickly at Natalie, whose face fell as she saw what was happening. Jari propped her up, leaning her against the wall, out of Renmark's sight, as Alex stepped up to the line drawn across the flagstones. He swallowed hard. This, he expected, was not going to go well.

"Begin!" Renmark roared.

A bright bolt of energy conjured by Natalie erupted

from Alex's hands, taking him by surprise. Jerked into action, he lunged forward, motioning to send it toward the professor. It barely reached Renmark before fizzling out feebly. A second bolt flew from Alex's palms, and he pretended to twist his hands in the correct manner. Renmark flicked it away easily with a bored look.

Glowering, Renmark sent spirals of liquid gold toward Alex, his hands barely moving, the conjurations sparkling with a mist of amber energy as they moved swiftly through the air. Alex did his best to get out the way, ducking and sidestepping, trying hard not to reach for the familiar icy comfort of his anti-magic, wanting badly to blow Renmark's magic away in a flurry of snow and hail. Looking briefly over Renmark's shoulder, he saw the strain gathering on Natalie's face as she tried desperately to help him, snatching away what magic she could and sending balls of energy flying toward the professor's head. But it was clear Professor Renmark wished to make another example of one of the students—and that student happened to be Alex.

Alex almost thought it'd be worth it, to take the hit and get Renmark to stop, but Natalie obviously wasn't willing to let that happen. Cheeks flushed and mouth set in a grim line, Natalie turned and flourished with her hands, forging shapes in the air, bringing her magic to life.

Blow after blow, a hail of magic swarmed toward Alex, until all he could see was golden light in a glittering screen before him—a veil of gauzy magic, sputtering and exploding as Natalie soldiered away. Renmark appeared irked by Alex's sudden improvement, his yellow eyes intensely suspicious, and he took his spells up a notch accordingly. The change was palpable. The room grew hot, the bolts of magic seeming more solid as they whistled past Alex's ear, the magic itself glowing brighter, becoming more streamlined and precise. This wasn't beginner-level playtime anymore, Alex knew, as he narrowly dodged a sleek-looking blade aimed directly between his eyes.

It had become too much for Natalie. Alex could see she was about to crumble, after he stole another glance at the wall. He raised a hand toward her, gesturing for her to stop. She shook her head weakly, her hands continuing to twist.

Without notice, the hazy galaxy of magic between student and teacher dissipated. A nervous-looking boy in a blue cap stood on the flagstones, looking up at the space where the screen of ferocious magic had just been. His lip was trembling, and his eyes were wide with fear.

Renmark turned to address the boy, annoyed by the interruption. "What is it?" he snapped.

The boy said nothing. Instead, he ran up to the professor and gestured for him to bend so that he might say something into Renmark's ear. Puzzled, Renmark did so. The boy whispered something rapidly. Renmark nodded a few times as he listened intently.

Alex glanced at Natalie, who was already staring in his direction, looking utterly panicked. Glancing back at Renmark and the messenger, Alex had a gut-wrenching feeling that the moment had come—Natalie and Alex were about to be called to the Head's office. The Head had finally discovered Finder was missing, and wanted revenge. Alex wasn't sure why, but he was convinced the Head knew he and Natalie were responsible, and that they were about to face the consequences of their actions.

Renmark stood, and Alex braced himself for his name to be called. Moments passed with painful slowness, but his name remained unspoken as the boy took off across the floor and out the door.

Renmark frowned, looking perplexed. "You are dismissed," he said absently, waving a hand at the students, his eyes following the boy's exit. "But don't get used to finishing early. I do not normally permit such liberties," the professor growled. Muttering under his breath, Renmark disappeared out into the hallway, letting the door slam behind him as he left the confused class alone within the chamber.

The other students began to file out of the room, but Alex rushed over to Natalie and Jari.

"Are you okay?" he asked Natalie. Her face was slick with sweat.

She nodded. "Do not mind me. I will be fine… Do

you think the Head knows?" she asked, her voice trembling as she spoke, though whether from fear or exhaustion, Alex wasn't sure.

"I guess we'll find out soon," Alex whispered.

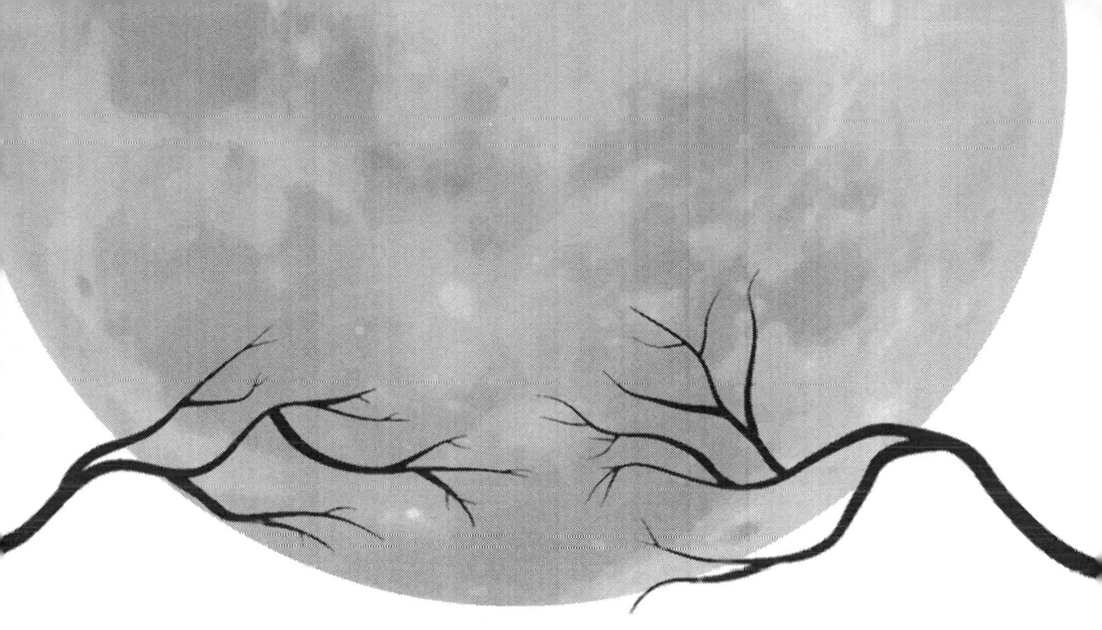

CHAPTER 7

STRIDING DOWN THE HALLWAY, DISTRACTED, ALEX did not see the figure walking toward him until they almost collided. Ellabell looked up, stunned, stumbling slightly as she tried—too late—to weave out of his way, but Jari and Natalie blocked the space behind him. Alex skidded to a halt, reaching out quickly for her, steadying her by the shoulders as she scrabbled for her books.

"Thank you," she said breathlessly, gathering the books to her chest.

"Sorry. I wasn't looking where I was going." Alex moved his hands away swiftly, realizing he still held her by the shoulders.

"Neither was I," Ellabell admitted with a flustered smile, checking the floor to make sure she hadn't dropped anything.

"I'm surprised you could see at all," Alex joked, noting the giant stack of textbooks.

"Just a little light reading." She blushed, trying to stop a few strays from escaping the hastily gathered books. "How did you get on, by the way?" she asked, with sudden interest.

"Get on?" Alex asked, confused.

"Yeah, you know…" She faltered. Alex racked his brain for what she meant, feeling the heat of his friends' eyes behind him.

It rushed back to him, just in time. "Oh, right. The mechanics stuff you wrote down? Yes, of course. Good, yeah. I got on great. Found lots to be getting on with. That's where we're headed now, actually—to the mechanics lab," he rambled, remembering the list of books she had given him, still stuffed at the bottom of his pocket with all the rest of his crumpled notes.

Her face seemed to brighten. "That's great. I'm glad they were useful." She smiled.

"They were—thank you." Alex smiled back, relieved he had remembered in time.

"Well, I won't keep you," she said, shifting the books in her arms. "I've got all this to get through." She laughed softly, her blue eyes sparkling with an infectious humor that made Alex's smile broaden into a grin.

"Happy reading. And sorry for almost knocking you over," he apologized again, trying to sound sincere as he reached out and touched her arm gently, giving it a light squeeze.

Ellabell's cheeks flushed a pale shade of pink, and she looked back up to Alex with a frown. Her sweater was soft beneath his fingertips, and he knew he had lingered a moment too long. Alex removed his hand slowly, wondering at the sudden rosy tint to her face. It made her look extremely pretty, her blue eyes piercing.

"Well, I really should be going," Ellabell mumbled, lowering her gaze as she skirted around the trio.

"Have fun," Alex called after her, feeling slightly lame as he heard the words leave his lips.

Ellabell glanced over her shoulder, smiling shyly, before heading up the corridor away from them, her brunette ponytail bobbing as she walked.

"We're going to the mechanics lab?" Natalie asked with a wry grin on her face.

Alex shrugged. "I thought it might take our minds off things," he lied. "Plus, I need someone with actual magic to try and make the clockwork function." He held up his own hands with a meaningful look. He was growing increasingly frustrated by how difficult it was to use his own powers, by constantly hitting a brick wall with his level of ability. With nobody around to teach him, it was proving tricky to be a self-taught Spellbreaker. After all, there were no textbooks on the matter to make it simpler. That moment in the cellar, when he had exploded Jari's conjuration, had been a fluke; Alex had tried to replicate it a few times, to no avail. It had happened in the moment, at the perfect time, but he still wasn't certain how he'd managed it. It was frustrating to watch his friends grow more powerful each day—Natalie shouldering some of the strain for him, doing the magic of two people—while he sat back, unable to show what he could do, or watch his own anti-magic grow in strength.

"You never mentioned the mechanics lab before," Jari replied suspiciously.

"It just came to me. I've been meaning to get down there for ages. Now seems as good a time as any," Alex replied brightly, remembering the small clockwork mouse he'd placed at the bottom of his pocket, smothered by countless crumpled-up bits of paper. He *had* been meaning to get to work on the mouse, and Ellabell had simply reminded him of it. "Why don't we build some clockwork things instead of moping about, waiting for something bad to happen?"

"I suppose. It's not as if we have much else to do," Natalie said. They were supposed to be with Renmark for most of the morning, but since he'd been called away, they had the luxury of some spare time.

"Good." Alex smiled, raising an eyebrow as he caught a sly look passing between Jari and Natalie. Ignoring it, he turned and led the way to the mechanics lab.

When they arrived, they were surprised to find the familiar figure of Professor Lintz sitting alone at one of the workbenches. He was the room's sole occupant, his round frame hunched over something shiny on the wooden work surface. On a tight elastic band around his head, he wore a monocle-like magnifying glass, flipped down over one of his small eyes, as he focused intently on a miniature cog held between tweezers.

Alex, Natalie, and Jari held their breaths as they waited for Lintz to place the piece within the inner workings of his clockwork creation, all of them fascinated by the delicacy in Lintz's pudgy hands as he maneuvered the piece into place. Lintz slowly removed the tweezers from the mechanical innards and used them to pick up the smallest screw any of them had ever seen, barely bigger than a grain of sugar, from a square of paper he had placed on the tabletop beside him. Gently, he placed the screw in the center of the miniature cog and twisted it skillfully into place, to hold the bits together.

Alex almost felt like applauding as Lintz laid the tweezers back down, wiping sweat from his forehead with the back of his robe sleeve.

Since Derhin's disappearance from the manor, Lintz hadn't been around much. Instead of his usual imposing figure, with his lively moustache jiggling on his upper lip as he spoke, the students had been left with instructions on a blackboard, the professor himself notably absent. Alex guessed this was where the professor had been—holed up in the mechanics lab, perhaps to take his mind off whatever it was he had done after taking his friend away that day.

As Lintz turned, becoming aware of their presence, the three students were quietly stunned by what they saw. His eyes had taken on a sad, vacant quality, his moustache sticking up at one end in a peculiar fashion, while the other curled downward. His rotund face was sunken in at the cheeks, adding to the fleshy jowls beneath his chin. His skin looked waxy and sickly, dark circles creating deep grooves beneath his eyes. He looked tired, but most of all, he looked finished—there was a lifeless quality to him, as if a curse had been placed upon him. Alex supposed there had been, in a way. Lintz must've been haunted by the ghost of a much-loved friend. He was almost a ghost himself, his robe tattered, skin an ashen gray.

Lintz barely acknowledged the trio as he turned back to the creature on his workbench, but they moved slowly closer to him, fascinated by the work. As they neared, Alex saw it was an elaborate clockwork owl, each gold and silver feather painstakingly put into place on the outer shell of the creature, forming layered plumage that gleamed in the light of the lab. Around the owl's wide eyes, exquisite carvings had been etched into the metal itself; sharp-edged fleurs-de-lis that flowed out into twisting vines and spiny leaves, coiling and curving around the edges of the eyes, appearing white or black, depending on how the indentations caught the light.

A hatch in the owl's stomach was open, and Lintz tinkered with the inside clockwork. A complex system of cogs and devices and metalwork made up the innards. Lintz twisted and checked the mechanisms, his focus never leaving the delicate handiwork. None of the three could take their eyes off the impressive creature. They watched Lintz insert and rearrange parts and pieces as he saw fit, his fingers moving dexterously, his hands steadier than a rock, without even a tremor to disturb his fine work.

Looking content at last, Lintz placed the tweezers down on his piece of paper and held his hands over the clockwork, closing his eyes. It was the closest thing to surgery Alex had ever seen. The familiar burning glow of magic appeared beneath the curve of Lintz's palm, trickling up his fingers like molten gold as he poured the spell into the clockwork; it dripped from his hands into the mechanisms, flowing through with an oily ease, and the elaborate, minuscule pieces began to move. A few turning cogs to begin with, until the whole being came alive beneath Lintz's hands, the neck moving from side to side, the wings flapping up and down, practicing the movement, the small beak opening and closing.

Lintz closed the hatch on the owl's stomach and locked it into place. He lifted the creature gently in his hands, the wings still flapping, and raised it into the air. It took a moment, but, after a rocky start, the owl flapped harder and faster, picking up a rhythm, until it lifted itself up, away from the safety of Lintz's hands. It flew through the air, swooping low and surging skywards again, making a low hooting sound as it performed a lap of the lab. The clockwork moved fluidly, the magic keeping the owl in the air. A weak smile played beneath Lintz's moustache as the beautiful metal owl began its second lap, the gold and silver feathers glinting with each ruffle of metallic plumage.

Finally, the exquisite bird came to rest on one of the shelves lining the mechanics lab, each one filled with endless boxes of screws and cogs and metal plates and solder—everything one could ever need to make whatever the heart desired.

Lintz scraped his chair back and walked over to the shelf where the owl had perched, reaching up to remove the magic from the creature. Within an instant, the golden pulse that gave the owl life had coiled back into Lintz's palm, the cogs ceasing to whirr. The neck stilled, the wings frozen mid-flap. He took down the owl and carried it gently over to a trunk in the corner, lifting the lid and placing it gingerly inside. Then he clipped a padlock to the front of the trunk and softly patted the heavy wooden surface as he pushed the lock into place.

"Did you like him?" Lintz asked, saying his first words to the trio as he slipped the key to the padlock onto a chain around his neck.

"He was beautiful, Professor." Alex nodded, awestruck by Lintz's undoubtable skill with clockwork.

"I've spent a long time on that one." Lintz smiled sadly. "Worth it, though, isn't he?"

"My goodness, yes, Professor—I believe he is one of the most beautiful creatures I have ever seen!" Natalie gushed.

"I'm glad you like him," Lintz remarked, an unexpected note of friendliness in his voice. "I don't think I've ever shown him to anyone," he added wistfully, patting the small key beneath the fabric of his robes. "Haven't had much chance to do any of this business, really, until recently. Nice to get back to it for a bit, you know?"

"Absolutely," Alex agreed.

"There's nothing like clockwork to calm the mind," Lintz went on. "What are you doing here, anyway? Shouldn't you be in a lesson of some sort?" The professor's eyes were drawn to one of the many clocks ticking away on the far wall. Alex thought the question was a tad hypocritical, considering that Lintz hadn't shown up to teach classes for weeks.

"We were supposed to have the morning with Professor Renmark, but he got called away," Jari explained.

A dark look passed over Lintz's face at the news. "Did

he now?" he muttered.

"Yes, Professor," Natalie said.

"I'm afraid I must be on my way," Lintz said suddenly, a curious look on his face, his mind seemingly already elsewhere. "Clear up after yourselves," he added as he disappeared into the hallway beyond. The three of them were left alone in the mechanics lab, with no sound but that of the endlessly ticking clocks for a long moment.

"That was weird," Alex noted as he wandered over to the trunk in the corner, checking the lock with a quick tug.

Jari hopped up onto one of the stools lined neatly around the workbenches. "Lintz *is* weird."

"That owl was beautiful, though, no?" Natalie smiled.

"It really was," Alex admitted. He checked out some of the shelves, reading the labels on the boxes. The bottom shelves seemed to be reserved for clockwork projects. Alex dipped down onto his haunches, running a hand along some of the creations—a frog, the metal tinted green; a small hummingbird, the metalwork tempered to be multi-colored, like the surface of an oil spill, pink and blue and yellow and green. A few others, though none of them were nearly as impressive as Lintz's owl.

At the back of one of the bottom shelves, hidden behind the bulk of a half-made cuckoo clock, Alex's eye was drawn to a cluster of clockwork creatures, gathering dust. A series of mice, all identical—five of them, their intricate, glinting metallic bodies smothered in a thick blanket of fuzzy gray. Beside the last of them was a clean outline on the dirt of the shelf, where something had protected the wood from the dust. The sixth mouse was missing.

Alex reached into his pocket and brought out the sixth mouse. It was exactly the same as the other five, the same size, shape, color, and design. Someone had taken the mouse from here and sent it to him, with the message tied to its back leg.

"Natalie?" Alex called, diverting Natalie's attention from a beautiful music box.

"Yes?"

"Could I borrow you for a second?" Alex asked. He wandered over to the workbench in the center of the room and set down the delicate mechanical mouse.

"Where did you get that?" Natalie asked as she drew herself up to the bench. Jari flanked Alex on the other side, peering over his shoulder to get a better look at the mouse.

"Over there." Alex pointed to the missing spot on the shelf.

"It is beautiful." Natalie ran her fingers across the fine metalwork.

"I was wondering if you could run your magic through it—see what happens. Like Lintz did with the owl," Alex said, setting the mouse up onto its dainty feet.

"I will try," Natalie said. She placed a hand against

the top of the mouse, a glow appearing beneath her palm. Smoothly, the misty fluid rippled through the mouse's clockwork, the cogs beginning to move as the mouse sprang into life, scuttling across the worktop. The ancient, dusty mechanisms creaked slightly as the creature ran the length of the bench. Natalie's face was bright with delight while she watched the mouse dart this way and that.

"Can you control it?" Alex asked, watching closely.

"I can try." Natalie moved her hand slowly, attempting to manipulate the magic inside the mouse. The mouse stopped, cocking its head at Natalie as it crept back across the workbench toward her, its golden tail whipping sideways as it moved. Natalie turned her index finger in a circular motion. The mouse followed, turning in a circle, lifting onto its hind legs. Natalie flicked her finger sharply, and the mouse went flying backward, only to come creeping back up to the young woman whose magic ran in its clockwork. It stood with its head cocked, awaiting instruction.

"I want to try something," Alex muttered, standing to fetch one of the toolboxes from the shelf. He pulled out some tweezers and reached out a hand for the mouse, which rolled easily out of the way. It was then that Alex noticed the eyes—no longer the glittering black he'd seen the night it came to him, but a dark gold shade.

"Shall I take my magic out?" Natalie asked, though she seemed to be having far too much fun with the clockwork creature for it to end.

Alex nodded. "Please."

Natalie beckoned the mouse toward her and placed a hand over the back of it, drawing the magic from the inner workings. The golden glow ebbed from within as the creature's eyes turned back to a dulled shade of darkened silver, closer to that of iron ore, the life gone.

Natalie handed the mouse to Alex, who held it gently in his palm for a moment, eyeing the clockwork closely before setting it down on the table, tweezers poised. It took him a while, his shoulders hunched in concentration, as he removed the parts and reinserted them, inverting the clockwork as best as he could—hoping it would mean what he thought it would mean. Jari chimed in with suggestions as he watched Alex work, and Alex was grateful for the fresh pair of eyes. After a few minutes, he fit the last few pieces back together again.

"Do you think it will work?" Natalie asked.

"There's only one way to find out." Alex grinned anxiously. Slowly, he placed his hand above the mouse's spine, as he had seen Natalie do with her magic, and closed his eyes, feeling the cold brush of his anti-magic as it gathered beneath his palm. Then he opened his eyes, seeing the curls of black mist and icy flakes flowing down toward the tips of his fingers when he touched the intricate clockwork of the mouse. Much like the golden flow of Natalie's magic, the darker anti-magic rippled liquidly through the mechanisms, beginning to move them slowly; a few cogs turned, though the mouse didn't seem to want to go anywhere. As he waited, a puff of smoke wisped up from the inside mechanics, the cogs jamming.

Alex lifted the mouse to remove his anti-magic before the thing broke entirely. As he drew it closer to his face, he saw the back leg twitch—just for a moment, a tiny movement, but enough. It twitched again, releasing another puff of smoke. Reluctantly, Alex removed the coiling black anti-magic, a sheen of frost licking the metalwork.

It was a small success in Alex's anti-magical clockwork endeavors, but it was enough to give him hope. He just had to figure out the inverted mechanics; if he could do that, he knew he might be onto something. He sighed heavily, his frustrations returning as he slipped the mouse back into his pocket. Yet again, without a guide, without a teacher, without a textbook, it was up to him to teach himself.

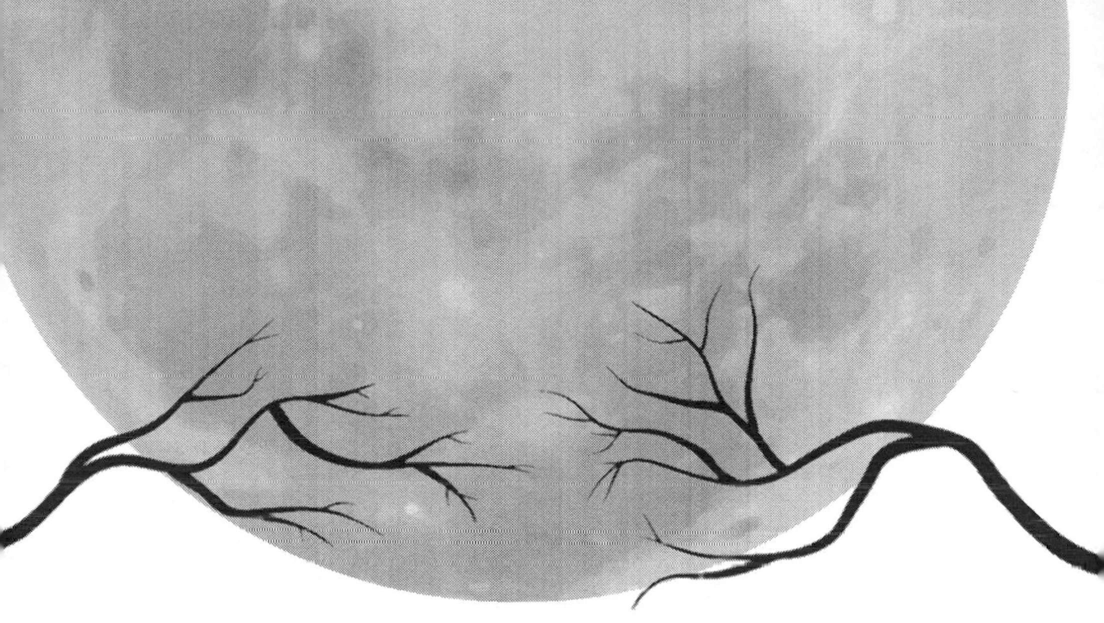

CHAPTER 8

Beyond the library window, the sky was a muted heather color, the first stars just starting to peek out as night crept slowly in. In the soothing warmth of the cavernous room, Alex and Natalie sat companionably in their favored armchairs by the window, gazing out every so often to see the soft twinkling of the stars in the twilight, growing brighter as the sun receded into night. Beyond the manor's boundaries, his hometown wasn't visible now, the landscape showing rolling golden hills instead, their gilded shine dimming in the gathering darkness. But home was still out there, somewhere.

Alex had a spread of mechanical and clockwork

manuals out in front of him and a notebook open on his lap, taking up most of the small circular table that lay between the two of them as he jotted things down he thought might be useful. He liked the intricacies of clockwork and the way its practical application calmed him and made him feel useful. Making the mouse's leg twitch had given him a taste for more. There were countless uses for clockwork, more than he had ever imagined, and reading over the instructions and possibilities made him feel like a kid in a candy store. He was also curious to know if there was any way of figuring out whose magic was inside a clockwork object, but so far he was having no luck with that avenue of enquiry.

Natalie, meanwhile, sat curled up against the deep-set, emerald-green cushion of her armchair, her legs dangling casually over the armrest, focusing solely on one leather-bound book entitled *Shielding Techniques for Intermediate Learners*. Occasionally, she would let out a small sound of understanding and tap the side of her head, as if something had clicked, and Alex would look across, having almost forgotten his friend was there, in his attempt to cram as much information as possible into his fried brain.

A fire crackled in the grate of the enormous fireplace that ran along most of one side of the library wall. Alex thought it was a strange place to have a fire so big, what with all the paper and potential kindling, but he presumed someone would know a spell to stop a raging blaze if it came to it. Plus, the flames brought him a curious kind of comfort. It reminded him of childhood holidays and summer camps spent around a fire, toasting marshmallows and singing songs, his clothes smelling of it for weeks after, that cinder scent of burning logs and warming smoke. He liked the sound of the fire, too, the erratic crackle and snap of the logs being consumed by the flames, the quiet scuffle as they charred and fell apart, collapsing in on each other, only to be replaced by fresh logs. It made the place feel even grander than it already was, as if they were hidden stowaways in a period drama or tourists in an ancient house, though the latter wasn't all that far from the truth, Alex supposed.

The cream pages of his notebook were sprawled with the black ink of reams and reams of information he thought he might be able to use in the mechanics lab. If he could invert the clockwork and the mechanisms in order to feed his anti-magic through the system, he might, hopefully, get something to work. There were crude diagrams, hastily drawn at the tops of the pages, and bullet points, alongside numbered, step-by-step instructions. Next to these instructions, Alex had written the inverse direction, knowing that was what he'd have to do with the clockwork under his construction, if he was to have any chance of creating a fully functioning clockwork creature. He thought of the mouse in his pocket, and reminded himself to keep it in the dormitory from now on, until he was sure he was going to be in the mechanics lab again. The last thing he wanted was to be caught with it, knowing full well he wasn't supposed to take things out of the lab, or anywhere else, for that matter. No teacher would believe the mouse simply ran to him in the night.

Alex jumped, startled, as a ball of paper hit him smack in the forehead. His mouth curved into a relieved smile when he saw Natalie grinning from her spot in the armchair opposite. She laughed softly, and he threw the paper ball back toward her. His own chuckle of amusement turned into a loud yawn as he stretched his arms out above his head, feeling his shoulder pop with a satisfying click.

Natalie looked sleepy too; the warmth of the library had settled like a blanket around them. It was getting late, and they had spent long enough on shields and mechanics. They were just beginning to pack up when Alex became aware of a commotion at the entrance to the library—the sound of feet pounding the floor and the sight of a figure scanning the vast room.

A flustered Jari came sprinting along the reading desks toward them, wearing a look of sheer panic.

"Where have you been? I couldn't find you," he said, bending slightly to get his breath back.

"Here. Why? What's up?" Alex asked, concerned for his friend.

"It's Aamir," Jari panted.

"What is it? Is he all right?" Natalie cut in, worry passing over her dark eyes.

"I'm worried—so worried," he wheezed, patting his chest. He had clearly been running for quite some time, trying to find them.

"What happened?" Alex pressed. Jari sat down slowly on the floor, holding his head in his hands.

"I was with Aamir—speaking to him in his classroom, once he was done for the day. It's the only time I get these days to just talk with him, you know?" Jari began. The other two nodded. It certainly hadn't been the same without Aamir around all the time; they had all felt it. Jari continued, speaking rapidly. "Anyway, we were just chatting, about nothing much, really, when some kid bursts in, looking all guilty and shaky. The kid didn't take the slightest bit of notice of me, but went straight up to Aamir and said that the Head wanted to see him immediately—that he was to go straight to the Head's office, as he was already waiting."

"The Head wanted to see him?" Natalie asked, her voice tight with concern.

Jari nodded. "Yeah, right away, and then the kid left and Aamir got all panicky and scared. You should have seen Aamir… He was a mess. He was shaking, and his face went white as a sheet. His eyes looked like horses' do when they're spooked, all wild and weird, and he was babbling. I couldn't make out any of it, but he just kept muttering things under his breath, and I couldn't get him to calm down. I tried to, but he was in such a state," Jari explained miserably. "Then he walked out. He said he was sorry and just left."

"I'm sure he will be fine, Jari," Alex said, trying to reassure both himself and his friend.

Jari shook his head. "I don't think so. You didn't see him. He was a complete mess. Even before the kid came in. He just looks so tired all the time, like that thing on his wrist is sapping the energy from him. He's in a bad way, Alex. I just know it. He kept trying to tell me things. But then his face would screw up like he'd been stung, and he'd just stop mid-sentence." Jari's voice caught in his throat as he spoke.

"What kind of things?" Natalie asked.

"Different things. He was telling me about how things were going, and then he just kept stopping, gritting his teeth in pain—then he'd just switch the subject." Jari shrugged. "We weren't even talking about anything we weren't supposed to be. Nothing to do with the Head or the teachers, nothing! That stupid line is sensitive to everything."

"Sounds like he was trying to tell you something," Alex murmured.

"What do you mean?" Jari asked.

"Maybe Aamir was trying to tell you something he wasn't supposed to, but tried to do it secretly and… well, the band on his wrist knew," Alex replied.

"You really think so?" he said.

Alex shrugged.

"Do you think he is in trouble?" Natalie spoke, her voice hushed to a whisper as she glanced around, conscious of being watched.

Jari gave a tense nod. "Yes, I do."

"Then what should we do?" Natalie said.

"We need to check that he's okay," Jari replied firmly.

"And how are we supposed to do that?" Alex asked, adopting the same hushed whisper as Natalie.

"We break into the teachers' quarters and make sure he is," Jari explained, matter-of-factly, as if the answer were a simple one.

"Seriously?" Alex did not like the plan one bit.

Jari nodded furiously. "Yes, seriously. We break into the teachers' quarters while everyone else is asleep and make sure he is okay," he repeated, as if it were obvious. "And, we can ask him what the Head wanted."

"Jari, I hate to say it, but that's insane," Alex said. "You know Aamir won't be able to tell us anything, even if he wants to. It's too risky! What about curfew?"

"What about it?" Jari replied, shrugging.

"It's a *huge* risk, Jari. I hate to sound like the killjoy here, but being out after curfew is a massive risk to take. What if we get caught?" Alex spoke firmly, a note of authority in his voice.

There had been much talk circulating about what happened if a student got caught after curfew: magical lashings with a golden cat o' nine tails, spells of long-lasting silence, powerful curses to sap the strength from a student, and torture spells that left the sufferer walking on pins and needles for weeks, unable to soothe away the continual stabbing sensation beneath their feet. The worst, though, was the threat of an audience with the Head and the tales of his mind control, used to punish and torture those who disobeyed the rules. He would bend the world around them, tormenting them with nightmarish visions of family and friends back home. Alex knew what it was like to have the Head force his way into his mind and didn't feel much like repeating the traumatic experience.

"If we get caught, we get caught. That's it," Jari replied with growing determination.

"No, Jari. I don't think you quite understand how high the risks are. If I get caught and they decide to lash me with some magical whip, don't you think the blizzard that will undoubtedly spring from my back will be a dead giveaway?" Alex asked, trying to make his friend see the problems in such a dangerous scheme. "And there's no telling what they'd do to the both of you. It's too risky, Jari. Surely you see that?"

"*I* don't mind taking the risk," Jari said desperately. "Our friend needs us. I don't care what the risk is."

Natalie glanced at Alex. "How about we all wait until

tomorrow, when it is our first lesson, and we speak with Aamir afterward—we make sure he is all right then, when it is much safer?" she suggested calmly.

Jari shook his head. "I have to know he is okay *to-night*," he snapped, keeping his voice low as he narrowed his eyes at Natalie and Alex. "If you had seen the state he was in, we wouldn't be having this conversation! We would already be making a plan."

"But the risks are—" Alex repeated, but Jari interrupted.

"Aamir would come for any one of us if we needed him. You know he would." Tears sprang to Jari's eyes. He wiped them away furiously, his voice thick with emotion.

It was hard to acknowledge, but both Alex and Natalie knew Jari was right. Aamir had been one of the first to befriend them and make them feel welcome at the manor, with his easy manner and his quick humor and his endless warmth. He had made them all feel safe. If what Jari said was true, then their friend was in real trouble. They owed it to Aamir to at least try to check on him, though none of them knew what state they might find him in.

"Then I suppose we are going to help." Natalie smiled tightly, the dread evident on her face.

Alex nodded, his throat going dry. "I suppose we are."

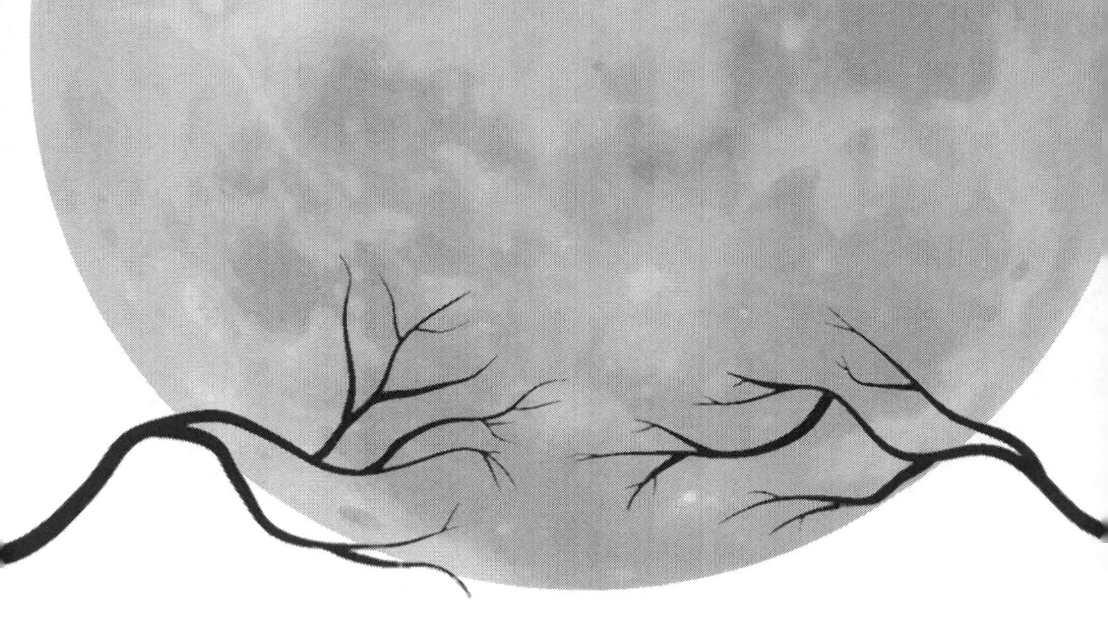

CHAPTER 9

THE CLOCK IN THE HALL WAS SOUNDING MIDNIGHT when Alex and Jari stole out of their dorm room, slipping from shadow to shadow as they made their way through the familiar corridors of the boys' section, pausing at each corner to listen for the sound of footsteps on the flagstones. In the silence, all they could hear was the distant rumble of other boys snoring, safe inside their rooms, and the steady tick of the clocks.

They moved quickly in socked feet, having left their shoes behind in favor of quieter fabric soles. Around the bottom half of their faces, they had wrapped black scarves, hoping it might make them less conspicuous, though they realized that, if they were caught, they'd have the scarves ripped from them regardless. Still, it made them feel more comfortable—stealthier somehow—as they tiptoed through the sleeping manor, toward the intersection where the two dormitories met. Natalie was supposed to be waiting for them on the corner, but neither of them could see her as they approached. Camouflaged in the darkness, Natalie startled the two boys slightly as she emerged, soundlessly, from the shadows. She, too, had socked feet, but no scarf around her face. She frowned at their rudimentary balaclavas.

"What are those?" she asked.

"Scarves," Alex whispered.

"To hide our faces," Jari added, muffled behind the fabric.

"You must take them off—they look ridiculous!" Natalie said. The two boys shuffled the scarves down, exposing their faces. They couldn't deny it felt nicer to breathe properly than to have their faces covered.

Faces fully visible, they began the stealthy journey toward the blue line of the teachers' quarters. They moved slowly through the dark hallways, the dimming torches barely shedding any light on the path ahead of them. They could have done with some moonlight, but the worlds and lands beyond the shifting hallway windows were having none of it; they refused to offer up any glimmer of light, giving only dark storms and savage tempests, clouds thick and furious, smothering any sunlight or moonlight that might have helped the trio find their way. It was as if the manor itself were angry at their disobedience.

Suddenly, Natalie's voice whispered back to the other two as a dim blue light appeared in the distance.

"There it is," she breathed, pressing herself flat against the wall. "We should check for any teachers."

They crept closer to the glow of the blue line and stopped beside it. Natalie peered around the wall and looked up through the darkened corridor beyond, squinting to try to make out any shapes lurking in the shadows. It was empty—as silent as the rest of the manor.

"It is all clear," she said. Alex shuffled past her to get to the blue line. He knelt on the ground, the stone cold beneath his knee, even through the fabric of his trousers.

Taking a deep breath, he found the energy coiled within him and felt it course through his veins as he willed it into his hands, the familiar sensation of it twirling around his fingers as he conjured a mass of anti-magic between his palms. Seeing the raw ball of anti-magic, rippling black and silver, he focused his thoughts upon it, manifesting it into something more useful. With a slight turn of his wrist, the anti-magic stretched out into a blade, the edge thinning to a point, as it pulsed and sparked with icy energy.

He lowered the blade toward the blue line, surprised to see the weapon holding its shape more easily as he focused his mind more intensely on what he wanted to see, using the turn of his wrist to build the definition of the long knife. As he touched the edge to the blue line, it cut through the stream of sapphire light as if it were butter, severing the connection as the two ends broke apart. Alex felt the push of the magic against his hands as he held the blade of anti-magic against the ground, but it did not creep through him or try to attack him. In fact, the blue line seemed to have very little effect at all on Alex, barely bothering him as he deflected it elsewhere. He moved the severed ends away, leaving a safe gap for the others to pass through.

"Nice job," Jari whispered. They walked tentatively through, into the unfamiliar territory of the teachers' quarters.

"Thanks." Alex grinned as he drew his anti-magic back into himself. It looked as though the self-teaching might be finally paying off.

The teachers' quarters were hopelessly steeped in pitch black as the three of them shuffled up into the first corridor. They could see nothing ahead of them, no light of any kind. Their only guide was the towering walls beside them.

"Wait one moment," Natalie whispered as Jari bumped into her.

"Sorry," he said softly.

A small golden glow trickled down toward the floor,

meandering delicately from Natalie's fingers. Suddenly, a thin stream of light shone beneath them, a snake of bright yellow, glowing in the center of the masonry below their feet. As they took a step forward, the snake of light moved ahead, showing them the direction they needed to go in.

"Nice trick," Alex commended.

"It is a new one," Natalie said.

They followed the ribbon of glowing energy, keeping an eye on it as it slithered along the floor, casting a dim glow on the walls on either side. It was not as bright as they might have liked, their eyes still squinting into the darkness ahead, but it was enough to see by, and the dim glow would provide some camouflage if they needed to cut and run. It was not bright enough for them to clearly see each other's faces.

Alex paused when the snaking torch lit up a series of frames on either side of the corridor. In them were pictures of people he had never seen—stern portraits, all painted in the same pose, wearing the same black robes that marked them as teachers. At the bottom of each portrait, set into the varnished wood of the frame, was a small bronze plaque, bearing the name of whomever the image resembled. Alex didn't recognize any of the names as his eyes glanced across the engraved letters. Some of the dates beneath went back decades. Picture upon picture of stuffy, stony-faced teachers lined the wall in a grim gallery. It wasn't until they moved into a different network of corridors that Alex saw a name he recognized.

The picture was in the same sort of frame as the previous one, the canvas gathering a sheen of dust. But the plaque at the bottom was shinier, as if it had only recently been placed there. The face was unmistakable, though younger and fresher. Barely any lines marred the smooth features around the figure's bright eyes, which jumped from the canvas in a deep, captivating blue. The hair was dark, untouched by the gray Alex had been used to seeing, and there was a half-smile of victory on the lips, though the pose was supposed to be a stern, serious one. He had been young and hopeful once—a force to be reckoned with. The proof was there, hanging from the wall, with his name carved beneath: *Professor R. Derhin*. Alex ran his thumb along the lettering, the engraving rough beneath his fingertip, and he felt a twinge of remorse for the young man in the portrait.

I bet he never thought he'd end his days still trapped here, Alex thought sadly.

Beside it hung a similar image, though the plaque at the bottom was missing. Still, it wasn't hard to see who the image was supposed to be. Lintz sat a little taller in the picture, with a shock of ginger hair and the beginnings of a reddish-toned moustache, nowhere near the monstrosity he had grown over the years. His hazel eyes were lighter, almost honey-colored, and there was a smile upon his lips too—a mischievous glimmer, twinned with that of

Derhin. His face was slimmer and almost chiseled in the rise of good cheekbones, the apples of them rosy and his jawline firm, no hint of a jowl, just the upward curve of a thick neck and a strong chin. He had been far better-looking than his older self suggested.

Alex felt sympathy toward Professor Lintz. The man had to walk past the image of his younger self, day in, day out, hung up beside his brother-in-arms—painted at a time when they had still had their whole lives ahead of them, their minds still racing with madcap schemes of escape and a spark of hope. A hope that had sputtered out long ago, no doubt, a world away from the crumpled old man they had seen in the mechanics lab, tinkering away with his owl to take his mind off what had happened to his black-haired friend in the picture beside him. To walk past that reminder every day, that notice of their failure to escape… Alex could not imagine the suffering it brought to Lintz. He felt a flicker of guilt, mingled with curiosity, wondering what sort of friendship those two must have had. It had lasted all those years, stayed as they aged from mere boys to old men. A sense of dread, too, ran cold up his spine.

If they couldn't do it, after all that time, how can we? Alex pondered, his eyes glancing to Natalie and Jari, walking just ahead of him. Their hopes were hauntingly similar to those of Lintz and Derhin, with their eternal optimism of one day breaking free from the walls of the manor and returning to the lives they'd had before, to the families and friends and dreams they had once taken so utterly for granted.

There was another portrait, down the line, just after the image of Lintz. The indent of a plaque remained at the bottom of the varnished frame, where the bronze had once been screwed in, but the plaque itself was missing. The figure sitting within the frame was familiar to Alex somehow, with a striking face and piercing brown eyes, dark hair combed neatly back. The man sat with a sense of pride and authority, a sardonic smile playing upon his lips. It certainly wasn't Renmark or any of the others. Nor was it any of the statues buried deep in the crypt, or reminiscent of the Head or anyone Alex had seen in the manor. And yet the man looked irritatingly familiar.

He would have stopped longer to look at the portrait, but the snake of light had disappeared around the corner, along with Natalie and Jari. Alex hurried after it, entering a broader corridor that stretched far into the distance, with doors on either side. The doors themselves were plain, boasting none of the elaborate etchings of the doors elsewhere in the manor, although some had small ceramic tiles hanging from the stonework beside them. On the tiles were different names and words, etched onto the smooth white enamel with black paint, perfectly curled into cursive lettering by a deft hand. They passed tiles which said *Common Room, Library, Kitchen, Storage*

Cupboard—all the usual dull necessities—spread out at the bottom end of the corridor.

Alex wanted to pause the group for a moment and duck quickly into the library, to see if they might get their hands on any contraband books, but he guessed what Jari's response might be. Their goal was Aamir; he could check out the library on the way back, when their objective wasn't quite so pressing. Still, Alex felt a pang of regret as they slipped swiftly past it.

As they moved farther along, careful to listen for voices coming from any of the communal areas, the tiles grew more personal. Natalie paused beside one tile with an anxious look on her face, barely visible in the hazy glow of the light-snake. On it were written the words *Professor A. Nagi.*

"Do you think this might be it?" Alex joked, trying to lighten the mood.

"Do you think we should knock?" Natalie asked, lifting her hand.

"No way," said Jari. He pushed forward, turned the handle, and stepped boldly into the room beyond.

Aamir stood near the door, his shoulders hunched as he examined an array of belongings laid out neatly on the bed in front of him—pants, shirts, socks, underwear. A black leather bag sat to one side, open.

When Aamir turned, his face morphed into a mask of horror as he saw them standing there, smiling at him with innocent joy on their faces. Alex closed the door behind them, and Aamir observed the trio with a flustered look of fear.

"What are you doing here?" he gasped, his voice tight with anxiety. "You shouldn't be here—you need to leave, right now." Aamir took Jari by the shoulders and ushered him toward the open door.

"We came to see if you were all right," Jari explained sullenly, resisting Aamir as he pushed him toward the door.

"You can't be here! You need to leave. You need to go. *Now*!" Aamir pleaded, diving for the door handle and opening it wide. He shoved them roughly through, back into the corridor, pressing a finger to his lips as they stood out in the darkness. He paused, listening intently to the silence. "You shouldn't have come—you really shouldn't have come," he whispered, his voice dripping with terror.

"We wanted to make sure you were okay… Jari told us what happened," Natalie tried to explain, but Aamir was restless, his eyes scanning the shadows, his neck jerking backward in sharp motions as he glanced anxiously over his shoulder.

"You need to leave," Aamir murmured again. "Come with me—you need to go. You really shouldn't have come here." He took hold of Jari's arm and set off down the corridor with the rest in tow. Beneath his palm, he held the dim glow of a ball of magic, casting a faint light as they walked.

"We came for you," Jari repeated, his face crumpling at his friend's disinterest.

"I know... but you shouldn't have." Aamir shook his head, picking up the pace as he strode onwards, obviously hell-bent on getting them out of the teachers' quarters as quickly as possible.

"If it's the curfew, then we're ready for that," Jari told him as he struggled against the pull of the older boy's strength.

"It's not the curfew. You just—" Aamir began, but Jari cut him off sharply.

"We shouldn't have come. I think we're starting to get the picture," he snapped.

As they passed the door with *Library* written beside it, Alex muttered his annoyance under his breath, wishing he had just made them stop for a second to have a look. It might not have been a wasted trip, then, he figured—they might have found something useful. Silently, he wondered if that was where the missing books were kept. Perhaps the censored gaps in the library's index were hoarded within the teachers' private library, giving them information students weren't permitted.

Looking at his friend-turned-professor, a sour thought popped into Alex's head. Aamir probably knew, now, about the inner workings of the manor, everything inside and outside of it. How much knowledge did their friend have, held back by that glimmering band around his wrist? Alex couldn't help but feel a touch resentful toward the new professor and the secrets at his disposal. For a brief moment, even knowing it was unlikely and unfriendly, Alex couldn't help but think that, perhaps, Aamir hadn't wanted Alex to try to remove the band because he didn't *want* to share his secrets. Alex pushed the thought away, knowing it was bitter and unfair, as he followed Aamir through the hallways, past the stern gallery of former and current teachers.

A figure stepped out into the light, blocking their path.

"And just *what* do you think you're up to, after curfew, in the teachers' quarters?" roared Renmark in his unmistakable growl, his eyes sinister in the pale glow of Aamir's feeble light.

"I had some personal matters to discuss with these students, Professor Renmark," Aamir said swiftly. "I asked them to my chambers, as they required some extra tutoring. We went on later than I anticipated, and I am just returning them now, to ensure they don't get into any trouble. It was entirely my fault."

"I know you're new here, Nagi, and you haven't quite gotten into your head how things work—despite being told time after time—but that doesn't mean you get to bend the rules to your liking. This is simply unacceptable. The Head might turn a blind eye to it, but I won't,"

Renmark said, eyeing Aamir with the look of someone who had just stepped in something unpleasant. "You want to provide extra tutoring, you do it in your classroom or study hall—you do *not* bring students into our personal quarters whenever you feel like it. We come here to get away from students, not be followed around by them. Is that clear, Nagi?"

There was a strong animosity between the young new teacher and the seasoned professor, Renmark visibly displeased with the manner in which Aamir had forced his way onto the faculty. After so long with the same lineup of teachers, Alex imagined it hadn't been an easy pill to swallow—to see Derhin replaced with some young upstart, especially one who seemed favored by the Head, at least initially.

Aamir tensed, a flash of anger passing across his eyes, as he leveled his gaze at Renmark. Touching Aamir's arm lightly, Natalie stepped forward, the dim glow of Aamir's magic glancing across her pale skin, revealing more of her face in the warm light.

"I am truly sorry, Professor Renmark. It was simply an opportunity to learn, and the time got away from us," she explained gently, her eyes wide with sincerity.

"Ah, Natalie—I didn't see you there," said Renmark, a puzzled look creasing his brow. "Well… be on your way, then, and be quick about it. Don't let it happen again," he added, his tone softening.

"Of course, Professor Renmark," Aamir spoke tersely. He skirted around Renmark, the others following quickly behind.

A melancholy air hung around the four friends as they slowly made their way down the corridors, toward the blue line at the entrance to the quarters, which was still broken at both ends. Nobody was willing to speak as the silence stretched unbearably, peppered only by the scuff of Aamir's feet on the stone and the soft pad of the others' socks. Aamir's gaze was always forward, never looking down at Jari or back at Natalie and Alex as he led them closer to where the blue line had lain, buzzing and crackling. It seemed to Alex that Aamir was beyond their help, his face fearful, his eyes constantly looking over his shoulder.

Aamir's urgency was palpable as he moved them over to the other side and knelt on the ground, before the broken barrier. Hurriedly, he began to repair it with his magic, the golden energy flowing from his palms and into the shattered ends of the line.

"I need to fix this before anyone else notices," Aamir whispered. "If someone were to see it, they would suspect a student and start a witch hunt."

"Sorry," Alex said. "I would've fixed it myself if I could."

"It's fine. You must—" Aamir made a choking noise. He lifted his gaze up to his trio of friends, a wide look of anguish in his eyes as he slowly began to mouth something. Alex felt a prickle of fear shiver through him as he understood the unmistakable shape of the words:

"*He knows.*"

As soon as the words had silently slipped from Aamir's mouth, his body doubled up in an instant burst of agony. He crumpled sideways onto the hard stone floor, clutching desperately at his stomach and raking at his lungs, as if the air was being squeezed from them by the pain. Aamir's face twisted, and his eyes bulged, his cheeks turning purple. He clawed at his throat, his breath coming in short, painful-sounding rasps, as he convulsed on the floor in untold agony—the golden line on his wrist exacting its punishment for his whispered warning.

The blue line was back in place, bursting into life, preventing the others from running over and helping their friend.

"Aamir!" Jari cried out in panic.

Alex skidded to the floor to place his hands on the sapphire pulse of energy, but Aamir raised a desperate hand against his attempts, shaking his head as the veins popped and strained beneath his neck, begging him not to. They watched, helpless, as Aamir writhed against the savage bite of the golden band.

"Go! *Go!*" Aamir commanded over and over, his voice frantic and thick with the pain.

Grabbing Jari and pulling him back, Alex retreated

with Natalie. Tears prickled Alex's eyes at the sight of his friend's suffering, knowing he could do nothing. Aamir's mouthed words haunted them from the shadows as they turned and ran, his tortured cries ringing in their ears.

It was the Head. The Head knew.

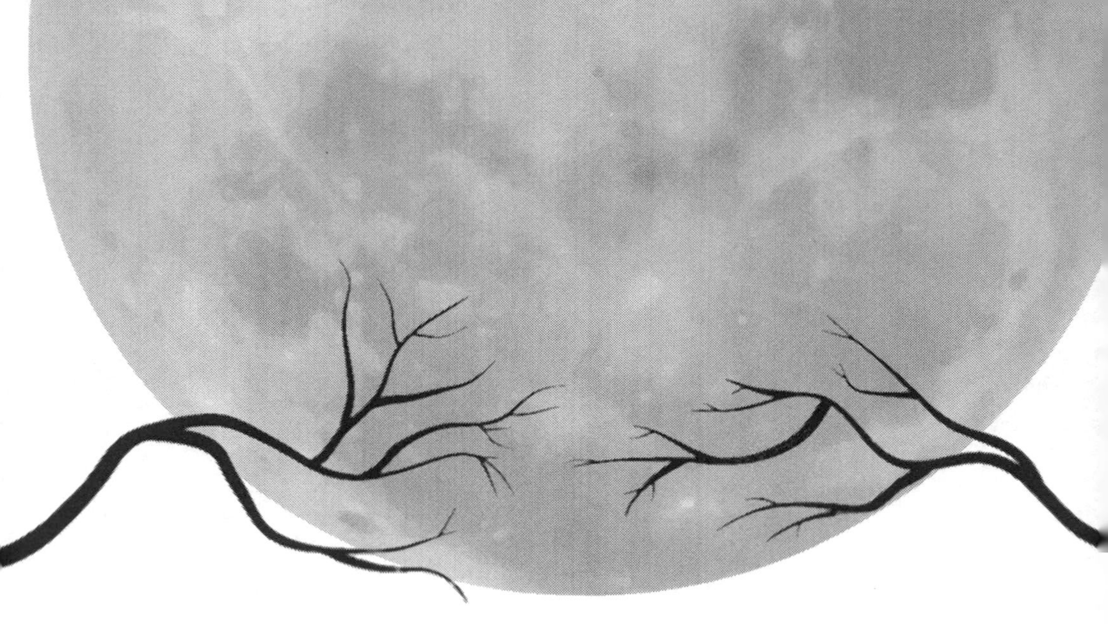

CHAPTER 10

Alex had lain awake long after they had returned to their dorm, and when dawn arrived, he realized he hadn't slept a wink. Across the room, he knew Jari had been the same, the boy uncharacteristically silent. Alex had spent the night staring up at the ceiling, his mind racing with the events of the night before, stirring up visions each time he had closed his eyes, a cold sweat trickling down his back and across his brow. Aamir's mouthed words had played again and again, on endless repeat, making sleep impossible.

How much does the Head know? was all Alex could think, his heart racing along with his mind as he envisioned the skeletal creature beneath the hood grasping for him, wanting to destroy the Spellbreaker history coiled up inside him.

Unable to stay in bed any longer, Alex sat up and rubbed his itchy eyes. Jari sat up too, and a look passed between them. Aamir's unmade bed drew their eyes, and Alex thought he saw Jari shiver as he turned his gaze away. The sound of Aamir's cries, echoing behind them, had been a disturbing one, and Jari certainly looked haunted. His face was drawn, dark circles shadowing the skin under his red-tinged eyes, his shoulders slumped.

The two spoke very little as they dragged themselves out of bed and dressed quickly, wandering dozily toward the mess hall to attempt to eat a quick breakfast before the trials of the day. Alex was on edge and couldn't help but imagine the Head breaking down the doors at any moment and dragging him to the room with the manacles that dangled from the ceiling.

Alex and Jari walked into the mess hall, expecting the usual buzz of morning activity, only to be met with a low hum of curious gossip. Natalie marched over to them, looking just as worn out as they felt, her eyes bloodshot and her skin far paler than normal. Nobody paid the trio any mind, their gazes distracted by the far wall, where an enormous noticeboard had been erected against the stonework. On it was a long list of announcements written on the black background in curling white chalk. The three friends stepped closer to get a better view of what was written there, joining the small crowd already gathered in front of it.

The first bullet point read that graduation had been cancelled, causing a few students to smile with relief, giving a quiet whoop as they patted each other on the back.

The next statement announced that Professor Nagi would be on temporary hiatus from the school while he worked with both Heads in pursuit of new student recruitment. Alex, Natalie, and Jari looked at one another in alarm. There was, at least, some comfort to be found in the word 'temporary'—a certain promise that Aamir would be returned to them, at some point down the line. There was little comfort to be found, however, in the rest of the sentence, as it brought to light some meaning in what Aamir had mouthed to them the night before.

The Head knows about Finder's death, Alex thought. *That has to be what the Head knows.* Alex didn't think the Head knew specifically that it was he who had disposed of Finder, but he knew the Head was onto something. The statement seemed intended to keep the students believing nothing had changed. To mention 'both Heads' kept the secret of Finder's disappearance from the curiosity of the other students, reminding them of the potency of their leaders, but Alex couldn't shake the feeling of what it meant to him.

The Head knew. That was the crux of it. He knew, but

he didn't want the truth to spread, though Alex guessed the Head must have known the perpetrators would see the statement and know it to be a lie. There was only one Head now, and they would have to wait and see if any vengeance would follow.

A ripple of quiet surprise spread across the rest of the students at this revelation. Nobody could remember a time when the Head had left the premises before. It was well known that the mysterious, invisible 'Finder'—the second Head—was the only one to venture outside the manor walls, in pursuit of new students. Though none of them had ever seen him, save for Alex and his anti-magical capabilities, everyone had seen the gate open and close, and the misty-eyed, hypnotized students he had brought through. The students of Spellshadow were proof enough of Finder's existence, but his sudden departure with the Head spurred both alarm and curiosity in the other students. It had never been done before, as far as any of them knew.

The students wondered what the reasoning might have been. Suggestions traveled around the mess hall in a haphazard game of 'telephone', all of them asking the same question: What was important enough to call both Heads away, with a teacher in tow?

Another note on the board explained that Professor Nagi's classes were to be covered equally by Professor Renmark and Professor Gaze, which caused a quiet groan amongst the gathered pupils—nobody wanted extra classes with Renmark.

The announcements grew worse as the list progressed. In the Heads' absence, a new curfew of nine p.m. sharp was to be introduced. The message stated that if anyone was caught out of their rooms after such a time, they would be subjected to severe punishments. It didn't elaborate, but the students could guess well enough.

Any former buzz of excitement had turned into an anxious ball of tension as the list went on and on, adding more and more rules to an already extensive list.

There would be an extra lesson put in place, after the evening meal, to prevent any lax behavior before bed, a time that ought to be used solely for study. Evenings were to be spent asleep, in the library, or in study hall—there were to be no alternative options. It also stated that students were strictly forbidden from spending their leisure time—what remained of it, anyway—on the manor grounds, as fresh air was to be taken within the lunch hour only, or not at all.

Beneath that was a warning that failure to attend lessons would lead to the same 'severe punishments', and tardiness would not be tolerated, under any circumstances. All of it seemed cruel and relentless, snatching away the final snippets of freedom they had clung to.

Surprise, concern, and worry spread through the gathered groups of students, the trio of friends included, as they read over the new announcements again, absorbing them with intense displeasure. The sullen murmur of discussion continued over uneaten plates of toast and soggy bowls of cereal, all appetites lost as the students watched tentatively over their shoulders, nervous that someone might be listening—the very someone who had put that board up.

Alex sat with his hands balled into fists, his knuckles whitening as he felt the manor closing in around him. Jari gazed listlessly down into a milky bowl of cornflakes, and Natalie stared blankly into a mug of tea, watching the teabag float idly. They felt the absence of their fourth companion keenly as they glanced back at the noticeboard, wondering where on earth he had gone.

The day passed slowly and uneventfully, nobody coming to get them mid-lesson or surprising them in the hallway as they moved from period to period, keeping their heads down. An atmosphere of uncertainty had infected the whole manor. Even the hallway windows weren't sure what to think, one looking out on a beautiful tropical beach with golden sand and turquoise waves, while the next showed a violent storm whipping around the jagged peaks of stony mountains, grim and desolate, lashed by lightning and rain and hailstones.

"Come on," Alex said to Jari and Natalie. They were at the end of their brand-new evening session, their minds exhausted from lack of sleep and a long day. It was eight p.m., and they had an hour to kill before curfew. Frustrated by the feeling of being hemmed in, Alex wasn't interested in spending his last hour in the library or study hall. He wanted to feel the kiss of fresh air on his face, draw it deep into his lungs, and shake off the antsy, irritated feeling crawling beneath his skin.

"Where are we going?" Natalie asked, a little anxiously, as Alex led the way, striding through the hallways toward the entrance of the manor.

"To try something out," replied Alex cryptically. His friends followed him.

In the hallways, they passed a few other students, who were rushing to their dormitories so as not to be caught by any marauding staff members. Renmark in particular had taken a perverse delight in repeating the new rules to the students during their first class of the day. It had fed his need for power, Alex was sure. They thought he had been strict in their first session, but Renmark had shown he was capable of much, much worse. Their two sessions with him that day had consisted of brutal duels and exhausting new spells that had sapped the energy of them all, except Alex, who had had to watch as Natalie plowed on, doing double the work, the strain evident on her weary face. He wanted her to feel the cool air on her face too—she had earned it.

Around every corner, they expected Renmark to accost them with his accusing tone and strange eyes. He had told other students he'd be roaming the halls most evenings from now on, just in case anyone thought it smart to flout the rules. Alex wasn't sure why, but he felt the act was aimed at him personally, or him and his friends, anyway.

Things were changing.

There was little sanctuary to be found in the new regime. If Renmark had his way, the school would be as close to a military operation as possible, and their lives would only become more restricted. The only comfort was in Lintz's lessons. He had returned to work in a much brighter mood after the owl incident. And their other new teacher, Professor Gaze, had proven to be an unexpected delight as well. She was a small, ancient woman with a love of laughter, and her warm, generous manner relaxed the students and made her lessons as close to fun as it was possible to have in the manor. Professor Esmerelda had become frighteningly volatile, swinging from pleasant to aggressive in a nanosecond, seemingly as on edge as everyone else under the new rules, though she hadn't exactly been her usual flighty self since Derhin's upheaval. Each lesson, she would prowl the classroom, evidently paranoid one of her students was going to challenge her to a duel and steal her place on the faculty. She told them as much, in a woeful voice, pleading with them not to, promising she was a nice person. It threw Alex a little to hear a teacher talk that way, to know the changeover between Aamir and Derhin had caused more concern than he had realized. Then again, Esmerelda had always been a bit strange.

Finally, the trio entered the large foyer that led to the manor's entrance. The sky beyond was a hazy purple as sunset gave way to twilight, stars beginning to twinkle. A flurry of a breeze rippled through the air toward them from the grounds. Alex longed to be out in the desolate landscape, so charred and twisted and broken, yet carrying a macabre beauty he had developed a fondness for. It was so close he could scent the metallic tang of ozone in his nostrils.

"Last one out is a rotten egg!" Alex said with a grin, about to break into a sprint, when he felt Natalie's hand close around his arm, pulling him backward.

She shook her head, pointing miserably at something glimmering in the doorway. He saw the dull golden glow of the same type of barrier that lay across the ancient tomb, and felt a flood of rage surge through him. He walked toward it, kneeling on the ground, ready to place his palms against the pulsing radiance.

"You cannot break it every time, Alex," Natalie said sadly. Alex sat back on the cold stone floor, gazing out at the grounds beyond, desperate to escape the stifling walls of the manor house.

"Just this once?" Alex smiled weakly, knowing it was futile. Natalie was right, he couldn't keep breaking barriers. He'd only run the risk of getting caught.

"Not today, buddy," Jari croaked, slumping down on the floor beside Alex. They let the light breeze wash over their tired faces.

It was then that Alex's eye was drawn to the outer edge of the front lawn, his heart gripping in his chest as he jumped to his feet and moved to the farthest edge of the entrance, trying to get a better view.

"*No,*" he whispered in heartbroken disbelief. Jari shuffled to see what Alex was looking at. Natalie followed, peering over Alex's shoulder.

Something was not right with the front lawn. It was like an optical illusion; it took a moment for the mind to realize what it was seeing. Alex had simply thought they were looking from the wrong angle, but as he peered around as far as he could to get a better view, he realized his worst fears had come to life. The walls really were closing in on them. On the far side of the lawn, where the vast iron gate should have been, there was nothing but wall. The gate had disappeared entirely, replaced by a giant wall, smothered in the same magic-sapping gray ivy that curled and stretched across the grounds. They were locked in, closed off completely from the outside world.

"No," Alex breathed again. He slammed his fist against

the masonry of the doorframe.

"It is gone," Natalie whispered, holding her hands to her mouth in shock.

"They've trapped us in here," Jari wheezed, his head in his hands.

Alex gazed out upon the thick, ivy-covered wall, not quite believing his eyes.

The manor truly was a prison now.

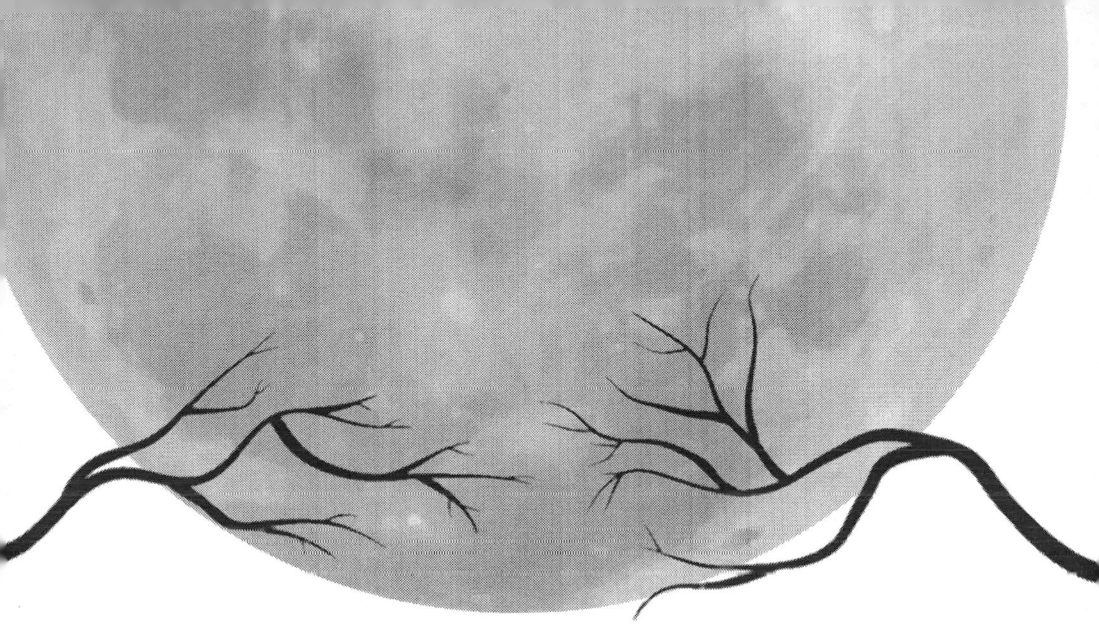

CHAPTER II

AS THE DAYS WENT BY IN THE CONFINES OF Spellshadow Manor, Alex came to realize the value of the brief time he and his friends had at their disposal. With the new restrictions in place, and Renmark's endless prowling, which he had somehow persuaded Esmerelda to join in, their only chance for a taste of freedom was lunchtime. On occasion, the three of them would pick up sandwiches and go for a wander, sitting on the broken fragments of ancient stone benches, or lying back in the dried-up grass, the blades prickling through their clothes as they wolfed down whatever they'd managed to pilfer from the mess hall.

One lunchtime, after forgoing the midday meal, Alex decided they should use the time to go and spar in the cellar instead. It had been a long while since they had sparred, and Alex had almost pleaded with his friends, knowing his skills were getting rusty with disuse. Natalie and Jari had agreed to come along with him, happy for the distraction of a good old-fashioned fight. What was more, during Renmark's lessons, Alex often felt the cold shiver of his anti-magic beneath his palms, conjured by prickling resentment toward the professor's teaching methods, until he almost couldn't control it. He knew he needed a safe place to practice defusing his knee-jerk reactions before they got out of hand.

"With all these weird things going on, I figure it wouldn't hurt for me to get a bit stronger," Alex explained as the three of them walked down the steps and out onto the grounds.

Natalie and Jari nodded in agreement. They walked through the desolate gardens, rubble skittering away beneath their feet, the skeletal trees reaching their clawed hands skywards, raking at the livid sky. A headless, limbless statue stood sentinel over a patch of dead weeds. Up above, a storm was picking up, shifting the dirt and rustling the draped gray ivy that hung all across the manor grounds, sprouting from holes in the stone walls, spewing from the innards of blackened trees.

"So, how do we get out now that there's no gate?" Jari

asked, kicking a stone against one of the cracked walls.

"We'll just have to think of something else. Besides, they weren't exactly going to let us just walk out, were they?" Alex replied, shoving his hands in his pockets, his fingertips touching the sharp edge of a forgotten square of paper.

"If you get strong enough, do you reckon you can break the manor's magic?" Jari ventured, staring up at the overcast sky.

Alex shrugged. "It's pretty strong, so… probably not."

"Maybe we could summon some ancient creatures to come help us, like a dragon or a griffon or something." Jari grinned at the idea. "We could control them and use one to bite off the Head's head!" He laughed, turning to Natalie. "Hey, you dabble in necromancy—you think you could try it with one of those stuffed ones in the hall?" Jari suggested, his tone only half joking.

"I don't think so. You would end up controlling nothing more than a scary bit of fur stuffed with cotton wool," Natalie chuckled.

"Maybe I could give the manor a try. What do you think?" Alex asked, turning to Natalie.

She shrugged. "I believe the manor's magic could indeed be broken, but it would take the most enormous amount of energy. I have read of such things—dark magic that may perform great things, more than you could ever imagine. I do not think I am strong enough to wield such magic yet, but I may be one day." Her eyes were bright with passion. "There are not many capable of such magic, but it can be done," she added wistfully as they neared the cellar.

Alex eyed Natalie suspiciously, noting the excitement in her voice as she spoke of this rare magic. Guessing from her dreamy expression, Alex assumed she wished she were one of those few. He hadn't heard her willingly mention dark magic before, and the thrill it seemed to give her worried him a little. Great power rarely led to good.

"Do you mean life magic?" Alex asked, leveling his gaze at Natalie.

She flushed. "I mean dark magic."

"But life magic is dark magic," Alex continued, growing more concerned by his friend's words.

"It can be controlled if you know how."

"It's dangerous, Natalie. You shouldn't dabble in life magic. No good can come from it. It leaves a scar on your soul. When you use life magic, it takes a piece of you with it. You know that," Alex said, wanting his friend to understand. "Promise me you won't do any life magic. Promise me, Natalie." She looked down, her expression sheepish.

"Of course not, Alex. You worry too much. I would never do such a thing," she said finally, lifting her gaze. "I would not be so stupid." She smiled reassuringly, but Alex wasn't convinced.

They stopped beside the familiar split tree. Alex

brushed the gravel and dust away from the trapdoor in the ground, and lifted it. A rush of musty air stung Alex's eyes as he glanced down into the room below. It was dark, the torches blown out.

They dropped down into the subterranean cavern, quickly lighting the lamps, which cast a warm glow around the room. A few scorch marks remained from the last time they had been in there, with Aamir, and Jari stared at them uncomfortably. Shaking his head, he went off in search of bottles.

"So do you think the Head has actually gone, then?" Jari asked, reappearing with two dusty magnums in his hands.

"What?" Alex turned, puzzled.

"Do you think he has actually gone?" Jari repeated. "Or do you think he's just playing tricks, tightening his hold on the school?"

"I'm not sure," Alex admitted. "But he must know Finder is dead by now. When the board said *both* Heads, I knew that was a message. It would only make sense to those who know Finder is gone."

Jari nodded. "I thought that too. So you think he has gone and taken Aamir with him?"

Alex shrugged. "Maybe the Head wants more students. And with Finder gone, that means he has to go out and get them himself, or find someone to take Finder's place. Maybe he wants Aamir to do it, or something. I don't know. The wall seems a bit like overkill if the Head *hasn't* left the manor, don't you think?"

"The wall is a weird move," Jari agreed, drawing a star shape in one of the dust-blanketed bottles. "Maybe he just wants to frighten us."

"Or maybe we have spooked him by killing Finder, no?" Natalie said evenly, her expression thoughtful as she leaned back against the earthen wall of the cellar.

"You think so?" Jari asked.

"I believe it is possible, yes," Natalie continued. "He perhaps felt as if he had lost some control, and so he has chosen to reclaim his control with these new rules."

"I don't think he'd need a wall if he wanted to leave, either," Alex began. "He's a majorly powerful wizard. I'm sure he has other ways… secret ways." He felt the pointed edge of the paper in his pocket, recalling the last time they had been in the cellar, and how he had wanted to tell his friends about the note Elias had given him.

"What kind of secret ways?" Jari asked, sounding intrigued.

Alex took a deep breath. "See, the thing is… a while ago, I found this note in between the pages of a book. An old thing full of pretty dull histories, but this bit of paper came tumbling out of it," he started, expecting his friends to assume he'd found the book in the library. He wanted to leave out Elias's role in delivering the message. The moment he even thought about saying the name, he felt a creeping sensation prickle at the back of his neck, the invisible gag keeping him silent on the subject of the shadow-man.

"And?" Natalie encouraged.

"Well, it said something about there being nine havens, and that wizards were to find these havens and lock themselves in there, away from some evil. It didn't really go into detail, but it said there were four havens left," Alex said.

"Havens?" Jari frowned.

Alex nodded. "Yeah, they're schools, like this one. The havens are the schools, and there are four left… or there were when the note was written. Do you remember the Head talking about that Blaine kid being sent to Stillwater House? You know, when he got caught and… and he just never came back?"

The other two nodded.

"Well, Stillwater House is one of the havens. It's on the paper I found, along with two others: Falleaf House and Kingstone Keep. Altogether, four. I've been trying to find information on them, but I keep hitting a brick wall. There are entries in the Index where the books should be, but the books themselves are missing from the shelves," he continued, feeling the intensity of their eyes on him as he talked. "So there must be other schools. The Head mentioned Stillwater specifically, so I was thinking, maybe, at least that school still exists, and the Head has some sort of dealings with them. So if he wanted to go anywhere, or needed something, surely he'd just go to them for help."

"Other schools?" whispered Natalie.

"I'm thinking that's where the Head might've gone. Stillwater," Alex repeated.

"You think there might be a way to travel there?" Natalie bristled with excitement.

Alex shrugged. "I think there's a chance. It's like everyone was saying at breakfast—nobody has ever really seen or heard of the Head going out on the grounds, so I think that's it. I think he travels there using some special kind of magic."

Alex could feel Jari's glare from across the room. Alex couldn't be certain, but he felt a strange energy coming from the blond-haired boy. He was narrowing his eyes as he scrutinized Alex. Shifting uncomfortably, Alex turned back to Natalie, who seemed far more excited, her dark eyes alert with curiosity.

"You really believe there might be a way to travel to these places?" She clasped her hands together.

"I think it's possible," said Alex.

"Why would you want to, if it's like this place?" Jari said, his face still sour.

"There might not be so many barriers on the other places, or there might be a way to reach one that isn't in use anymore. A stepping stone to getting out," Alex replied, frowning at his friend.

"Do you think the other schools might help us?" asked Natalie.

"I couldn't say. You know as much as I know, now." Alex shrugged apologetically, cracking the knuckles of his right hand beneath his palm as he tried to ignore the displeasure on Jari's face.

"How long *have* you known?" Jari asked. It sounded more like an accusation than a question.

"What do you mean?" said Alex, attempting to play dumb.

"How long have you known about these havens? When did you find this note?" replied Jari, waving his hand in the air.

Alex shrugged. "A week or so, I can't remember." He ran a hand through his hair as he answered. Cold sweat prickled the back of his neck.

"Why didn't you say something sooner?" Jari pressed.

"There hasn't exactly been time," sighed Alex. Though he knew he could have told them sooner, and had intended to, there was honesty in his words. What with Aamir and Derhin and the Head's disappearance, other things had taken precedence.

Still, guilt bristled in the pit of Alex's stomach, and he resented the feeling of being called out. He hadn't meant to keep the information from them, not really. Had he? The paper *had* been in his pocket for weeks, and Elias's name still wouldn't spring willingly from his tongue. They had no clue the mysterious shadow-man even existed, because Alex had kept him secret. From day one, Alex had kept Elias to himself. However, it didn't seem fair to Alex that he was the only one being dissected because of a single secret, not when Alex knew there were other secrets being kept by the two friends beside him. There was the matter of Natalie's shiftiness every time dark magic or Renmark's private tutoring was brought up, as well as Jari's solo visits to Aamir after lessons, before their failed rescue attempt.

"You could have found time," Jari said, raising an eyebrow. Alex grappled with the growing twist of guilt in his gut.

"When?" Alex could feel the flare of his temper. "Look, I found the piece of paper and I meant to tell you, but things kept getting in the way and I forgot. I'm only human," he explained wearily.

Natalie smiled. "It's okay. Sometimes it is not so easy to tell things," she said. "To find the time, I mean," she added quickly, though the peculiarity in her previous words made Alex curious, and there was an unmistakable conspiratorial note in her voice. She turned away before he could question it. Alex frowned, feeling tension building in the air around him. Natalie wouldn't look at him, and Jari looked too intently at him.

"Well, I think it's a waste of time," Jari stated. "Even if these 'havens' are out there, they aren't going to lift a finger to help us."

Though Alex hated to admit it, Jari probably had a point. Those books were missing for a reason, and Blaine had never come back from Stillwater House—assuming he really had been sent there. It seemed like either a one-way ticket to another school with another wall and another Head, or a one-way ticket to something far worse.

Whichever outcome contained the truth, Alex knew he had opened a can of worms he could never get closed again.

CHAPTER 12

THE NEXT EVENING, ALEX FOUND HIMSELF HAULED to the library after the last lesson of the day, pulled along by Natalie's eager hand. The sun was setting through the far window as they entered. He was tired and groggy, dreaming of the soft pillow on his bed, but she had been insistent that he come with her, not taking no for an answer as she dragged him through the hallways.

"I have had a breakthrough," she explained, ushering Alex over to their usual spot in the corner. Stacked high on the table were columns of leather books, in various colors with brightly embossed lettering, teetering crookedly to one side. They reminded Alex of a game of Jenga, and he smirked as he sat down, wondering if he dared pull one from the tower.

"With what?" asked Alex, his brow furrowed in confusion as he sat back in the armchair, trying to resist the comforting pull of the soft cushions and the fire crackling in the grate.

"What you told us yesterday," she began excitedly. "It made me think about the possibilities of magical travel."

"Mmhm." Alex's eyes drooped shut as he sank deeper into the chair. Natalie smacked him lightly on the arm. "Magical travel, I was listening!" he yelped, rubbing his bicep.

"Well, I found out some things. I have been reading much on travel and transportation," said Natalie gleefully, sitting down in the chair opposite.

"I can see that." Alex grinned, still tempted to pull one of the books from the middle of the stack.

"Here."

Alex couldn't see Natalie over the vast array of literature as she spoke, but he saw the book coming as it flew through the air toward him, landing with a smack against his hands as he reached up and caught it, just in time.

"What is it?" he asked.

"Just read it, see if it has anything about travel in it," she demanded, peering around the stack to shoot Alex a look.

"Sorry," he muttered. He opened the book to the

first page: *The Limitations of Clockwork Machinery and Other Uses* by R.B. Moxam. Before he even read a word, Alex knew the book was going to be dull. He wondered if Natalie would notice if he took a little nap. A second book flying through the air toward him gave him the answer to that question; even if she couldn't see him to tell him off, the thrown artillery of books would certainly keep him awake.

"Ah, here it is!" he heard Natalie proclaim breathlessly as she rushed over to him. Perched on the armrest of his chair, she shoved a book under his nose, her finger pointing to one of the lines. Alex read it, but couldn't quite make sense of it. As far as he could tell, it was simply a brief explanation of a group of spells that required a huge consumption of energy, and how they might be achieved.

"I don't get it," he said.

"Spells which require a huge amount of energy," repeated Natalie, her gaze expectant, as if waiting for the cogs to click into place inside Alex's head.

He smiled apologetically. "I have nothing."

"Alex, the magic of the manor!" she squealed, rolling her eyes at his slowness. "The manor requires a huge amount of energy to function, no? It is always shifting places, from one land to another to another. Do you not think that must use up a lot of magic?"

"I suppose so…"

"Of course it does! A huge amount, Alex. One of the

other books explains that to move a big object, such as an elephant or a truck or a building, you need a vast magic source. It is not easy and uses much magic. So imagine the magic needed to move this place," she whispered, gesturing around the library. "It must take an *exorbitant* amount, even to just do it once! And this place moves every day. Can you imagine?"

"I have no idea," he said, trying to take in the enormity of what she was saying.

"It takes a lot of magic just to move a pebble or a beetle or something small. Imagine how much magical energy is needed to move the manor, the grounds and every person within it, every single day!" Natalie explained, her voice quietening to a hushed whisper. "That would require a whole other level of magic, Alex. One which I am not certain any one wizard can possess."

Natalie's words began to make some sense to him. The shifting inner hallways of the building, with their windows showing foreign skies and wild landscapes, one moment in Southeast Asia, the next, who knew where. The changing view beyond the manor's boundaries that he often looked out on from the library window, the building and its compound uprooted from one place to another, never settling. Alex didn't understand how it all worked, and hadn't thought about the energy needed to accomplish such a feat. Since he hadn't even known magic existed until about a year ago, he supposed he had thought it par for the course—that all magical buildings and magical people could be moved and replaced at will. If any wizard was capable of such a feat, the Head was surely a contender; he had already shown Alex what appeared to be the whole world within his palms.

"So not even the Head can move the manor? Really?" he asked Natalie.

"Not even the Head, I do not think. Not without a lot of other wizards to help or extra magic to boost his strength," she replied, shaking her head.

Alex frowned. "Then how is it possible?"

"There is no mention of any magic so large as this," explained Natalie. "I have my thoughts on how it can be done, but I think I need more time to study it. When I have more to tell, you will be the first to know, but I have a feeling it is to do with the other side of the magical spectrum," she whispered, her eyes gleaming as they leveled with Alex's, her excitement rippling from her like static electricity. Alex could feel it.

"Life magic?" he asked, his voice growing stern.

"Perhaps," was all she would say, much to Alex's chagrin. He watched her wander back to her seat.

So much of what he had learned disturbed him. Natalie's apparent fixation with spells requiring life magic and the thought that the manor moving might have something to do with that kind of magic—it chilled him to the core.

Reading the passage beneath Natalie's finger more closely, it did indeed seem physically bizarre that the manor should be able to move at all, and yet it did; there was no denying that it did. Windows looking out on Australia and Europe and deep South American jungle were a dead giveaway. Somehow, it was managing to do the impossible.

"What's this?" he murmured to himself, picking up a large, intriguing-looking tome from the pile. The dyed pink leather caught his eye, the cover vivid against the plain wood of the table and the dull-toned books beneath. On the front, in purple lettering, was the title *The Trouble with Travel,* by Benjamin Cornwell.

He opened the book on his lap, the ancient cover creaking at the spine. A few pages in, Alex came to the contents page, not expecting the pleasant surprise that awaited him there. Laid out neatly, in uniform print, were names and descriptions of magical travel techniques and how to use them. Alex was stunned, wondering how on earth this one had slipped through the Head's net of library censorship.

"Look at this," he whispered excitedly to Natalie, beckoning her back over.

"What is it?" she asked, peering down.

"A how-to guide to magical travel." He almost laughed. The book was so perfect, each mode of travel resting neatly on the yellowing paper beside a helpful page number, begging to be read.

"Can this be?" She grinned, and Alex nodded as he flipped to the first of the numbered sections.

It was entitled "Simple Teleportation for Beginners." A sense of triumph ran through Alex's veins, a smile spreading across his face as he read the brief introduction. The magic seemed easy enough; what he was reading certainly wasn't beyond Natalie's powerful skillset.

"What do you think?" he asked her, lifting the book so she could get a better look.

"It doesn't look too complex, I don't think," she agreed, confirming Alex's suspicions. "I can certainly give it a go." Her face broke into a childish grin of excitement.

The clock on the wall of the library chimed a quarter to nine, distracting Alex; curfew was almost upon them. Alex felt a flicker of annoyance. He still wasn't used to the new restrictions, and each reminder of them grated on his nerves.

"I'll put this somewhere safe," whispered Alex, checking the surrounding area before shoving the pink book beneath the main cushion of the green armchair. It made the center rise up in a wonky fashion, but Alex pushed the book farther back until it rested in the gap where the back of the chair met the base, covering any remaining strangeness in the fabric with the smaller cushions.

"Shall we try tomorrow?" asked Natalie.

Alex nodded. "Tomorrow at lunchtime. See if Jari wants to come this time," he said, sighing as they made their way quickly out of the library.

Jari had proven difficult to pin down after Alex's revelation in the cellar about the havens. Though Alex had tried to speak with him, feeling he ought to attempt to explain himself better on the matter of keeping the note to himself, he was met with short replies and a suspicious look that Alex couldn't quite work out. In lessons, though Jari hadn't gone so far as to move away from Alex, the blond-haired boy barely made conversation, though Alex tried relentlessly. It stung Alex to see his friend become so distant over so small a thing as a forgotten scrap of information.

Even Natalie had attempted to get Jari to come to the library, but he had flat out refused, claiming he had other work to do, passing Alex that curious expression as he went in the opposite direction. Returning to the dormitory, Alex guessed Jari would be pretending to sleep, not realizing the lack of snoring betrayed him every time. He wasn't sure what he'd done to deserve such cold treatment from his friend, but how could he find out if Jari wasn't willing to talk about it?

"Tomorrow at lunchtime," agreed Natalie, and they parted ways.

Sitting out on the crisp grass, his crossed legs flattening the dry blades of faded green, Alex looked grimly up at the high wall, which now surrounded every part of the manor gardens. He was still getting used to the absence of the gate, which to him had been the central feature of the manor's grounds for so long.

He sat in the shade of the wall so as not to be seen, and because it was an unusually balmy day. The sun shone brightly down on the desolate gray of the gardens, warming his face as he closed his eyes against it.

Alex had the pink book open in his lap, a musty scent rising from the pages as the mildew dried out in the sunlight. He had pinched the book from its hiding spot in the library earlier that day. Natalie was setting up nearby, awaiting Alex's instruction from the manual. He had decided they should try teleporting from one place to another, keeping it small to begin with. The title said "Simple Teleportation," but Alex wasn't sure such a thing existed.

"It says to focus on the place you want to teleport to. Using your magic, you need to create a shield both around yourself and within yourself, and compress that magic," he explained to Natalie. "Once it's compressed, you should have morphed into a ball of energy. Move that ball of magic from where you are to where you want to be, and then decompress it back to your full form." It sounded a lot like gibberish as he spoke the words aloud. More than that, it sounded potentially dangerous. "Does that make any sense to you?" he asked.

"Not much," admitted Natalie. A sheen of golden energy rippled through her body and lay slickly against her as if it were a second skin, her whole self glowing. Alex watched, focusing on Natalie's steady glow, ready to step in with his anti-magic if something went wrong. She radiated light, the image an ethereal one, but she didn't seem to be going anywhere or turning into the proposed ball of light.

A few moments passed before Alex realized something was wrong.

"Are you all right?" he asked, kneeling.

"Yes, it's just not working," said Natalie, her face scrunched up in concentration.

"In what way?" he pressed.

"I keep trying to draw my magic upward, but I cannot. I keep focusing on the stairs, willing myself to move, but… it is like something is pressing back against me," she explained, the golden sheen fading from her skin as she ceased her efforts.

"What does it feel like?" asked Alex. He skimmed through the manual to see if it said anything about environmental resistance.

"It burns," she muttered.

"It burns?"

"Yes, it is hard to explain," she said quietly.

"How about some flight?" encouraged Alex. He

flipped to another section of the book he thought they might try.

Scanning the list, he eliminated the travel techniques that required any equipment they didn't have, such as a standard-issue cape, a pair of griffon's wings, the scales of a dragon, or the tail feather of a 'Thunderbird,' to name a few. That left only a handful that needed solely magic, but enough for Alex to be hopeful of success. He wondered if that was how the book had slipped past the Head's notice: the students had no access to any of the things required for most of the travel methods.

"Is it not simply like in the library?" Natalie frowned, reminding Alex of the graceful leaps from the towers that everybody except him seemed able to do.

He shook his head. "No, I think that's more like jumping and falling. This is a bit more of a long-distance thing," he explained, reading quickly through the "Introduction to Flying" section. "Okay, so you need to force your magic into your feet, while holding streams of magic in your hands, sort of like a marionette puppet. Turn the streams in your hands with your index and middle finger in opposite circles, until you create a cushion of air beneath your feet. Then raise your thumb with the other fingers and control up and down by pinching your two fingers against your thumb," he rambled, holding up the diagrams to Natalie so she might see better.

This one seemed a little easier, Alex thought, as he

watched her begin to move her fingers in the correct motions, her feet glowing amber as rippling streams of golden energy lifted from her toes to her hands. Slowly, she lifted from the ground, floating a short distance above it. Alex flashed her a thumbs-up as she glanced over to him, an anxious smile playing on her face. As she moved her three fingers into the right position, she pinched them together slowly.

Nothing happened, the cushion of air holding her just above the singed grass of the lawn. Alex pointed upward with his fingers, gesturing what she should do. Natalie nodded, swiftly moving her fingers apart, breaking the circle of the pinch. The effect was immediate as she soared into the air at hurtling speed. Alex's heart was in his mouth as he watched her shoot upward, almost as high as the roof of the manor. She was doing well, moving smoothly, seemingly in control.

Then, in a split second, everything went wrong. Natalie smacked hard into a barrier, invisible to the eye, running parallel from the tallest spire of the manor house across the grounds. Her body crumpled against it, frozen for a moment, before she began to tumble from the sky, the golden aura around her feet falling away like glittering dust.

Alex jumped to his feet, focusing on the falling figure as he sent a stream of black and silver toward her, trying to snatch her out of the sky. But he knew his anti-magic wasn't strong enough to catch and hold her, and he was unable to latch on to anything. Thinking quickly, he raced toward the point of her imminent impact, placing his palm down against the ground, squeezing his eyes closed as he formed a cushion beneath his hand. The familiar cold smothered his fingers, and he pushed the anti-magic higher and higher, inflating it.

Plummeting fast, Natalie collapsed into the deep drift of snow created by Alex's hands, the soft substance breaking her fall. Rushing to her aid, Alex couldn't help glancing over his shoulder to make sure nobody had seen the act. The grounds were empty, save for a few spiny bundles of tumbleweed that bounced lightly along the barren earth.

"Natalie! Natalie, are you okay?" He dug through the snow to get to her, though it was melting quickly in the sunlight.

"Ow." She winced, sitting up, showing surprise at the sight of the snow around her. She looked to Alex. "This was you?"

He nodded. "I had to improvise."

"Thank you," she whispered, holding a hand to the back of her neck.

"Are you okay?" asked Alex, watching his friend as she checked her limbs for broken bones.

"I think so. A few bruises." She smiled feebly, though her sudden, sharp intake of breath when Alex reached out to help her up told him that she was putting on a brave face.

Indeed, a purple welt was coming up beneath the apple of her cheek, and her upper lip was cut, fresh blood welling to the surface as Alex got her to her feet, the snow now a pool of water soaking into the thirsty dirt.

"Anything broken?" he asked.

Natalie brushed off the damp seat of her pants. "I do not think so."

"That was lucky," said Alex, a worried look in his eyes.

Natalie nodded. "A close call, no?"

"Very close." Alex sighed. "I don't think we should try this anymore." He helped Natalie across the derelict gardens, back toward the manor. She was limping slightly and leaned heavily against Alex as he walked with her.

"Neither do I," Natalie admitted, wincing as she lifted a hand to her cheek. "The manor's magic is far stronger than I thought," she added, looking up at the sky, squinting to try to see the invisible barrier she had smacked against. It explained why he'd never seen any birds within the manor walls.

After dropping Natalie safely outside Professor Lintz's

classroom for their next lesson, Alex ran back to the library with his contraband book in tow, feeling responsible for the way things had gone outside. He had been so intent on finding a way to travel from the manor that he had pushed away all acknowledgement of the risks, putting Natalie's life in danger.

Alex raced up the ladders to the farthest tower and pounded across the levels, pausing at a gap in a shelf. He shoved the pink leather book into the empty slot. It didn't matter that it wasn't the right place; it would eventually find its way back where it belonged.

As he made the slow climb back down, his gaze wandered to the sunlight beaming down on the lawn outside, glinting from the wall and glittering against the horizon where the real world lay. He wondered curiously if the travel techniques might be inverted with his anti-magical abilities so that he could twist the methods for his purposes. The gray ivy could prevent him from leaving, but he wasn't convinced the invisible barrier could. He didn't think anybody had thought in that much detail when designing the manor, of forging a barrier to keep *Spellbreakers* in. Then again, maybe they had. His people were the enemy after all.

The outside called to him, tempting him to try.

But what good would it do? Alex thought.

It would mean abandoning his friends and every student within these walls to save himself. The selfish notion left a bitter taste in Alex's mouth, and yet it was undeniably enticing. It wasn't as though he could fetch help, Alex realized; the manor was no place for non-magical people, and they wouldn't even be able to get close to the school, should they plan to launch any sort of rescue mission. People might even lock him up if he started babbling about magical manors and wizards, thinking he'd lost his mind, wherever he'd been the past year.

His mother would welcome him home, though. Alex's heart wrenched at the thought of her. She had been so ill before he'd disappeared. Who was to say she was even still alive, out there, waiting for him? Tears spiked the corners of his eyes as the morbid idea crept into his brain. He wondered if he'd know if she were dead—if some anti-magical part of himself would know, deep down, that she had gone. He had felt no such thing, at least to his knowledge, but he knew that didn't mean his mother was okay. Maybe it just meant his anti-magic didn't stretch that far.

A large part of him wanted to jump ship that instant, damning everyone else. He just wanted to make sure she was still alive. But he doubted whether he could have the best of both worlds. After all, he wouldn't be able to find his way back to Spellshadow if he left. He thought of Natalie and Jari, despite their ongoing differences, their families and their homes and their lives before. Of Natalie's family, especially, who had sent her away to America under the assurance that she'd be safe with Alex and his mother, only to have her disappear off the face of the earth.

Gritting his teeth, Alex knew he couldn't just walk out, no matter how desperately he wanted to see his mother again. It was a tough pill to swallow, but there it was. Alex just wished fervently that time didn't work the same out in the real world as it did within the manor walls—that a year to them was mere minutes to non-magical people. *That would be ideal*, Alex thought, hoping his mother wouldn't have to miss him.

Magical travel and anti-magical escape would have to wait. However, one technique close to the end of the tome had piqued Alex's interest. The section title read "Portals and How to Find Them." It did not require a spell, as such, but gave a short explanation on their usage: 'Often appearing as still passageways or doors with strange auras, these portals lead to other realms and destinations. Portals require a vast amount of magic to create and keep open, but many can be found by chance, usually those that have been forgotten. To use them, one need only walk through.'

Alex had committed the small section to memory, the words conjuring images of the shifting windows and the doors that led to nowhere within the manor. A slithering sense of despondency wriggled uncomfortably through his nerves, the realization dawning that it would take him years to check every single one. And by then, no doubt, it would be too late.

They had been duped again. It was so obvious to him now. He felt a bubble of rising resentment ripple through his body. How he loathed the Head for dangling such a tempting carrot of hope, only to swipe it away. Then again, Alex realized, that book would never have been in the library if they could actually have used it.

CHAPTER 13

A BLAST OF BLACK ENERGY, FLECKED WITH SHARDS of silver, thudded against the cellar wall, exploding in a burst of ice and snow. Alex grinned as he watched the ball shatter mere inches from Jari's head, a surprised expression appearing on the other boy's face as cold flecks of snow landed on the back of his neck.

Alex had finally managed to convince Jari to come and spar during the lunch break, after days of stilted conversation and frosty tension. He didn't want to speak too soon and jinx himself, but the break from the norm seemed to be doing a world of good for their strained relationship.

Alex thought he almost saw Jari smile as he sidestepped a well-aimed javelin of ice.

Sparring was a slightly different beast where Alex was involved. He couldn't simply throw his anti-magic in the direction of his opponent and expect them to snatch it away or deflect it with their magic; it would slip through their fingers, the anti-magic hitting home with a nasty sting at best, a deeper wound at worst.

To prevent accidental injuries, Alex had suggested they draw crosses in the dirt for him to aim at, with the sparring partner standing between the markings; he would try to hit the targets instead of his opponent. So far, he had only made impact once, a stray shard of black anti-magic skewering the front of Jari's boot, fortunately missing any toes. Otherwise, he had been on target, hitting the markings with a precision and focus that surprised even him. Jari and Natalie had been taking turns firing their magic at him. Alex had to swipe their attacks toward the wall with his anti-magic or attempt to dive out of the way when it came to particularly quick spears of golden light. Pleased with himself, Alex found he could snatch the stronger balls of magic in mid-air and make them evaporate into a flurry of snowflakes, where once he would have had to duck. Slowly, he was gaining some real control over his powers.

It was thrilling to see the black and silver mingling with the gold and white as the elements crashed together in the vacant space between Alex and his opponent. Direct impact resulted in a loud bang of an explosion, the two contrasting energies hovering together for a moment before erupting into a rush of bright white light that burned the eyes to look directly into, the breeze from the blast whipping over their faces as it swelled outwards. A few times during the sparring session, Alex paused to watch it when he should have been ducking, but he simply couldn't tear his eyes away from the sight.

A distinct improvement in Alex's focus and the strength of his summoning was evident to all, and he felt pride in the anti-magic he could conjure beneath his palms, molding it more easily to his will. The cold ripples coiled more effortlessly from his fingers, and he found he could spend less time with his eyes squeezed shut in concentration and more time looking at his opponent, surer that his anti-magic would do what he wanted as he watched for the moves and conjurations of his challenger. He had only been struck twice that session—a new record—the blows bruising him a bit as they disintegrated into snow, but doing no real harm.

Even Jari seemed impressed as they finished up, both drenched in sweat, Alex finally on the way to being evenly matched with his magical counterparts. They stepped forward and shook hands. Alex grinned as he wiped the sweat away with the back of his forearm.

"Good match," said Jari, giving Alex a half-smile.

"Well played," agreed Alex.

"You are getting much better!" Natalie chimed in from the side of the cellar, clapping gently.

Alex beamed as he picked up a towel from the cellar floor, wrapping it around his neck. He felt pleased with his progress.

"I've had a thought," said Jari unexpectedly as he dabbed the last beads from his brow.

"About what?" Alex asked, taking a sip from a mug of cold tea he had smuggled from the mess hall.

"About the Head." Jari slid down the wall of the cellar, landing in a heap on the floor as he sat against the earth, his legs extended.

"What about him?" Alex felt a sense of dread at what was to come from Jari's mouth.

"I want to know if he's still here or not," Jari said simply.

"It will not bring Aamir back." Natalie spoke softly, sitting down beside Jari on the floor.

Jari shook his head. "I want to find out if the Head is still within these walls, and, if he is, what he has done with Aamir. I need to know when Aamir is coming back," he insisted, his voice tight. "I can't rest until I know he's okay," he added quietly, looking far younger than his years as he dipped his head.

"You think they punished him?" Alex wondered aloud. The thought had been plaguing him too, each night as he lay in bed, struggling to drift off, wondering if Aamir's mouthed words to them had caused him extra trouble.

"I don't know. I just need to find out if the Head is still here," Jari repeated. "I have my reasons."

"Well," began Alex, pausing uncomfortably as he recalled the last time they had been in the cellar. "I'm having doubts about the Head leaving. He hasn't left before, as far as anyone can remember, has he? I think it's a trick to keep us scared." Alex shook his head. "I don't think Aamir has gotten into as much trouble as we fear. Or that the Head knows as much as we think he might. We're still here, aren't we? If he knew, we'd be gone for sure—I definitely would be. I think he just knows Finder is gone, but doesn't know why or how," he added, with an anxious shrug.

"He would certainly have come for us, if he knew it all," said Natalie. "If the Head truly is out there, though, then it is strange that he should go out of the manor with Aamir. If they have both gone, I wonder what it is they are up to. Surely, they would not both need to go if it was a matter of recruiting students?" she mused, her expression puzzled.

"Or maybe he's showing him how?" suggested Alex, the thought a chilling one. He did not like to think of Aamir out there, doing the job of that tattered gray ghost, using hypnotic whispers to draw young men and women into the trap of the manor, sentencing them to a life of imprisonment. Aamir was no Malachi Grey.

"I just need to see that the Head is physically within this building. I *have* to see it for myself," said Jari, with a determined grimace.

"Why do you have to actually *see* him?" Alex pressed, worried for his friend.

"It's just something I have to do. It might be exactly what we are looking for," muttered Jari, his voice barely audible.

Alex stared at Jari intently, wondering if the boy could be right. If the Head *was* gone, it very well could be their only chance at taking control. A prime opportunity, not to be missed.

"If I wanted to check, would you help?" asked Jari, sheepishly.

Alex glanced at Natalie, but her expression gave little away as she shrugged a response.

"It would depend on the plan," Alex replied, understanding the subtle implication in Jari's question. If Jari wanted to break into the Head's quarters, he would need Alex. Maybe that had been the only reason Jari had agreed to come and spar, to get Alex back on his side.

"I'll work on it," promised Jari as they all stood to leave, the manor calling them back.

True to his word, Jari raced off to the library after classes were over for the day, leaving Alex to wander through the hallways by himself on his way back to the dormitory. Alex was glad Jari was speaking to him again, even if his reasons weren't entirely honest; he had missed the quick humor and infectious laugh of his friend.

Stepping through the door of the dorm, Alex could sense something was amiss. He glanced around the room, walking cautiously over to his bed.

A figure slipped from the farthest shadows and sidled up to him. With a smirk etched across his black mouth, Elias perched on the bedpost, as solidly as a creature like him could, his shadow-draped body in constant fluid motion.

"Well, well, hasn't it been a long time," he said.

It felt bizarre to admit, but Alex had been worried for Elias; it had been weeks since he'd last seen him. With Malachi Grey gone, Elias was looking to be one of Alex's only hopes for any grasp on his heritage or his anti-magic. It wasn't as if the Head was going to tell him anything.

"Hello, Elias," replied Alex, trying not to let on that he was pleased to see his shadow-guide.

"I believe congratulations are in order," Elias

whispered, his words like silk.

"Congratulations?" asked Alex, confused, wondering if Elias had been in the cellar watching them. He hadn't felt the eyes of the mysterious creature.

"You disposed of that vile gray *thing*." Elias grinned, a sinister quality in the pleasure of the words as they glittered in his endless black eyes, the whole of the universe seemingly compressed within two dark almonds. "You got rid of Malachi Grey, achieving what decades of your kind couldn't." He chuckled slyly. "Surely that has to feel good?" he said, his voice oozing like honey from the shadowy cavern of his mouth.

Alex shrugged. "I haven't really thought about it," he lied. He got the feeling Elias wouldn't take too kindly to his admission of second thoughts over the death of Malachi Grey.

"And off the Head runs, like a scared little boy," cackled Elias, the sound startling. It was hard not to hear the thrill in Elias's voice. Alex couldn't be sure, but he thought Elias seemed more excited about that than the actual disposal of Malachi Grey.

"So, the Head really has gone?" asked Alex, wondering if he might get a straight answer for once.

"That's not for me to say," Elias tutted.

"Well, has he or hasn't he?" Alex pressed, trying again.

"Who can say?" Elias replied, the liquid slope of his shoulders rising in a shrug.

"Have you just come back to annoy me?" Alex snapped. "Where have you been, anyway?" He eyed the shadow-man curiously, looking for a hint of honesty on the peculiar, ever-shifting face.

"Oh, you know, here and there and everywhere. Watching this and that, getting under peoples' feet." Elias grinned, whipping his shape up suddenly into a wisp of black shadow before emerging against the post as a cat, his fangs pointed. Brushing his fluid form against the wooden frame, he stretched out, yawning loudly.

"You *have* just come back to annoy me," muttered Alex, lying back on the bed to stare up at the ceiling as the cat pounced up onto the mattress beside him, peering down with those alarming onyx eyes.

"Oh, come now, there's no need to be like that," said Elias, the words rumbling at the back of his throat. Alex ignored him, watching the darkness play across the rafters.

There was a snap in the air, a dark mist swirling as Elias-the-man reappeared. The stars in his eyes seemed to burn as he glanced down at Alex, his smile ebbing. "In fact, I brought you some things, though I'm not sure I want to hand them over now."

Alex sat up on his elbows. "You brought something?"

"I certainly did," said Elias, delving into the dark robes of his shadowy cloak, his hand seemingly disappearing into the starry expanse of his chest, a sight Alex wasn't sure he could ever get used to. From within the crevasse of his ribcage, Elias withdrew two books. He handed the first to Alex—a red, leather-bound book. "I thought you might enjoy this one more," he quipped as Alex read the cover. It was a non-fiction book, similar in style to the *Historica Magica*, but the title simply read *A Comprehensive Guide to the Great Battles* by Reginald M. Boyd.

Alex smiled. "Another history book?"

"Of sorts. Much more interesting than the last," sighed Elias. "And this. A rare thing." Elias handed Alex another book. This one was a notebook, slim and black, with barely any pages inside and no title embossed on the front to hint at what was held within. "You *might* find this useful." Elias smirked.

"What is it?" Alex asked, opening the middle of the notebook to find a scramble of symbols scattered across the thin paper, browning at the edges.

"A thing that took me great pains to acquire for you. A fitting payment for a job well done, ridding the manor of that hideous creature," murmured Elias, a note of unexpected sincerity in his voice.

"You're a veritable library of stolen goods," joked Alex, turning the slender notebook in his hands.

"And who says they are stolen? The ingratitude! Anyway, you cannot steal something which already belongs to you," said Elias.

"These are yours?" Alex frowned, perplexed.

"In a sense. Ownership is a vague principle when you

can melt through walls." Elias cackled, grasping the fluid bottom of his twinkling ribcage and pulling upward sharply, his flowing form folding back in on itself, imploding in a mist of eerie darkness.

"Elias?" called Alex, but the shadow-man was gone.

Each time Elias appeared to him, Alex grew more and more aware of how little he knew about the spectral shadow creature who was always slipping into the darkness, appearing as he pleased. It was hard to imagine Elias as anything other than a fluid being, and yet there was a humanity to him, albeit buried deep in the peculiar galaxy of his strange, shapeshifting body. When Elias had said 'you cannot steal something which already belongs to you,' Alex had believed him, picturing a human version of the slippery shadow holding those books in hands of flesh and blood.

The thought made Alex curious. What had Elias been before he was a shadow-man?

Sitting alone in the empty room, Alex flipped through the *Great Battles* book with some interest, but his eye was continually drawn to the slender notebook. Opening it up to the first page, the paper yellowing with age and worn by time, Alex saw nothing written there except a small signature in the bottom right corner, the ink faded… It read *Leander W*. He couldn't stop looking at the signature, running his finger over it, feeling for any residual magic, but there was nothing. Pausing with the half-moon of his thumbnail beneath the *W*, Alex wondered if it was merely hope that made him think twice about the letter, or if it meant something much closer to home. Could it be? *Leander W. Leander W...*That *W* antagonized him, toying with him, as he read it over and over.

Desperately, he flicked through to the next page, only to find the same smattering of jumbled symbols, too small to be diagrams but not neatly placed enough to be sentences. He didn't recognize the symbols as any language he knew, and, as he flipped through the rest of the notebook, he realized the whole thing was made up of these doodles; there was no other complete word within the book that he recognized, save for that first page with that infuriating name on it.

Alex knew Elias had given it to him for a reason. There was a purpose to everything Elias did, even if it took a while for that purpose to become clear. A chill shivered through Alex as he thought of the shadow-creature. He knew how Elias worked. These weren't gifts with no strings attached. There was a price for every prize.

CHAPTER 14

WITH THE NEW RESTRICTIONS KEEPING A TIGHT leash on the students, there was little sanctuary to be found within the walls of the manor. One of those fleeting moments of refuge was in the lessons of Professor Gaze, a curious woman of undetermined age, who moved swiftly despite her bony limbs and hunched back. Her slim, craggy face was framed by tendrils of curling silver locks that shot out wildly in places from beneath a moth-eaten beret of black wool.

Alex had not had Professor Gaze as a teacher for very long, but had taken an instant liking to the crooked old woman and her mischievous grin. She was an affable sort, with a cheerful laugh and a natural way with the students that bordered on the maternal. There was an undeniable, deep wisdom about her that drew people in—something in the strange quality of her eyes and her voice that commanded attention. During class, she would zip between the desks, robe swishing, and rush to the aid of whoever was struggling with a spell, crying out good-naturedly at the royal mess they had made of it.

Gaze's classes and manner were unlike any of the other professors', in that they lacked the undercurrent of anxiety. Alex never felt as if there were eyes on him, sizing him up for an imagined duel in the near future, nor did he feel pressure to achieve, which took the strain off Natalie somewhat. They could all relax a bit in her lessons. It was easy to warm to the old woman; her lessons were useful and to the point, never trying to trip anybody up, but they were also filled with laughter and jokes and stories of her youth.

Everyone, Alex included, would listen, enthralled, as she spoke of herself as a young wizard, struggling with spells and the nonsense she and her friends would get up to inside the manor walls. Once, she even spoke of a roasting summer day spent on a riverbank, splashing and swimming in the deepest parts until a current snatched at the legs of a friend, forcing Gaze to perform a daring rescue mission. After Gaze had hauled her friend safely onto the bank, they shared a bottle of cold ginger beer and ate cupcakes from a wicker picnic basket she had been given as a present, with red-spotted napkins and real silverware to eat with. It dawned on Alex that this particular story was from *before*; before Malachi Grey had come for her and torn her away from her childhood days spent on riverbanks with friends and bottles of ginger beer and red-spotted handkerchiefs. A sad expression had flashed across her wrinkled face as she recounted the tale, but she had shaken it off with a whispered, "Anyway, that was a lifetime ago."

Alex wondered where her wizard friends were now. Gaze was far older than Esmerelda or Lintz or Renmark or Derhin, so it seemed unlikely any of those spoken-about pals from her manor stories were among the faculty. She must have lost them a long time ago, Alex realized with a pang of pity. Alex couldn't understand how she remained so cheerful. Yet, other than those brief moments of wistful sadness, she was a bundle of humorous energy, always ready to tell them a new tale. In her classes, Alex found an escapism unlike any other to be found within the manor.

Professor Gaze had an innate sensitivity to the world around her, seemingly able to pick up on small undercurrents in the atmosphere. Whenever she was near, Alex could sense her observing him—not in an aggressive or intrusive way, but simply as if she could sense something was amiss in him and was trying to pinpoint it, like a puzzle in need of solving.

"How peculiar," she muttered to herself one day as she passed so close to him her wrist almost brushed his shoulder.

"What is?" asked Alex.

"Are you quite well, child?" she asked.

He frowned. "I think so."

"Are you cold? You seem cold," she said. "I must offer you a hot beverage. Can I fetch you a hot beverage? I have a variety of exotic and flavorsome teas." That puzzled expression played upon her lined features as she waited for him to accept.

"Oh, I'm honestly fine, Professor," insisted Alex, recalling the chill in his bones. He'd endured it for so long now that his Spellbreaker body had somehow adapted to it, and he barely noticed it anymore.

"But you are cold. You seem cold," repeated Gaze. "Please allow me to fetch you a tea. Something simple, perhaps. Peppermint?"

"Uh, okay," he conceded, watching her as she rushed off to fix him a mug of peppermint tea. She knew he was cold. He couldn't help but find that curious. He didn't shiver anymore; it was more of a dull numbness in the pit of his stomach, never really coming up to the surface of his skin like it used to. But Gaze had sensed it in him.

He drank the peppermint tea, mulling over the thought, as Gaze rushed around, helping students with their magical tasks. The hot liquid heated him from the inside out, and he was glad of it as he drained the mug. He guessed he must have been colder than he'd realized, though the tea only gave him a momentary respite from the insistent chill.

On many occasions after that, Alex came into the lesson to find a mug of steaming tea already waiting for him on the desk, in countless exotic varieties. Often, there was one waiting for Natalie, too.

Alex had overheard Gaze several times noting that Natalie seemed fatigued and should take a rest. When Natalie refused, claiming to be fine, Gaze had zipped off to her tea chest in the corner and whipped up a mug of pungent tea that wafted across the classroom, sour-smelling and heady. She had insisted that Natalie drink the infusion. For days, Natalie had been telling Alex she was fine, though Alex had his suspicions about her wellbeing. With her doing so much, studying all hours of the day, helping him out in lessons, on top of her extra tutoring with Renmark, Alex knew she had to be exhausted, though she was too stubborn to ever tell him she was struggling. He watched Natalie drink the tea, his eyebrows rising in surprise as she downed the entire mug. Her mood seemed to instantly lighten. Alex could see Natalie's tiredness fall away as Gaze gave a pleased grin.

"Excellent. You feel better?" she asked Natalie.

Natalie nodded, smiling. "I do, thank you."

"Good. You let me know if you need more, and I'll

brew you up a batch of the good stuff," cackled Gaze as she zipped away to help another student in need.

Even Jari could not escape Gaze's perceptive energies. She moved past him one lesson, remarking with a high whistle that his aura was particularly angry that day. Unfortunately, she did not appear to have a tea that cured anger. At the end of the lesson, she simply asked that he stay behind for a moment. Jari had waved Alex and Natalie on, promising to catch up as he stepped back into the classroom. He never told them what she had said to him, but his mood had seemed to brighten.

It was undeniable that, as well as being a kind, compassionate teacher, Professor Gaze was also a powerful mage. There was an ancient quality to her, an imperceptible aura that pulsated with raw magical ability. Complex spells wove deftly from her fingertips as if they were a beginner's glamor, moving like molten gold at every subtle whim. In her lessons, she focused on teaching them defensive strategies that could be used against Mages of all strengths and abilities. The spells themselves were intricate and mind-boggling, but she made them seem easier. She took the time to stand with every student and explain the ins and outs of the defensive design, making them understand what they were capable of.

When she paused beside Alex's desk to watch the magic thread spool from his fingers with Natalie's assistance, Gaze frowned, an amused smile on her thin lips.

"*You* can do this," she said to him in a low tone, touching his hands. "*You* have the ability, child. A powerful ability," she added, her voice barely above a whisper as she gave him a secretive wink. It didn't need explanation; at first he felt terrified that she'd guessed his secret, but then he felt confidence swell in his chest as he took what she'd given the class and thought about how he might use it for anti-magical purposes. He and Natalie kept up the charade, but, always, Gaze would stop beside him and whisper the same words, touching his hand lightly, before offering up another cup of tea to combat his chill. It gave him more hope than any teacher or textbook in the school had done so far.

Every pupil seemed to adore her, and she had time for each and every one. No problem was too small, and she did not shy away from teaching them powerful magic that could very well have been used against her. At her age, Alex mused, perhaps she no longer cared if anyone challenged her. He watched as other students learned to deflect and snatch magic, but the thing that truly intrigued him was the creation of great, powerful shields. None were as powerful as Gaze's, which seemed forged from pure, solid metal, but others had successes of their own, some conjuring screens of light that thrummed powerfully in curved arches around them. Alex made a mental note to try to inverse the method to create his own extra-strong anti-magical shield that night, in the peace of his dormitory; it was too cool not to.

With a conspiratorial glance around the room, Gaze rapped on the edge of the blackboard with her bony fist and waited for the students to fall silent.

"I've got a treat for you," she whispered gleefully. "I'm going to show you something very secret and very rare—something none of you will ever have seen, I guarantee it! It's so very exciting, so very, very special… but before I show you, you must promise not to breathe a word of it. That's the deal, my little chickens."

The room bristled with anticipation, wondering what it could be.

"Do you promise?" she asked as she flashed them an irreverent grin.

The room chorused a "yes," their eyes focused on her as they waited to see what she would do next.

She stood perfectly still. The room nearly crackled with tension.

For a moment, nothing happened. Then, from nowhere, a ripple of golden light surged into existence, manifesting rapidly into one of Gaze's impeccable shields without so much as a flicked wrist or a twirled finger. It fizzed in the air for several minutes, then disappeared with a snap. As it faded, Gaze grinned, and the room erupted into rapturous applause. Magic like that did not come along every day, and Alex felt honored to be in the same room as it, wondering if he'd ever be able to conjure without using his hands. He could only guess how long it had taken her to conquer the skill within the walls of the manor, though he imagined she had had nothing but time.

She performed another. This time, a shivering ball of amber light crackled into life, exploding into the air as she threw it left and right, never moving from her spot at the front of the class. Her arms remained by her sides, and the ball spun, faster and faster, shards of glittering magic spinning off in fiery sparks. Smiling, she launched the ball into the audience. It stopped inches from the face of the closest student before being whisked back toward her again.

Professor Gaze swirled the ball in a figure eight, the energy leaving a glowing echo in its wake, like waving sparklers on the Fourth of July. The whole classroom was enraptured as she compressed the magic with a loud hiss, sputtering it out without so much as a wink or a gesture or a twitch.

As Gaze gave a kooky little bow, Natalie flashed Alex a look of excitement that screamed envy. Alex chuckled, though he felt the familiar creep of worry beneath his skin. Whenever Natalie witnessed intense power, Alex saw a concerning hunger in her eyes that he did not like one bit. Natalie was already proving herself to be a formidable Mage, but it did not seem to be enough; her hunger was unyielding.

It was all she could talk about as they left the classroom and headed to dinner. Alex listened as she whispered of Gaze's abilities, her dark brown eyes glittering almost manically as she spoke of what they had witnessed, wondering how it was done and how she might gain the same skills. He had to bite his tongue, wanting to remark that it had most likely been the years of incarceration that had brought Gaze those skills. It was uncomfortable to watch his friend get so hyped up over powerful magic.

In the end, he could listen to no more. He got up and made his excuses to head to the dormitories. Jari asked if Alex wanted him to come too, but Alex shook his head, telling Jari to enjoy the extra bit of free time. Their evening class with Lintz had been cancelled, giving them an extra hour to themselves. Alex decided he would use the time proactively, instead of having the early night he had previously planned to indulge in.

In the quiet stillness of the dormitory, Alex pushed Aamir's old bed back against one wall, opening up the space a bit. Encouraged by Gaze's daily words to him, he stood in the center of the wider space and attempted to recall Gaze's shielding spell. As it came flooding back, he began to invert the instructions.

First, he created a ball of silver and black between the palms of his hands and slowly let the anti-magic slip back into his body, a tendril at a time, instead of flowing outward in spirals. Next, instead of sucking the energy in to form the concave shield around him, he exploded the anti-magic out through his skin.

He felt a rush of cold around him as the shield surged forward, creating more of a barrage than a dome, which slammed hard against the far wall in an eruption of silver and white flakes. Useful, Alex thought, but not quite a shield.

Undeterred, he tried again and again, slamming barrage after barrage into the far wall until it glistened with melted ice.

It didn't seem to be working. He racked his brain for the part he was missing. Then, it dawned on him: he had to hold the barrage in place to make it a shield. With magic, it was a pull and hold motion, so with his anti-magic, perhaps it would work if he *pushed* and held.

He forged the ball once more and let the icy tendrils snake up through his arms, before releasing them back outward. Quickly, he held the anti-magic in place by clenching his hands inward and down, instead of turning them up and opening them as if surrendering, like he had seen the magical students do. It held steady, becoming a tangible shield in the air before him, rippling and thrumming with overlapping silver and black as he kept it there. Without an opponent attacking him, he wasn't sure if the shield would hold up in a fight, but it felt good in his hands—a strong defense against anything that might want to harm him.

Excited by the progress he had made, he clapped his palms together, the shield disappearing in a flurry of snow around him. Flakes landed on his skin, but he did not feel their cold.

Silently, he thought of Gaze's words. He *could* do this. He *did* have the ability. He had just needed some encouragement.

CHAPTER 15

ALEX LAY BACK ON HIS BED, DEVOURING THE book on *Great Battles* Elias had given him. It was full to the brim with intense conflicts and heroic battles that read like the most nail-biting action novels, and yet they were non-fiction; they had actually happened, often to Alex's disbelief. It told of vast numbers charging across battlefields as gold and white met black and silver, as sparks flew and the very air trembled amid the vibrations of clashing energies. It told of Spellbreakers riding through the skies on the backs of mythical winged beasts as the Mage cavalry thundered along the earth, churning up mud and dirt as they sent bolts upward toward the wings of the griffons and Thunderbirds who flew overhead, trying to bring them down to fight at ground level.

There were great warriors in both armies, sometimes locked in single combat—a fight to the bitter end, with only one destined to walk away. Some of the fiercest warriors on both sides were terrifying women who fought more ferociously, more boldly than many of their male counterparts. These formidable women called themselves the Howling Valkyries on the Spellbreakers' side and the Gilded Vipers on the Mages' side, and they roared and screamed as they stormed into battle, their powers piercing the air. It made Alex shiver to think of the sound they must have made, curdling the blood of any warrior who heard it.

The image of one Spellbreaker in particular, Kira the Merciless, stuck in his mind because of how the book described her on the battlefield. *A savage woman, more demon than Breaker, her eyes burning red as she gazed down upon the sea of blood she had drained from the bodies of two thousand men, struck down by her hand. She stood atop her mountain of flesh and bone and lifted her godless face to the sky, screaming loud for all to hear as she pounded the armor plate on her chest, the sound inciting fear in all who heard. There was no part of her person that was not drenched in the blood and ash of others. In her hands, she held up great clusters of glowing red fronds, far more frightening than any spilt blood, for they were the souls of the departed, their life magic torn from within them and held aloft by Kira's dark energy. It is said her eyes burnt bright red for all the souls she had stolen.*

She sounded horrific to Alex, and yet he knew the Mages had done worse to his kind, knew they had had more vicious wizards and witches than her among their ranks.

The book was different from the ones he had picked up in the library in that it didn't take sides; there was no good versus evil, only Mages versus Spellbreakers, and Alex couldn't get enough. It was addictive, reading the tales of ancient soldiers and their daring feats of life and death. Naturally, he rooted for his side, but he was not without sympathy for the Mages. They had lost big numbers too, in some of the most notorious battles, like the *Struggle for Elder's Edge* and the *Battle of King's Rock*, but they had never lost as many as the Spellbreakers. Each Spellbreaker victory was met with harrowing deeds beyond the battlefield—the torture and murder of innocents who barely had the strength to put up a fight. Punishing the Spellbreakers for winning with their continued persecution.

Jari had disappeared off to the library, and Alex decided he'd like to get Natalie's opinion on a few of the battles he had read within the leather-bound tome, thinking she'd appreciate some of the legends around the Howling Valkyries and the Gilded Vipers, if nothing else. He was curious as to whether she might know anything about the 'great sacrifices' that were mentioned, whether that meant the use of some sort of darker magic, and how that might have been used in battle. If anyone knew about the intricacies of dark magic, it was Natalie.

He got up and made his way through the hallways toward the girls' dormitories, moving easily through the apparent barrier that had been put up to keep boys away without a female escort. Arriving at number twenty-eight, the brass numbers dulled, he knocked lightly on the wood and waited, the book tucked beneath his sweater to avoid any unwanted attention.

Alex's eyes went wide as Ellabell answered; they hadn't spoken much of late.

"Is Natalie in?" he asked, feeling stupid at his initial surprise. It seemed he had almost forgotten she was Natalie's roommate.

Ellabell shook her head, her brown curls bouncing. "She's at one of her extra sessions with Renmark," she answered stiffly.

Alex wasn't exactly pleased to hear Natalie was with Renmark yet again, but still, he smiled, seeing the valuable opportunity he had been stupid enough to overlook until that moment. Ellabell was infinitely more knowledgeable about these historical matters than anyone Alex knew. She was the perfect person to ask.

"How did you get here?" she questioned.

"Well," Alex replied smoothly, "you must know I have my methods by now..." He smiled, trying to act casual, before quickly moving on. "Anyway, forget Natalie—now I'm here for you," he stated, and a frown passed across her arched eyebrows.

"Me?" asked Ellabell, sounding suspicious.

Alex nodded. "Yes, you're perfect," he said, and Ellabell's cheeks turned an interesting shade of pink.

"Perfect for what?" She spoke hurriedly, lowering her gaze.

Alex realized what he had said and felt his throat dry up a little as he looked at Ellabell's downturned face, noting her flush. He felt the sudden urge to touch her shoulder, encourage her to lift her chin so that she would look at him again, but didn't dare reach out to do so, worried how she might react.

"You know all there is to know about magical history, and I need a bit of help with some magical history," he explained, wanting her to meet his eye, for this awkwardness to be over.

"What kind of magical history?" she asked, peering over the top of her spectacles and leveling her gaze once more in his direction.

"I was hoping you could tell me some stuff about the great battles of the magical world." He smiled, pleased to see the discomfort gone from her face and replaced with curiosity.

"Which ones?" she asked.

"Well, I stumbled across some books and thought they were pretty cool. I hadn't really seen anything like them before, so I'm not sure what to make of them. They're all about the battles between the Spellbreakers and the Mages, but not any I'd read before. I just wanted to learn a little more about the biggest ones. You know, the most important ones in our history." He shrugged, hoping she wouldn't see through his white lie. If anyone had read through the entire contents of the library, it was Ellabell, and Alex wasn't sure he could pull the wool over her eyes.

"You're really interested in magical history?" Ellabell frowned, giving him that look of suspicion he had come to associate with her. There was uncertainty too beneath the glint of her blue eyes, as if his concerns were valid and she didn't quite believe his story.

"I really am," he insisted.

"Fine," she said curtly.

Alex was a little surprised. "You'll help me?"

"Yeah, I'll help you." She stepped back into her dorm room and gestured for him to come in.

"Oh, we're staying here?" Alex faltered, his voice catching in the back of his throat.

"Unless you want to go somewhere else?" Ellabell asked, an amused smile pulling at the corner of her full lips.

“Well, I was thinking the library, but I guess this is okay,” he said quickly, trying to recover his nonchalance as he stepped past her into the room.

The room was more or less the same as it had been the last time he’d been there to visit Natalie when she was practically dying from the chokehold of Derhin’s curse, but it looked a little more homey. A few more lights had been strung up on the walls alongside sketches and watercolor paintings of what Alex guessed was home for both Natalie and Ellabell. He didn’t dare ask, but they were pretty to look at. On the far window, cut-out shapes of multi-colored material clung to the glass, casting streams of vibrant light onto the floor and beds that furnished the sparse room.

“Welcome,” teased Ellabell, as she sat on the edge of her bed. Alex pulled up one of the desk chairs and sat down beside the window, feeling weird about sitting on one of the beds.

“So?” he said, trying not to sound too impatient as he waited for Ellabell to begin.

“So, you wanted to know about battles?” she asked.

He nodded. “Yeah. The biggest ones.”

“Well, there are a few big battles in our known history, but there is one very famous one. It is sometimes referred to as the ‘greatest battle of them all,’ if that’s what you’re interested in?” she began, looking to him for confirmation.

Alex was intrigued. "Sounds good."

"It was the biggest battle in recorded history, and also, funnily enough, the last one. It happened in the winter of 1908, and is known more commonly as the *Fields of Sorrow* due to the number of dead. Huge losses on both sides, but it's said that this was where the last Spellbreaker fell," she explained, her voice enthralling Alex as he listened.

Fields of Sorrow rang a bell in Alex's head, but in that moment, he couldn't quite place where he had heard the name before. He almost had it, when Ellabell's words distracted him from his thoughts.

"It was a vicious battle that raged for almost a fortnight, with severe casualties every day from both sides. Thousands of infantry Mages and Spellbreakers were wiped out within the first week, along with the beasts that served as cavalry and air support," she continued, her memory an awe-inspiring thing as she recounted the tale, remembering it perfectly from whichever book she had absorbed the knowledge from. "Bodies were strewn across the battlefield, unable to be moved, as magic and anti-magic flew between the two sides. Now and again, they would charge one another, attempting to smoke out the strongest, but usually it was the charging side who suffered against hidden traps and buried clockwork ballistics."

Alex was astonished, feeling the familiar spark of

anger beginning to glimmer into life in the pit of his stomach. Frowning slightly at Ellabell, he wondered how it was that she had come to know so much. Curiosity encouraged the question to his lips.

"How do you know so much about this?" he asked, sounding a touch suspicious.

Ellabell looked at him strangely. "I have my ways."

"What ways?" He couldn't help but press her for an answer.

"This manor has secrets—they're useful if you know where to look," she replied cryptically, pushing her spectacles higher onto the bridge of her nose. A nervous tic, Alex thought. He had touched a nerve.

"Where would you look?" His attempt at nonchalance fell flat.

"It wouldn't be a secret if I told you that." She smiled, but there was a hint of a warning in her sparkling eyes not to press further. "Look, are you okay? You seem distracted. If you want to talk about this another time, we can," she ventured.

"I'm fine. Sorry, I was just curious—I am invested in what you were saying, I promise." He smiled shyly, trying to push away the itch of resentment and the tingle of intrigue as he continued to listen to her story.

"Are you sure?" She frowned, seeming to test him.

He nodded. "Please, go on."

"Well, by week two, the numbers had dwindled

away to barely more than a small band of each as the battle reached its final days. The greatest warriors from each side were all that were left. On the magical side, the twenty crowned princes and princesses of the eight Royal Families, battling alongside some of the most famous heroes and heroines in history. On the other side, the Heads of the six main Spellbreaker bloodlines and their grown children, fighting along with some of the most terrifying Spellbreakers that have ever been known to walk the earth. If you get a chance, look up Kira the Merciless; she was a monster," Ellabell said in a hushed tone, as if Kira might somehow hear.

Alex kept quiet, not wanting to admit he had already read up on the infamous Spellbreaker. It was strange to hear Ellabell mention the Spellbreaker bloodlines when he had kept them so close to his heart. He wondered suddenly if Ellabell might know any more about the Spellbreaker families. He made a mental note to ask her later.

"Go on," encouraged Alex.

"So, these two remaining sides fought fiercely over the final two days, until only two remained on the battlefield, locked in single, one-on-one combat. Malachi Grey and Leander Wyvern," she explained, the names sending two sharp shivers down Alex's spine.

Leander W., Alex thought. *It had to be the same one.*

"There was only one difference… Leander was the

very last of his kind, whereas Malachi Grey was merely the last of the Mage army. It was a futile fight, but Leander fought valiantly to the bitter end. It is thought the battle raged for six hours, the pair evenly matched almost to a stalemate. Witnesses have said it was in fact Leander who was the victor, standing over a wounded and half-dead Malachi, with a blade of anti-magic held in his hand, ready to deliver the final blow to Grey. But then Leander was ambushed by a newly arrived platoon of Mage infantry, sent from a different battleground.

"They jumped him from behind and held him to the ground, shackling him with specially crafted manacles that absorbed the power of any magical or anti-magical being. They strung him up in the center of the battlefield, to the top of a crudely built scaffold, and tortured him to death. A hundred wizards against one powerless Spellbreaker, though he stayed alive far longer than any of them imagined he would, his cries chilling the blood of any who watched as his eyes seemed to burn with a blinding silver light, his broken body punished by wave after wave of magical artillery. They say it was Malachi Grey who dealt the final blow, with the last bit of strength he had." A misty glitter of something like sadness hung in Ellabell's eyes as she glanced across to Alex.

Alex was speechless. He could not bring any words to his mouth. Rage gripped his chest in a vice, blood rushing in his ears. Nausea and distress fought for precedence within him as his gaze dropped to the ground, the hatred searing through his veins.

"It wiped the Spellbreakers from existence, but there was a price to pay. Historians aren't exactly sure of the meaning, but the last sentence of *Stormholt's Essay on the Fields of Sorrow* says 'a great evil was set free that day, as the essence of the last Spellbreaker soaked the battle-ground.' Nobody is quite sure what that means, but I've always imagined it to be a metaphor for the genocide of the Spellbreakers," she added with a bashful shrug, adjusting her spectacles as she gave Alex her educated opinion.

Still, Alex said nothing. However, his thoughts were distracted a little by the word 'essence.' It intrigued him; they could have picked 'blood' or 'body' or any such word, but they had chosen 'essence' instead. Why would they choose that word over any other? It felt wrong to Alex—out of place, somehow.

He looked to Ellabell. "Why 'essence'?" he asked, his voice tight with emotion.

"What do you mean?" She frowned.

"Why did they use the word 'essence'?" he repeated, his eyes narrowing.

"It's just a word, Alex. Writers like to use interesting words," she said simply.

"It's a strange word to use, though, don't you think?"

"Not particularly. It's just a word," sighed Ellabell.

"Where did this happen?" He changed the subject

quickly, feeling the burn of his anger threatening to break loose.

"Here," she answered solemnly.

"What?" spluttered Alex, his pulse racing.

"Well, not right here, obviously, but you can see the last stronghold of the battle from the manor. The final battlefield from the *Fields of Sorrow*. There were others where the battle was fought, but the one you can see was where it all ended—the place where the last Spellbreaker fell. It's in a bit of a state, but that's the place," she said.

Alex felt his body tense up as he envisioned Aamir, standing beside him on a hill overlooking a desolate, smoking field, more than a lifetime ago it seemed. It was the last vestige of a war that had raged, seemingly, since Mages and Spellbreakers had been placed on opposite sides of an invisible line. This was one last field in countless fields, playing host to the final gasp of his people. The place Leander had made his last stand with those who were left, backed into the corner of this wretched, scorched piece of earth, knowing everyone else was dead across the other battlefields. Alongside the burning anger for the murder of his people, he felt a sudden sadness for the loss of his friend, who had shaped so much of his first year at the manor.

"Why did Mages hate… the Spellbreakers so much?" asked Alex in a whisper, the word 'us' almost slipping from his lips.

Ellabell shrugged. “Natural-born enemies, I suppose. Magic and anti-magic, good versus evil,” she said evenly, her expression thoughtful.

“Maybe you’re right,” sighed Alex, though he couldn’t say for sure which side was which.

CHAPTER 16

ALEX WAS IN NEED OF DISTRACTION AFTER Ellabell's storytelling. His mind was overwhelmed with what she had told him, and it was proving difficult to sift through it all to focus on any one fragment in particular. There was so much to take in. He had all but run from her dorm room, his head foggy with confusion and sadness. Pain and anger had made his sudden departure from Ellabell an awkward one, but he hoped she would forgive him. He had stood up quickly, his eyes misting, making his excuses as kindly as he could through gritted teeth, claiming he was overdue at a private tuition. But he wasn't sure he had convinced her. He at least hoped she wouldn't bear a grudge against him for his sharp exit.

The knowledge that Malachi Grey had been the last on the battlefield with the mysterious warrior Leander Wyvern haunted Alex, a shiver running through him as he thought of the gray ghost in the flesh and what he had done to Leander. The ambush dashing Leander's last hope. Alex knew it couldn't be coincidence that the notebook Elias had given him bore the same lettering as Leander's name, and he wished the shadow-guide would stop being so elusive so that he could ask a few blunt questions and get some straight answers for once.

It seemed a sick tribute to have the battlefield itself behind the school, for all the young wizards to see. At least it wasn't used as a method of teaching—to march the students up the hill and make them look at the devastation as they basked in the victory of the Mages and the death of an entire race. At least there was that, Alex thought; the old Mages had the decency not to gloat. It reminded him of history lessons back in the world beyond the manor, whenever World War II came up in the curriculum. Students had stared wide-eyed, shifting in their seats with discomfort as the teacher showed grainy pictures of yellow stars, striped clothing, and concentration camps, horrified that the scenes had once been reality.

Alex was frustrated and in need of somebody to talk to, but he could find neither of his friends anywhere. Pacing the corridor outside Renmark's classroom, Alex waited, but Natalie never appeared. He checked the library, the dull study hall, and the empty mess hall, but could see no sign of Jari. By the time he had done two laps around the manor, he was at the end of his tether. He needed to speak with them, vent his pain and get their opinion, but his friends had all but disappeared from the face of the earth.

At a loss as to what to do with himself, Alex stormed through the hallways toward the mechanics lab. It was the only place he could think to go, to try to blow off some of the steam gathering fiercely inside him. He recalled Lintz's words: *"There's nothing like clockwork to calm the mind."* That was exactly what he needed—something to calm his racing mind. There was so much he wanted to say, and nobody to say it to.

He burst into the lab, unsurprised to see the place empty. Since the curfews and extra sessions had been in place, the other students had been unwilling to spend their free evening hours doing even more work. Alex had been the same, until that moment.

Moving over to one of the workbenches in the far corner, out of sight of the door, he scooped the five mechanical mice from their dusty shelf and placed them on the wooden tabletop. Checking his pocket, he realized, much to his dismay, that he had left the damaged sixth one back in his dorm room. Still, he figured five clockwork mice would be enough for him to practice on.

His hands were shaking as they held the miniature screwdriver he needed to get into the clockwork of the small golden creatures. Adrenaline still pulsed through his system, making his heart thunder as he struggled to calm himself down. With some difficulty, he managed to remove the mechanisms from the first mouse and began to plot how he would reinsert them so each piece was an inversion of its previous form. On a scrap of paper, he wrote instructions and sketched the design. Just the focus of that minor task steadied the tremor in Alex's hands as he lifted the first few pieces of sleek metal clockwork with a pair of tweezers and reinserted them into the mouse's body. The methodical nature of it permitted a blanket of calm to settle slowly over Alex as he fixed the mechanisms to his anti-magical requirements, piece by tiny piece.

When the mouse was suitably whole again, Alex held his palm over the delicate arch of its golden back and let the icy anti-magic flow from his fingers into the clockwork. He watched it ripple fluidly, like oil, and moved his fingers gently to try to manipulate the energy within. The mouse's back legs twitched, giving Alex a glimmer of hope before the discouraging sight of smoke dashed it entirely.

Undeterred, he moved on to the next mouse. This time, he managed to get three limbs twitching and the turn of one ear before the plume of acrid blue-tinged smoke rose from the inner clockwork. He was getting better.

The third mouse was the closest to success. The hind legs moved forward and backward, pushing the mouse across the splintering tabletop, though the front legs refused to budge. It lasted a good while, zipping along the surface, until the cogs jammed and disheartening spirals of thin smoke wisped in the air.

Realizing he had the rear legs figured out, Alex played around with the clockwork mechanisms of the front section, rearranging them before he was satisfied enough to run his anti-magic through the metal cogs. The mouse sprang to life, racing around the bench with its black eyes glittering. Alex grinned, watching the tail whip from side to side and the ears twitch as the delicate nose snuffled. He tried to manipulate the mouse again, drawing his fingers into a fist to get the creature to stop. To his delight, it did. As he released his fingers, the mouse set off again, scurrying lightly across the wood, easily navigating the dips and cracks in the bench with its graceful feet.

It had the same strange realism that the mouse in his dorm room had displayed, brimming with the magic of whoever had sent it, only it was *his* handiwork that had given the mouse renewed life. He instructed the creature to walk up into his hand and held it closer to his eye line, observing the intricate inner workings and the swirl of black anti-magic that spiraled within the small eyes. It was a beautiful sight to behold, and, as he removed his anti-magic from within the clockwork, he realized he no longer felt the course of anger and frustration rushing through his body, nor the foggy chatter of a thousand questions in his head. Lintz had been right; clockwork *did* calm the mind.

Alex was intrigued by the possibilities as he glanced around the room more closely. Lintz's trunk lay in the corner, and Alex wondered how easy it would be to break the lock. Never mind magic, a hammer would probably do it, he thought. After a moment of half-serious contemplation, he pushed the idea away, knowing the chest was probably full of Lintz's private creations. It certainly wasn't for Alex's eyes.

Seeing the mouse work had inspired him. He still had the list Ellabell had made him, of suitable books for learning more about clockwork and magical mechanics. The *Battle* book had spoken of bombs and traps, made from clockwork, being thrown across a battlefield or buried beneath the earth for wizards to fall into, setting Alex's mind alight with all the possibilities that lay in the practical application of his hands and some metal. It wasn't necessarily the defensive or offensive potential of the clockwork that drew him in, but those aspects certainly weren't off-putting. In a place like the manor, Alex knew he needed all the help he could get, especially if it was something small enough to fly under the radar. Like a mouse, for example.

Frowning in thought, Alex picked up the fourth mouse he had experimented on and refueled it with his anti-magic, watching in childish delight as the creature burst into life once more. As it skittered across the workbench, Alex gathered the fingers of his right hand into a fist and made the mouse freeze. Concentrating, he turned his other hand in a circular motion, watching as the anti-magic within the clockwork spun, faster and faster. Finally, he extended the fingers of his left hand in a quick gesture and watched with a mix of awe and regret as the mouse exploded violently in a shower of glowing metal particles.

Where the mouse had previously been, there was a deep scorch mark burnt into the desktop, and the smell of singed wood and spent fireworks permeated the room. The glittering ashes of the clockwork creature settled on the workbench. Alex hastily swept them up in case someone should walk in. He felt bad for blowing up the one mechanism he had managed to get working, but he had the successful instructions written out on the sheet beside him, should he desire to try again. Slipping the piece of paper into his pocket, he put the remaining mice back in their place on the dirty lower shelf and smiled to himself as he lined them up in a neat row, two spaces now empty.

Indeed, the possibilities were endless.

CHAPTER 17

As morning dawned, Alex awoke slowly, rubbing his eyes against the sunlight glancing in through the curtains. He was mid-yawn when he noticed the bed opposite was empty. Alex frowned; Jari hadn't been there when Alex had gone to bed, either, though he had been disturbed at some point in the night by the sound of soft footfalls on the dorm room floor. It hadn't been enough to fully awaken him, but Alex remembered the sound and the sleepy guess that it was his friend, returning from wherever he had been all evening. Alex had no idea what time that might have been.

He checked the ticking clock on the bedside table.

It was early still, and he had an hour before breakfast. Yawning again, he moved over to the edge of his bed and hung down over the side, reaching underneath the bed-frame for the notebook he had hidden away. Pulling it back up, he propped himself against the headboard and opened the thin pages.

Since he'd been to see Ellabell, Alex hadn't had much of a chance to read through the notebook. But as he held it in his hands, he felt a wave of sadness flood through him, knowing the fate of the man who had once owned the book. To have come so close to winning a fight, only to be ambushed and strung up… It didn't bear thinking about.

He flipped to the first page and noted the familiar jumble of sketched shapes and symbols. It made little sense to him, though he knew they couldn't be random. Elias wouldn't have given him a book of nonsense; it wasn't the shadow-man's way.

As if hearing himself being thought about, Elias appeared in the darkest corner of the room with a silent quiver of frosty air. He poured himself from the rafters in one slick movement, shaping into an almost-human form.

"Good morning," greeted Elias, keeping to the shade of the walls, unable to get too close to Alex as the sunlight dappled the graying flagstones.

"Elias." Alex nodded in the shadow-man's direction, surprised to see him at such early hours of the day. He wasn't sure if it was the light playing tricks on him, but

Alex was certain he could see discomfort in Elias's movements and the contortion of his peculiar human face. "What brings you here?" Alex asked, curious.

"Can't a shadow visit his friend?" Elias's mouth twisted into something resembling a grin, and his inky teeth glittered.

"It depends what the shadow is after," said Alex.

Elias frowned. "Perhaps the friend should remember that I am only ever here to help," replied the shadow sourly.

"Sorry, it's early," Alex said, raising his hands in apology.

The gesture seemed to appease Elias as he leaned fluidly against the wall, most of his body sinking into the shadows there, until only his face stood out against the darkness.

"I came to see how you were progressing with my gifts." Elias nodded toward the notebook in Alex's hands.

"Not too well. I can't make any sense of it." Alex shrugged, tossing the notebook onto the bedcovers in front of him. "I think it's a dud," he joked.

Annoyance flashed in the endless black of Elias's eyes. "It is no dud, Alex. You are simply not trying hard enough." He peeled his form away from the protective shade of the cold stone walls.

"It doesn't make sense," insisted Alex.

"It might," growled Elias, "if you bothered to try."

"I've tried. I've looked at it and looked at it. It's just scrappy little patterns that don't mean anything," exclaimed Alex, exasperated.

"And so you give up?" Elias glared in Alex's direction, irritation evident in the shadow's voice.

"I haven't given up. I'm just… figuring it out," Alex explained, picking the notebook up again. He felt bad for throwing it.

"You should be further on with it by now," hissed Elias, wringing the wispy tendrils that served as his hands. "You went to visit that curly-haired do-gooder yesterday, yes?" His impossible eyes flashed at Alex with borderline menace.

"What if I did?" said Alex defensively.

"She told you about that last battle?" Elias pressed.

"Yes," Alex admitted.

"And off you ran to your little mice, when you should have come straight here. Perhaps I have misplaced my trust. Perhaps you are not as capable as I thought," said Elias bitterly, running his wispy hand through the flowing locks of pure, liquid shadow that framed his face.

"This doesn't make any sense, Elias," snapped Alex, waving the little notebook at the shadowy figure in the corner.

"If only you had the same sense of urgency and dedication as your friends," spat Elias, his eyes burning brightly as they made Alex squirm. "Day by day, they grow stronger, while you stay the same. The French girl is delving into deeper, more dangerous magical arts and cares not for the consequences, so long as she may have the knowledge. The other one—the Greek one—is forever in the library reading up on powerful magic and how to do useful things, like break locks and cloak himself. What do you do? You wait to be handed things on a silver platter."

The disappointment in Elias's voice stung. Alex was startled by the truth rolling from the shadow-man's contorted lips. He had suspected Natalie was wandering into dangerous territory, but to hear it confirmed stunned him. Jari, too, going above and beyond. What on earth did he need to break locks and cloak himself for? Alex couldn't help thinking that perhaps he *was* getting left behind.

"That's not fair," murmured Alex.

"Nothing is," sighed Elias, the sharp edge to his words softening slightly.

The silence stretched between Alex and Elias. A low, musical whistle trilled from the cavernous depths of the shadowy figure's form as he moved forward a step or two, held back only by the gathering sunlight. Listening to the tune pierce the air, Alex got the not-so subtle hint that Elias was waiting for him to speak.

"Did you bring me something else?" Alex asked, still confused by Elias's early visit. Was he just there to chastise him?

Elias scowled, the expression terrifying on his fluid

face. "No, I did not bring you anything else. Do you see what I mean? Always expecting the answers on a silver platter—hand delivered in a box with a ribbon on top, no doubt," he grumbled. "You have done little enough with the books I have already given you. Perhaps I will not be so generous in future."

"I've read the *Battles* book," said Alex tersely.

"And done nothing with the other!" cried Elias, the sound vibrating through the walls and up the very bones of Alex's body.

"What am I supposed to do with it? I can't read it!"

"Figure it out, without having to be spoon-fed," Elias said coldly.

This wasn't the Elias Alex was used to, and he couldn't help feeling a tremor of fear as the room grew cold around him, Elias's voice pressing in from all around. There was menace in Elias's face, and Alex could not ignore it.

"It belonged to Leander Wyvern, right?" said Alex quietly, running his thumb once more across the faded lettering of the name he had feebly hoped belonged to his own heritage.

"It belonged to a great warrior," replied Elias, giving his usual brand of slippery answer.

"Wyvern was a Spellbreaker?"

"That depends—what do the books say?" Elias remarked tartly.

"That he was," said Alex, resisting the urge to snap.

Elias clapped the viscous extensions of his hands together, the motion making a thudding sound that quaked through the ground, as his starry eyes rolled in dramatic exasperation.

"Now what?" Elias taunted.

"I have to figure out a way of reading it?" Alex shrugged, feeling victimized. It was like a flashback to middle school—the teacher asking him an exceptionally difficult question he didn't know the answer to and watching him squirm regardless.

Elias gave another sarcastic clap of his wispy hands, and Alex glowered at him. The shadow-man only seemed amused by Alex's annoyance as he swooped as close as he dared to the edge of the sunlight's boundaries.

"How might you unravel such a *puzzling* mystery?" Elias whispered.

"It's a code," said Alex suddenly, the markings making sense. He still couldn't read them, but he had an idea what they were. It was obvious, thought Alex. If a Spellbreaker wanted to write notes or secret entries, it was only natural they'd want to use a cipher of some sort. A code only another Spellbreaker could crack…

Elias grinned. "Now you're getting it," purred the rippling figure, his expression twisting into one of glee.

"A code," mused Alex.

"I'm certain you'll figure it out," whispered Elias as he

reached for the edges of his cloak. "And perhaps there will be a reward. There are so many other books, Alex. Books you could not even dream of," he said euphorically. "Oh, such rare tomes, filled with spells nobody should see… spells that helped me, long ago," he breathed, the last part barely audible as the air bristled with mystery, Elias seeming to withdraw into himself as he spoke the words.

"Wait! You're not going yet, are you?" said Alex, not finished with the shadow-man. There were questions he wanted answers to, that nobody else seemed able to answer. The time was now.

"Why should I stay?" Elias shrugged the cloaked slopes where shoulders should have been.

"I have questions for you."

Elias's face crumpled into a frown. "I'm not sure I can help," he said simply, "but go on."

A thousand thoughts raced through Alex's mind as he tried to figure out what to ask first. This was his opportunity, and he did not want to blow it. Elias was rarely so openly amenable, but Alex found he could not quite focus once the spotlight was on him. It was hard to find the question he wanted answered the most when he wanted them all answered.

"Who are you?" asked Alex, finally settling on a line of inquiry. There was a niggle in the back of Alex's mind that had been there almost since the first moment they met—a curiosity to know more about the peculiar, impossible being that made up Elias. He had always wondered what Elias might have been before he was the shadowy homunculus. There was undeniable humanity in the way he spoke, and in the fluid mannerisms of his apparent limbs, until he turned into a cat and Alex's whole understanding of him went out the window.

"Elias made me, and I am Elias," came the rehearsed sentence from between Elias's lips; Alex had heard it before, in the early days at the manor.

"But who was Elias before this?" Alex pressed, gesturing at the shadowy form. "Did somebody do this to you?"

"In a way," replied Elias cryptically, his voice colored with something Alex couldn't put his finger on. A tightening of what would have been Elias's throat, lacing the words with emotion.

"Did somebody hurt you? How long ago was this done to you? Where do you keep finding all these books?" Alex fired questions at Elias, watching as the shadow-guide's face turned even darker than it already was, discomfort looming over his shifting form. Alex didn't want to push Elias too far, but the opportunity to ask everything was overwhelmingly tempting.

"You misunderstand," was all Elias was willing to say. "And these books, I find them where they are left," he replied.

"How did you end up like this?" Alex ventured,

waggling his arms to try to emphasize what he meant.

"Elias made me, and I am Elias," hissed the shadowy figure, the tone in his voice a warning to Alex. Elias smirked, flashing inky teeth. "Though you should not be so fixated on my state, considering your own position. You have read the book on the great battles; you have been told almost all there is to know about the *Fields of Sorrow*. Surely, you are beginning to understand?" he breathed, the whisper of it pricking the hairs on the back of Alex's neck.

Alex shook his head uncertainly.

"They *hate* your kind. Mages—they hate you. If they knew… Perhaps you should be a little less trusting with whom you share your information," growled Elias. "You think you are safe so long as your secret is unspoken, but you will never be safe, Spellbreaker. You will spend the rest of your life looking over your shoulder," he warned, a tense trace of pity in his words.

"Is that the great evil?" asked Alex, remembering the line from the essay Ellabell had spoken of. "Their hatred of my kind? Is that it?" he added, thinking he had hit upon something.

Elias released a low, bitter laugh that chilled Alex's blood. "A great evil was indeed set free that day, but it is nothing as insignificant as their hatred of your kind. It is far worse." His starry eyes took on a distant look that unnerved Alex. "Their hatred was the cause, but not the result. They left a void behind that day, and voids must be filled," he said vaguely, a sudden sadness appearing in the black, glittering depths of his piercing eyes. "Just remember, Spellbreaker: a desperate Mage will do anything to win a battle."

"What do you mean?" asked Alex.

"The specifics do not matter, Spellbreaker. They are all the same. Desperate wizards do desperate things. Just look at what desperation made your friend Aamir do, pummeling the face of poor Professor Derhin." Elias lowered his voice, a strangely joyful note to his words. "Some will even resort to life magic. You saw for yourself." The cheerful glint continued, Elias's words reminding Alex of Derhin's panicked, last-ditch attempt to survive by using life magic.

"So, what is this 'great evil,' then, if it is not the hatred between Mages and Spellbreakers?" pressed Alex, returning to his previous train of thought.

"There you go again, always wanting things on a silver platter! Such a shame… I thought we'd made progress," snapped Elias suddenly, his mood shifting in an instant. "I have spoiled you with my gifts. Well, no more. I have already done and said more than I should have, to help you. How can you learn if I lay it all out for you so easily? If you are so desperate, perhaps you should seek out the Head—he has plenty of the answers you seek."

Elias's figure twisted in the air, shifting smoothly into

the form of a cat. Alex only caught the glint of sorrow for the briefest moment, but it was long enough for it to trouble him.

"What happened to you?" Alex called, but the shadow-cat was already gone, lost once more to the depths of the manor, leaving Alex with the worrying feeling that his secret guide was never coming back.

CHAPTER 18

Elias's words stuck with Alex as the day wore on, leaving him distracted and unfocused in classes and snappy during breaks. The shadow-man had made him feel inferior, and Alex didn't like it. Also, despite the questions he had been able to ask, Alex had come away from the encounter feeling as if he had even more that needed answering.

In the evening hours, Jari and Natalie were once more absent from his company. Natalie had brushed him off, saying she had an extra session to get to, and Jari had made an excuse about wanting to look over some ideas he'd had. Alex hated to admit it, but he was feeling a little put out by their continued absence. Besides, there were things he wanted to ask them, in the wake of Elias's revelations. He was worried, and he couldn't even tell them. Natalie concerned him the most, as he wondered what dark and dangerous arts she was getting into, exactly. He hoped she had been telling him the truth when she'd said she wouldn't be stupid enough to dabble with life magic, but there was a gnawing doubt in his stomach.

Jari, too, so fixated on his scheme that he seemed not to notice anything else going on around him—not seeing that Alex also needed his help. Even if it was just the willingness to spare an hour to listen to the insanity of what had been going on lately in the ever-developing strangeness of Alex's world.

He wasn't ashamed to admit he missed them. The manor could be a lonely place.

Equally pressing was the idea that he was falling behind in some intangible way. With an hour on his hands and Jari absent from the dorm, Alex pulled the notebook back out from its hiding place and scanned the pages. It was a code—he knew that. He just had to figure it out. Surely, that would be easy?

Alex looked across the sketched symbols, seeing no continuity or repetition in any of them. Had he expected the answer to jump out from the page, just because he was a Spellbreaker? No matter which way he turned the book or looked at the inked markings, no epiphany came.

He lay his hand over one of the pages and brought the tendrils of his anti-magic creeping out onto the yellowing paper. It did nothing but dampen the fragile page ever so slightly. Perplexed, he tried uttering random words like "Spellbreaker," "Leander," and even "open sesame," in case a password unlocked the code. The symbols remained exactly as they were.

Frustrated, Alex lay back on his bed with the notebook open on his chest and stared up at the sky, just visible through the curtains, as he tried to come up with something useful. It reminded him of rainy days when he was a kid, the heavy droplets pattering softly against the window as he would pull a box full of jigsaws and puzzle books from beneath his bed. His grandmother had taught him how to do the ones where you had to unfocus your eyes to see a shape beneath a pattern.

He tried it with the notebook, crossing his eyes slightly. It just made him feel stupid, squinting cross-eyed at the pages.

He racked his brain, trying to think of other solutions to puzzles from his childhood. Jigsaws were easy; they just required the missing pieces. But as far as Alex could tell, there were no pieces to be found here. There had been crosswords and code words, but he had tried those already with the book. The symbols didn't seem to represent letters or characters of any sort. They were just randomly spaced on the paper, each one different.

What else? What am I missing? Alex thought, frustrated by the shapes on the page.

An image of Christmas Day flickered into his memory. He couldn't have been older than seven or eight, wearing a bright orange paper hat as he sat at the dinner table with his mother and his grandparents, from her side of the family. They had never had any of his father's side around the dinner table, from what he could remember. His grandparents were dead now, but he could picture them vividly, laughing and smiling as his grandmother served the Christmas meal that sat in the center of the table, a Santa hat on her head. He watched the scene as if it were playing on an old reel. His grandfather reaching over with a dark green package, spotted with golden snowflakes, wiggling it in front of the younger Alex for him to open. Little Alex grasped the wrapped parcel eagerly and began to tear into the wrapping paper, opening the present quickly to see what was inside. A small booklet fell from within the package, followed swiftly by a small magnifying glass made of red plastic. The younger Alex snatched up the magnifying glass and unfolded the booklet onto the first page to reveal a blue, red, and white pattern dotted across the sheet. As the smaller version of himself held the magnifying glass up to his curious eye, the pattern shifted, revealing the words *Merry Christmas*. The Alex in his memory whooped in delight at the neat trick.

It seemed like a random, useless memory, until it gave

the present Alex an idea.

Scanning the room, he made sure he was alone as he pressed the notebook flat on the covers of the bed. Certain that he was, he allowed his anti-magic to flow slowly into the palms of his hands before stretching it into a thin square of glittering black-and-silver energy, much like the shielding spell he had tried the other day but far smaller, held in the space between his palms. A thrill of excitement coursed through him as he lowered the screen of anti-magic over the top of the notebook, like his younger self had done with the red magnifying glass.

Beneath the glittering square, the symbols sprang to life, each sketch spreading across the page in a series of sentences and diagrams and bullet points. There was no real structure to the writing itself, but the screen permitted him to see it as it had been intended. It was a scrappy sort of journal, really, with thoughts jotted down as they had come to the writer. Sometimes, the work was dated. Other times, it was not.

Alex had to re-conjure the screen every time he wanted to turn the page, but what he saw made his eyes go wide in fascination. The work was written by an actual Spellbreaker. It was a fact Alex already knew, but the information within was designed specifically for Spellbreakers. A true first for Alex. It was like a well-fitting shoe after years of wearing a too-small boot.

On some pages, there were lists of spells and what

they were used for. Others told of control techniques, to make the best out of anti-magic abilities—actual, specific instructions on attack and defense methods and how to forge anti-magical weaponry that could be thrown or maintained in a duel. It was all aimed at his kind. There was no figuring out necessary; the words were right there, in bluish-green, on the page, spelling it out.

Though Alex had discovered how to form certain types of weaponry, the notebook described kinds he had never seen before, some of them positively medieval. There was a delicate sketch showing an anti-magical longbow and arrows, with a side note that it was often far more effort than it was worth. Another showed a spiked mace and a double-edged axe, though Alex thought those looked a bit too vicious for his liking.

Just having the notebook in his hands, with the humorous side notes and inner monologue of the writer, Alex felt slightly less alone. It was the most tangible relic of Spellbreaker heritage he had come in contact with, and it soothed a dull ache within the caverns of his heart.

He devoured the book quicker than he had the *Battles* tome. Every page was filled with something new and exciting that thrilled Alex, making him antsy to try out some of the spells and techniques described within.

However, as he flicked further through the fragile pages, coming to the last section, the writing began to change. No longer formally informative, it took on a more thoughtful, less practical tone. The sentences were scattered more haphazardly, penned wherever the writer could find space. Alex was surprised to find bullet points that noted previous wars and battles between the Spellbreakers and the Mages, repeating the ones mentioned in the other book Elias had given him. At the bottom of the page, beneath the long list of battles, there was a hastily written note within a sketched square:

My father has fallen in battle. My brother has fallen with him. I feel it will soon be my turn. There are not many of us left now. I look to my brothers and sisters in arms and we are growing few. We still hold our defense, but we cannot last much longer. Most of the Houses are already gone, wiped from the face of the earth. I do not simply mean we soldiers. I mean all of them—all of them, gone. Men, women, children, elderly, all. Of the Six Great Houses, three hold fast. I am the last of House Wyvern. On the field, the two remaining daughters of House Volstag fight with the savage fury of the Banshee. Beside us, the head of House Copperfield and his three sons. Never have I seen braver or bolder men and women than these few, who fight as one with me.

I wonder what will happen when we are gone? We are the last.

The pages only grew scrappier as the notebook came to its sorrowful conclusion. The writing was rushed and spiky, Alex having to squint to make out some of the words as he read them. There was something macabre about reading words written by a dead man, but Alex could not tear his eyes away.

I do not know what it will mean for the world, when the last of us falls. The world demands balance. There has to be light with dark, dark with light. Without one half, what will be left instead? It will create a void.

Alex heard Elias's words echoing in his head, poignantly recalled. *"They left a void behind that day, and voids must be filled."*

A void has to be filled.

The notebook parroted Elias. Or had Elias somehow gained those words from these very pages?

A world cannot exist in which there is only magic. It cannot simply be the Mages without the Spellbreakers. If you take one away, you leave a void; something has to replace it. It is like digging a hole in the sand—water will fill it, no matter how far from the sea you are. When a void is created, something has to fill it. Something has to restore the balance.

When the last of us falls, I wonder what will come to balance the scale?

Alex flipped the page over, finding it to be the very last one. He had never thought of it like that before, in terms of a balance that needed to be kept even. Nor could he imagine the terror of knowing his time was running out. And yet it seemed he and Leander had something in common. The tragic title of *Last* they shared.

We are desperate.

The daughters of House Volstag have sacrificed themselves in the hopes that we may hold out a while longer. I begged them not to, but they used the last resort of their death magic. They could not be stopped, and though it broke my heart to watch them, their last moments proved a fantastical sight. To see their bodies shimmering with bright, blinding silver light as they stormed across the field, channeling their souls into a single pulse of raw destruction, was something I shall never forget. Still, we miss their presence more keenly for their loss. I wish they had not done so, but they were as desperate as I am now, as I write this. It is no easy task, to use one's death magic, and I wish there had been another way. But those ferocious Howling Valkyries would not be swayed. They did not wish to end their days cowering behind rocks, as we do.

I envy their courage. We all do.

I heard the others talking of performing a similar ritual, but I know they will not.

The aura of the Volstag sacrifice still ripples across the field like ice on a river, almost liquid to the touch, evaporating any Mage who sets foot on it. But they will wait us out. The aura will not remain forever, and they will come for us before long.

I do not wish to use the essence of myself in battle, yet I know I will, should they push me to it. I will take down as many as I can before the end, though I do not imagine the end is far off. We are so very few now. Dillane of House Copperfield fell yesterday, and his sons are bereft.

All hope is lost.

We are the final players in the game of life and death. We are the final weights holding everything steady, before the scale tips. We are all that stands between balance and the void.

I hope they are ready to pay the price for what they have done. May their wrongdoing haunt them to the ends of the earth.

There were only four more words on the page, with the date written rapidly at the very bottom right corner. 1908. Alex's heart was in his mouth as he let the words sink in. He knew the outcome of the story, and yet Leander had still been alive when he had written those sentences. Leander could not have known what would happen to him. The ambush, the scaffold, the death by magical firing squad. He pictured Ellabell's description of a burning silver light in the eyes of Leander Wyvern and wondered if it was the same silver light the daughters of House Volstag had radiated as they had walked to their deaths. A flicker of a Spellbreaker's essence.

It was the first Alex had heard of this mysterious death magic, though he guessed it to be similar to the life magic of the Mages. Everything in balance. Every magic having an anti-magic counterpart. A kind of dark magic that took something from your soul in order to use it—a high-stakes, high-cost power. One to be used only in desperation.

Elias's words came creeping back—*"a desperate Mage will do anything to win a battle"*—though relevant, it seemed, for Mage and Spellbreaker alike. It had certainly sounded like desperation in Wyvern's description of the Volstag women. A last-ditch effort to buy time for the others by using their essence. By bartering their souls as payment. Alex shuddered.

His eyes prickled as he read Leander Wyvern's final words, feeling them resonate powerfully within the depths of his own heart.

I am the last.

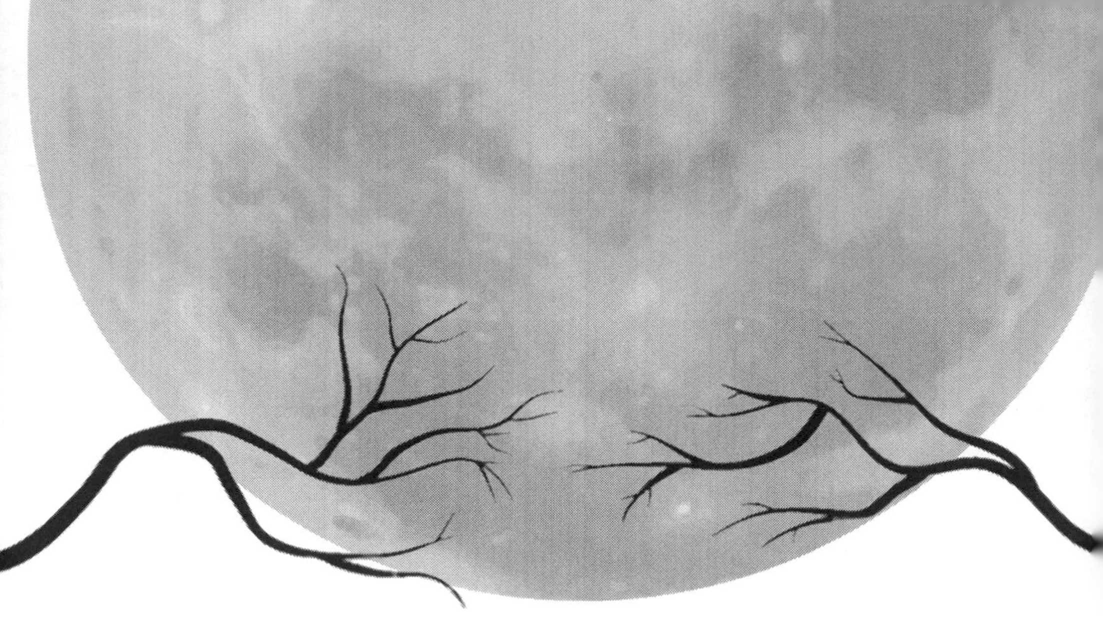

CHAPTER 19

"ARE YOU READY TO GO?" ASKED ALEX AS HE SAT down opposite Jari and Natalie in the mess hall, taking a small bite out of a rosy apple.

"What?" Natalie replied sleepily, looking up from her plate of congealed lunch. Her eyes, so dark brown in color they were almost black, were bloodshot, and the bruised-looking bags had reappeared beneath them.

"Are you ready to go to the cellar? We've only got about forty-five minutes," clarified Alex, checking the clock on the wall.

Natalie shook her head. "I am sorry, Alex, but I cannot go today. I have a session arranged at half past with

Professor Renmark." She stifled a yawn as she pushed the remains of a mushroom through the gelatinous mass of cream sauce with the prongs of her fork.

"But we said we'd meet today," said Alex, crestfallen.

"I'm sorry, Alex," repeated Natalie, her brow furrowed in apology.

"Can't you just brush Renmark off for once?" Alex tried a different tactic, trying to keep the annoyance from creeping into his voice. "You've been spending too much time on these extracurricular things, Natalie. You're exhausted. Come on, just take some time off and come with us to the cellar. You don't have to spar or anything, just sit with us for a while." His gaze fixed on Natalie's so she might see the concern that lay there.

"I'm sorry, but I cannot go today. I really cannot." She sighed wearily. Alex knew she had seen the look of worry in his eyes and heard the troubled note in his words, because she would not look him directly in the eye. Her shifty gaze only added to his concern. It was as if another curse had settled over her, except Alex could not feel the physical presence of a coiled snake gripping her insides as he had the last time; it was a far subtler affliction than that. It was hunger. Not the gnawing hunger of an empty stomach, but something far more sinister—he could see it in her vacant stare and agitated manner.

"Yeah, I can't either. Sorry, man," added Jari guiltily.

"What do you mean?" replied Alex with as much

serenity as he could muster, despite the frustration running through his veins.

"I forgot," Jari admitted quietly.

"Well, what else have you got going on?" Alex asked, exasperation slipping through his mask of calm.

"I've got a few things I need to look over while I have the chance. The library is usually pretty empty at lunchtime, so I'm afraid I have a lunch date with some dusty old pages." Jari flashed a hopeful grin, but Alex was in no mood for humor anymore. He had been looking forward to spending some time with his friends, if only to find out more about how they were and to see if he could be of any use to them.

With them keeping very much to themselves and their personal projects, Alex couldn't help but feel out of the loop with them both. Jari had his scheming, but never seemed inclined to ask Alex to join him. Natalie had her extra work, but never wanted to talk to Alex about it, shunning the issue if he brought it up. He saw them mostly in lessons, and, though they didn't say anything to confirm it, Alex felt like they had begun to view him as a hindrance, needing them to cover for him. Slowly but surely, Alex felt himself being pushed away, constantly held at arm's length.

"Can't you just leave it for one lunchtime?" asked Alex tersely, trying to keep the hurt from his eyes, not wanting to let on how wounded he felt by their apparent ambivalence toward him.

Jari shrugged. "It's too important, man. Sorry." He at least had the decency to look ashamed as Alex scraped back the legs of his chair and stood sharply.

"If you need me, you know where I am," said Alex, discarding his apple. He turned and walked from the mess hall. The temptation to look back at the small circular table was compelling, but he managed to resist as he strode out into the hallway without so much as a glance over his shoulder.

It was a lonely walk toward the entrance of the manor. The corridors were empty of students, all of them still eating in the mess hall or catching a moment to themselves in the library or study hall. Alex did not pass another living creature as he walked along the familiar route, his footfalls echoing between the cold, damp stone of the walls.

Each day, the duty rested on a member of staff to remove and replace the golden line around the steps into the manor, to give students the opportunity to go out into the gardens. Hardly anyone took the offer up, but Alex liked that. The gardens were still a place of peaceful retreat from the restraints of the manor, and though they weren't exactly classically beautiful in their gray desolation, Alex loved to roam the ruins of what must once have been an exquisite feat of horticulture.

With a wry smile, Alex recalled the stern, displeased expression on Aamir's face as he had shown Alex the gardens for the first time, before accusing Alex of not taking magic seriously. Alex couldn't help wondering if Aamir had been right; perhaps he *still* wasn't taking it seriously enough. Elias's sour words of reprimand crept in, leaving Alex with a sudden surge of motivation as he walked across the scorched earth, the skeletal trees bowing against the strong breeze whipping up around the gardens. He refused to be left behind.

Overhead, the sky was an even, dull gray, the monochromatic shades blending into one another without much definition. It felt as if it might rain.

Uncovering the hatch in the ground, Alex dropped down into the familiar subterranean vault. It was chilly at first, but the room warmed up quickly once Alex lit the torches that stood in the brackets on the earthen walls. The flames flickered and danced, casting lively shadows across the hard-packed floor.

Without Jari or Natalie to help, Alex knew he'd need something to practice on. As he wandered over to the crumbling wine racks at the back of the cellar, he could still make out the indentations in the floor where they had sparred last time, and felt the returning pang of disappointment that his friends were not there with him. Pushing it stubbornly away, he brushed a finger over the remaining bottles that lay within the disintegrating honeycomb of shelves until he found one he liked the look of.

Carefully, he pulled the dusty wine bottle from the

rack, sending up a puff of dirt as he did so. A small brown tag was tied to the neck of the bottle. Curious, he turned the card over and read the name. *Fields of Sorrow, 1908.*

Alex felt a sudden pulse of fury as he turned the bottle over and read the label, which bore the same foul name as the tag. He had seen it before—he *knew* he had seen it before. It was all coming back to him. He had seen the name when Aamir had brought him down here and left him alone that first time, when Elias had appeared to him. The name had meant nothing then, but now it meant everything.

The sudden realization made Alex feel sick with disgust. The Mages had celebrated the genocide of his people, had even named a vintage after it. Blood-red wine to toast the blood-soaked battlefields that had wiped out his kind. He wanted to smash the bottle then and there, but, breathing deeply, he moved it into the center of the room.

Pulling the slim notebook from his pocket, he formed the familiar square screen between his palms and read over a number of the techniques, wanting to put them into practical use on the vile bottle and its abhorrent name. Shaking off his anger, he stood at one end of the cellar, close to the old indentations on the ground, and let the anti-magic flow through him. The tendrils of black and silver rippled smoothly around his fingertips, awaiting instruction. Pinching the vaporous substance between his fingers, he forged shards of glinting ice that shone with dark menace in the torchlight. Then, with a flick of his wrist, he sent the shards hurtling toward the bottle on the floor, creating a *whoosh* of air as they shot across the room.

With some disappointment, Alex saw they had missed the bottle, but pride washed over him as he noted the shards sticking out of the ground nearby, holding their form for a moment or two before they began to melt. The savage tips had been sharp enough to cut into the hard ground, where before they would have shattered and snapped before they had even reached it. He was definitely making progress.

His confidence boosted, he kept his eyes on the bottle as he forged a dense shield around it, using the inverse technique he had figured out from Gaze's class. Once he was certain it was strong enough, the anti-magic pulsing and crackling with vivid silver sparks, he held the shield steady with one hand as he conjured the body of an ice spear with the other. Brow furrowed, he focused on how he wanted the weapon to look, the anti-magic flowing and shaping with each turn of his fingers and each instruction from deep within his mind. The triangular point sharpened as he turned his fingers anti-clockwise. The tip of the long, shimmering rod glowed with an almost pearlescent quality as Alex held it in the air above him.

Still holding the shield steady around the bottle, Alex launched the icy spear with full force at the thrumming barrier, watching as it rebounded, the spear shattering into a million glittering pieces that fell to the ground in a shower of diamonds. The shield had held, protecting the object within. Alex grinned, feeling a trickle of sweat running down the side of his face from the exertion of performing two complex anti-magical tasks at once. He had focused his energies, and he had done it—he had performed two things at once, protecting and attacking at the same time.

It felt good, and he knew he had the notebook to thank for it. The ghosts of his heritage had steadied his hand and focused his mind. It occurred to Alex that Leander might've used those very skills on the battlefield, perhaps even in the final moments before the ambush that sealed his fate.

As Alex imagined the carnage, he felt a pull of somber empathy, and the shield around the bottle grew suddenly stronger, pulsing with a vibrant silver energy that rippled across the room in shimmering waves, like heat rising up from desert sands. The almost-liquid current undulated from the glittering barrier. His emotions, he realized, were tied to the fabric of his anti-magic, making it stronger and more potent, depending on how he channeled it and how keenly he felt that emotion.

Alex dropped the shield from around the bottle and set about attempting to make a barrage. He had done it by accident when trying to forge a shield for the first time, but wanted to see if it could be done more powerfully to create a useful tool in a fight.

The anti-magic swirled in the air as he lifted his hands and forged a ball of silver and black, the glinting sparks making the energy resemble a faraway galaxy. Alex slowly let the anti-magic slip back inside his body, one wisp at a time, feeling the peculiar sensation of it running through his veins, piggybacking on his blood, as he held it inside for a moment. Moving his hands sharply outward, he focused on the power of the barrage, his muscles tense, and released the fury of his anti-magic out into the cellar.

A rush of cold air whipped up about him as the wall of snow and ice surged forward in a dense mass, more of a blockade than a simple barrage, and exploded with a bone-shaking bang against the far wall, the small room filling quickly with a blizzard of detonated flakes. Alex whooped with excitement, punching his fist into the air as he felt some of the snowfall land on his cheek, the cooling sensation welcome as it melted against the heat of his sweaty skin.

Sitting down to take a breather, Alex flipped through the pages of the notebook, considering what else he might like to try while he had the time. He paused on the note about death magic. He knew the basis of his 'essence', but wondered how it could be physically used, when it was tied so intrinsically to the inner soul of a person. For a brief second, he thought about reaching inside himself and trying to find the corners of this 'essence,' but couldn't bring himself to do it, feeling a tremor of fear shiver up his spine as he recalled the sacrifice Leander had mentioned, in using this mysterious death magic. It was a valid fear—one Leander had shared.

Alex stood back up and held out his palms, contorting his fingers to conjure the body of a sword. He started with the blade, shaping it to his requirements. It emerged from the twisting energy of black vapor and silvery shards, the edges thinning to razor-sharp points that seemed to tremble with power. A radiance shone through the length of the blade, glinting almost like real steel as it stretched out from the bare bones of a hilt.

The notebook had mentioned a focus technique in which the Spellbreaker pinpointed the very center of the object and forced the mind to feel the weight of the weapon it wanted to manifest. Alex concentrated on the sword until he imagined he could see the icy radiance firming up, becoming more tangible. Grasping the weapon, he could feel the weight of an actual hilt in his hand, cold like metal on his skin. The freshly forged blade gleamed as Alex swiped it through the air. Experiencing the sheer weight of the weapon, he held it in both hands as he cut through the atmosphere, feeling the icy rush and powerful vibrations that pulsed down his forearms with each slice.

He practiced for a while, getting comfortable with the weight as he whirled the sword around. Alex was surprised to see that the weapon maintained its shape far longer than any previous attempt had achieved. He liked the feel of it, imagining himself a warrior of old, taking down a Mage on the back of a savage beast.

Eventually, the sword disintegrated, but the bottle still lay unbroken on the floor. With his mouth set in a grim line, Alex held out both hands and turned them upward, moving them in a perfect mirror-image of one another as he created a crackling, violent, snapping ball of black energy, flecked with glimmers of silver. Raising the ball into the air, he snatched his fingers into fists, and the projectile hurtled toward the bottle on the floor. Alex watched in delight as it smashed with an audible crack of glass, the contents erupting in a wave of sour, blood-red liquid that seeped into the ground.

A small vengeance against the *Fields of Sorrow, 1908.*

CHAPTER 20

ALEX YAWNED AS HE MADE HIS WAY BACK TO THE dormitory, tired after a brief spell in the library looking up the many uses of clockwork. Unable to focus, he had called it a day and decided to go for an early night instead. His muscles ached a little from his lunchtime sparring, but it was a good pain—it was the ache of progress.

As he opened the wooden door to the dormitory, he was surprised to see Jari sitting on the bed. Jari hadn't spent any evenings in the dormitory since the curfew had been placed upon the manor, spending what few hours they were permitted elsewhere. Alex was often asleep by the time Jari crept in with a few minutes to spare before the curfew came into action, and he was usually gone again by the time Alex awoke in the morning. After being let down at lunchtime, Alex couldn't help but feel a lingering annoyance toward his friend, and he struggled to muster a smile as he walked over to his own bed. Jari jumped up and wandered over, his brow furrowed.

"What's the matter?" asked Alex, seeing the nervous twist of Jari's hands.

"I need your help," he whispered, glancing over at the door.

"With what?" Alex tried to stop the irritation from creeping into his voice. Of course Jari would only want to talk these days when he needed something.

"I need to break into the Head's quarters," explained Jari, his voice shaking slightly as he met Alex's eyes with earnest. "The time has come. I have to be certain the Head is gone." He mumbled something incoherent beneath his breath as Alex sank down onto the mattress.

"Does it make a difference?" said Alex wearily, trying to ignore the tense atmosphere of Jari's desperation.

"It makes every difference, Alex. There is information we can gather to use against him. This might be our only chance, if he has truly gone." Jari perched on the edge of the bedframe as he cast anxious glances in Alex's direction.

Jari made a good point. The Head's office was a source of untapped knowledge, Alex knew, as he recalled the bookshelf behind the Head's desk, the one ringed in a glowing red protective barrier. Alex was stronger than he had been the last time he had broken the defenses. Perhaps he could break in more easily a second time, to pilfer whatever he wanted while they had the chance.

Alex remembered Elias's teasing tales about rare books. If those books were going to be anywhere, they would be on that bookshelf in the Head's office. Of that, Alex was almost entirely certain.

He heard the disappointed frustration of Elias's voice once more, replaying in his mind, telling him to go and find the Head if he wanted answers. Even if the Head truly had gone, who knew what answers Alex could find left behind? The risk would definitely be worth the reward if he uncovered something about the Head or the history of the manor. Alex hoped he would uncover something within those secret tomes that would help him in his ongoing plot of escape or that might shed more light on who he was. If there were any Spellbreaker books in the manor at all, they would be in the Head's office. The stolen books on the Havens might also be hidden there, locked away from prying eyes.

It was too tempting an offer to turn down, though Alex knew the stakes were high.

"Fine," he muttered.

"You'll really help?" asked Jari.

Alex nodded. "I could do with checking out his book

selection," he said with a half-hearted smile as Jari's face visibly relaxed with relief.

"There's something I might need too," explained Jari, his tone secretive, though he didn't elaborate as Alex waited patiently for him to say more.

"Like what?" Alex pressed, when Jari said nothing else on the subject.

Jari shook his head. "I'll tell you if I manage to find it," he said, the response frustrating Alex.

Trying not to let it get the better of him, Alex lay back on the pillows and took out the book on the *Great Battles* that he had stuffed down the back of his mattress. Absently, he began to read, going over the familiar names and skirmishes before he became aware of Jari's eyes staring intently in his direction.

"What?" asked Alex, looking up from the page.

"Well, are we going or not?" said Jari sternly, a small black bag slung across his shoulder as he nodded toward the door.

"We're going *now*?" replied Alex, shocked. He knew Jari had been planning something for a while, but he hadn't expected to have such little notice where his part was concerned.

"Yeah," said Jari simply.

Alex got up, putting the book back behind the mattress as he glanced down at himself. He wasn't sure what else he could wear to make himself less conspicuous; most of his clothing was already black. His eyes lingered over the black scarf hanging from the back of the wardrobe door, but he remembered Natalie's response the last time and thought better of it. Looking over, he saw that Jari had on much the same as him and figured he'd be okay.

"Are we getting Natalie?" Alex asked, as they stepped out into the hallway of the boys' dormitories. It was dark, and he could hear the low chatter of other voices coming from behind the doors that lined the corridor.

Jari nodded. "I didn't have chance to tell her it was tonight, but she should be good to go."

Although it wasn't yet nine o'clock and the curfew hadn't come into action, the hallways were pretty much deserted as they took the familiar route toward the girls' dormitories. As an extra precaution, they kept to the shadows, anxious not to set off any alarms or get in anybody's way as they stealthily went to find Natalie. They were just turning a corner when they almost ran headfirst into the very person they wanted to see.

Alex stepped out of Natalie's way just in time, but it didn't stop her from shouldering into Jari as they collided. She looked up with an air of surprise, and Alex was alarmed to see the state she was in. Her face was deathly pale in the weak light cast from the torches. Beneath her eyes were deep, dark circles of fatigue, made all the more worrying by the drawn, sunken look of her features. Her shoulders were sagging, and she looked dead on her feet with exhaustion, her hair dull and bedraggled, but she managed to muster a feeble smile as she asked them what they were up to.

"We're heading to the Head's quarters tonight to see if he has truly gone," explained Jari quickly, giving her the simple version. "We were just on our way to get you, to see if you were good to come with us?" he added, frowning at her.

"Sorry, guys… I am simply too tired to help you this time," she said reluctantly, though her reasoning needed no explanation. Her exhaustion was clear for anyone to see, etched on her face and in her limp posture. "If you were to go tomorrow or another day, I could almost certainly help. I would very much like to help," she whispered.

Alex glanced down at Jari, wondering if they *could* postpone their trip until Natalie felt more up to the task. He didn't want to go without Natalie, but she was deathly pale, and a grip of worry for his exhausted friend twisted at his insides. He knew she was pushing herself too hard, and he was fearful she might break. Her pursuit of magical triumph seemed to be taking its toll, and Alex wasn't sure what he could do to help. He had already tried to get her to stop, with little success.

"We could wait," said Alex, flashing a reassuring smile at Natalie.

Jari shook his head. "No, it has to be tonight. I'm

sorry, Natalie, but it is now or never," he replied firmly. Natalie's face fell.

"Why does it have to be tonight?" asked Alex, eyeing Jari suspiciously for any hint as to why. Jari was already twitchy, and this apparent delay only seemed to make him more agitated.

"It just does! We can't wait any longer," he snapped, giving no further explanation.

Alex knew time was against them. It had been a while since the noticeboards had appeared with the new rules and regulations written on them, and the likelihood of the Head returning, if he had gone away, was increasing with each day they didn't investigate. Still, Alex knew it would be far more dangerous with just the two of them than it would be with three. Natalie was a strong, powerful Mage, and she had skills neither of them did that could be useful in the sort of high-pressure situation they were about to walk into. But Jari didn't seem to care. His only concern seemed to be getting into the Head's quarters that night, come hell or high water. Alex wasn't even certain Jari was worried about getting out, as long as he got in.

"Well, we'll need to get somebody else to help, then," insisted Alex.

"Why? We're good with just us," replied Jari, the anxiety clear in his voice.

"It'll be safer with three," explained Alex. "We need a third to help watch our backs."

"Who can we trust?" asked Jari, his brow furrowed in thought.

Alex smiled as an idea came to him. "We could ask Ellabell. She knows some great, powerful shielding spells that could be good for defense if we need it."

Glancing across at Natalie, Alex saw a flash of hurt pass across her wide eyes. He watched as she tried to muster a smile, but knew she was upset by the notion of someone taking her place. He couldn't blame her; he had felt the same when they hadn't wanted to spar with him. It wasn't nice to feel left out.

"It is fine," Natalie insisted. "I thought I was tired, but I am all ready to come with you. I can do it." No matter what she said, her exhaustion was undeniable, Alex thought. Bravery would not cover the weariness sapping her strength.

"No, Natalie. You're exhausted," said Alex kindly, patting his friend on the shoulder. "We'll tell you what we find as soon as we get back, okay?" he promised, though Natalie still looked crestfallen as the suggestion of Ellabell hung in the air.

"You had best come with me, then," she murmured as she turned and walked with them toward her dorm room.

Ellabell seemed a little confused as to why there were two boys in her room as Natalie ushered them quickly in. It was getting closer to curfew, and Ellabell was holding her pajamas over the crook of her arm, as though she had just been about to get ready for bed. Her brown curls were tied up into a messy bun, though a few sprang loose about her face, and she seemed less than pleased. Alex hadn't spoken properly with her since he had made his excuses and run from her dorm room, and she cast him a peculiar look as he stood against the wall, waiting for Natalie to explain.

At first, Ellabell didn't seem to like the idea, shaking the curls on top of her head.

"That sounds pretty dangerous to me," she said, holding her pajamas to her chest.

"Aren't you curious?" asked Jari eagerly. Time was slipping away, and the longer it took to make Ellabell come around, the less time there would be to actually get going with the plan. "Don't you want to know if the Head is really gone?"

"Does it really make a difference?" replied Ellabell, echoing Alex's earlier sentiments.

"We need to check. It's for Aamir's sake," explained Jari, his voice bordering on pleading.

"Professor Nagi?" said Ellabell, her face surprised.

Jari nodded. "Yes, it's for Aamir. We're trying to help him out."

"Is he in danger?" Ellabell frowned, glancing at Alex, who had yet to say a word.

"He might be," said Jari, his voice pinched with emotion.

"I would go with them, but I do not feel so well," murmured Natalie, sitting wearily down on her bed. "I would be most grateful if you would help them out for me and make sure they are safe. I wish I could go with them, and I am sorry to ask such a big favor," she sighed.

The sight of Natalie, so pale and sickly, seemed to affect Ellabell, chipping away at her aversion to such a dangerous scheme. Slowly, she put her pajamas down on the covers of her bed and folded her arms.

"Why do you need me?" she asked simply.

"We need a third to watch our backs," said Alex, leveling his gaze in Ellabell's direction. "I know how good you are with shielding spells, and I suggested you might be able to help us out because you're one of the strongest, most knowledgeable students in this place and you're more than capable of helping defend us if anything bad happens," he explained softly, his mouth curving into an encouraging smile.

"*You* suggested me?" Ellabell frowned, pushing her spectacles back up to the bridge of her nose.

Alex nodded. "Plus, there are stacks of forbidden books you could always have a glance through while we're there." He shrugged casually, hoping the temptation of the rare tomes would seal the deal.

It felt as if an eternity had passed as they waited for Ellabell's answer. Her face was etched with concern and there was a nervous energy about her, but Alex hoped she would say yes. He knew it was a lot to ask of her, but her skills would be invaluable if they got into any trouble behind the golden line.

"I'll help," she said hurriedly, as if deliberating any further would change her mind.

Alex grinned as the newly formed trio said their hushed goodbyes to Natalie, and he and Jari ushered Ellabell out the door. There was no more time to waste. It was already past curfew, and they had to get to the golden line without disturbing anyone or setting off any booby traps.

"Can you put a shield around yourself and Jari?" asked Alex in a whisper. "A strong one that can protect you both as well as possible?" he added, his eyes darting to the darkness at the end of the corridor.

Ellabell nodded, her eyes wide with fear as she began to conjure golden streams of light from beneath her hands. "You as well?"

Alex shook his head. "Just you two," he insisted, hoping he was right about his anti-magic protecting him from any magical traps that might be in place throughout the corridors. The barrier to the girls' dormitories didn't work on him, and he was convinced none of the unseen curfew spells would either, should there be anything out there, hidden in the darkness of the hallways. It was a big risk to take, especially since the Head suspected something was amiss about Finder's disappearance, but it was one Alex was willing to try. If he got caught, he knew it would be a catastrophe. He'd cross that bridge if he came to it.

Slowly, Ellabell's magic spread out in a glittering lattice across the pair of them, golden threads interlacing with other threads until a gleaming screen covered them entirely, lying lightly over their skin. Pulling her hands tightly inward, her face stern in concentration, she suddenly dimmed the radiance, and Alex couldn't see them against the shadows of the hallway. The shield had worked, hiding Jari and Ellabell mostly from sight. It wasn't foolproof, but it was better than nothing.

"Follow my lead," whispered Alex as they moved through the empty manor, his eyes darting cautiously into the shadows ahead of each corner to scan for anyone moving about in the darkness. He didn't want to come across Renmark by accident, or his new right-hand woman, Esmerelda. There would be no leniency from either of them if they were caught—Alex knew that for sure.

Eventually, they reached the entrance to the Head's quarters, the golden line glinting menacingly from the floor, where it snaked up the walls and across the ceiling. As Alex paused, Ellabell removed a small square in the lattice of her camouflage, the shield glowing dimly for a moment as her face appeared in the gap. Alex wasn't sure it was a good spot for a conversation, but he held his tongue.

"How are we supposed to get past?" she asked nervously. Alex could see Jari smirking behind her.

"Close the gap in your shield and turn around. This shouldn't take long, but it might be dangerous, and I don't want you to get hurt. I'll call you when it's safe," said Alex.

Reluctantly, Ellabell wove the gap back together with glowing threads around her peering eyes, and he heard the sound of shuffling feet on the flagstones, as if the hidden figures were turning around. Alex squinted into the shadows, hoping they weren't looking, before kneeling in front of the golden line. Concentrating hard, he conjured the body of a silver sword above his hands, feeling the twist and swirl of the energy as it sharpened the edges and gave weight to the blade. Remembering the tip from the notebook, he focused on the central pulse of the sword and flexed his fingers inwards until the weapon glinted solidly in the air. Only then did he dare to reach out and take the hilt in his hands, feeling the delicate balance and heft of the sword.

With a deft swing, he brought the blade down on the golden barrier, watching with surprise as it fractured in one clean break, each end rebounding off the blow of the blade and hitting the sides of the corridor walls, leaving a big gap in the center through which a person could slip through unnoticed.

For a moment, the hallway was still. Then, out of nowhere, an artillery of golden-tipped arrows and icy blades soared upward and turned toward Alex, glinting in the low light as they rushed in his direction. Alex dropped the sword and threw up a frosty shield around himself with one hand, the arrows smashing to pieces as they impacted. With his other hand, he grasped at the icy blades and snatched them from the air, hurling them into the slick stone of the walls, where they shattered harmlessly. His only concern was the noise they made as they hit the stone, the sound chiming in his ears as he held off a second wave.

Alex caught sight of something slithering across the floor from the point of the initial cut he had made with his sword. Tentacles snaked rapidly up Alex's body, darting through the gap left between his shield and the floor. He could feel the bitter frost of the magical tendrils nipping at his skin as they wrapped about his neck, tightening and constricting as his hands passed helplessly through the golden vapor of them. They took hold of him, squeezing the air from his lungs, making it impossible to draw in another breath as they coiled tighter.

Panicking, Alex forged a small, glittering black knife with his hands, pinching the blade into a sharp point as quickly as he could before lifting it beneath the tendrils that strangled him. Concentrating hard on the central pulse of the weapon's energy, his eyes bulging, he poured a layer of darker power into the blade, strengthening it as he felt the anti-magic meet the magic with a tense push of resistance. The tendrils' magic didn't feel exactly like regular magic; it was cold and defiant, more like his own. But the extra layer of force seemed to do the trick as the blade sliced savagely through the tentacles, breaking them apart until they shriveled away into small wisps of amber energy that floated downward through the air, disappearing as they touched the flagstone floor.

Chest heaving as he drank in the stale air of the manor, Alex made sure none of the attacks had reached the place where he knew the shielded Ellabell and Jari stood. Frowning, he wondered how much they had seen, secretly, from within their camouflage. Alex hoped Jari had kept Ellabell from peeking.

"You can come out now," he said breathlessly, wiping the sweat from his brow as the shield fell away.

He could sense nothing in the way Ellabell looked at him that would suggest she knew what he had just done, but perhaps she had a good poker face. Alex wasn't sure, but he was eager to move on, and gestured for them to walk through the first corridor.

Ellabell paused in front of the space where the golden line had been, her eyes darting suspiciously toward the walls as she stepped forward on tiptoe, like she was checking the temperature of a pool. Alex laughed softly as he watched her, his amusement fading as she turned and glowered at him. He held up his hands in mock surrender as he followed her through the gap and up into the unmapped shadows of this area of the manor.

Picking up the pace, they ran as swiftly as they dared

through the hallways toward the main body of the Head's quarters, Ellabell producing her shield every so often at the sound of something scuttling across the floor or a flash in the darkness ahead. The corridors remained eerily empty as they rushed through, pausing at corners, expecting the Head to appear at any moment and swoop down on them like a hawk. Nobody came.

When they reached a fork in the hallways, Jari came to a halt.

"I'm going this way. You guys should go explore the rest," he announced without warning. He took off toward the right-hand route. Alex frowned, knowing the Head's office was through the corridor that lay straight ahead.

"We shouldn't split up!" Alex called after Jari, wincing as he heard his voice rebound off the walls in a loud echo, worried it would bring somebody to investigate.

Jari didn't reappear from the darkness of the tunnel, his footfalls fading away to nothing as Alex stood at the fork, wondering whether to go ahead or turn left, to investigate some more. Who knew when he would next get the opportunity to roam around these parts so freely? But the purpose had been to seek out the Head. If he went left, he was going against that purpose. While he couldn't understand Jari's detour, Alex knew he had to at least keep to their target. It also helped slightly that what he was after lay within the Head's office itself.

"Are you okay?" he asked Ellabell, who trembled

beside him. It didn't matter that she was a fierce young mage; he could understand anyone being scared of the Head.

She nodded. "I'm fine," she whispered, her voice shaking.

"Straight ahead or left?" He gestured toward the two tunnels, leaving it up to Ellabell to decide.

"Straight ahead," she replied firmly, glancing up at him with concern.

"Good choice." He smiled warmly as he stepped toward the hallway ahead, with her following close behind.

It looked much the same as any of the corridors in the manor, although it lacked the grim portraits that could be found elsewhere. The only decorations were torches hanging in elegant golden brackets on the walls, the metal twisting up into the elaborate heads of serpents, which seemed to hiss at passersby with darting silver tongues. Alex speculated about who lit those torches when nobody was around, and his thoughts cast back to the plump, toad-like figure of Siren Mave, with her excessive blush and drawn-on red lips. He wondered if it was her—above everyone, she had seemed to have free rein of the place. Concern from this forgotten threat crept slowly through him, refusing to be brushed off, heightening his wariness as they moved stealthily through the halls. He very much hoped he didn't end up bumping into her in the shadows.

In the low light from the flickering torches, doors

began to appear in the walls. They were marked with brass lettering that had gone crusty with age, and, as they passed a door marked *Library*, Ellabell paused.

"Are you going on ahead?" she asked.

Alex nodded. "Yeah, the Head's office is up there." He pointed up into the abyss beyond the comfort of the torchlight.

"Then, would it be okay if you left me here?" She rested her palm against the stone wall.

"Are you sure?" he replied, his voice laced with worry. He didn't like the idea of leaving her alone in this place.

"I know my way back from here—just in case anything happens. Plus, I don't like the idea of going where you're going," she admitted shyly.

"I don't blame you." A hollow chuckle caught in the back of his throat as he gazed up toward the rest of the vacant hallway, though he still felt a twist of reluctance at leaving her by herself. "Are you sure, though? I don't feel right leaving you alone," he explained, hoping she didn't think he was being too overbearing.

"I'll be fine, but thank you. Now go on, we haven't got time to chat." She grinned at him, the expression lighting up her face. Not for the first time, Alex noted how pretty she was, with her bright blue eyes sparkling behind her spectacles and her curly brown hair bobbing as she spoke. Across the bridge of her nose, soft freckles dusted her skin, just above the deep cupid's bow of her rosy lips. Her sharp intelligence and ready smile were captivating, and Alex felt his voice catch in his throat as he spoke again.

"Well, you know where I am if you run into trouble. Just yell or something and I'll come running," he told her, hoping he sounded confident.

"I'll be sure to yell. Knock for me on your way back," she replied, moving her hand to the handle of the library door.

"I will. Be careful, and keep a close eye on the door," he warned, reaching out to take her hand and give it a light squeeze of reassurance.

"I will be. Take care." Her cheeks flushed a deeper shade of pink at the touch of his hand on hers. She gave him a strange look, the expression turning into an anxious smile as she hurriedly opened the door and stepped inside, leaving Alex alone in the hallway.

As he walked on alone, he remembered the last time he had come this way, with the chambers of rotting four-poster beds with moth-eaten drapes that smelled damply of age and mildew. The rooms of people who had long since departed. He almost didn't stop as he came to the door of the small chamber he had seen before—the stone chamber with the manacles dangling from the ceiling above a slickly covered grate. The pull of the strange room was magnetic to him. Alex pushed open the door. The metallic tang of blood and fear still rose pungently from within, filling his nostrils with the nauseating scent as he stepped inside. He couldn't help but revisit this place, curiosity getting the better of him.

Yeah, and curiosity killed the cat, he thought dryly as he closed the door quietly behind him.

The room was little changed. Above the center grate, smothered in gray ivy, were the grim manacles, dangling limply from the ceiling. Beneath, the ground glinted with the same sticky, sinister residue as before, the smell of blood growing stronger as Alex drew closer to the grate. To the side of the room, the same foul painting of a gaping mouth with layer on layer of savage teeth and a lashing tongue still hung above the small wooden table, which was strewn with tools and something new that made Alex's stomach turn. A wide-brimmed hat lay on the very edge of the tabletop, tattered and frayed at the edges—undeniably similar to the hat Derhin had worn on the day of his last battle, the hat that had given him a brief advantage over Aamir. Beside it were the bladeless knife and the ordinary-looking clipboard.

Alex wandered over, glad to be away from the grate's sickening stench and the slick substance that glistened in the semi-darkness of the chamber. Cautiously, he picked up the steel hilt of the bladeless knife and felt a sudden rush of energy course through his forearm, oddly cold, as a blade appeared at the end of the handle. The silver blade glowed with radiant white light, solid and menacing. Holding it up in awe, Alex caught sight of something peculiar as the brightness of the knife's blade cast a silvery glow across the room. At the opposite end of the chamber, buried beneath a dense mass of gray ivy, stood a thin wooden door, the black handle just visible beneath the layered leaves. He must have missed it in the rush of his last, hurried visit to the chamber.

Putting the knife down, Alex moved toward the door, skirting around the grate and feeling his foot slip in something vile. Shuddering, he rested his hand on the door handle, trying to avoid the ivy that hung across the wood as he pushed against it, but the door wouldn't budge. It was locked.

Slowly, Alex covered the lock with his palm and conjured a small ball of black-and-silver anti-magic, focusing the blast of it into the center of the lock. There was a quiet crack as the door gave against the shove of his shoulder.

In the room behind the first stretched a long antechamber, filled with row upon row of wooden shelves, stacked neatly with small black bottles. Though there were no windows, the room was somehow filled with a dim light, just bright enough to see by. Alex squinted into the long room, wondering if it was another wine cellar. As he ventured farther along, he realized the bottles were far too small for wine, and they seemed to glow dully from within, like fading fireflies, pulsing with a dimmed red color behind the black glass.

Leaning closer to some of the racks, Alex saw they

were labelled with dates. One rack had *1909* written in curling black ink underneath, but there weren't any bottles on that one. Frowning, he saw that only the most recently dated racks were full—the shelves closest to the door. Behind those, many were empty.

Horror gripped his stomach as he hurried back up the length of the room and reached for a bottle on the first rack. Illuminated by the dim red glow within, Alex almost dropped the bottle as the letters on the label lit up. In the dim pulse, he felt sick as he read the name over and over, wanting to be sure.

It read *R. Derhin*.

As he closed his hand around the bottle, gripping it tightly in his palm, Alex felt the energy radiate from within as color rippled out from the dark glass, causing the world around him to bend and distort as the ground rushed away from him and his body tumbled through darkness, into oblivion.

CHAPTER 21

As the world stopped spinning and the rush of air slowed to a light breeze, Alex found himself floating unseen above a familiar setting. Students rushed past below him, dressed in black, their laughter echoing down the hallways as they pushed and shoved in small groups, chattering away about the trials of the day ahead. Everything seemed more colorful, with only narrow patches of gray ivy creeping from the chilly stone walls and cracks in the flagstones, hardly noticeable and easily kicked away by a stray foot as students trod over it. There were more students than Alex had ever seen at the manor, the corridors crowded with young men and women.

As he scanned the students below, his eyes were drawn to two boys, on the border between boyhood and manhood, laughing mischievously as they perched side by side on one of the deep windowsills. They were faces he had seen before, though slightly older than these iterations. It was unmistakably them. Lintz and Derhin, smiling and joking, laughing about a mishap Lintz had had with one of his bombs in the mechanics lab, Lintz gesturing to the two ungainly bandages wrapped tightly around his hands where he had managed to burn himself. Derhin was grinning, his face youthful and boyish, his hair jet black and his dark blue eyes glittering in amusement as his friend recounted the tale. Lintz was wincing through a belly laugh as he explained how the bomb had gone off just as Professor Gaze had come into the lab, doing a dramatic impression of the scream she had given. Derhin howled beside him, holding his ribs as the laughter pealed from them both.

Lintz's ginger hair flopped over his lightly freckled face, smooth and fresh with youth, as he tried to wipe away the giddy tears with his bandaged hands, like bright white mittens on the ends of his wrists. He was athletic-looking, and his chiseled cheekbones flushed pink with humor as Derhin tried to copy the sound of Gaze's scream, causing Lintz to collapse into another fit of hysterics.

Alex felt an instant warmth toward the two boys in their own hilarious world, not caring about the looks of disdain they were being thrown by other students. Some teachers, too. Alex squinted as he noticed one particular individual, clad in the instantly recognizable cloak of a teacher, standing at the corner of the corridor, watching the pair intently. His eyes were narrowed into slits, and the expression on his face was one of intense displeasure, the muscles in his cheeks twitching each time their laughter pierced the air in a raucous wave. There was something about him that niggled at the back of Alex's mind. The face was familiar somehow, but Alex couldn't quite place him. He wondered if he could move closer to the figure to get a better look, but, as he floated forward, a bloodcurdling scream shattered the image.

As the piercing cry vibrated through Alex's body, the world of Derhin's memory broke apart, rushing away again as the colors bled away to darkness. Alex returned to the dimly lit antechamber with the glowing red bottles, Derhin's still clutched in his hand. He shoved it back onto the shelf and tore out of the room, back through the rancid stench of the chamber and out into the stale corridor. He sprinted, his footsteps echoing loudly on the flagstones, until he reached the door of the library. Ellabell sat huddled against the wall by the entrance, her whole body trembling and her eyes wide in horror as blood trickled down her chin. Her hands were clamped tightly over her mouth, her fingers shaking violently. Her spectacles lay crushed on the floor beside her, little shards of glass scattered out from the wire frame.

Alex glanced around the medium-sized chamber, feeling eyes on him, as he reached down to pull Ellabell to her feet. She shrank away from his hands with a whimper, not wanting him to touch her. He tried again, lifting her by the arms, ever conscious of the deafening scream inviting unwanted visitors, but she thrashed against him desperately, tears falling from her wide blue eyes.

"Hey, hey, it's me. It's only me," he whispered in soothing tones, trying to calm her as he held her to him. Eventually, she stopped thrashing, her fists no longer pummeling his chest as she rested limply in his arms.

Suddenly, Jari appeared in the doorway, an expression of panic on his face. His face was pale and sweating, his chest heaving with exertion as he looked down at the sight of Ellabell clutched in Alex's arms.

"We better run," he gasped, as Alex heard the first echoes of footsteps on the flagstones behind Jari, gaining speed.

Gathering Ellabell up in his arms, Alex burst from the library and ran with her, Jari only slightly ahead of them as they raced through the corridors toward the main body of the building, hurdling over debris and clusters of tangled gray ivy that threatened to sabotage their escape. Alex felt a fleeting moment of frustration that he hadn't managed to see the Head's office, but knew there was no point worrying about it now. If it was the Head in pursuit, he would no doubt be seeing the inside of the Head's office soon enough.

Glancing over his shoulder for the briefest second, Alex caught a glimpse of the figure running behind them. He was tall and dressed head to toe in black, with a pale, haunting mask covering most of his face. It wasn't the Head, but it was someone equally terrifying. The black holes in the mask, where the eyes ought to have been, stared coldly and intently as two gloved hands lifted and sent glittering bolts of golden magic snaking rapidly after them.

Turning a corner, Alex placed Ellabell down and yelled for Jari to get her to safety as he held his own palms up and felt the tendrils of shimmering black and vivid silver slipping easily across his fingers in vibrant tendrils, made more powerful by the pulse of emotion rising through him. Pressing himself flat against the wall, he drew the anti-magic back into himself, feeling the strange tingle of it in his bloodstream as he peered around the corner, his heart pounding as he witnessed the figure gaining ground quickly.

"Stop!" called the figure, in a strict, sharp voice that wasn't familiar to Alex.

Alex extended his hands and sent the blockade rushing toward the figure. It was densely packed with ice and snow, ripples of black and silver energy twisting and turning within the frosty interior, far stronger and more powerful than the one he had practiced in the cellar. It knocked the figure backward with a loud thud, its body hitting the stone floor hard. Watching the blockade disintegrate, Alex moved his hand in a rapid figure eight, creating a fog of condensation that rose up thickly from the icy remnants, distorting the escape route from view.

Alex didn't wait for the figure to get up as he raced after Jari, who was a short way ahead with Ellabell's arm draped around his neck. Taking up Ellabell's other arm, Alex gripped her waist and ran, holding her up as they raced past the golden line that lay cracked and broken on the floor. Spying the dull, painted red wood of one of the empty chambers in the adjoining corridor, Alex headed for it and burst through the door, dragging them all inside. He gently set Ellabell down and touched his finger to his lips, ensuring she and Jari understood his meaning as he crouched low to the floor and crept back over to the door, placing his eye close to the keyhole to watch the hallway beyond.

He heard the figure before he saw it, the hurried beat of shoes hitting stone sending jolts of panic through Alex's heart as he waited for the figure to come into view. The dark-clad pursuer passed close by the door without pausing to check it, permitting Alex to get a closer look. The figure looked tall and menacing as he ran past, with a distinct masculinity in the broadness of the shoulders, though his face was shrouded by a hood. Alex frowned as he sat back from the keyhole; he had never seen the figure before, and the notion made him wonder how easy it was to hide a stranger in the manor. Perhaps the Head was hiding an army in this labyrinth of a place.

Looking back at his fellow escapees, he noticed that Ellabell had curled up against the wall with her eyes staring out into space. He felt a wave of protectiveness for the curly-haired girl, wondering what on earth had happened to her.

"Ellabell?" he whispered, his hands reaching out to hold hers as she trembled uncontrollably. "Ellabell, what happened?" he asked, but she only shook her head and lowered her gaze.

Her entire body shivered, the blood drying and flaking from where it had trickled from the corner of her mouth down to the edge of her chin. Tears streamed silently from her big blue eyes as she clutched the broken spectacles in her hand, the splinters of glass pricking her skin until Alex took them carefully from her desperate grasp and placed them on the ground.

"Ellabell, tell me what happened. You can trust me," Alex reassured her earnestly, squeezing her hands lightly as he spoke.

She shook her head, a choked whimper escaping her throat as she looked up to the darkness that crept across the chamber ceiling, her pupils darting rapidly as if she thought someone was watching her. Alex glanced up, following the direction of her gaze, but could sense nothing in the shadows that might want to hurt them.

Only when the coast seemed clear did Alex give the go-ahead for them to re-emerge, some hours later. Gently, Alex picked up the wilting, terrified form of Ellabell and carried her carefully back to her dormitory like precious cargo. Jari headed back to the boys' dormitory at Alex's insistence, leaving Alex to tiptoe through the vacant halls, checking around every corner to make sure he was alone. Nobody stopped him as he made the slow trek back to the girls' dormitory, and he felt a keen sense of relief when he reached the door with the brass number twenty-eight on the front. He rapped quietly on the wood and waited for Natalie to open it.

She answered it quickly, and Alex realized she must have stayed up all night, anxiously awaiting their return. Natalie gasped when she saw Ellabell and helped Alex carry her to her bed.

"She needs professional help," said Natalie, pressing her hand to the back of Ellabell's forehead to check her temperature.

"No," whimpered Ellabell. "I'm fine," she insisted, curling up into the fetal position as Natalie pulled the covers over her.

A look passed between Alex and Natalie. He hadn't heard Ellabell speak properly until that moment, and the strangeness in the curly-haired girl's voice was deeply concerning; it was thick and distorted, as if her mouth were filled with liquid.

"You should see someone. One of the professors should be on duty," pressed Alex, but Ellabell looked up at him in horror.

"No. I don't want to see anyone. I'm fine," she repeated, her odd voice catching in her throat as she began to cough violently. Natalie handed her a handkerchief from the top drawer of her bedside table, and Alex was certain he saw blood as Ellabell spluttered into it, the deep red staining the pale pink of the fabric as she held it to her mouth, though she tried to hide it with her hands as she smothered the handkerchief with her fists.

"You should go. I will make sure she is okay," whispered Natalie as Alex tried to get another look at the handkerchief. He was growing more worried about Ellabell with each fact he didn't know.

"Are you sure?" he asked, frowning.

Natalie nodded. "I will make sure she is okay. I promise."

"I hope you feel better soon," Alex murmured, not knowing what to say to Ellabell as he moved toward the door of the dorm. She didn't respond, turning beneath the covers to face the wall.

"You can tell me everything tomorrow," Natalie said as she led Alex to the door and ushered him out into the corridor.

Alex nodded, passing her a wave of goodbye as she closed the door on him.

Back at his own dormitory, Alex changed quickly out of his dusty, dirty clothes and into his clean, crisp pajamas, lying wearily back on his mattress as he stared up at the ceiling, his limbs aching a little from the run. Across the room, Jari was a mirror image, staring up into space with his arms folded across his chest.

"What did you find?" asked Alex, propping himself up on his elbows as he looked over toward his friend.

"The Head is gone," replied Jari with a low sigh, "but I couldn't get my hands on what I was after." There was regret in Jari's voice, and a subtle hint of anger rippling just below the surface.

"The Head is gone?" Alex was curious that Jari didn't seem more pleased by the revelation. "How can you be sure?"

"He's definitely gone. It's a long story, but let's just say a little bird told me," he explained with a vagueness that frustrated Alex. "What happened to Ellabell, by the way?"

"No idea. She won't say, but it was definitely something bad," said Alex, wishing he knew what had happened so he could help her. He couldn't get the image of her wide, terrified blue eyes out of his head.

"Looked it," mused Jari. "Poor girl."

Alex nodded. "Yeah, I hope she's okay." He didn't want to admit it, but he felt responsible for what had happened to Ellabell. It was his suggestion that had led her down that rabbit hole and caused her whatever trauma she had experienced. If he had just gone with Jari, like Jari had wanted, it would never have happened. Guilt gnawed at his stomach as he thought of the terrified girl, huddled beneath the covers, scared of the shadows.

"Did you get anything?" asked Jari, breaking Alex's train of thought.

Alex shook his head. "Not really."

He wasn't ready to tell anyone what he had seen and felt in the antechamber—not until he was able to process it in his own mind. The rows on rows of glowing black bottles, glimmering red within. The labels, the dates, the slick floor of the chamber beneath those menacing manacles. It haunted him, flooding his mind as he lay back to go to sleep.

What was that place? Alex wasn't sure he wanted to know.

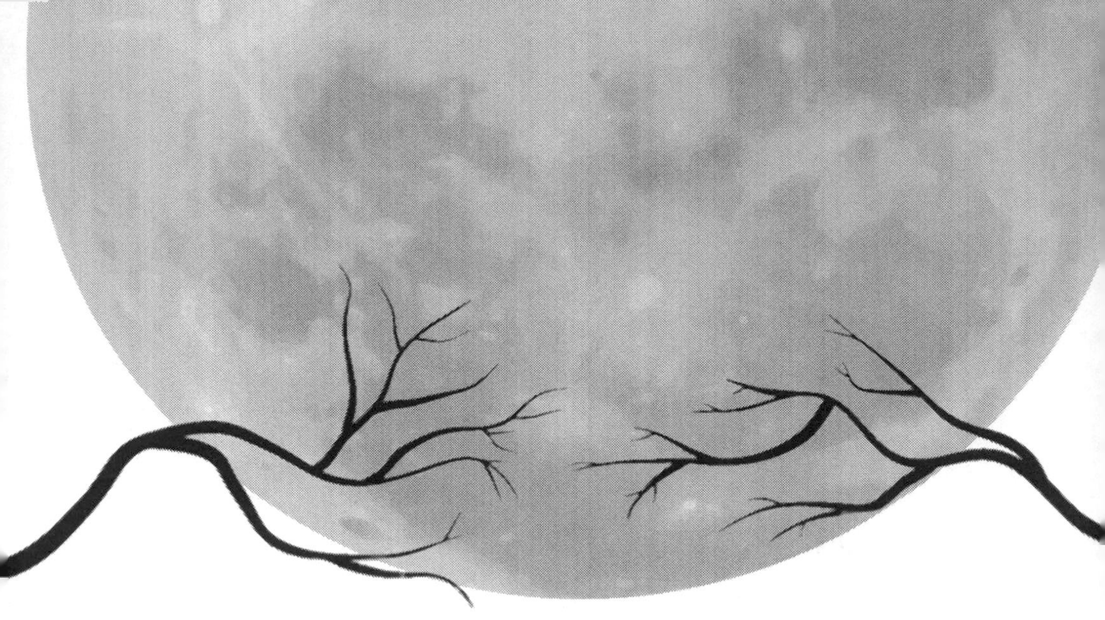

CHAPTER 22

ALEX AWOKE WITH A CHURN OF NAUSEA IN THE pit of his stomach. He had slept fitfully through the few hours left between their hasty return to the dormitory and the customary wake-up call, and he knew he was going to struggle to keep anything down that morning.

Blood rushed in his ears, and his hands took on a clammy, sweaty texture that would not be wiped away no matter how hard he tried. He felt as if he could see his heart pounding through his chest as paranoia coursed through his waking body like a virus, his mind recalling the previous night's events with a sickening dread. He had tried to tamp down any fear or anxiety while the events were happening, but they had caught up with him and were all the more potent for having been kept at bay. He envied Jari, who was still snoring away across the room, once again spread-eagled on top of the covers with his limbs sticking out over the edges of the bed. While Alex had tossed and turned for most of the night, he had heard the snores of Jari's slumber within moments of his blond-haired head hitting the pillow.

In the cold light of day, the memory of the night's close shave with danger seemed all the more worrying. Alex's heart raced as he thought of the dark-cloaked figure with the chilling mask, wondering how much the stranger had seen of Alex and what he could do. Obviously, he knew Alex could create a blockade of ice and snow, but Alex wasn't sure if the figure had seen his face. If the dark-clad figure had recognized them, Alex knew they were in for a world of trouble. But, if what Jari had said was true and the Head was definitely gone from the premises, then he wasn't sure who could be hiding behind the mask.

Alex wiped away the cold sweat that trickled down the back of his neck and prayed silently to whoever was listening that the fog and the blockade had been enough to stop them from being recognized, as much for Jari and Ellabell's sake as his. If someone *was* out for blood for the trespass into the Head's quarters, they could punish the other two to get at him, and Alex didn't think he could bear the thought of Ellabell suffering any further because of their futile excursion.

After shaking Jari awake, Alex waited for his friend to throw on some clothes, and the two headed to breakfast. Jari wasn't particularly talkative but didn't seem too fazed by what had gone on, much to Alex's chagrin, as they walked to the mess hall. Alex dragged Jari with him as he took a slight detour, wandering as casually as possible past the golden line in front of the Head's quarters. He was surprised to see that it had been swiftly repaired, as if nothing had ever happened. It was crackling and buzzing as powerfully as it ever had, warding off any advancing students.

If the masked figure had gone to the effort of putting the line back together so quickly, perhaps there would be no more said on the matter, Alex thought nervously. His paranoia was off the scale as he stepped into the mess hall, convinced everyone was looking at him oddly as he picked up a bowl of fruit salad and hurried over to where Natalie was sitting, in their usual spot by the window overlooking a particularly bleak section of the gray, desolate grounds. He sat down, eager to speak to her.

"How is Ellabell?" asked Alex, testing the nausea in his stomach as he forced a grape into his mouth and chewed slowly.

"She is much better. She is just a bit shaken up," she assured him, though her tone was somewhat distant as she sipped from her coffee cup.

"That's good. I can't help feeling responsible for what happened to her," he admitted, swallowing the grape with some difficulty.

"She is fine, Alex. Nobody was hurt. You were lucky," she replied, with a coldness Alex hadn't heard before.

"Is everything okay?" Alex glanced at Natalie with concern, wondering why she was speaking with that tone of voice.

"Everything is fine. I am just tired," she explained, her expression relaxing. "I am sorry, Alex. I was just worried about you all, and it has worn me out," she added with a sigh.

"Sorry. We didn't mean to scare you," Alex said with a worried frown. He knew she was already exhausted most of the time, and they had gone and made matters worse by staying out all night doing dangerous things.

She gave a tired smile. "You are forgiven."

As Jari sat down with his plate piled high with fried breakfast, Alex launched into a series of questions to ease his paranoia. He wished he could be as blasé about the whole thing as Jari seemed to be.

"Do you think we were seen?" quizzed Alex, feeling the grape rolling around uncomfortably in his stomach.

Jari shook his head. "We weren't seen," he said, shoving a forkful of omelet into his mouth with hungry glee.

"How can you be sure?" pressed Alex.

"I know we weren't seen. We got away with it,"

repeated Jari in between mouthfuls.

"Do you know who that man was?" Alex asked.

Jari shook his head again. "No idea, but he was a scary-looking thing," he laughed casually.

"What man?" Natalie chimed in, her eyes glinting with curiosity.

"Some figure in black chased us, but I have no idea who he was," said Alex thoughtfully as he attempted to chew a slice of apple, the sweet, fruity sugars turning sour on his tongue. "He didn't look or sound familiar. Must be someone the Head keeps around for when he goes away or something."

Jari nodded. "I think you might be right," he said, swallowing an enormous bite of buttered toast.

"How did he get in?" asked Natalie, but neither Alex nor Jari could answer her.

"The back door?" suggested Alex, feeling acid rise in his throat as he forced the apple down.

"You think there may be one?" questioned Natalie with a sudden flair of excitement in her voice.

Alex shrugged. "Who knows? There are stranger things in this manor than a back door," he mused with a grim smile.

At that moment, Alex's attention was distracted by a student bursting in through the doors of the mess hall. The boy ran up to one of the small groups sitting closest to the entrance and whispered something urgently. A murmur spread like wildfire through the room. Alex waited for it to reach their table.

"The gate has reappeared," muttered Billy Foer as he leaned back to pass on the message.

"What?" asked Alex in disbelief.

"Just now, the gate has come back," replied Billy with a concerned look on his pallid face.

Alex jumped to his feet, abandoning his fruit salad as he and the other two raced from the mess hall and headed toward the front of the manor, just in time to see the huge iron bars of the gate swing open. The glowing golden line that usually blocked the way out into the gardens so early in the day had disappeared, permitting the students to congregate on the steps as they all rushed to see what was happening.

It was true—the gate had reappeared, settling back into its position between the high brick walls, draped in flowing clusters of the omnipresent gray ivy. With the shrill creak of rusting metal, the vast iron gates swung wide to reveal the very real form of a black-clad figure stepping onto the front lawn. The same one that had chased them through the hallways the night before.

He was tall and broad-shouldered, his posture drawing him up with a certain dignity as the drape of his dark cloak moved elegantly with the movement of his body. Taking his time, he walked across the lawn with a new student in tow. The same misty-eyed hypnotism of every newcomer was evident in the face of the young boy beside him, who did not seem to know what was going on, let alone where he was or what he was in for.

The black-clad figure wore a hood, much like the Head's, which shrouded his face from view, not that it could be seen beneath the delicate artwork of the mask he wore, painted gold and white in a distinctly Venetian style, his eyes made more menacing by the dark holes cut into it.

Seeing the gathered crowd of students, the masked figure stopped short of the steps with the new boy by his side. The boy swayed slightly under the trance that had been placed upon him, much like the one Natalie had been in when she had been taken to the manor. Tension bristled through the crowd as the glittering eyes assessed the students before him. Silence stretched unbearably as the figure chose his moment to speak, the students fidgeting beneath the discomfort of his intense stare.

"It is excellent to see your enthusiasm for your new classmate," purred the masked figure, his voice rich and deep and without accent, though distorted ever so slightly by the mask over his mouth. "This young man beside me is Felipe Cortez, and he is to be the newest member of our fair school. I hope you shall welcome him with open arms and teach him the ways of this place. As you may have realized, he is not the only new face amongst your ranks. I must be a stranger to you also. Well, wonder no more—I shall be the new Deputy Head here at Spellshadow Manor while the venerable Head is on important business for the benefit of our beloved school. You shall refer to me as Professor Escher. I am to manage this manor, and, if you comply with the rules, we shall get along just fine. If you do not, you must not expect leniency. Rules are in place for a reason, and I expect them to be followed to the letter." His voice curled elegantly into the air, sending shivers down the students' spines. There was an oddly sinister quality to it, despite its sophistication.

"I am not just to be your Deputy Head, however. I shall also be taking over some of the teaching duties in the wake of young Professor Nagi's ongoing work outside the school, assisting our much-respected Head. You will find me firm but fair, and I expect nothing but your finest work in my lessons. I do not accept lax attitudes regarding education, and I will push you to work your hardest toward the glorious goal of graduation," he continued, his arms gesturing with the fluidity of a dancer as he delivered his eerie speech. He clapped his hands lightly, making a few of the students beside Alex jump. "Now, back to work, all of you. The day has just begun, and we must get young Felipe oriented before his first day." There was the hint of a smile in the way Professor Escher spoke the last words, sending a chill through Alex as he watched the new professor walk the poor boy up the steps and usher him into one of the side rooms, closing the door behind them with a firm slam.

The students on the steps disbanded in a buzz of curious chatter, but Alex and his friends remained on the top step, staring out at the huge gate with its sapping ivy and thick iron bars. The gate didn't look as if it was going anywhere soon, with the arrival of the new professor to take the Head's place. More students would be snatched from their lives into a trap they could never escape, and the realization made Alex burn with anger.

"Who the hell is he?" seethed Alex, hoping fervently that his icy blockade had caused a bruise or two on their new dictator's graceful body.

"I don't know, but you can bet things are going to change around here," said Jari sullenly, sitting down on the stone step with his head in his hands.

"Do you believe he saw your faces last night?" asked Natalie, fresh anxiety lacing her words.

Alex shrugged. "If he did, we'll soon know."

CHAPTER 23

THOUGH THEY SHARED LESSONS AND SAT IN THE same mess hall for their meals, often walking the same hallways, Alex could not get Ellabell to speak to him. She seemed determined to avoid him at every turn, her gaze permanently lowered to the floor, her manner jumpy. The smallest scrape or whisper of a spell sparking would make her head jerk upright in alarm, her eyes scanning the room with an anxious flicker. Alex watched her as closely as he could, worried by her behavior. The more withdrawn and agitated she became, the more he held himself responsible for the change in her demeanor, wishing he had stayed by her side on that night.

Each time he saw her at the end of the corridor, knowing they would have to cross paths, she would look at him for the briefest moment before turning swiftly and walking the other way, scurrying along with her head down. If they stood closely in the line for dinner, Alex would watch her remove herself and loiter toward the end, only rejoining it once Alex had moved away and taken his seat elsewhere. He had tried to speak to her a number of times, but she didn't seem to want him anywhere near her. The realization stung him a little, but he could hardly blame her; he still wasn't sure what, exactly, had happened to her, but the trauma of it lingered. Every time he thought of the thick sound in her throat and the blood soaking through the delicate pink fabric of the handkerchief, his stomach turned, knowing it was his fault. He wished she would at least let him hug her or help in some way, so that he could ease her suffering.

Clambering up the rungs of one of the library's giant columns, Alex stepped out onto its middle platform and walked along the rows of books. He wanted to find out more about shielding and defensive techniques so he could try to invert them—but, as fate would have it, at the end of the row, drawn up against the stacks with her knees to her chin, was Ellabell. She looked as if she was muttering something to herself, her lips moving but barely a sound coming out as her eyes flitted distractedly across the pages of a book open on the ground beside her. She was wearing new glasses with square black rims that made her look as studious as she was, her fingers toying anxiously with strands of hair that had escaped the tight ponytail at the back of her head as she read over the book's words, completely absorbed in the task.

"Ellabell?" said Alex softly, not wanting to frighten her.

Startled, she jumped back against the stacks of books, the shelves shaking beneath her desperate hands as she struggled to get to her feet. Her blue eyes were wide with panic as they looked up at him.

"Ellabell, wait," Alex pleaded, but her gaze had shifted toward the barrier of the walkway.

Without saying a word, her book still open on the floor, she vaulted the banister and sailed through the air, landing with a light thud on the ground. Alex watched her go, feeling crestfallen as she raced off toward the entrance to the library, not once looking back up to where Alex stood.

Reluctantly, he tidied away the open book on the floor. It was a heavy thing bound in a peculiar, soft, silken cover that read *Mistress Bodmin's Guide to Mythical Creatures* in uniform black lettering that seemed to have been seared into the jacket. Alex flicked through the first couple of pages, which featured intricate drawings of dragons with jeweled scales that glinted in a thousand facets of color and fierce jaws that grinned menacingly. Closing it again, he put the book back on the shelf, reaching up to fetch the volume he had been seeking on magical defense. As he descended the tower, walking past the spot where Ellabell had landed in her hurry to get away from him, he made a silent promise to himself to keep out of her way, until she was ready to talk to him. If that was never, then so be it.

Fate, again, it seemed, had other plans. As Alex took his usual seat at the back of Professor Gaze's class, Gaze announced they would be doing something a little bit different, just to mix things up. With a cheerful grin, she explained that she would be pairing the class up to do a week-long project, to work on some of the shielding techniques they had been learning. They would duel and test the weaknesses in their defenses. The class groaned. Alex's one of the loudest as he wondered how he would get around his magical shortcomings if he was paired with someone other than Jari or Natalie.

Gaze strolled around the classroom, shouting out the named pairs she had decided upon. Alex waited on tenterhooks as Gaze neared him.

"Alex and Ellabell," she announced, frowning as she caught Alex's wince of concern. "Something wrong with that, Webber?" she asked, lifting a scraggly gray eyebrow in his direction.

Alex wondered if Gaze had sensed the discomfort between the two of them, in her keen, perceptive way, and decided to step in. It seemed like a scheme to him, to get him and Ellabell together, especially as it meant separating him from the two people who could conjure for him. Gaze wasn't stupid. There was more to this pairing than met the eye. In the meantime, he'd have to hope Jari and Natalie were paired with each other, giving them a chance to help him out, taking turns as he underwent his lesson-time counseling session, courtesy of Gaze.

Alex shook his head. "No, Professor. I just had a twinge in my neck," he lied feebly, pretending to massage the inner corners of his shoulders. Gaze snorted with amusement and walked away. Alex didn't dare look over to see Ellabell's reaction, knowing it wouldn't be a particularly favorable one.

She was sitting at the front of the classroom with her back to him, her shoulders slumped and her head hung low. There was a mug of something steaming in front of her, hand-delivered by the professor. As Gaze yelled for them to sit with their partners and begin, Alex was surprised to see Ellabell scrape back the legs of her chair, gathering her things from the worktop and placing the mug precariously on top before making her way slowly toward the back of the classroom, where Alex sat. Placing her things on the table, she pulled back the chair of the vacant seat to the left of him and sat down, keeping her gaze forward and her hands wrapped tightly around the ceramic of the mug, warming them.

Able to observe her more closely, Alex noticed two

small, healing scabs at each corner of her mouth, thin, like papercuts. He frowned, only to be distracted by the sight of a large, discolored bruise on the side of her head closest to him, just above her ear and half-hidden beneath the curling sweep of her hair. He desperately wanted to ask her if she was okay, but the vibe she was giving off wasn't exactly friendly. There was a frostiness to her manner, and Alex didn't want to cause her any further distress with unwanted questions.

"So… where do you want to start?" asked Alex, flipping open one of the textbooks Gaze had laid out for them.

Ellabell shrugged.

"We could start with handheld shields?" he suggested, turning to the right page. It showed pictures of sketched wizards holding a small circular disc of a shield on their forearms, to rebound any incoming magic.

Ellabell nodded.

"Do you want to go first?" he offered, pointing to the page.

Ellabell shrugged again, lifting the mug to her lips to take a long sip.

"What did she give you?" Alex asked, attempting to divert the conversation.

"Tea," she answered, her voice muffled and peculiar, as if her tongue were swollen.

"Peppermint?" He tried to smile, but she wouldn't

look in his direction.

"No," she replied, shaking her head lightly. Her mouth moved like she was in discomfort, and seeing it made Alex's concern want to burst from his lips. Pushing it down, he remembered his silent promise to himself and swiftly changed the subject back to the topic of shielding. At the end of the lesson, Ellabell bolted from the room before Alex could even say goodbye.

As the week drew on, she began to relax ever so slightly in his company during Gaze's lessons. Not by much, but Alex could sense a subtle shift in her comfort around him. She was still twitchy and jumped at the smallest sound, but was more forthcoming with her words as they worked on their project.

Natalie and Jari *had* been paired together, much to Alex's relief, meaning one of them could help Alex out when it was his turn to throw magic or defend himself against Ellabell, since he couldn't put up his real defenses.

The first time the golden streams of light had poured from his palms and snaked through the air toward Ellabell, she had looked at him through her glistening amber shield with suspicion. When he had put up a latticed defense, much like the one Ellabell had used the night of their adventure in the Head's quarters, she had paused for a moment, forgetting to send out any magic at all. Seeing him using the golden flow of magic seemed to confuse her somehow, and Alex could feel a spike of concern. It was as if an unspoken question lay on the tip of Ellabell's tongue too, but she dared not say it out loud. Each session, Alex thought she was about to ask that question as she turned to him with her brow furrowed, but she never did, leaving Alex to worry that she had seen more than he thought she had, that night in front of the golden line.

"How are you feeling?" asked Alex one day, watching Ellabell sip from a fresh mug of tea that smelled faintly of lavender.

She turned to him, looking directly in his eyes. "I'm getting there."

"I promised myself I wouldn't ask you anything until you were ready, but I can't help worrying," he admitted, feeling a twinge of anxiety as he finally spoke the words aloud. He gestured toward the side of her head, and she quickly raised her hand to the bruise, moving her hair to cover it.

"I'll speak with you if you'll promise me one thing," she whispered, her hand still pressed against the side of her head.

"Anything," answered Alex, grateful for the opportunity.

She sighed heavily, the sound rattling in the back of her throat. "If I agree to talk, you have to promise you'll leave me alone once I have," she stated, coughing a little into a fresh white handkerchief pulled swiftly from her pocket.

Alex was taken aback by the request, but her eyes were staring at him earnestly, awaiting his response. He supposed it was the least he could do.

"I'll leave you alone, if you'll tell me about what happened," he agreed reluctantly.

"Not here," she whispered. "Meet me in the library, on the middle row of the second column, after the lesson, and I'll speak with you then." She stepped back, putting up a glittering shield around her body, and gestured for Alex to send magic toward her.

She ran away as soon as the lesson was finished, and Alex followed, heading toward the library as he had been instructed. He climbed the ladder up to the middle section of the second tower and walked along to the very end, until he found her sitting up against the stacks in her favorite place. He sat down beside her, keeping a comfortable distance between them. She seemed calmer than the last time Alex had found her up in the stacks, but knew she could still be a flight risk.

"Are you okay?" he asked, glancing at her.

"I'm much better," she replied, but her voice faltered slightly. It still had that thick, distorted quality that seemed to cause her pain.

"That's good to hear," he said softly, though he had a sneaking suspicion she was lying to him. "So, what happened back there?" he ventured, wondering if he'd get a straight answer.

"At the Head's library?" she asked.

Alex nodded. "What made you scream like that? And who did *that* to you?" he pressed, gesturing toward the side of her head that hid the vivid purple bruise.

"It's silly," she whispered.

"I won't think it is, I promise," he said reassuringly.

Ellabell's gaze rested on the two points of her raised knees. "It was dark in there, and I stumbled into a bookshelf when I was reaching for something. There was a mirror hanging on the wall, and I caught sight of myself in it and thought—" She chewed her lip. "Well, I thought it was a ghost or a teacher, and I just spooked myself and ended up smacking my head against one of the shelves. That's why I screamed—I thought I'd seen a ghost. At least, I think that's what happened."

Alex listened intently, but the story didn't add up. Nobody was that afraid of their own shadow that they would spend days in a twitchy, agitated shock. He had seen the panic in her eyes. It was not because of some self-inflicted accident. It didn't take a rocket scientist to figure that out. And yet, as he watched the worried expression on her face deepen, he sensed it would be difficult to get another story out of her. It was the truth she had chosen to go with, and Alex had to try to respect that, though curiosity and guilt still raced through his mind. He knew *somebody* had hurt Ellabell, and though he had his suspicions of figures who kept to the shadows, he couldn't be certain who it had been.

"Did somebody attack you, Ellabell?" he asked softly, trying again.

Her eyes went wide in panic.

"Is that what really happened?" he pressed. He didn't want to scare her away, but he wanted to know who or what had done this to her.

"I don't know… I didn't see," she murmured, her gaze darting around anxiously.

"I'll find whoever did this to you and make them—"

She shook her head rapidly, her face etched with terror as she grabbed Alex's hand. "No, you can't… Anyway, it was an accident, like I said—just an accident. I need you to forget about it."

"Is that why you've been avoiding me?" he asked suddenly.

She turned her face away, hiding her expression. "I haven't been avoiding you."

"In the corridors, in lessons, you seem to want to do anything to get away from me," he said, hoping she couldn't hear the wounded tone in his voice. "Did I do something to offend you?"

"I guess it's because of what I saw and the things I know," she whispered, turning back to him with a stern expression in her bright blue eyes. All traces of fear had gone, as if she had placed a mask over her face.

"What?" Alex drew back from her, alarmed by the

sudden shift in mood.

"I know what you are, Alex," she announced, her voice hushed. "I saw what you did. I know you're one of *them*," she added, a note of something close to displeasure in her voice.

"I don't know what you mean," he replied, playing the nonchalance card.

"You're a Spellbreaker, Alex. I saw you," she hissed.

Alex laughed. "That's ridiculous. You said so yourself, there aren't any of them left… You must have hit your head harder than you thought." He felt his throat tighten up as he lied through his teeth, hating himself for using her bruise against her. It felt strange to hear himself called out for what he was, and he wasn't sure he liked the sensation of hearing his secret out in the open.

Ellabell sighed, her disappointment evident. "Don't worry, I'll keep your secret, and maybe even help you out if I can. But I meant what I said. I want you to leave me alone from now on. I don't want you near me unless we absolutely have to be in each other's company, do you understand?" she asked, her voice trembling.

Alex knew he had been caught in a lie, and no amount of subterfuge would convince her otherwise. She knew the truth; he could see it in her eyes that she knew. It was out there, and Alex hoped fervently that Ellabell could be trusted with the secret. She seemed keen enough to keep her own, so perhaps it would be safe with her.

"Do you understand?" she repeated gently, her face oddly sorrowful.

Alex nodded. "I understand."

"It's for the best," she whispered as she leaned in toward him and kissed him softly on the cheek.

As she stood up to go, Alex reached out to grasp her hand and squeezed it lightly. Squeezing it back, she flashed him a sad smile, then turned and walked toward the barrier of the walkway, leaping over it in one easy movement.

For once, Alex didn't follow her to watch her leave.

In the pitch black of the dormitory, something awoke Alex with a start. He rubbed his eyes, checking the clock on his bedside table; it read two in the morning. Wondering what on earth had awoken him, his eyes fixed on a flash of gold and silver darting across the end of the bed, weaving and ducking behind the folds of the sheets as the creature made its way up and over the bent limb of Alex's leg.

Curiously, he checked the top drawer of his bedside table to find it already open, the motionless mouse inside missing. A shiver shot up Alex's spine. He turned back toward the scuttling clockwork creature. His heart pounded loudly in his chest as he waited for it to make its way up the rest of his body, once it recognized the familiar shape of him with its glittering black eyes. It was the same mouse that had been tucked away inside his drawer.

On the golden hind leg, Alex saw the small shape of a curled note, attached with a thin piece of twine. He gulped, holding out his palm for the mouse to run onto. Its feet were light on his skin. He lifted the creature up and carefully untied the miniature scroll from the back of its leg. Settling the mouse down on the mattress beside him, Alex lifted up the scroll and unrolled it slowly, squinting to see the words in the moonlight that glanced in through the curtains above his head.

Fear prickled at the back of his neck. His blood ran cold.

I warned you, was all it said.

Turning swiftly back to the mechanical creature on the mattress, he saw that the eyes had already gone dead.

CHAPTER 24

Alex sat alone at one of the tables in the mess hall, trying his hardest to eat a bowl of gristly, bland stew that left a greasy residue on his lips with each forced mouthful. Natalie and Jari had been up to their old tricks again, still off doing their own things without him. He tried hard not to feel annoyed by their disappearing acts, but it was starting to wear thin on him. He missed the old days, when they would all gather for lessons and lunches and dinners and in any spare moment they had, to laugh and joke and chat together, as friends should.

Since the night in the Head's quarters, Jari seemed to

have redoubled his work, whatever it was, even though his reasoning for visiting the Head's abode had been resolved. They knew the Head had gone. In fact, if they had simply waited a day longer, Alex thought bitterly, they'd have found that out without any harm or risk to anyone. He was still paranoid that the new Deputy would call him up at any moment and make an example of him, but so far, the new professor had been quiet. The masked man had yet to take up his teaching duties, leaving the extra sessions still in Renmark and Gaze's hands, but he had begun to make some changes within the manor. Good ones, as far as Alex was concerned.

The morning after his dramatic arrival, a new noticeboard had appeared announcing that the extra evening lesson would be removed in favor of independent study. Alongside it, to encourage exercise, the golden line would be lifted from the manor's entrance between the hours of six and seven in the morning and six and seven in the evening, for the students to have access to the gardens. However, the curfew of nine p.m. would remain, as would the golden line at all other times. Tardiness and the skipping of lessons, and any bending of the rules, would remain a punishable offense.

Despite the slight relaxation of the restrictions, Alex still couldn't help fearing the dark-clad figure, with his eerie mask and commanding voice. There was something deeply disturbing about Professor Escher, as if there was something not quite human lurking below the surface, shrouded from view by cloaks and hoods and masks. Alex wasn't sure he could trust a man who hid himself.

Natalie had been absent, too, much to Alex's disappointment. His worry for her increased daily, as she was showing no signs of slowing down in her studies. Rather than use the extra free time to relax, Natalie had thrown herself into more sessions with Renmark, emerging at dinnertime with sweat beading on her forehead, her clothes soaked through, and her hands trembling from sheer exertion. Alex tried to encourage her to take it easy, but she would simply wolf down as much as food as she could and then disappear again, chattering from time to time about something exciting Renmark was going to teach her from a book students were rarely allowed to see. Each time Alex mentioned life magic, she shrugged it off with the same practiced lines that she wasn't stupid enough to dabble in such things. It grew less and less easy to believe.

Giving up on his stew, Alex got up and left the mess hall, heading through the echoing hallways toward the front of the manor. He needed a break from the stifling indoors, and the cellar was calling. Perhaps he'd shatter another bottle of *Fields of Sorrow*, he thought grimly as he stepped out into the crisp sunshine. He'd had enough of the library, searching endlessly through the stacks for censored books that had been taken from their rightful places. Recently, he had even moved on to fiction books, in the hope that they might shed some light on havens and 'great evils' and voids, but they proved as fruitless as the gaps in the shelves.

It was a warm day, the sun bright on his face as it sat hazily in the middle of an azure sky. A few pale clouds moved slowly across the steady blue, wispy and almost translucent. Alex smiled, noting that even the gardens looked more beautiful beneath the sunshine's golden glow. Though they were crooked and warped, the rich light lent the skeletal trees and raggedy bushes a bright sheen, and danced across the waxy gray leaves of the ivy that clung to the walls and crumbling ruins.

Pulling up the cellar's trapdoor , Alex was met by a gust of roasting hot air. Worrying that he had left the torches lit the last time he was there, he jumped down into the vault beneath and stood with surprise as he saw that the room below was already occupied. There were five pairs of students in the middle of a duel, with Jari standing at the far end of the cellar barking out orders. Natalie stood beside one set of duelers with her arms behind her back, watching them perform an intricate spell Alex had never seen before, involving a mist that seemed to cling to the eyes of the opponent, making it hard for them to see. The pair beside them were practicing a spell that seemed to take control of the opponent, using their magic against them with varying degrees of success.

They all stopped and turned as Alex brushed the dirt

from his clothes, narrowing his eyes at the scene before him.

A thought rushed coldly into Alex's mind. He wondered if this was what they had been doing all along, on those days when the two of them had been impossible to find. He felt as if the air had been knocked out of him as he leveled his gaze toward his friends, waiting for an explanation that didn't come.

Natalie's mouth went wide in shock at the sight of him standing there, her expression molding into one of guilt. Jari, meanwhile, seemed to shrug off Alex's sudden presence, ignoring him with a determined expression as he barked further orders, trying to regain the duelers' attention.

Alex couldn't help the hurt and confusion that rose up through his veins. They had kept this from him, and he didn't know why. He almost climbed straight back up the ladder and out into the gardens, but Natalie moved toward him.

"Alex, please wait," she insisted.

The other students glanced at each other awkwardly, as if they could feel the tension in the room. One of them turned to Jari, asking if they should go, but Jari shook his head.

"No, you have to stay. You have to prepare to fight," he explained tersely.

Alex felt frustration pulse through him, wondering

again why his friends had kept this secret from him and why Jari did not seem to care. He wondered desolately if it was because they thought he was useless. After all, Jari hadn't seen him use the blockade or the fog the other night, what with being too busy dragging Ellabell to safety and running on ahead. Then there was Natalie, who was so busy with her own extracurricular sessions that Alex hadn't had the chance to talk to her about the notebook and his vastly improving skills as a Spellbreaker. They hadn't given him the opportunity to prove what he was now capable of, because they simply hadn't been around. There had been so many occasions lately when he had needed them and wanted their advice, and they just hadn't been there. But then, when Jari had come begging for *his* help, Alex had stepped up to the plate, despite the dangers. There was an imbalance, and Alex was becoming painfully aware of it, feeling the fracture of their group in the tense atmosphere, making him bitter and bewildered.

"I should go," whispered Alex. He turned to climb back up the ladder and out into the sunshine. The hazy glow had lost its joy, the twisted trees and wretched shrubs no longer taking any beauty from the sun's rays.

Natalie came up behind him, grasping him by the arm. "Alex, you must wait. Let me explain," she pleaded, her voice earnest.

"Fine," muttered Alex as he wandered toward one of the crumbling gray walls of the garden and slipped through a passageway he had never seen before. It led out into what must once have been a walled garden, with plateaued steps of fringed cobbles leading down to a water feature, long dried up. Bleak-faced cherubs stared out at the grim garden in various states of decay, some missing their pudgy stone faces or a few chubby limbs, while most of their bows had been smashed away. A thick layer of spongy white lichen and dark brown mulch carpeted the bottom of the water feature's bowl, which might have been made from fine marble. It was barely recognizable now. Alex walked toward it, leaning up against the crimped lip of the basin, curved to look like an oyster shell.

"Alex, you mustn't be upset," said Natalie as she leaned beside him on the oyster basin.

"Who said I was upset?" he muttered, kicking a pebble away with the toe of his shoe.

"I understand how it must have looked," she explained. "I know we have not been around so much, and I know what you must think, but we are doing it for the good of the others." She let out a low, regretful sigh.

"Then why?" he asked.

"Why haven't we asked you to join us? Or why have we not been around so much?" she replied, fidgeting anxiously.

Alex shrugged. "Both."

"The first is more simple, though I see now that, perhaps, it was not the best plan. We did not invite you along for your own benefit—to keep your powers a secret, I suppose. It did not seem wise to let everyone know what you are, because you cannot be sure who you can trust in this place," she began, her words a touch mysterious as she gazed off into the middle distance.

"You could have told me, though," said Alex steadily.

"I see that now. We were silly not to have told you," she agreed, flashing Alex an apologetic smile.

"How long has it been going on?" he asked, out of curiosity, trying to smother any residual hurt. A note of deception still lingered in the air between them, and he could not brush it off. Given the chance again, he sensed they still would've lied to him. He wondered silently if an invitation would be extended once they left the garden—he wasn't convinced it would be.

"We have not been doing this for as long as you might suspect. A few lunchtimes while the rules were in place, and more often now that many have been lifted," she said.

"And the new spells?"

"Well, actually, that is part of the second question, in a way. Some of the spells Professor Renmark has been teaching me, I have taught to the other students. We must get them prepared for what may come, and the magic I have learned is very powerful and will be very useful if we must fight," she explained grimly.

"A fight?" murmured Alex.

She nodded. "If the time comes when we must rise

up against the Head, everyone must be prepared. If we all fight, we may have a chance to win. If it is only a few, we will surely lose," she said firmly.

"What has he been teaching you?" asked Alex.

"Professor Renmark?"

Alex nodded.

"Many things, from many books that other students do not see. He has promised to teach me from a book of dark arts, but we have not yet begun," she whispered, her eyes glittering with excitement.

"You promised me you wouldn't delve into the darker arts, Natalie. You said you'd never be so stupid as to take those risks," said Alex with alarm, trying to keep the chastisement from his voice.

"You should not worry so much, Alex. I am getting stronger every single day." She smiled reassuringly, but Alex wasn't convinced; he had read of life magic and death magic, and neither ended well. The price of a piece of the soul could never be worth the prize. "How are your skills coming along, by the way? Jari tells me you are improving," she said, her voice bright with genuine enthusiasm.

Alex frowned, wondering how Jari knew his skills were improving. Perhaps his blond-haired friend had been paying more attention than Alex thought.

"I'm getting much better," admitted Alex. He wondered whether to tell Natalie about the notebook, but a warning shiver prickled up the back of his neck, keeping the words from slipping out of his mouth. "I'm teaching myself a lot," he half lied.

"That is wonderful to hear!" She gave him a cheerful grin. "I knew you would figure your powers out eventually."

"Yeah, I'm getting there," he replied dryly.

"Well, I must be getting back," said Natalie.

"Yeah, me too," said Alex.

They set off up the steps and slipped out of the walled garden. As they parted ways, Alex couldn't help but watch as Natalie walked in the direction of the cellar, his invitation still nonexistent. They neither wanted him nor needed him, despite what he could do.

As he wandered back toward the manor, he pondered why he hadn't told Natalie about the notebook. He knew it wasn't just the invisible gag of Elias's stern retribution; there was something else, running alongside it. An uneasy feeling in the pit of his stomach.

It seemed everyone really did have their secrets.

CHAPTER 25

THE FOLLOWING DAY, FOR THE FIRST TIME IN A long while, Alex was surprised to see Jari and Natalie waiting for him in the mess hall at dinner. In their usual spot by the window, they sat down to eat together, though the tension from the previous lunchtime's discovery still lingered in the air between them.

Alex didn't bring it up again, but as they ate, Jari seemed to have an air of passive-aggression about him, skewering a buttered potato on the end of his fork and biting savagely into it as Alex asked how they were both doing. Alex was frustrated by Jari, but refused to let his friend see. At least Natalie had tried to explain why they had kept the cellar training from him, but Jari seemed set on brushing off any guilt he might have felt, not caring about Alex's feelings. Alex tried to talk to Natalie instead, but Natalie was too tired to really speak. He knew she had been in another of her brutal lessons with Renmark, and it had clearly left her on the brink of exhaustion. Even lifting a forkful of mashed potato to her mouth left her hands shaking.

So, they ate in almost complete silence, peppered by snippets of small talk and the clink and scrape of cutlery on ceramic.

"Alex Webber?" a voice asked. Alex turned to see a boy beside him, small in stature, with reddish-brown hair. It was the new boy, Felipe Cortez.

"Yes?" said Alex, frowning.

"Please come with me. Professor Escher would like to see you right away," he explained nervously, brushing an anxious hand through his hair.

"Me?" asked Alex, his heart in his throat.

The boy nodded. "Yes, right away. Follow me."

A wave of dread crashed over Alex as he stood to follow the boy. Casting a worried glance back at his two friends did nothing to still his nerves: their faces were as pale and horrified as he imagined his to be. Paranoia piggybacked on the rush of dread. Alex wondered if it had come—if this was the moment he had been fearing.

Had he finally been found out? He had been cocky,

allowing himself to be reassured that he had gotten away with breaking into the Head's quarters and firing a blockade of dense ice at Professor Escher. He had been arrogant, thinking he could keep his secret forever, within the walls of the manor. He had allowed himself to be fooled, when there was, in truth, no place to hide in the manor.

He followed the messenger through a labyrinth of hallways, heading toward a part of the manor Alex wasn't familiar with. Gray ivy hung in clumps from the stone walls, snaking down and creeping out across the floor, where it reached up to brush against Alex's leg as he walked through the corridors. It prickled him like a nettle, a cold sting against his anti-magic. He didn't recognize any of the doorways or portraits that hung in this section of the building, but Felipe seemed sure of his route as he scurried on ahead.

Eventually, they reached a broad set of double doors that stood ominously at the very end of a long, wide corridor. They were made of thick, varnished oak with two black iron knockers roaring out from the center of each, sculpted into the shape of a lion and a unicorn, though the unicorn was not the type seen in fairytales. Its mouth was open wide in a scream as it bared its teeth, the eyes narrowed and savage beneath a brutal spike that served as its horn. Alex felt as if the lion might snap his hand off if he lifted the great circular weight that dangled from its fanged jaws.

"I'll leave you here," insisted the boy as he tore off in the direction he had just come.

Breathing deeply, Alex steadied his nerves, picked up the bottom curve of the iron rung, and knocked it hard against the dense oak. The impact thundered around Alex, echoing up the hallway behind him. The lion glowered down at him with burning black eyes.

"Enter," called a voice from within.

Heaving against the hefty door, Alex pushed the unicorn side open and stepped into a large, empty room with a single table and two chairs in the center. Above the room hung a beautiful chandelier, half-covered with a dustsheet, the crystals glinting in the torchlight and casting shattered silver petals of radiance onto the black marble floor. It was polished to a high shine, reflecting the artwork of the ceiling. Alex's breath was taken away by the beauty of it; whoever had painted it had been a virtuoso. Scenes of battle lay splayed out in minute detail across the whole length and breadth of the ceiling—armor-clad warriors on the backs of savage unicorn warhorses hurling golden spears and wielding sharp-edged blades of pure magic at crooked figures dressed in flowing gowns of crimson and white. Dragons and Thunderbirds soared in a technicolor of scales and feathers, breathing bursts of fire and rippling bolts of jagged lightning down upon the armored knights.

Alex wondered if the room had once been a ballroom or a great dining hall of some kind. It certainly looked grand enough, with suits of ancient armor rusting on the walls and twisted marble statues, god-like in their poses, flanking the room.

Two huge portraits hung on each of the four walls. On two sides, Alex felt watched by the eyes of stony-faced old men with white hair, staring out over the top of golden pince-nez, their expressions haughty and proud. On the third wall, two ancient crones peered out from glassy blue eyes, wearing golden bands across their foreheads, their gray hair twisted up into an elaborate style above it. On the fourth, two much younger individuals watched Alex. A man of around thirty with autumnal hair and golden eyes looked out upon the black marble and glittering chandeliers, a small smile upon his lips. In the painted waves of his hair, a silver band was just visible, intertwined with his lustrous locks. Beside him on the wall, in the next portrait along, a young woman watched Alex with sparkling gray eyes, her flaxen hair so long that it disappeared into the frame of the image. A silvery twist of a tiara wove in and out of her flowing hair, glinting with the delicate touch of jewels.

Alex wondered who they were, these special figures.

"It's beautiful, isn't it?" asked the cloaked man in the middle of the room, standing with his back to Alex.

"What is this place?" Alex said nervously.

"It used to be the grand ballroom," explained Professor Escher, whose voice oozed across the room like molasses, making Alex's skin crawl. "Come, sit," he instructed with an elegant flourish of his arm.

Alex paused, a million hurried thoughts racing through his mind as the distance between himself and Professor Escher seemed to stretch impossibly ahead of him. Foolishly, he wondered if he had time to run for it—if there was time for him to get out onto the front lawn and have a crack at anti-magical travel or to push all of his anti-magic into the gate and hope for the best. He knew it was ridiculous, but he was beginning to feel desperate.

"I wouldn't try running if I were you," purred Escher in a soft, amused tone that seemed vaguely threatening despite its quietness.

"I wasn't going to," lied Alex.

"Good. Now come and sit."

Alex walked toward the table and chairs and sat down in the one closest. Professor Escher still had not turned, and the sight of the still, black shape was an unnerving one. Carefully, Alex placed his hands beneath the table and began to conjure the familiar prickles of ice against the skin of his fingers, forming the beginnings of some anti-magic, just in case.

"I know what you are, Alex Webber," whispered Escher suddenly, his back still to Alex.

Alex could barely move as fear held him to the chair. "I don't know what you mean," he said.

Escher chuckled coldly. "Oh, I think you do. You are a

Spellbreaker, Alex Webber. One of a kind, these days," he said slowly, a hint of amusement in his silky voice.

Alex was speechless, stunned into silence. His heart hammered in his chest as he let the words wash over him in uneasy understanding of what had just been said. The Deputy Head knew his secret. He was doomed; he was certain of it. It was a Mage's destiny to dispose of Spellbreakers—Malachi Grey had said as much. How would they dispose of him? Alex wasn't sure he wanted to know.

"How—" he began, but Escher cut him off swiftly.

"How do I know? That is not important. What is important is what happens next," he said, turning to face Alex for the first time. Glittering eyes moved menacingly beneath the eyeholes of his mask, and Alex could hear the faint hint of a grin as he spoke. "I must assure you, Alex, that I do not intend to harm you," he added with a twist of his wrist.

"What?" whispered Alex, dumbfounded by what was happening.

"I do not intend to harm you, nor do I intend to tell anyone what you are. Your secret, I suppose, is safe with me. I do not wish to get you into any more trouble than you are already in," hissed Escher, his voice momentarily menacing.

"What kind of trouble am I in?" asked Alex, flinching as the glittering eyes bore down on him through the white porcelain of the mask.

"A great deal of trouble… perhaps," he said, lighting a flicker of hope within Alex. "It all depends on you, really. You are the master of your own destiny. Here's the deal: I will not say anything or harm you in any way, under one proviso," he added casually, extending his gloved index finger to illuminate his point.

Alex waited for the fine print.

"You are a disruption, Alex. It is my duty to remove disruptive students, but my plans for you are somewhat different. I have an offer for you. In exchange for keeping your secret, you must leave the manor." The words sat heavily in the air between teacher and student as Alex let them sink in.

"Leave?" asked Alex, confused.

"Yes, leave. This is my offer. I will take you back into the real world—only you—and restore you to your mother and your old life," proposed Escher quietly, a note of surprising gentleness in his voice. It was unnerving to Alex, how Escher could shift between emotions so swiftly, surprising him at every turn, but hearing Escher mention his mother with such softness was almost more than he could bear.

Memories and feelings rushed vividly into Alex's mind as he thought of his ailing mother, out there beyond the twinkling spires of the horizon, waiting for him. He pictured her at breakfast, the morning Natalie had arrived at their house, beaming over freshly made pancakes and ripe red strawberries. She had been so pleased to see him socializing with someone his own age, even if she had had to drag them across an ocean. It broke his heart to think of her in that moment, so happy and brimming with life. He knew he would give anything to see her again, but that same guilt toward leaving everyone behind twisted at his insides—the conscience that had kept him within the manor walls thus far. It was an unfair balance that tipped one way and then the other with each passing moment.

His feelings toward the other students were marred a little by the furtive behavior of his so-called friends, but still he knew in his heart that their secret-keeping was not enough reason for him to leave everyone else to their fates. He had kept his own secrets from them, hadn't he?

"That's all I have to do?" asked Alex quietly.

"That is all, Alex. You must leave, this moment, alone," Escher repeated, but with no hint of haste in his words.

Closing his eyes, Alex thought about his options. He tried to picture his mother, but the image of her remained blurry in his head, the edges undefined and grainy. Part of him wondered if he might just slip out for a moment, just to leave a note for her, to let her know that he was okay and that he hadn't abandoned her. Even if it was just to see her for a while, to make sure the grief hadn't made her worse. Just to make sure she was alive; that was all he wanted. Plans and schemes raced through his mind as he felt his time slipping away like sand through his fingers. Ideas of how he might deliver his message and return to Spellshadow Manor flitted half-formed through his mind, and yet Escher's offer was clear—this trip was a one-way ticket. A tempting one.

Miserably, Alex shook his head. "I can't accept," he said through gritted teeth.

"I beg you to reconsider. Think of your mother," Escher said, almost tauntingly, picking up the painful threads of Alex's heartstrings and yanking hard on them. "She is all alone out there, Alex. With your father gone and now you, she has nobody. She is sick, and losing you has only made her worse. I have seen her for myself, Alex—"

"Liar!" snapped Alex savagely.

Escher shook his head. "I have nothing to gain by lying to you, Alex. I am telling you the truth when I say I have seen your mother. She is not doing well without you. Each day, she grows weaker, her eyes forever on the door, awaiting your return. Each day that you don't come home, her spirit is sapped just a little, and her strength wanes," he said softly. "She needs you, Alex. She needs you far more than anyone in here does."

Alex wasn't sure if Escher was telling the truth, but the professor had certainly played on just the right insecurities. Alex's heart ached at the continued thought of her out there, sick and alone and missing him. In his head, he knew he couldn't leave. It was his sacrifice to stay and help in any way he could, but the sentence was a long one. He thought of the dream image of Lintz and Derhin as much younger men. They had spent nearly their entire lives within the manor's walls. Was that his fate if he didn't take Escher up on his offer? To see his mother again was a sacrifice of another sort. And yet, either way, somebody was going to lose. Alex wasn't sure if he was ready to let that person be his mother.

He knew what he had to do.

"I have my answer," said Alex softly.

"And what is your answer?" asked Escher, taking a seat in the chair opposite. He leaned closer to Alex, waiting patiently.

Alex looked up at Escher, his gaze fierce.

But when he opened his mouth to speak, the roar of an explosion crashed through the air as the ballroom's heavy doors split open with a sudden rush and splinter of wood. Natalie and Jari burst in through the falling debris and sprinted across the polished black marble, sending shards of magic hurtling toward Escher.

Escher had little time to think as Natalie charged him, conjuring intricate webs of magic with her hands, her fingers moving rapidly as she sent glowing tendrils of her own golden magic up beneath Escher's sleeves and down into his skin. He froze, juddering as Natalie's magic took over his body, controlling him. His hands tried to move, to fight back, and it looked as if he might break free.

A coil of crackling golden magic erupted from Escher's palm. He pushed Natalie's magic aside, but Jari was ready with the cavalry. He sent a ripple of glowing amber toward Escher in a thin wisp that struck the professor in the shoulder. Tremors shook Escher's body as the spell did its work, wrenching Escher's limbs into violent spasms that sent him crashing to the floor.

Natalie sent the tendrils snaking back beneath Escher's skin and gripped her fingers tightly into her palms as she held her magic inside him, controlling his body and his magic, preventing him from fighting back.

Alex watched in amazement as Natalie lifted Escher to his feet and jerked him back toward the chair, throwing him down with a graceless thud. His eyes glittered furiously beneath his mask as he struggled to break free of Natalie's hold, but she had truly become an exceptional Mage. Nobody could deny it—her magic was extraordinary.

"Don't mind the intrusion." Jari grinned as he undid a silvery coil of rope and tied Escher's hands behind his back. Alex was confused, knowing a simple rope wouldn't keep Escher at bay, but it seemed Jari had learned some new tricks too as he fed a weaving pattern of magic into the rope itself. It seemed to keep Escher frozen to the spot, just as Natalie's control magic had done.

"What the hell?" cried Alex, gesturing toward the door.

"Apologies for the surprise. We saw an opportunity and we improvised a little." Natalie grinned, though her brow was creased with the exertion of holding Escher in place.

"Yeah, it was a bit scrappy, but it seems to have done the trick," said Jari as he fastened a tight knot into the last bit of rope. "You can let go now," he told Natalie. She released her tightly clenched fists with a sigh of relief.

Alex moved to the other side of the table. Professor Escher was oddly silent as he sat there, bound by the enchanted ropes. He stiffened as Alex approached.

Alex reached down for the edge of the delicate mask, with its complex pattern of gold and silver vines that curled elegantly across a white veneer. Escher tried to strain away from Alex's touch, but he could not escape.

The man's almond-shaped eyes glowered as Alex slowly lifted the mask. Shock shivered through Alex as he stared at the face before him, losing his grip on the mask. It tumbled to the floor, the porcelain cracking down the center.

Aamir stared back.

CHAPTER 26

"AAMIR?" WHISPERED ALEX IN DISBELIEF.

All along it had been their friend. He did not know how any of them could have missed it, but Aamir had changed in the time since they had last seen him. He had aged, grown taller and broader, his face bearing a thin trace of stubble along his grimly set jawline, though his brown eyes and black curls were the same as ever. It was definitely Aamir; it was not a glamor or a trick of the eye. It was definitely him.

A still silence spread across the ballroom as the gathered friends glanced at one another. Aamir gnashed his teeth as he strained against his bonds, his eyes flashing angrily.

"You will let me go!" he barked. The mask must have been altering and distorting Aamir's voice, as it no longer sounded the same as it had beneath the eerie porcelain. It was closer to the voice Alex remembered. Even so, it was not quite the same; there was a rich, deep authority that had not been there before.

"No, Aamir," said Alex, shaking his head.

It was hard to look at Aamir and not think of their old friend, buried deep beneath the savage exterior of the man who sat before them. He was the Deputy Head, and the only person who stood between them and the opportunity they had been waiting for. It would be foolish to remove his restraints, and Alex knew that Aamir was no longer to be trusted. There were going to be some tough choices ahead, and it would be easier to pretend Aamir wasn't the boy they had known. Even watching him strain and pull and growl against the ropes that held him was hard enough.

He was working for the Head now. He was no longer on their side.

Suddenly, Aamir broke free of the bonds holding his hands. Golden shards shot from the coiling strands that wove about his fingertips as he lashed out against his former friends, narrowly missing Jari's heart with a sharp blade of glinting gold. Jari cried out, his face crumpling in a wince of pain as the bolt hit him just below his shoulder blade.

Alex ducked a spear intended for his head as he rallied on Aamir. The brown eyes of his old friend were narrowed and alien, his face twisted viciously into a changeling version of Aamir as he released wave after wave of destructive magic. He was as far from the Aamir they knew and loved as it was possible to be, a throaty growl emitting from the depths of his lungs as he shouted his defiance.

"You will not get away with this! There is no escape from the manor, and there is no escape from the Head! He will discover your treachery, and he will punish you brutally for it. There will be nowhere you can hide from his vengeance! The Head will crash down on you all, and you will rue the day you thought you could defeat him!" roared Aamir, his brown eyes shot through with threads of red. His face was contorted by a terrifying rage as he let out an inhuman howl. "LET ME GO!" he screamed, pulling against his leg restraints.

Alex watched Natalie as she struggled to regain control of Aamir. Sweat ran down the side of her face, the strain seemingly taking its toll. Aamir was stronger than he had been, and Natalie was struggling against his defenses as he fired golden artillery in her direction. As she turned quickly, avoiding a nasty dart of energy, Aamir seized the opportunity and snapped the ropes keeping his legs bound.

Stepping in, Alex conjured tendrils of black and silver beneath his palms, focusing hard on Aamir as he let his power slither undetected across the floor and up over the towering figure. As he had done with the wine bottle in the cellar, Alex forged a dense shield of pulsing silver light, shot through with swirls of a deep bluish black. The shield swooped across Aamir, who thrashed against it, unable to fire any magic from within his glittering prison. Sparks rippled from the points of impact where Aamir was trying to conjure magic, but the shield held. It seemed to work both ways, protecting the person inside from any outside harm and protecting those outside from the person within.

Alex gripped his hands tightly, holding the shield in place, feeling confident that it would stay standing as long as his focus remained. It took a vast amount of energy, but he could feel the flow of it holding more easily than he had expected.

He caught sight of Natalie and Jari staring at him in quiet awe. They had not had a chance to see his newly learned skills.

Jari gave a low whistle. "Nice trick," he muttered, a strange look on his face.

"Thank you," replied Alex, his mouth set in a grim line.

"Where did you learn this control?" asked Natalie, her voice oddly envious.

Alex smiled. "I've had a little help."

It was clear to Alex that they had all been acting

badly toward one another, keeping secrets and telling half-truths, but he felt as if this sudden union—this need to work together—was a small step in repairing the fractures in their friendships. He made a note to come clean with everything, once they had a moment to themselves.

"From whom?" asked Natalie, wiping away a sheen of perspiration with the back of her hand.

"I'll tell you another time," promised Alex. "Now, what are we going to do with him? I can't hold him forever."

Furiously, Aamir hammered against the ripple of the dark shield. Alex knew his powers still weren't as strong as they could be, but the barrier seemed to be keeping Aamir at bay. Curious, Alex knelt down onto the floor and pressed his hands down into the polished, cold surface of the black marble. Gathering his energies, he sent a pulse of anti-magic through the floor and up through the smooth, fluid fabric of the shield, anchoring it to the ground. As he removed his hands, the shield held.

"Natalie, you and Jari should go and see if you can prepare the cellar and use it to keep Aamir locked up, until we can come up with a better way of keeping him restrained," said Alex firmly as he glanced anxiously toward the rooted shield. "I'll stay and watch over Aamir. I don't know how long the shield will hold, but hopefully it'll stay until you get back. If it doesn't, I'll think of something," he added with a dour smile.

"Good plan," Jari said as he cast a miserable glance at

his beloved friend. It was uncomfortable for anyone to see Aamir like that, but Alex knew it must have been hitting Jari the hardest.

"Work as fast as you can!" Alex said. Natalie and Jari nodded and jogged to the two vast doors. Pulling the hinges open, they staggered backward as a swarm of students flooded into the room. Alex stared in surprise, recognizing a few from Jari's lunchtime training sessions.

"What are you doing here?" yelled Alex.

"We are here for the Uprising!" shouted a tall, slim figure at the very front of the group. His name was Jun Asano, and he stood a good head taller than most of the other students. Alex knew him to be a final year, one of the students who was on his way to graduation.

Jari turned toward Alex, looking sheepish. It seemed there were even more secrets that had been kept from Alex, just when he had thought they were all out in the open. He had never heard the word 'Uprising' mentioned, but the group seemed riled and ready for action, their collective glare directed at the shrouded figure of Aamir.

"We want retribution! Kill Escher!" cried a blond-haired girl beside Jun. The group bellowed behind her. Alex could see they were already in the throes of full-blown mob mentality, waving their fists and yelling at the top of their lungs, baying for the blood of whoever was closest to the Head—whoever could offer them the revenge they thirsted for. At that moment in time, that title fell upon Aamir.

They could not see that the man behind the shield was their one-time classmate and friend. They saw only Escher, the Deputy Head, and he was close enough to the real thing to slake their thirst for blood.

Alex ran across the marble toward them, standing in front of Natalie and Jari.

"Stop! Your anger is misplaced," Alex stated. "The person in there is not who you think he is. He is not some faceless, masked monster who wants to hurt you, and there is no Professor Escher. That man in there is Aamir—your friend and classmate. He is suffering under a curse, laid upon him by the Head. He is not responsible for any of this." Alex gestured toward the walls of the manor. "Your anger is with the Head, not with Aamir, who needs our help as much as anyone."

"This could have happened to any one of us," Natalie declared, nodding to Alex before turning to the mob. "Aamir was only doing what the Head made him do. He could not say no, the same way none of us could have refused if we had been in his position."

"You're only saying that because he was your friend!" sneered Jun. The group behind him grumbled in agreement.

"It's not Aamir's fault!" snarled Jari.

"Of course you'd say that. You were his pet. Always tagging along behind him like a lost puppy," laughed Jun with a cold mockery.

"You shut your mouth!" yelled Jari as Alex held him back.

"All of you, stop!" Alex shouted. "We have to work together and use this opportunity. Aamir could know something we can use against the Head, and you can be sure that if any of you harm him, the Head will come running."

Jun frowned. "You're lying," he hissed.

The mob shouted insults and angry slurs behind their leader, howling for Aamir's comeuppance, furious at being held back by three upstarts. It didn't matter that two of them had helped train them; they seemed hell-bent on their revenge.

Jun raised two cupped hands with a sneer, posed to strike. But before he could even twist his wrists to release a spell, Natalie had formed a shining shield of gold between them. It thrummed powerfully as the mob stepped back with a cry of discontent.

"Give us Aamir!" Jun shouted, those behind him echoing the call.

"Do you really want to wait here until my shield falters?" Natalie challenged.

"It'll be days," Alex said, casting Natalie a wry smile.

Jun snorted and formed a ball of energy between his palms, throwing the glowing orb toward Natalie. The blow ricocheted off the shield, crackling above the gathered heads of the mob and frying the top of the doorframe with a sharp sizzle, blackening the wood. No one else dared attempt to break the shield after that, though a few shouted brazenly that they might.

Jun motioned for his entourage to gather around, and they set into a hushed debate about their next plan of attack, flashing furtive glances toward Natalie and her glinting barrier. Her own gaze never faltered.

Alex gave a low sigh at the raging voice of Aamir, who was screaming abuse from across the ballroom, doing himself no favors. Unfortunately, it seemed the shield did not silence the person within, only kept their magic from doing any harm.

"You'll all pay for this! You are nothing! When the Head returns, he will punish you all! You will wish you had never set a foot out of line, you fools!" he bellowed from within his pulsing cell, his words descending into a bitter cackle.

Alex stepped into Jari's place as the blond-haired boy moved quickly back toward his friend and knelt on the floor in front of the rippling barrier of his prison. He could not reach Aamir through Alex's anti-magic, which burned his hands with a sharp wince as he attempted it. Alex felt the judder of Jari's impact, feeling sorrowful as he watched Jari try to grasp his dear companion by the shoulders. Alex would have lowered the shield, but was too worried about what Aamir might do. He watched Jari sit cross-legged on the floor and talk softly to Aamir.

"I am your friend. Aamir, it is me. I have been with you from the beginning, through thick and thin in this place. You have to listen to me. You have to know it is me," begged Jari, his voice heartbreaking to hear. "Remember my first night, when I was terrified and had been chucked into the room by Siren Mave? I couldn't stop crying, do you remember? Remember me, Aamir. Remember all the times we have shared together, as the closest of friends," he whispered, reaching his hand up as if he were about to test the barrier again. He held it there, frozen, instead.

Aamir smashed against the shield, bouncing back. He roared up close to the very edge of the barrier, screaming in Jari's face. Alex saw Jari flinch, but the younger boy was not deterred.

"Please, Aamir. I'd still be a shivering wreck if it hadn't been for you," he whispered.

Alex listened as Jari recounted colorful tales of laughter and mischief from before Alex had arrived. A prank gone awry, leading to Renmark emerging from the teachers' quarters in nothing but his underwear. Races with clockwork beetles along the wooden benches in the mechanics lab. Jumping from the stacks of the library for the first time and seeing who could land the farthest. Aamir always helping Jari out of a situation, like his futile attempt at wooing Ellabell. With each story, Jari's throat tightened, the emotion evident in his voice.

But none of the stories seemed to be getting through

to Aamir, who thrashed wildly against the shield. Alex could feel the ripples coming from it, but didn't dare add another layer of anti-magic to the barrier until the mob had dispersed. Who knew what they would do to him if they discovered his secret? They were already hungry for a lynching.

"I know you're in there, Aamir," Jari murmured earnestly, his eyes squeezed tightly shut. "It's not you speaking. It's that golden line playing tricks with your mind. It's not you—it's the Head controlling you."

Alex frowned at Jari's whispered words, and a thought rushed into his head. He turned to the gathered students.

"It's not Aamir speaking," Alex repeated. "It's the golden line they put on his wrist, controlling him. You know, like the ones they put where we're not supposed to go?"

The mob nodded uncertainly. Natalie looked at Alex and tentatively lowered her shield, the relief clear on her face as the angry tension in the room dissipated and morphed into an atmosphere of collective curiosity.

"Well, they can use them on us, too. They used one on Aamir. They put it on his wrist and made him do as they pleased," Alex said, his voice rising. He had to make his argument convincing enough to rile them up against the Head instead of the Head's innocent avatar.

Alex still didn't know how much control the golden line had over Aamir, but he guessed the Head must be using magic through the golden band to distort Aamir's emotions. It made Alex uneasy, wondering what else the Head knew through the golden band.

"The Head may know what has gone on here," declared Alex, his voice rich with gravitas as he stood before the crowd of murmuring students. They quieted at his words, and he continued. "Through the golden line, the Head will know that Aamir has been apprehended, and now we're running out of time. The Head will return to regain control of the manor. We must make sure we're ready for when that happens."

A murmur of worried surprise rippled through the mob, their gazes turning from Aamir to Alex, waiting for him to speak again. Alex wasn't sure if what he said about the golden line was true, but he had an inkling it might be.

"We must prepare ourselves for the return of the Head, because he will be coming," Alex went on, feeling their eyes on him, watching him intently. "You can count on that. We must be ready if we are to overcome him. *This* is our opportunity. *This* is what we have been waiting for. This moment may be our only chance to break free of this place." His voice was thick with emotion as he thought of his mother and the offer he had been given to see her again. "Think of your families, out there beyond the horizon. Think of those people you were taken from, against your will. Think of them, left to wonder what happened to you. This is your chance to go *home*."

The mob's voice rose in a rush of agreement, the glitter of tears prickling in the eyes of many gathered there.

"Think of your mothers' tears and the empty caskets that bear your names, on headstones, in cemeteries miles from here. They don't know what happened to any of us," Alex said, his eyes burning with a bright fury. "Imagine the joy on their faces when they see us again, after so long—all that heartbreak forgotten in an instant, to see our faces again. This might be the only chance we ever have. We must prepare for a great battle ahead—we must be ready for *his* return."

Alex felt the shift in the mood of the room as the mob's anger diverted wholly toward the Head and the battle that lay ahead.

"We'll lock Aamir away," Alex stated, gesturing to Jari and Natalie. "The rest of you should gather in smaller groups and practice sparring, all hours of the day, as much as you can, until I make a call-to-arms. I will rally you when the time is right, and, until then, you must prepare. Ransack the library, find all the spells you can to help in the battle to come. Try spells you never dared. Go to the mechanics lab and build bombs and traps and set them at every corner." He leveled his gaze with several of the older students. "You must rally the younger students. Spread the message and take charge of the groups. If any student is too scared to fight, do not force them—they are the ones who will need our protection in battle. If they do not wish to fight, we must not make them."

The students nodded, though there was fear among the hope.

"Learn as much as you can about attack and defense. Knowledge is power. Ask for help from the teachers you think you can trust," Alex said, knowing he didn't need to spell out their names. The only ones Alex was certain of being trustworthy were Lintz and Gaze. The other two, he couldn't be sure whose side they'd be on, when the time came. "Go! Prepare yourselves!" he commanded.

The mob split apart at Alex's final instruction. Alex watched as his fellow students retreated, hopeful that they might have a chance. They had the numbers, and, if everyone studied hard, maybe they would have enough power to overcome the Head.

"The shield is breaking," called Jari, his voice panicked. "I don't know how much longer it can hold!"

Alex turned and walked cautiously over to Aamir. The barrier sputtered, and thin slits had appeared in the anti-magical fabric of the cell, tearing the energy apart piece by piece. Alex poured an extra layer of glittering power into the barrier, repairing some of the shield's gaps, but he knew it wasn't a permanent solution.

Suddenly, an idea came to him. He couldn't believe he was even contemplating it, but it seemed to be the only way, with what little time they had at their disposal. What he was about to suggest saddened him deeply, twisting at his heart, but he was convinced that in this moment, it was the only solution.

"I know a place," he said miserably, not daring to look his friends in the eye, "where Aamir will be safe."

CHAPTER 27

ALEX LED THE WAY. BEHIND HIM FOLLOWED Natalie and Jari with Aamir between them, his hands tied with the coiled ropes, glittering with black and silver from the anti-magic Alex had fed through the interwoven threads. Around his mouth glowed a golden gag Natalie had conjured to keep him silent; Alex's anti-magic would only have burned.

The hallways were empty, the students using the rest of their evening to do as Alex had instructed: ransacking the library, dueling in empty chambers, building weapons in the mechanics lab, and strengthening their skills. Some had even taken to the grounds, as far from corridors and prying eyes as possible.

"Alex?" said Jari as they helped Aamir along.

Alex turned over his shoulder. "What is it?"

"About back there," Jari muttered sheepishly, "with the others."

"What about it?" Alex shrugged, feigning ignorance.

"I feel like I need to apologize," he explained, shifting Aamir's weight slightly. There was discomfort in the boy's voice.

Natalie nodded. "Me too."

"It's fine," said Alex quickly.

"No, we left you out, and I'm sorry—I want to explain." Jari seemed sad, imploring Alex to listen. "I wasn't myself, with him gone," he murmured, nodding at Aamir. "I needed to fix this, and I didn't think you could help. I thought you were weak. I didn't know you were capable of what you *are* clearly capable of. I left you out without thinking, and I didn't bother to ask if you were up to it or even how you were doing. I was consumed by this. I was self-centered, and it was wrong. When you came into the cellar that day and caught us, you made me feel guilty about what we were doing in secret, and I got defensive. I reacted badly, and I should never have done that—I'm sorry. We should never have left you out of it or let it get as bad as it did."

Alex glanced at Jari, trying to gauge the blond-haired boy's sincerity. There was a deep look of regret creasing his brow, and his eyes glistened as he returned Alex's gaze.

"I thought your powers needed protecting, when what they really needed was nurturing and for us to understand your strength," chipped in Natalie with a remorseful expression. "Now that we've seen them, we know how stupid we have been. I never stopped to ask, and neither did Jari, and we're sorry for that."

"I didn't exactly help matters. I know I kept the havens from you," said Alex, shoving his hands into his pockets as awkwardness stilted his speech. "I know you must have thought you couldn't trust me. I'm sorry for that," he added, sighing heavily as he felt a prickle of guilt in his heart.

"We trust you," murmured Natalie.

"Of course we trust you—you're our friend. *I* behaved badly. I overreacted and let other things cloud my judgment... I'm sorry." Jari nodded, mirroring Alex's awkwardness.

"I appreciate it," said Alex quietly, feeling the ties of their fractured relationship coming together again. "Anything else I should know about? The student uprising, perhaps?" he added, with the beginnings of an irreverent smile playing upon his lips.

"The Uprising was just an extension of the training you saw. We aren't keeping anything else from you, we promise," Jari replied swiftly, looking to Alex with encouragement. There was something earnest in his friend's behavior that Alex sensed was genuine—a very real sorrow for what had passed between them all.

Alex wanted to believe them, wanted to know their apologies were sincere, and he hoped time would reveal them to be honest. It felt a touch hypocritical, knowing his own secrets bubbled just beneath the surface, but there would be time for his apologies and his truths later. He would come clean. Silently, he promised himself he would, soon.

"That's good to know," said Alex, the smile reaching his eyes at last. It felt nice to be united again.

"You forgive us?" asked Natalie.

"There is nothing to forgive." He would have hugged them both had they not been holding up the limp, angry figure of Aamir between them. Smiles spread across their faces as they continued on toward Alex's destination. Once they saw where he was taking them, Alex knew, those smiles wouldn't last for long. He only hoped they didn't think him a monster.

Passing the familiar door to Renmark's classroom, Alex could hear the gruff tones of the professor within, grumbling something incoherent, his voice rising threateningly as he spoke to himself. Alex stopped to listen, Natalie and Jari nearly running into him as they too halted.

"I've had enough of these *blasted* students and these God-forsaken walls!" Renmark shouted. There was a dull thud, as if something had hit one of the walls. "…taking it to the Head. I'm tired of teaching these imbeciles and their constant disrespect for authority! Punishments are what we need here. Yes, punishments…" He seemed to relish in the possibilities as he weighed the pros and cons of each kind of reprimand. Alex was certain he caught a mention of the word "Escher" somewhere in the tirade.

"The Head should have left *me* in charge, not some young, useless upstart!" Renmark cried out to his apparently imaginary audience. "Decades of my life I have dedicated to this place! For what? To be overlooked time and time again!"

Another thud rumbled through the wall. Alex took it as a sign to hurry onward. He beckoned for the others to quicken their pace as they rushed past the classroom doors, not wanting to disturb any of the inhabitants within.

Aamir still fought against his restraints, but he could make no sound louder than a muffled groan through his gag. The anti-magic within the ropes seemed to have sapped Aamir's energy somewhat, leaving him more compliant as they hurried him through the hallways.

Reaching the familiar golden line, Alex paused.

"Stand back," he told Natalie and Jari. He conjured the body of a sword above his hand, the spell weaving habitually through his fingers in icy streams. It was an easy spell for him now. The blade sharpened to a thin edge that glinted with menace as he poured anti-magic into the center of the weapon, solidifying it so he could pluck it from the air.

Alex brought the sword down hard on the golden line, which instantly shattered. Moments later, he sent a dense, powerful blockade charging down the hallway, wiping out any of the hidden magical defenses, his icy blast rushing into the darkness and disappearing from sight. It was almost second nature to him now, breaking into the Head's quarters. He had definitely become something of a pro, anticipating the next issue before it arrived.

"You won't like my suggestion," muttered Alex, as he gestured for them to follow. He knew it was the only way to keep Aamir safe, from himself and from hurting others. Alex had seen the suspicion in the other students' eyes as they observed Aamir, knowing their old classmate wasn't behaving like himself. Despite their misgivings, Jari and Natalie seemed convinced the real Aamir was just beneath the surface somewhere, but Alex wasn't sure how deep the real Aamir was buried.

Alex walked along the familiar hallways, coming to the fork in the path and heading straight on. He kept going until he reached the eerie wooden doorway to the chamber that reeked of fear and blood. Pushing the door open, he stepped in and waited for the others to follow. The wide-brimmed hat still lay on the table at the side of the room, but the ivy-covered door to the antechamber, which he was sure he had left open in his hurry to leave before, was shut. He leaned back against the tabletop, his hand resting close to the bladeless knife, as the other two entered, with Aamir held between them.

"What is this place?" asked Natalie, horror lacing her words, her eyes wide with shock and disgust.

The manacles dangled from the ceiling, the metallic tang of dried blood permeating the room.

"You can't be serious," hissed Jari.

"What other option do we have?" replied Alex, looking up at the manacles.

"You're insane. We're not leaving him here," snapped Jari, shaking his head.

Alex sighed. "This place was designed to hold wizards," he explained grimly, gesturing around the room at the tools and devices that looked intended for torture and confinement.

"What is this place?" repeated Natalie, her voice barely above a whisper.

"*This* is graduation," Alex said, his voice thick with anger and sadness as he tapped the ledger that lay on top of the table behind him. "I don't know why or how, but this is it. This is where the students come, on the same day each year, to be strung up, their essence removed. It's a final test of some sort." He swallowed hard. "So far, it seems no one has passed."

His eyes hardened as the certainty cemented itself in his heart. He had guessed as much, but it seemed so obvious now. In the depths of his chest, his anger burned with a renewed fury. The blood on the floor was the blood of broken youth, used for some unknown, foul purpose.

"What?" gasped Natalie.

"I don't know what the test entails or what it's for, but there's a reason it's done, and this is the place where it happens," Alex said, remembering bitterly the comment in the notebook, telling of the desperation of wizards.

Is that what this is? Alex thought. *The Head's desperation? But to do what, and why?*

"Let me see that," said Natalie cautiously, pointing toward the ledger. Alex handed it to her and watched as she flipped through it. Her face was horrified. A pang of sorrow rippled through Alex as Natalie's mouth shaped the names written there. Jari moved beside her to read over her shoulder, his features darkening as his eyes scanned the pages.

"Raul Gallico. Odette Narcisse. I knew them," Jari said, his voice trembling with wrath.

"We need to get him up there," said Alex reluctantly as Natalie set down the ledger.

Awkwardly, they removed the coiled ropes, expecting Aamir to fight back. Sapped of his energy, he made no effort to retaliate as Alex pulled the heavy bolts out of the cuffs. With some difficulty, Natalie and Jari held their friend up while Alex closed the manacles around the coppery skin of Aamir's wrists, sliding the bolts quickly back into place. Stepping back, the sight was a horrifying one—to see Aamir's body dangling limply, an echo of so many students before.

"Please, let me go," he begged as he hung there, his head lolling to one side.

Alex felt the pull of guilt. He knew they couldn't help Aamir until they were sure he had returned to his former self, but that didn't mean he didn't want to break the cuffs right there and then. His friend dangling there like a prisoner was a gut-wrenching sight, and Alex could not believe the idea had come from his own mind. He felt appalled with himself, yet unable to tear his eyes away.

With his arms above his head, the sleeves of Aamir's robe had peeled away, revealing the golden band on his wrist. It was glowing brighter and more vividly than before, seeming to thrum and crackle in the air as it burned with renewed ferocity. If he could break the golden line on Aamir's wrist without alerting the Head, he'd do it in a heartbeat. But it was too risky. Alex didn't know if the Head was already aware of everything that was happening around Aamir, but destroying the line seemed like a surefire way to attract attention.

"What do we do now?" asked Jari miserably, unable to look at the hanging figure of his friend.

"He'll be safe here on his own, but we should try to spend as much time watching him as possible. He could do with the company," replied Alex, staring at the glittering band as it glowed angrily in the darkness of the chamber. "We'll take it in turns, and when we aren't here, we train. We get better, we hone our skills, and we prepare for what's to come."

"I'll watch him first," said Jari.

Alex nodded. "You'll have to stay until morning, to avoid any curfew issues," he warned.

"I don't mind." Jari shrugged and tried to look up at his friend, who was staring at the trio with mournful eyes.

"You sure you'll be all right?" Alex frowned at Jari, wondering if he was the best person to leave alone with Aamir. Surely, if anyone was to be persuaded by Aamir's sad expression and weary pleas, it would be his best friend?

"You can trust me," whispered Jari, as if reading Alex's mind. "I won't let him loose, no matter how much he asks," he added sadly.

"Okay. We should go," said Alex, turning to Natalie. She nodded, hurrying toward the door, clearly eager to be away from the stench of blood and the sight of Aamir hanging from the manacles.

Almost without thinking, Alex reached out for the bladeless knife on the tabletop and slipped it discreetly into his belt. A sad, bitter terror followed him as he made his way back through the vacant halls. The true extent of the lies being told within the manor was finally being realized. Suddenly, escape seemed a far more pressing matter.

There could be no escape at any other time, only a one-way ticket into that chamber, making this one opportunity all the more important. The Head was away, and the manor had been left without a master. Alex guessed that, for some reason, Aamir had been sent back and was now supposed to be the leader in the Head's place, but they had managed to overcome him, leaving the manor vulnerable. The Head was still out there fulfilling his vile task of student recruitment, not realizing the manor was under threat, thinking it in the safe hands of his masked avatar. If they didn't rise up, Alex knew those headstones he had spoken about would have a reason to be there.

"Do you think we will win?" asked Natalie in a whisper as they walked together.

"I think we'll try," replied Alex worriedly, putting his arm around her.

It all seemed too real, suffused with a very tangible sense that not everyone would make it out alive. Still, Alex knew his fellow students shared his stoicism and steadfastness; they would not give up, and they would not give in. After all, there couldn't be a plan B now.

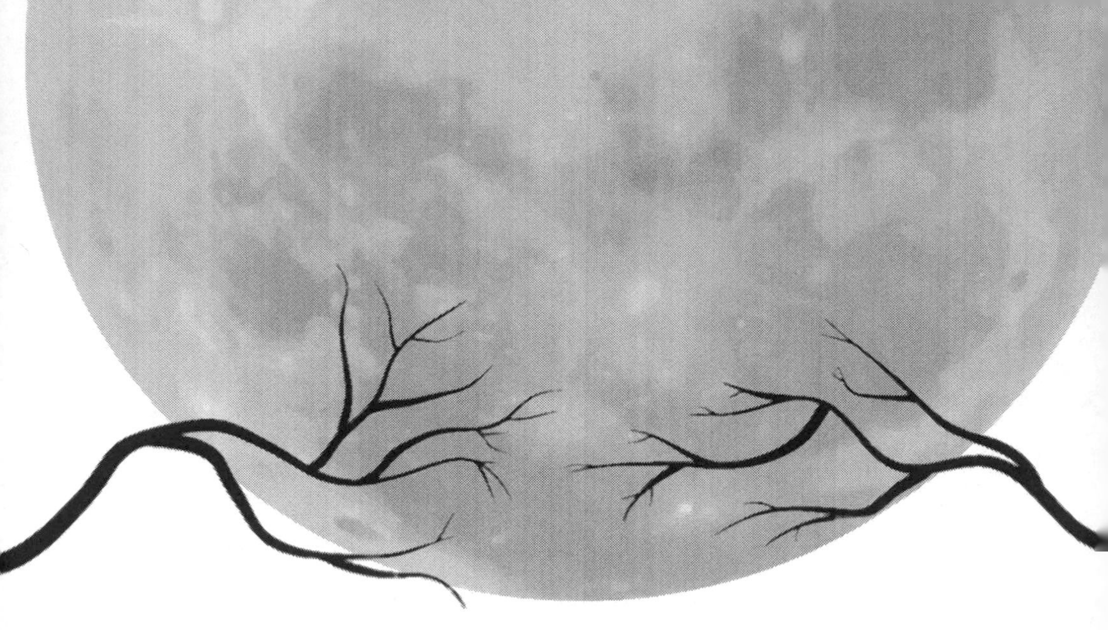

CHAPTER 28

In the following days, Alex was pleased to see that the others had taken heed of his instruction. Lessons were skipped in favor of training, and the bookshelves in the library had been looted for spell books and manuals. Without a Deputy Head to carry out any severe punishments for late curfews and missed classes, the fear had lifted a little from the manor, everyone able to breathe more easily. Alex wondered if his fears about the golden band listening in had been unfounded. Days had passed, and still the Head did not come. He hoped tentatively that they might have more time than he'd thought.

Walking quickly down the hallway, intent on reaching the wine cellar for a private training session, Alex jumped as a head appeared around the corner of one of the classroom doors. It was Lintz, his brow furrowed and his mouth set in a stern line.

"What's going on?" he asked sharply. "Where is everyone?"

Alex had known this time would come. The classrooms had been growing progressively emptier, and so had the dormitories, with students scattered throughout the manor, trying to keep as much distance between themselves and the teachers as possible. As yet, it seemed, nobody had asked for Lintz or Gaze's assistance. Perhaps they were too afraid to judge their trustworthiness wrongly, Alex thought, as he narrowed his eyes at Lintz, weighing whether or not he *could* trust this particular professor.

"Staging a coup," said Alex bluntly.

Lintz nodded with a tight smile. "I thought as much. About time, if you ask me." He grinned, his moustache twitching. "Any room for an old codger like me?"

Alex widened his eyes, pleasantly taken aback. "There's room for anyone who's on our side," he replied, hoping his gut feeling to trust Lintz was right. There was a lightness in Lintz's manner that made Alex curious; he seemed keener than Alex had anticipated. He knew how long Lintz had been waiting for an opportunity like this, and perhaps he had finally come to realize that there was only really one mode of escape left to him, after what had happened to Derhin. They had been friends, from young men to old men, and Alex had to wonder if Lintz felt there was anything left to lose. It certainly didn't seem that way.

"Count me in. I'll go fetch some things. You call on me when the time is right—I'll be barricaded in here until then." He chuckled, a genuine warmth spreading across his face.

"Professor?"

"Yes?" said Lintz.

"Do you think any of the other professors would help us?" asked Alex sheepishly.

Lintz flashed a smile. "Only one," said Lintz. "I will ask her."

"Thank you," sighed Alex, hoping he meant Gaze.

"Well, this is very exciting," muttered Lintz as he closed the door of his classroom behind him and headed off down the hallway, whistling loudly. Alex watched him go, a broad smile on his face, before he carried on toward the cellar.

Alex had just returned from a sparring session in the cellar when a loud explosion sent him running back through the manor. The rumble rippled through the flagstones, the ground shaking. Another loud bang knocked him sideways into the wall, but he scrambled to his feet and kept running, determined to reach the place the explosions were coming from.

"How dare you!" roared the biting voice of Professor Renmark.

Alex rounded the corner and saw a maelstrom of energy chasing a small group of students down the corridor ahead.

"How dare you go against the Head! You are not worthy!" Renmark yelled after them, shards of golden spears sailing past the shoulders of the fleeing students.

Beside him stood Esmerelda, wearing a striking, sequined purple dress that glimmered with each burst of magical energy that soared from her delicate hands. Alex saw her gazing up at Renmark's face with an expression that lay somewhere between adoration and hero-worship, her blue eyes shining.

It seemed Renmark had decided to seize back power, in the absence of Professor Escher or the Head. Alex recalled the muttered conversation overheard through Renmark's door. It was the moment Renmark had been waiting for—the chance to prove himself to the Head. It looked as if the students had tried to take him on, underestimating his strength and overlooking his partnership with Esmerelda, who was a far more powerful mage than anyone had suspected. Beneath her delicate exterior lay a ferocious force of raw energy, and the pair made formidable foes. Alex ducked into a doorway, watching the fight from afar but not daring to toss himself into the line of fire just yet. Perhaps he could initiate a surprise attack when the professors were least expecting it, or could run to get Lintz, knowing his classroom wasn't far.

A few of the students sent streams of golden energy trailing over their shoulders, some even using spells they'd been taught in Renmark's classes. But he seemed to always be a step ahead, swiping the futile magical attempts away with a flick of his robed wrist.

The magic thundered between the walls as the fight tore through the corridor, close to the classroom doors. Fierce blades and great, mystical birds of prey dancing within a flame-like aura raced after the students, lashing out at their skin, trying to inflict pain, as Renmark and Esmerelda walked slowly in pursuit of their quarry. They didn't need to run; their magic was doing the legwork.

Alex lifted his hands, preparing to form a blade of anti-magic, but he was distracted by the sound of rusted metal scraping the floor as a door across the hall flung open. Lintz jumped out of his classroom, the students rushing past him. A look of disgust flashed across his face, his moustache twitching angrily as he beheld the two teachers at the far end of the corridor. Across his body, he wore a leather satchel that bounced awkwardly against his back. He didn't seem to mind it, though, and stood his ground.

Deftly, Lintz conjured a blockade, a magical version of the inverted one Alex liked to use, and sent it rushing through the hallway—only it seemed this one was intended to combat magic alone and not inflict damage on human bodies. It swallowed up the magical arsenal of Renmark and Esmerelda's combined forces, rendering it useless.

"Stop!" yelled Lintz. "What on earth do you think you're doing? You do *not* kill the students!" he bellowed as the group tore past him, leaving him to face Renmark and Esmerelda head on.

"Get out of the way, old man!" shouted Renmark.

"I will not!" Lintz sent another blockade to dispose of the fiery eagles trying to dive-bomb him.

Forging vast spears and swirling balls of raw power, Renmark hurled his weapons in Lintz's direction. Lintz, in turn, ducked and flicked the attacks away, a spear narrowly missing his face, singing the tip of his moustache. A low growl emitted from the back of Lintz's throat as he retaliated with a wave of thinly made arrows that sliced through the atmosphere, slipping quickly toward his aggressors. One hit Renmark in the shoulder, eliciting a shrill howl as it made his arm shake uncontrollably. Esmerelda gently touched Renmark's elbow, her magic flowing into his skin and sucking away the hex as his arm ceased to shudder.

Enraged, Renmark fired a flat disc of amber light that spun through the air between them, skimming over the top of Lintz's head as he ducked, his old knees cracking.

So far, the two men looked almost evenly matched, but the added power of Esmerelda seemed to put a strain on Lintz. Alex wondered if he should step in, but hung back with the other students as they watched the fight continue. They all shouted encouragements to Lintz as he rallied his strength and sent a shimmering dragon toward his two opponents, the golden mouth opening wide as a stream of hot, white fire erupted from between the glinting fangs.

Esmerelda combatted the dragon with a rush of amber mist. The whole corridor was glittering with the sheen of building magic, the air growing hot and stifling. Beads of sweat had appeared on Lintz's brow, and Alex could feel the chill within him intensifying as he watched the battle.

Renmark's hands twisted and turned with violent speed as his mouth moved silently. His eyes seemed to glow with an unearthly radiance as Alex observed his unorthodox conjuring, wondering what he was doing. A sliver of a shimmering, navy substance rippled between the mist of the golden magic, snaking toward Lintz. Alex tried to call out, to warn Lintz, but the professor could not hear him above the din of the fight. The substance creeped down into Lintz's skin.

Lintz froze, his hands grasping at his chest as if trying

to remove something, his body doubling over in pain.

"Don't you dare!" a voice called from behind the gathered students.

Gaze pushed through the small crowd and stepped into place beside Lintz, her hands moving quickly to remove the bluish-tinged magic Renmark had slipped beneath Lintz's skin. She flung it away like it was a poisonous creature, compressing it until it exploded into harmless vapor.

"You coward, Renmark! Who uses dark magic in a battle?" she crowed.

Gaze sent small, delicately made balls of fire toward Renmark and Esmerelda. The miniscule projectiles seemed feeble but held a dangerous secret—as they neared their target, they exploded in a wide, savage burst. They went off in a series, flashing in the air with a blinding white light and sending out a pulse of violent energy that surprised the others as they staggered back.

Gaze didn't give her opponents a moment to catch their breaths. She sent a stream of gold toward Esmerelda, creating a barrier around her that seemed to drag her back into the corridor. The younger professor flailed against the strength of Gaze's magic. Professor Gaze smirked and shot another barrier toward Renmark, but he managed to fend it off. It kept him busy, though, as Lintz regained his strength from whatever had been sent creeping into his body.

"All of you, run! Go to the front lawn!" yelled Gaze, turning momentarily with a fierce expression on her face. She wasn't even looking at Renmark, but managed to flick his magic away easily. The students didn't need telling twice—they sprinted off down the halls.

Alex lingered around the corner, knowing he could help.

The two pairs were evenly matched as they faced off in the corridor, magic billowing and spiraling and sparking. Gaze had created a latticed barrier around herself and Lintz, keeping away the dark magic Renmark was using while allowing them to release magic of their own. A two-way shield.

Alex was mesmerized as he watched Gaze work. Her magic was flawless. Twisting her hands gracefully, she managed to weave a loop of magic around Esmerelda and Renmark, reducing the impact of their attacks. But Renmark's dark magic was strong. Alex could see that each rebuff and blow from the viscous streams of navy liquid drained Gaze. It took a lot to protect the hallway, but it had given the students time to get away safely. The corridor behind Alex was empty; everyone had made it out.

Lintz reached into the leather satchel around his body and pulled out two mechanical bombs. He threw them wildly at the opposing pair, just as Gaze forced a moving blockade of strong, fierce magic in their direction. The dual hit sent their opponents flying backward onto the flagstones as Lintz and Gaze turned and ran, following the direction the students had taken.

Gaze reached out a claw-like hand and grasped Alex's arm.

"Run, boy!" she shrieked, dragging him along with her as they headed toward the front lawn. At least, Alex mused, glancing at Gaze and Lintz, they now had two powerful allies to help with the stand they were about to make.

CHAPTER 29

Alex's lungs burned as he sprinted out of the manor, other students spilling out behind him after hearing the ruckus inside. It wasn't safe in there, with Renmark and Esmerelda on the loose. Gaze and Lintz followed wearily, Gaze stooping for breath as she leaned against the manor's vast doorframe. Lintz patted her gently on the back, though a sheen of sweat glistened across his own forehead and his chest heaved with the exertion of the battle and their swift escape.

Gathering himself, Alex walked through the gathered group who stood out on the front lawn, making sure everyone was okay. A few of them had burns lacerating their backs and shoulders, but nothing a bit of salve couldn't fix. Renmark had clearly been saving his more vicious spells for more formidable enemies.

"What happened in there?" asked Jun Asano, his jet-black eyes peering over Alex's shoulder with barely suppressed anxiety.

"A fight," said Alex simply. "The first of many, I would imagine," he added grimly.

Jun nodded. "We are ready."

The small, lanky boy standing in Jun's shadow suddenly went pale, his eyes wide, his mouth opening and closing like that of a beached fish. His terrified gaze was looking at something over Alex's shoulder.

The hairs on Alex's arms prickled. He didn't need to turn around to see who it was the boy was staring so fearfully at—he could feel the creeping cold of the Head's skeletal form, the otherworldly eyes burning into the back of his head, willing him to turn and show the same fear found on the other boy's face. Alex would not give the Head that satisfaction.

With agonizing slowness, he turned to the Head.

Finally, he had returned.

Thoughts raced through Alex's mind as he faced the Head, who was standing by the gate, still with some distance between them, but close enough to instill fear. Alex wondered where he had been and what had finally brought him back to stand against the rallied students.

Had someone told him? He knew Aamir was still strung up in the manacle chamber, so it couldn't have been him. Had the band finally sent out a beacon of help to him? Was he taunting them, letting them believe they had the higher ground only to crush them? Alex wouldn't put it past him. The Head was an impossibly strong magical entity, and they were an army of half-formed wizards. Perhaps he thought he had nothing to fear from them.

Already, Alex had streams of black and silver shards running between his fingers, ready to use in the battle ahead. His eyes locked with the hooded demon, narrowing in determination as he gathered his strength. On every side of him, he felt the other students move into defensive stances, ready to go on Alex's command.

Nobody fled and nobody stood down in terror, not even the young man beside Jun, who stepped forward, moving into a position beside Alex. The boy's face was determined, even though his small hands shook. A sad smile pulled at the edges of Alex's mouth as he watched the boy, hoping he wouldn't have to shoulder the responsibility of this young man coming to harm. Alex had understood the risks; he understood that not everyone was going to make it out. But he hoped, despite himself, that the boy would.

Seeing the younger student so stoic spurred Alex on as he stood firmly before the hooded figure. A smirk played on the Head's pale, unnatural mouth, the rest of him shadowed beneath his robe. Alex remembered his feelings about the mask of Professor Escher, before they knew he was Aamir—a man who hid himself could never be trusted.

The same was infinitely more true of the Head. Whatever the reasons for the Head's vile 'graduation' ceremony, whatever secrets rippled beneath the earth of the manor, Alex knew none of it was excusable. There was no cause great enough for what the Head had done and would continue to do if they did not stop him.

Strength surged through Alex on a wave of adrenaline as he moved his hands slowly upward, the anti-magic swirling icily around his fingertips. He was focused and he was ready. But before he could even lift his palms to perform the strongest anti-magical move he knew, something heavy and ungainly fell at the Head's shrouded feet.

The metal ball landed on the ground with a thud, rocking gently on the sweeping black train of the Head's robe. Confusion crossed the Head's shadowed eyes as he looked down at the object, just in time to get the full force of Lintz's magical trap in his face as it exploded around him, sending his skeletal form flailing backward as he tried to kick the trap away. It bought the students time and the element of surprise they so desperately needed.

Alex glanced back over his shoulder to see Lintz grinning wildly, looking like a much younger man, standing tall and proud at the top of the manor steps with a mechanical ball in each hand.

"Now!" cried Alex, his head snapping back to the main event.

The handful of students around him—a fraction of their main number, perhaps a quarter—did not need to be told twice. Turning on the Head, they bombarded him with their most elaborate, intricate spells, firing them off in perfect unison, preventing him from edging any closer to the school. Gold shards filled the air in a hot rain of glittering embers, the thunder of clashing magic ricocheting through the ears of all present. Streams of fierce gilded light shot through the miasma of misty glimmers, striking the Head with a peculiar fizzing sound. The sound of his pain hissed above the din of magic exploding and students roaring their war cries, audible enough to give the warriors the courage to persist.

Alex ducked through the fighters, running up to the top steps of the manor, where he stood side by side with Gaze and Lintz. Gaze seemed to have recovered somewhat, as she launched attack after attack in the Head's direction, hitting her target every time. Her aim was deadly, and her power was more immense than Alex could ever have guessed from such a small, ancient creature. Every spell was one he had never seen, her hands moving with disturbing speed, her eyes burning with ferocious intensity. Lintz, still grinning, lobbed bomb after bomb at the Head, watching in delight as they exploded close by, startling the robed figure each time.

Natalie appeared in the doorway, her eyes wide with concern as she took in the newly forged battlefield.

"I left Jari to watch over Aamir," she explained quickly.

Alex nodded. "We need you out there."

There wasn't time for much more in the way of conversation as Natalie slid into the ranks and shaped magic beneath her hands, firing spells and hexes in the Head's direction. For a moment, Alex thought he saw a thin stream of blue-tinged magic leave her fingertips, but wasn't sure if it was a trick of the light.

A moment later, a spear with a pinkish hue at its center rippled from Natalie's palms, and she threw it with great force. A bellowing roar rose up from the Head as the point hit him square in the shoulder, and Alex knew Natalie had moved away from the basic, everyday magic everyone else was using. He didn't like it, but he knew it wasn't the time to stop her. Whatever she was doing, it was working.

Lintz passed Alex bombs and traps from a bag clipped to the side of his leg, watching with gleeful pride as Alex proved himself to be a superb shot.

Barrage after barrage of magic artillery thundered across the front lawn, making the very ground tremble as the energy battered against the Head's skeletal form. It kept him at bay, but it was nowhere near enough to defeat him. Alex wasn't sure if the Head was just biding his time, but he knew the ancient wizard had more in his tank than he was currently revealing; he was luring them into a false sense of security. The Head fought back, of course, glistening streams of energy pouring fluidly from his clawed hands, knocking students back and snatching away their projectiles—but he did not seem interested in attacking them with all the strength he had within him. He seemed more intent on defending himself and letting the gathered students tire. Alex frowned, unsure why the Head was holding back.

The small force held him off successfully for a while, but they were starting to wear out. The explosions grew quieter as the dripping sweat on the forehead of every soldier glistened slickly in the glow of their magical fallout. The barrages were fewer and farther between, wizards staggering their spells to try to cover those who could not conjure any more. Each blast and bang was a whimper of its former self. The students were not as quick with their energy, wrists and fingers moving more slowly as aches began to set in. The only ones who seemed as fresh as ever were Natalie, Gaze, and the Head himself.

"Gaze, take the students and regroup! Use the hallways!" ordered Lintz, shouting to his colleague above the rumble of exploding bombs. He seemed to have an endless stash stored about his person, and as he turned back to the fight, he spun his satchel around to the front of his body and flipped open the leather flap. Inside, to Alex's awe, the satchel was full to the brim with mechanical, magical bombs and traps. Clockwork animals, too—a tiny mechanical army within the battered leather bag.

Lintz delved into the depths of the satchel and pulled out the owl Alex had seen him working on what seemed like years ago. The professor launched the winged creature into the air. It flapped vigorously as it weaved around flying spells and hurled projectiles, stopping above the Head's hood, where it circled and dived, dropping tiny explosions of magic onto the target below.

"I shall stay with you," said Natalie, standing beside Lintz.

"Me too," agreed Alex.

"Students, with me!" roared Gaze with startling volume. She beckoned for the students to follow her as she sent a rippling barrier of fierce, white-hot energy in the Head's direction. It seemed to pour from the very core of her body, her arms raised outward to the sky as it surged in a violent blast that seemed to skip the students, destined only for its one victim. With a crackle, it wrapped around the Head, incapacitating him for the briefest of moments as Gaze rallied her students to her.

She nodded at Alex, Natalie, and Lintz, tipping the frayed rim of her hat to them before darting off into the darkness of the manor, the rest of the students running behind. Gaze was a powerful wizard; they were in the best hands they could be, Alex knew.

He hoped fervently they wouldn't run into Renmark and Esmerelda on their journey back through the manor. They hadn't followed Lintz and Gaze, but Alex knew the blast they had sent at the other two professors wouldn't have kept them knocked out for long. He pictured them like beetles scuttling through the hallways, sending their brand of nasty, lashing magic at the backs of any students unfortunate enough to encounter them.

Gaze can handle them, if it comes to it, thought Alex quietly, praying he was right.

As the sheet of white magic wore off, Lintz hurled his bombs, each one crackling and exploding in a different, more elaborately destructive way, and Natalie forged the intense spells of her ill-learned dark arts, her golden light tinged pink and dark blue in succession. Alex knew it was time for him to use what he had learned, to keep the Head at bay.

"I've been waiting decades to do this!" bellowed Lintz with a broad grin on his face, his moustache twitching with excitement as he launched bomb after bomb, his arm never seeming to grow tired. It was like watching a machine—one hand reaching for a bomb as the other threw it with impressive speed.

Conjuring the familiar black and silver beneath his hands, Alex sent a shivering stream of anti-magic at the Head. It swirled, snaking between the galactic mist of the magical remnants that still glimmered in dust-like particles in the atmosphere. The whole front of the manor was drenched in a fine golden fog, and the anti-magic cut through it easily.

Alex noticed Lintz looking at him oddly with an expression of interest and understanding, his gaze moving from Alex to follow the snaking dark ripple of the conjured anti-magic. The professor smiled, casting a conspiratorial wink in Alex's direction as he returned, with satisfaction, to his bombs. Twisting his hands with swift dexterity, Alex launched some of the spells he had read in the notebook. A spell of anti-magical incapacitation, designed to make one's opponent freeze solid. He saw the spell hit the Head, but frowned as it seemed to do very little. It annoyed the Head, but no more than that. Alex sent another new one—a corkscrew of energy that was supposed to burn the skin and inflict intense pain on the victim. Again, it didn't seem to do more than irritate the Head, like a minor itch or a bug-bite. Alex knew it should have done far more than that, but it wasn't reacting the way it would on an ordinary magical individual. Perhaps it didn't work as well on more powerful beings, thought Alex with a twist of annoyance and panic.

Frustrated, he conjured the sparkling silver shape of a longbow and filled the center with dark energy that solidified the weapon. He held it tightly in one hand and manifested arrow after arrow with his other as he touched it to the glittering black string. Leander had been right—the bow was difficult and tricky, but the arrows were worth the effort. They fired at the Head with deadly accuracy, hitting him hard in the shoulder and arm, jerking his body with each impact. They didn't seem to hurt him much, but they knocked him back time and time again.

A hoarse cry erupted from the Head's throat as an arrow hit him in the heart, the pain evident in the pitch of his scream. From that moment, Alex aimed for the heart, but the Head was ready for it.

Dropping the bow and arrows, Alex forged a hefty spear, crafted from the purest energy. It buzzed and thrummed as Alex swiftly shaped the weapon to a razor-sharp point and poured his focused power into the very center, instilling the spearhead with an added layer of anti-magic that would explode on impact. Launching the spear, Alex watched its glittering, streamlined body as it glided along with thrilling speed. He was certain this was the thing to cause some real damage to the Head. As it neared, however, the Head snatched it and gripped it frozen in mid-air, before turning it around and sending it straight back toward Alex.

Alex ducked just in time, the spear shattering against the doorframe behind him, but he was hit in the shoulder by the stream of golden energy that quickly followed from the Head's other hand. The magic didn't harm Alex, though, as a flurry of frosty flakes drifted down from the small tear in Alex's pullover and a scorch mark tainted his skin beneath.

Alex stood, a deep frown furrowing his forehead as he brushed off the burn. Two weaving tendrils rippled along the Head's hands, so starkly contrasted, and yet moving in perfect harmony across the paper-thin skin of the hooded figure's fingers.

Black and silver still surged beneath Alex's palms. The Head eyed Alex with a curious glint in his inhuman eyes. It was as if they were frozen within the battle, focusing only on one another.

Alex held his breath. He was beginning to understand what the Head was. A mix of light and dark, gold and black. An impossible thing.

"We should run," whispered Natalie. She looked drained of all energy.

Alex nodded. They were overpowered. At this rate, they'd be dead in minutes.

"You go!" shouted Lintz defiantly, with a look of heroic resignation on his face.

"We can't leave you," insisted Alex, but Lintz batted him away.

"Go!" he repeated, as he turned to face the Head with a roar that boomed like overhead thunder. "I should have done this years ago!" he cried as he began to throw two bombs at a time while skidding magical traps along the floor to snatch at the Head's feet. His hands moved so quickly they were a blur.

Alex faltered, but Lintz shoved him and Natalie roughly toward the manor doors during a brief few seconds of quiet in the middle of a particularly brutal barrage.

"I said go," Professor Lintz whispered with a bittersweet smile.

Reluctantly, Alex and Natalie did as he asked and sprinted back inside the manor with the sound of exploding bombs echoing in their ears. They tore through the hallways, Alex shouting his call-to-arms at the top of his lungs as they ran.

"WE MUST FIGHT! JOIN US! THE TIME IS NOW!" His voice rang through the corridors, imploring any and all remaining students to come out of their rooms and join him.

The Head was back. Lines had been drawn. Sides had been taken.

The war had begun.

CHAPTER 30

A LARGE GROUP OF STUDENTS HAD GATHERED AT the entrance to the Head's quarters, students who hadn't been out on the front lawn, but Alex frowned as he counted the number of people present. There weren't as many as he had expected from his rallying cries, and yet no one else seemed to be arriving. The last few stragglers had trickled into the ranks.

"Is this everyone from the manor?" he asked.

Ellabell stepped forward from the group, her sparkling blue eyes prickling with the glitter of held-back tears.

"This is everyone," she said firmly.

"How can this be everyone?" whispered Alex in disbelief.

Ellabell sighed heavily, a hand raised to her heart as if she were physically trying to stop it from breaking. "A big group of us were hiding in the library when Renmark and Esmerelda came," she began. "We weren't expecting them, and they ambushed us. It didn't matter that we begged and pleaded for our lives. They were… merciless. Only a few made it out."

"You were there the whole time?" asked Alex, his stomach twisting in knots.

She nodded, wiping away tears with the palm of her hand.

The news of this attack stung Alex afresh, a wave of guilt washing over him as he looked toward the scared faces of those still with them. They had relied on him, and he had let them down. He hadn't been there when they had needed him—but he knew who truly deserved the blame.

"Where are they?" he growled.

"Esmerelda is dead," Ellabell said, the anger in her voice mirroring Alex's own. "A second group came to our rescue with Professor Gaze, but it was already too late to save everyone. They took out Esmerelda, but Renmark was nowhere to be found. I think he had already escaped by the time we went searching for him."

All too easily, Alex could imagine the bodies of his peers spread across the library floor, could picture their glassy stares and silenced screams. The grief and guilt and horror were overwhelming. Students were dead because they had followed his lead. They had been ambushed, and he hadn't been there to save them. He should have known Renmark and Esmerelda couldn't be trusted, with how they had teamed up after the Head's disappearance. He should have done something to stop them, but he never thought they'd do something as evil as *kill the students.* He knew Renmark relished power, and Esmerelda seemed to look up to Renmark, but he had never thought them capable of cold-blooded murder. Injury and punishment, perhaps, but nothing as horrifying as what they had done.

The *should haves* and *what ifs* charged through his mind, deafening his thoughts to anything else. It was all he could think of, but there were eyes on him, begging him to lead them—to tell them what to do next. They were terrified and grief-stricken, and so was he.

Gaze sat at the side of the corridor, perched on the edge of a windowsill that showed a vast, exotic desert of shifting golden sand with a hot sun baking down on the dunes. Her head hung low between slumped shoulders, and there was sadness in her eyes.

Alex walked over to her. "Professor Gaze?"

She looked up with clarity in her expression, as if she already knew what Alex was going to say.

"I need you to take the rest of the students and put them somewhere safe. Myself, Natalie, and Jari will cause a diversion to lure the Head away," he said softly, just out of earshot of the other students. He didn't want them to argue. He wanted them away, where they would be safe. He didn't want anyone else's death on his conscience.

He understood now that they were too few and too weak, but there was a glimmer of hope left—they might stand a better chance if they tried to fight on the Head's own turf, where the narrow corridors and darkened shadows could work to their advantage. Just himself, Jari, and Natalie. They could be enough, he hoped. They could be strong enough to overcome the Head at close quarters. He was just a man, after all. A powerful one, but still just a man beneath the cloaks and mystery.

Plus, Alex thought darkly, he could always use the essence within himself, if it came to it. He was prepared to make the sacrifice of creating a tear in the fabric of his soul. From what Alex had been able to garner from his brief brush with death magic knowledge in Leander's notebook, the enormous pulse of pure destructive force was in the same style as the life magic used by Mages, just the opposite version—the inverted form of his people. It seemed a small price for their survival. If the fight called for it, he would use his death magic; he would deal with the pain and disjuncture in the aftermath.

Gaze reached out and took Alex's hand. A silent moment of understanding passed between them. "I will take them, but I don't wish to leave you here to fight alone," she said, frowning. There was grief in her ancient eyes.

"I won't have another death on my conscience," he replied quietly. "It has to be this way. We know how to protect ourselves, and I'm… not exactly like the others."

"I know what you are." Gaze met his eye with a soft smile. "If I cannot dissuade you, then I will lead them to safety and do what I can. For them, I have one last trick up my sleeve."

"Where will you take them?"

"I can move and scramble the hallways behind me so that none of them will lead to this section of the manor, and we'll be harder to reach. Once I have done this, you will be on your own—I must know that you understand that?" she said hurriedly, her tone sorrowful.

Alex nodded. "I understand."

"Then we will go," she sighed, the weight of the world on her old shoulders. "And if I come across that snake Renmark, he will get what is coming to him. You mark my words," she added bitterly, her eyes shining with angry, heartbroken tears for all the lives lost.

She gathered the remaining students and explained what was about to happen. A murmur of confusion rippled through the group, but Gaze would not take no for an answer. It seemed she was not ready for any further losses either. As the news of the new plan settled, many of the students' expressions shifted to anxious relief, clearly grateful for a way out of this mess. Alex was pleased to see that; at least he could grant them a faint flicker of hope.

Ellabell stepped up beside him.

"Alex?"

Alex turned with a sad smile. He wasn't sure he'd see Ellabell again, and the thought made his heart ache. "What is it?" he asked kindly.

"I was wondering if I could help in any way? I can shield you and protect you, if you need," she said slowly.

Alex shook his head. "No way." She had just escaped an attack on her life; he wasn't going to put her in harm's way again. Memories of the cuts on her mouth and the bruise on her head came flooding back to him. She was in danger around him. There was no way he was going to let her come with him.

"Well, I'm not leaving," she said with a stubborn smile as she reached out and took his hand in hers. She squeezed it lightly. "I'm staying right here. I'm going to fight with you. I'm not afraid anymore," she stated, boldness in her blue eyes.

"Ellabell, you have to go with the others. It's too dangerous where we're headed," Alex urged, gazing at her with concern.

"I don't care. I want to help," she replied, her face defiant.

"Please, Ellabell—"

"I can't just run, knowing your life is on the line," she murmured, holding his hand more tightly. "I'm staying, and you can't change my mind."

Seeing the stony expression in her shining eyes, Alex knew he wasn't going to get her to budge. She was determined, and yet he wished she weren't. If anything happened to her, he wasn't sure what he'd do. At least, he thought grimly, he'd be able to see her and protect her if she was with them, but it didn't mean he was happy about it. With Gaze, he was certain she'd be safe. With him, he was less certain.

"Why?" he asked, wanting to understand.

"I can't hide while you fight. It's not fair, and I don't want to leave you," she whispered softly.

"Are you staying?" Gaze interrupted, addressing Ellabell from the edge of the adjoining corridor as she ushered the last of the students through.

Ellabell nodded.

"Very well," Professor Gaze said reluctantly. "Stay safe. I'll be thinking of you all." She tipped her hat one last time before disappearing into the hallway after her wards, leaving Alex, Natalie, and Ellabell alone in the vacant hallway.

The golden line that barred the way to the Head's quarters was already broken, yet to be repaired after their last adventure into the forbidden zone, although it still buzzed where the line remained intact.

"Well, here goes nothing," breathed Natalie, raising her eyebrow at Alex as she spoke the Americanism she had learned from him. She stepped toward what remained of the barrier line and touched it cautiously, wincing as she made contact. It wouldn't be long, if the plan worked.

Moments later, there was a cold rush of air as the Head whipped his cloak around and appeared in the hallway before them, called by the touch of a student's hand against the line. A menacing grin rested on the pale, skeletal features of his face—what was visible, anyway, beneath the hood.

"And where," the Head growled, his voice rasping, menacing and unnatural, in the back of his throat, "do you think you're going?" He stalked toward them with a smirk, already raising his hand to form a thread of energy between his fingers.

Thinking fast, Alex plucked the bladeless knife from his belt and wielded it at the Head. The blade shimmered to life as soon as Alex's hand wrapped around it, crackling with metallic energy, the sharp edge ready to bite. The energy that pulsed through the arm wielding it was cold, pulling at the twisting tendrils of his anti-magic to draw into the blade. Alex's gaze flashed toward the knife, wondering what powered it. It seemed to be using him—his anti-magic. Natalie and Ellabell fell in behind him with their palms raised, ready to fight. With a cry, Alex charged forward, brandishing the knife.

The Head hissed as the glowing blade swept the air close to his face, the light reflected in the deep, sinister pools of his eyes.

"How can you—hand me that knife at once!" he demanded, his voice pouring from an unnatural place deep beneath his cloak. "It does not belong to you. You should not be able to wield it! Give it to me!" The Head reached for the blade. Alex slashed a warning slice between them, stopping the Head in his tracks.

"Never," replied Alex.

"Where did you steal it from, you vile little thief? How dare you!" the Head seethed, the whispering sound sending a shiver up Alex's spine.

"You know very well where I took it from," said Alex in a low voice, the knife's silvery energy emboldening him. "I will make you *pay* for what you've done."

As Alex's anger rippled out from the epicenter of his heart, the blade began to glow more brightly. It strengthened with every pang of emotion felt through the hand that held it, burning more fiercely as it connected to the soul within.

The Head gave a hollow laugh. "You," he whispered, pointing a bony finger toward Alex. "What *are* you?" His foul gaze leveled with Alex, but Alex refused to look away.

"You know who I am," growled Alex, slashing again with the blade as the Head took a step toward him.

A vicious smile appeared on the wizard's emaciated lips. "Can it be, after all this time, that *you* have come to *me*?"

He lunged toward Alex, but Alex was ready for him,

swiping at the Head's bony arm with the knife. His mind focused on the pulsing center of the Head's essence, feeling the coiled creature within the Head's body. It was cold and uninviting, pushing against Alex's mind. He pushed back, teeth gritted, and lunged forward once more.

The knife made contact with the Head's arm, and the scream that erupted from the hooded figure's throat pierced the air in a bloodcurdling howl—the cry of a demon, guttural and raw. Snarling, the Head recoiled in searing agony.

As Alex withdrew the knife, he noticed a tiny bead of something red, glowing at the end of the blade, diluted against the shimmering silver. Before he could examine it more closely, Ellabell grabbed his arm.

"Run!" she cried, pushing him forward.

They broke into a sprint. The knife still glowed in Alex's hand, and as he ran, a wave of clarity crashed through his mind. After what he had witnessed on the battlefield and with the blade, he knew now, with great certainty, the man beneath the hood was a creature of both magic and anti-magic—a hybrid of the two, forged from light and dark.

But Alex couldn't wrap his head around how the Head had come to be. Could it be as simple as the Head being the offspring of a forbidden love? The abominable result of a Spellbreaker and a Mage, defying tradition and propriety to bring him life? Or was he something worse, created and not born?

He heard the thud of Natalie and Ellabell's feet close behind him as they made it to the fork in the corridors. They had just entered the main hallway leading toward the Head's office when a great blast surged from behind and knocked them flat on the floor. Alex's face slammed against the hard ground as the blade went skittering across the flagstones, just out of reach. He scrabbled for it but could not reach it as a second blast exploded over his head, keeping him down.

Jari burst from the chamber next to them, a war cry howling from his lungs, only to be sent flying, seconds later, by the eruption of a third blast. He landed on his back with a heavy thud. A fourth blast followed, more forceful than the last, knocking the air clean out of their lungs as the Head's voice filled Alex's ears.

"You will never escape me," the malicious voice breathed.

"We will," spat Alex, his face pressed down against the cold stones, the taste of blood in his mouth.

"It was an excellent attempt, but it was never going to work. I am far stronger than you will ever understand. You have merely annoyed me. Thanks to your foolish endeavors, you have set me back years. Do you know what that means, Alex Webber?" hissed the Head, the voice somehow coming from inside Alex's own skull.

Alex did know what that meant. "I will stop you," he

seethed through gritted teeth, speckled red.

"Thanks to you and your ill-favored uprising, I will have to find double the students. I will need to bring in more to replace what that idiot Renmark disposed of."

The Head's displeasure surprised Alex; he would have thought the Head, in all his vile glory, would have relished the death and suffering of so many students. Wasn't that what the whole purpose of the chamber was? To see so many students die, year after year, as they failed a test they could never win?

"He should have known better. So much work to be done," muttered the Head, apparently not realizing Alex was still privy to his thoughts.

Out of the corner of his eye, Alex could see the Head was still a fair way away, standing at the entrance to the main hallway. But in the skeletal palms of his hands he was beginning to manifest a rippling ball of black and gold. It was like no energy Alex had ever seen, and he was certain it spelled out the end for him. Pinned to the floor, unable to move, the blade just a fraction too far away, there was nowhere to run, no way to win.

Suddenly, the very shadows around Alex and the others shifted. The darkness became liquid, whirling from the deepest recesses of the hallway. The air crackled, and a rush of frosty air sent icy fingers running through their hair. Alex lifted his head in time to see Elias appear, floating in vaguely human form before them.

He flashed his glinting teeth at Alex. "Why do I always seem to be doing the heavy lifting?" he quipped with a starry grin.

The sight of the shadow-creature startled the Head, his inhuman mouth twisting into a grimace of confusion and wry amusement as he and Elias prowled around each other. Only it wasn't clear which was prey and which was predator.

"Oh, Elias, you are a thing of beauty, aren't you? Just look at you. Still so powerful. You had such potential. The finest wizard I had ever seen—the only one who might have been of vital use to me, and yet you chose to waste it on this half-life. Such a shame," the Head taunted.

"You have no idea," snapped Elias, his voice brimming with bitterness. "I would have been more powerful than you could ever have dreamed if it weren't for that sniveling little weasel Derhin. He was so desperate to take my place, and you listened! *You* are the fool here. Together, we could have fought and found another way out of this mess, but you were too much of a coward for that! As if I was just going to give myself up," he growled, the rage building in his shadowy throat. "I would rather watch you burn. I will see it one day. I will watch your destruction and I will smile, as you did," he spat, his sharp teeth glinting with menace.

"Now, now, Elias. No need to be so sensitive. It was all such a long time ago," chuckled the Head.

"I am patient. I have been patient. Your days are numbered." Elias smirked, as if he knew something the Head didn't. "You have realized too late," he whispered.

The Head sneered and conjured a spear of ice and fire, aiming at Elias's head. The shadow-man evaded it easily, coming back at the Head with a rippling swarm of pure, dark energy that billowed in a mist toward the Head's face.

"This is the end of you!" yelled the Head with a snarl, as he delved into the depths of his cloak. From within, he pulled out a bottle of black glass. Alex's eyes widened in horror, knowing the bottle's purpose. Elias froze too, his starry black eyes glittering with violent rage.

"Did you forget I had this?" the Head sneered, as he ripped the stopper from the top and tipped the contents out onto the palm of his hand. Within, Alex could see the dull red glow of something tiny. It was far smaller than the coiled, glowing essences he had seen stacked like condiments in the antechamber. It was only a section of the larger whole.

"That's mine!" shouted Elias, lunging toward the Head.

The Head waved his pale hand over the small, glowing ember, and a ripple of pale pink light shot through the shadowy form of Elias's body. Elias cried out in agony, slivers of his fluid form fading and slithering away from him, back into the darkness. Clawing the threads back into his shifting figure, Elias drew himself up and launched another attack at the Head. Jets of the purest black fired from Elias's shadowy form, the Head unable to snatch them or push them away. They were made from another energy entirely.

With a sweep of his arm, the Head passed his hand over the small coil of Elias's essence. Another cry shivered from Elias's shadowy throat, echoing between the walls and chilling Alex's blood. It was unearthly and inhuman and made goosebumps prickle along every inch of his skin. It seemed to come from another realm, the scream trembling the fabric of the world around them.

Elias swept backward, gathering up his errant shadows as he leveled a furious gaze at the Head. Alex had never seen rage like it. He was almost sure he saw a red glow burning, replacing the black, galactic irises of Elias's peculiar eyes.

Elias rallied again, flowing back on the wave of pain. This time, the Head was not as fast. The black mist of Elias's mysterious energy engulfed the hooded skeleton, blinding him for a moment as Elias swooped in with a rush of shadow and knocked the ember from the Head's palm. It fell like a marble, bouncing across the flagstones. Elias scurried after the ember, sweeping along the floor until his fluid fingers settled across the tiny red glow. Alex watched with wonder as Elias buried the glowing red marble deep inside the glittering cavern of his chest, where he seemed to store all of his most precious possessions.

"Go!" hissed Elias as he slithered along the floor, a triumphant grin on his strange face. Alex understood. Now nothing stood between Elias and the Head. Without the glowing particle of Elias's essence, the Head had no further control of the shadow creature. It was the moment Elias had been waiting a long time for, Alex realized, feeling a niggle of confusion in the back of his mind. Had this been the goal all along? The reason for the gifts and the books and the visits? Alex knew it would plague him later, but for now he had other things to worry about.

Alex scrambled to his feet, running to the others, who were doing the same, dragging themselves back up. He paused for a moment to pluck the almost-lost knife from the floor and slide it back into his belt.

The fight, so close to where they stood, intensified between Elias and the Head. All bets were off. Without the Head's advantage, the two seemed to be more than evenly matched, even with Elias's less-than-solid form.

Ellabell seemed frozen to the spot by the sight of Elias, her eyes staring at the shadow-creature in abject horror.

"Ellabell! You have to run!" Alex told her, grabbing her hand. She shook her head as if brushing off a trance.

"We can't leave Aamir," insisted Jari, just as they were about to break away from the fight.

Of course, Jari was right. They couldn't just leave Aamir to whatever fate might befall him if left within close proximity to the two superhuman opponents down the corridor.

Running into the foul chamber, a bolt of guilt sliced through Alex. Aamir was still hanging from the manacles, a cold sweat glistening on his sickly, waxy-looking face. Without thinking, knowing their time was precious, Alex reached up with the blade of the knife, watching it sear into life, and severed the golden line on Aamir's wrist.

A howl of agony erupted from Aamir's mouth as the line shattered, some of the energy seeping into the skin beneath, making his veins glow amber beneath the coppery outer layer as the rest fell, like iridescent confetti, to the floor. His face twisted and his entire arm glowed a molten gold, the overwhelming pain evident on his half-conscious face. Mid-cry, Aamir collapsed in the manacles, his body completely limp. Alex lifted his fingers to check for a pulse in Aamir's neck. He was still alive, just unconscious.

With the help of the others, Alex grabbed Aamir and unchained him as Jari and Natalie looped his arms around their necks. Running as fast as they could with their ungainly charge, they ducked out of the chamber and fled toward the Head's office as the battle raged violently on at the end of the corridor, sparks of black and gold flying against a glistening slick of oily mist.

"What now?" asked Natalie as the sound of the battle ebbed. She looked fearfully to Alex, her face damp with sweat, her eyes panicked.

"We need to barricade ourselves in the Head's office.

I don't know if Elias will be able to hold the Head off forever, and if he can't, it's going to be up to us. We'll have to make a last stand against him," said Alex, wiping the moisture from his forehead. The name *Elias* slipped from his mouth with a comfortable familiarity he hadn't experienced before, taking him by surprise.

"Elias?" asked Jari, his eyebrow raised in suspicion.

"The shadow creature?" echoed Ellabell.

The truth had caught up with Alex at last. "Elias is a strange friend of mine," he began. It felt odd to say Elias's name out loud. With the others finally seeing the shadow-man, the invisible restraint binding Alex's tongue seemed to have faded away. "It's a very long story, and right now we don't have time for it, but I promise I'll tell you all about him later, when we're…" He trailed off, as realization gripped his heart in a vise. He didn't know if there would *be* a later.

Alex had so many questions for Elias, having heard the exchange between the shadow-man and the Head. He wanted to know what Derhin had done and how the Head had come to have only a piece of Elias's essence. Where was the rest of it? He wanted to know what Elias had been before, when he was powerful and human and not a shadowy substance flitting from there to here and back again. He wanted to know what the Head had meant when he said Elias could have been vital, and what Elias had meant when he said they could have fought together in a different way. He wanted to know so many things, but he wasn't sure he'd ever get the chance to find out any more than what he already knew.

Their hope was a very weak flame now, moments from going out. The understanding settled in a cloud of melancholy around the small group.

"We can still get through this. All of us," whispered Alex. "Once we're in the Head's office, we're going to ransack the place for anything and everything we can use. We will find something, and we *will* make it out of this," he said, trying to comfort the despondent faces of his friends. "There might be something in those rare books we can use against him."

Natalie and Ellabell nodded silently. A smile grew across Jari's face, and Alex knew he was thinking the same thing.

Knowledge was power, and they were going to find it.

CHAPTER 31

ALEX LED THE WAY AS THEY RAN UP THE REMAINder of the corridor toward the Head's office and burst into the room. Moving quickly, knowing they didn't have much time, Alex instructed the others to set the still-unconscious Aamir up against the gnarled tree trunk that sat in the well of the fireplace. It was easily viewed from all areas of the room, in case Aamir awoke and still felt bound to the Head in some deep, disturbed way and tried to lash out at them. Who knew what side Aamir would be on. Even now, Alex wasn't sure how much Aamir was responsible for and how much the golden band was responsible for. He had so many questions for the unconscious young man that would have to wait for an answer.

Like those notes, warning him in the middle of the night; Alex still didn't know if it was Aamir who had sent them or someone else entirely. Then there was the mystery of his presence in the Head's quarters that night, now so long ago. Why had he been there, only to appear soon after through the gate with the new boy Felipe? Had the Head called him somehow? How had he moved so quickly from one place to another? Alex's mind flitted momentarily to the ill-fated magical travel attempts he and Natalie had made, wondering if that was how Aamir had done it, and if he had permission to move freely outside the manor's restraints.

Shaking his head, Alex returned his attention to the room and how to defend it. There would be time to ask those questions later, if they made it out alive. Secretly, Alex hoped Aamir would stay unconscious; he couldn't focus on that, too, with everything else he had to worry about.

With the others joining in, Alex blocked the door to the office with a few heavy chairs and a bookshelf laid diagonally across it. He knew it was a silly thing to do—it wouldn't hold the Head for more than a second if he came for them—but there was comfort in the practical action of keeping the skeletal figure out.

With the door barred and Aamir somewhere safe,

Alex turned to the red-lined bookshelf. Jari was already sitting on the Head's desk, swinging his legs with an irreverent grin on his face. It cheered Alex to see his dear friend still smiling, when there was so little left to smile about.

Alex knelt on the cold, hard floor, careful not to get in the way of Jari's swinging legs as he took out the anti-magical knife and touched it gently to the red line that glowed from within the ancient wooden structure.

Nothing happened.

Alex tried it again, but the knife did nothing. It could not cut through the red barrier.

Alex realized the knife must only have specific abilities. The knowledge was a little disappointing as he slid it back into his belt, but he wasn't defeated yet. Already grimacing, he moved his palms toward the thrumming red line and touched his anti-magic against it. Pain tore through his body, white-hot and searing through every cell, seemingly gripping at every organ and trying to crush every bone beneath his skin. It bit and twisted and ripped, leaving Alex bent double on the floor with his arms wrapped around himself, trying to hold the burning pieces of his body together.

Jari jumped down from the desk as Ellabell rushed to his side, asking if she could help, but Alex was in too much pain to speak properly. His jaw felt as if it had fallen away, and his teeth throbbed and stung around a swollen tongue. With whatever resilience he had left, he tried to focus his anti-magic in a last-ditch attempt to control the agony that shredded through every nerve.

Ellabell reached to grab his hand, but he pulled it sharply away.

"Don't… magic…" he gasped, worried about the residual energy hurting her. Her face showed she understood, although her brow creased with concern.

All they could do was watch Alex as he writhed on the stone, battling with his anti-magic and the pain that had taken over his body. Eventually, the pain ebbed just enough for him to regain jurisdiction over his own senses. Feeding his anti-magic through his veins, he felt the savage sting cooling down with an icy relief, though a dull ache remained as he struggled to sit up. Shaking it off, he looked to the bookshelf. The red line had shattered, leaving the books ripe for picking. Alex tried to read some of the titles, but many were in Latin or other ancient languages that he didn't recognize.

"Natalie!" he called, his throat still constricted and thick with discomfort.

Natalie hurried over. "You broke it?" she asked with a hint of excitement.

Alex nodded, feeling the pulse of pain throbbing behind his eyeballs. "Just about," he replied with a grimace. "See if you can figure any of these out," he added, gesturing to the ancient, rare tomes.

Natalie ran her fingers along the dusty spines with

a gentle caress, her lips moving as she silently mouthed the names. As she went along, she picked out a few she thought looked interesting, explaining what they were as she laid them out on the top of the desk. *The Rare Spells of Clarita von Bismarck. The Dark Times. Spells from the Otherworld.* All of them curiously named and meaning very little to anyone but Natalie, whose eyes glowed with that same worrying glee. Alex supposed it couldn't do any harm now. They might as well use the power they had if it meant they might survive.

He watched as Natalie took the books over to the corner of the room and sat with them open in front of her, flicking rapidly through the pages, trying to take in as much information as she could, while she could.

"Anything useful?" asked Alex.

Natalie shook her head. "I am still looking," she sighed bleakly.

Through the thick door and down the hall, Alex could hear the fight raging on, knowing it meant they still had time. He picked up a few books with English names and placed them on the desk to read. Jari took up a few too and went to sit beside Natalie on the floor, turning to her now and again to ask what something meant as they studied side by side.

"Aren't you going to read?" Alex asked Ellabell, who was sitting on the desk, focusing her shielding magic at the door, to strengthen the barrier. He had never known her to give up the opportunity to read.

She shook her head, her brown curls bouncing. "My powers are better used here," she said simply, never taking her blue eyes off the door.

Nodding, Alex turned to where he had left his short stack of tomes. He picked the top one up and flicked it open to the first page, but his eye was caught by the great window that stood before him. The stretching expanse of emerald field leading up to the midnight-blue lake that glittered beyond, on the horizon—the very same lake that held the bodies of thousands of his brethren. He could not tear his eyes away from it, nor could he understand why it was always there. It was the only view of foreign scenery that never seemed to change. Giving up on the book, he walked toward the window and its abhorrent image, pressing his palms against the glass as he neared.

Suddenly, the sound of fighting ceased. There was only the sound of footsteps echoing on the flagstones, growing closer. Dread surged acidly up Alex's throat. Natalie and Jari jumped to their feet, panic flashing across their faces as Ellabell poured more magic from her palms toward the shield rippling across the doorway. Her slender hands were shaking with fear, but she did not let up; her focus was steady.

"What are we going to do?" she whispered with terror as she did her best to bolster the shield.

"We wait. It might not be the Head," Alex lied. It had

to be him. He knew it wasn't Elias walking up to the door. It could only be *him*.

They had run out of time.

Alex ran an anxious hand through his hair. They were looking at him with such hope, and he wasn't about to let them down, but he wasn't sure what he could do. The books hadn't proved all that useful, and there weren't any weapons hanging helpfully from the walls.

The lake caught his eye again. Moving to touch the glass, he wondered grimly if he was about to join his fellow Spellbreakers beneath the glittering surface, buried in a watery grave. There would be no *last* after him.

Uncertainly, he searched within himself for the semi-familiar glow of his essence, coiled up within him. He knew what he had to do, if it came to it. If it would save his friends, he knew he'd risk a piece of his soul.

As he turned to join the other three, something drew him back. Beneath his hand, he felt a peculiar sensation prickling at the skin—the same cold numbness he felt from anything magical.

His head snapped back as he saw, for the first time, the tiny shimmer of a delicately thin red line, barely wider than a strand of hair, lining the outside of one of the window panels. Then the memory of the book on magical travel came flooding back to him once more. Glorious disbelief coursed through Alex's body.

"Come here!" he hissed to the others. "Bring Aamir."

The window was a portal. A still, unmoving passageway that seemed strange, just like the book said. Of course, Alex thought, his mind racing, the view from every other window in the manor changed, except this one. This was the only window that didn't go zipping off to Southeast Asia or the Amazon Rainforest each day—like in the hallways—or have an ever shifting landscape in the distance, as was the case in the library. It was forever looking out on the cemetery of his ancestors, always gazing upon the glittering lake.

The others looked at Alex in confusion, not understanding his sudden excitement.

"Bring him!" he yelled again, this time with more urgency.

They obeyed this time, dragging Aamir's limp body over to the window, Natalie tucking a few books about her person as they rushed over.

Just then, there came a knock at the door.

"Little pigs, little pigs, let me come in," jeered the Head through the wooden door. His voice was newly tinged with malicious amusement.

Alex pressed his fingers to the improbably thin red line and felt the familiar surge of agony pulse through his veins, though he guessed it must have been an old barrier, because it broke apart with a rapidity he had not expected. It fell to pieces with no added nasties, only the usual twist of his nerve endings being shredded with pain. An altogether unpleasant experience, but nothing he couldn't handle. He had been bracing himself for extra defensive measures, but none came.

Knowing there was no time to force the pain away, no matter how viciously it seared through his body, Alex gritted his teeth and soldiered through the agony, tasting blood in his mouth as he bit into his cheek.

With great force, he pushed open the window. The panel swung outward as a cool whip of wind blew in through the gap, soothing the damp perspiration on Alex's face. He peered out and saw, to his relief, that there was only a small drop between the ledge and the ground below. It would sting the ankles a bit, but it wouldn't break anything.

"Jari, you and Aamir will go first," he breathed, with no real time to explain as he bundled Aamir toward the open portal.

"This is wild," Jari whispered, awed, as he clambered up beside Alex and sat on the edge of the windowsill, wrapping his arms around Aamir.

"Ready?" asked Alex.

Jari nodded. "As I'll ever be." He grinned broadly, peering down to see the distance for himself.

"I'll huff and I'll puff!" mocked the Head, rapping more loudly on the dense oak of the door. The sound made Alex's heart pound faster as he gave Aamir and Jari a light shove. They tipped over the edge, disappearing into the darkness below.

"You okay?" called Alex, careful not to raise his voice too loudly, in case the Head heard. From the sarcastic, teasing quality in his mocking tone, Alex guessed the Head had no idea what they were up to in here. He wanted to keep it that way.

"In one piece," came Jari's voice from beneath the window. Alex heard the soft sound of Aamir's body being dragged along the grass, followed by Jari's labored breathing.

"Little pigs, I know you're in there," the Head chuckled.

Alex knew their time was quickly disappearing. It wouldn't take long for the Head to realize something was amiss and come barging through the door, but he needed to think. He needed to figure out a way to cover their tracks.

An idea popped into his head. He didn't like it, which seemed to be a recurring theme, he thought dryly, but he knew it might be the only way to give them a decent head start.

"Natalie, do you think you can close the portal behind us?" he asked with trepidation, hating himself for the question. He knew the dangerous magic involved in opening and closing portals, but it was a risk they had to take. Natalie had been learning rare and complex magic; surely there was something in her arsenal they could use.

Each moment they wasted was peppered with the

menacing sound of the Head's voice, oozing through the door, intent on delivering the message from his nursery rhyme.

She frowned and glanced toward the door. "I know a trick that is not portal magic, that I read in one of the darker arts books, but I think it might possibly work for this," she said, a gleam of excitement in her eyes. "Yes, I think it could."

"Good. Close the portal—or whatever it is you're going to do—as soon as I've jumped, okay?" he instructed hurriedly.

She nodded. "I will do my very best."

"Good luck," he whispered.

Natalie climbed up onto the ledge and jumped gracefully, her feet barely making a sound as she landed on the field below. Alex peered out to make sure she was okay and saw the glimmer of her magic working beneath her hands. The golden streams of energy were tinged with a much brighter pink and shot through with bolts of sapphire blue. Seeing them, he knew whatever she was conjuring came from a much darker place than he was happy with, but it was too late now; he needed her dark magic, whether he wanted to admit it or not.

Hastily, he hurried over to where Ellabell still sat, perched on the edge of the desk, focusing on the door. Golden light still flowed elegantly from her hands.

"Ellabell, you have to stop," he said, but she shook

her head, her eyes glittering with defiance and frightened tears.

Slowly, he placed his hands over hers and stemmed the current of her power, turning it into soft flurries of snow. It burned his palms a little, but it snapped her out of her intent trance.

"Ellabell, we have to go," he whispered, still holding her hands in his.

She nodded, terror flaring in her eyes as another loud knock echoed through the room. Beneath his hands, her fingers trembled.

Making sure she didn't turn to glance back at the door, Alex led her over to the window and helped her up onto the ledge. With a graceful leap, she followed the others out and down onto the field below. It was only Alex left now.

As he began to climb up onto the ledge, a thud of magic jarred against the door, making the chairs and diagonal bookshelf shudder violently. Alex knew with a rush of panic that he had mere seconds. Ellabell's residual shield would hold, but not for very long.

Hearing another blast, followed instantly by the sound of splintering wood, Alex stepped onto the windowsill.

Natalie was below him, her eyes closed tight in concentration. The others stood far away from her, and Alex could see why. A vortex whirled wildly in front of Natalie, swirling with a myriad of colors, from the brightest cyan to the deepest purple and all the colors in between. In the very center of it was a stationary ball of energy, glowing with a dark pink pulse that seemed to suck in all the light around it. Shadows poured into the radiance, pulled with magnetic force.

Alex glanced back to see a crack ripping through the surface of the doorway. He turned and jumped, dropping down onto the grass beside Natalie as the window closed behind him. A loud blast erupted from within the manor, shaking the earth beneath him.

"Now," he whispered.

Natalie gave a barely discernible nod as she lifted the vortex up toward the window, the expanse of it growing wider, sucking in more shadows and more light as it rose up. Everything it touched was drawn into the glowing center, and it seemed the portal was no different.

Another explosion blasted through the earth as Alex caught sight of a shadow rushing toward the window. Hands seemed to fumble at the catch, before swinging it open. At that moment, Natalie surged the vortex forward with greater ferocity, catching the figure in the swirling magic. A blood-curdling scream pierced the air as the grasping magic reached for the strong power at the Head's very core. He pulled away with a furious roar, stepping back from the window, though Alex was convinced he could see the burning glow of red eyes beneath the hood.

Alex looked anxiously at Natalie, his heart thundering. Although the portal resembled an ordinary window to the untrained eye, Natalie's magic quickly seemed to sense there was something magical about it, and stretched toward it hungrily. Before the Head could come at them again, the pulsing epicenter floated from the middle of the vortex and burned with blinding ferocity against the dim light coming from the office above, sucking a dense stream of a dark gray substance from the center of the window. The vortex pulsated again, ablaze with opalescent fire as it engulfed the very last of the dark mist, pulling the portal forcefully from its stronghold and swallowing it whole, until the window was no more. In its place were dew-soaked fields rolling away into the distance; the manor wall and window were gone from sight, moved away under Natalie's skillful hands.

Now that the vortex had folded in on itself, disappearing in a silent swell of energy, Alex wondered if the window would still look out on the lake, or if the Head would see something else now.

He was staring up at the sky where the window had been when Natalie crumpled before him. Her legs gave way beneath her, but Alex reached out quickly, catching her just in time.

"Natalie, talk to me. Are you okay?" he asked, shaking her gently as he held her.

Her face was pale and her lips were colorless. She looked dead.

Alex shook her more vigorously. "No..." he begged.

"Natalie. Natalie, wake up!"

She whimpered quietly, her eyes blinking open with a painful slowness. Her face and her clothes were drenched in sweat, and her black hair clung to her skin in damp tendrils. Her mouth moved slowly, as if she wanted to say something.

"Are you okay?" asked Alex gently, as the others gathered around Natalie's slumped form.

She nodded slightly. "It… was very… powerful… magic," she whispered as a small smile appeared on her cracked, bloodless lips.

"You took the portal away." Alex was impressed and infuriated with his dear friend, in all her recklessness. She had no doubt saved the day, but Alex wasn't sure at what cost.

She shook her head slowly. "I… moved it," she breathed, the smile breaking into a broader grin.

"Promise me you didn't do something stupid," Alex said, his voice thick with emotion. He knew he would not be able to forgive himself if she had used a piece of her soul to help them escape.

She laughed quietly. "Not… life magic… just big… magic."

"Do you promise me?"

She nodded, wincing slightly. "I… promise."

"I think we should get out of here. Wherever *here* is," said Jari, saying exactly what Alex was thinking. Aamir, still unconscious, was slumped against the blond-haired boy.

"You took the words right out of my mouth," said Alex as he looped Natalie's arm around his neck, pain still surging through his body like an all-over stitch.

Ellabell stepped toward Aamir's dangling arm and pulled it around her shoulders, propping him up between herself and Jari.

"Let's go," said Alex, with hesitant relief, as the five of them took off across the pitch-black field, lit only by the dim glow of distant stars.

It was foolish, Alex knew, to hope they had found a portal leading to the normal world. All around them, the air buzzed with magic. They were no longer at Spellshadow Manor, but they had escaped to somewhere utterly foreign to them.

They looked only toward the glitter of the lake ahead as the grass crunched underfoot. The thin crescent of a selfish moon was out, offering little in the way of visibility, giving no indication of what could be lurking in the dark, waiting for them. It didn't matter. It wasn't important that they could see, just as long as their legs could run. That was all Alex was certain of. They had to run—only time would tell how much of a head start they had.

Though what they were running into, Alex wasn't sure.

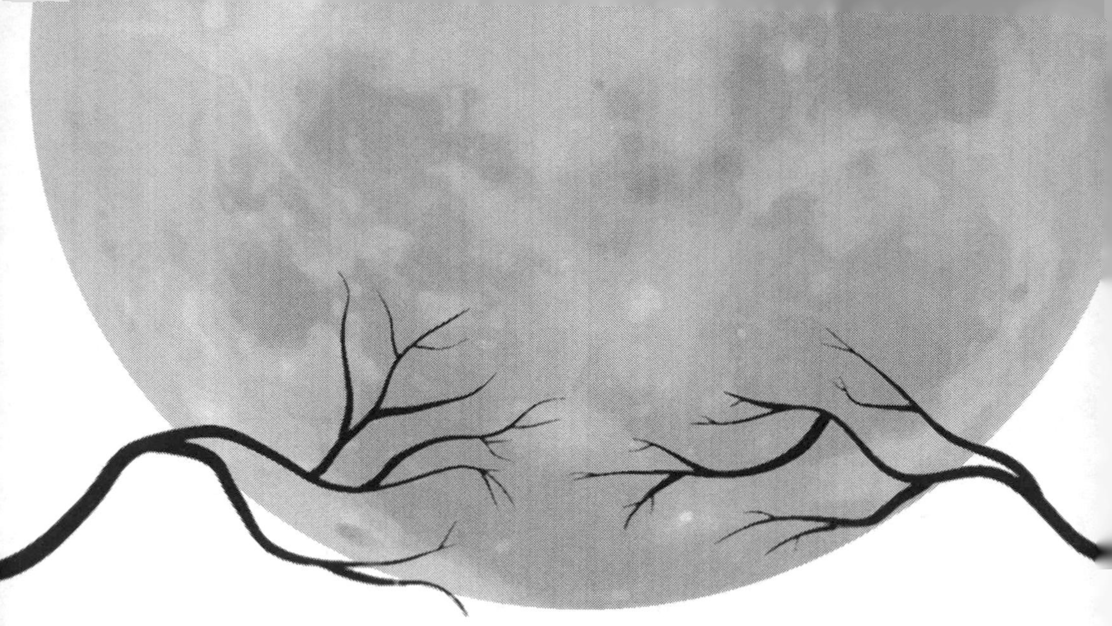

EPILOGUE

Elias slunk furtively from shadow to shadow, battered but undefeated, licking his wounds with the lashing tongue of his shadow-cat form. He pouted with remorse, knowing he could have fought for longer, but the Head had almost clasped his skeletal fingers around the dull red glow of his essence once more, reaching straight into the starry abyss of his chest. And he hadn't been about to let that happen again, not after he had just gained it back. Running away would seem cowardly to others, but Elias wasn't bothered by others. He had the glowing particle back, and it burned inside him, though he couldn't feel its warmth.

He slithered in the darkness, peering down upon the grim aftermath of the uprising, looking over the wreckage, sliding from corridor to corridor to seek out the remaining students, his curiosity piqued. He was amused by the higgledy-piggledy state of the hallways, left in a jumbled mess by one of Gaze's powerful spells.

Very clever, he thought, though it didn't much affect him. He could still go where he pleased. It just took a bit longer.

Eventually, he found the rest of the survivors huddled in the mess hall, as safe as they could be beneath the protection of Professor Gaze. He had always liked Gaze. It was sad to see her so old and still here, all that power wasted.

He purred with amusement as a weary Professor Lintz entered the room, his large figure covered in deep lacerations from the magical beating he had taken at the Head's hands. He was limping slightly, too, but he was, surprisingly, alive. Elias wasn't sure how happy he was about this turn of events. Though Lintz had never given him reason to dislike him, Elias had found him guilty by association. A sniveling weasel by association. Still, he couldn't help feeling a touch impressed by the sight of the old codger still standing.

He watched a while longer as Gaze moved from student to student, trying to fix up as many as she could with the limited tools she had. It bored him. He smiled sardonically, stretching his shadowed mouth across starry teeth as he tried to force an insincere pang of sorrow for the students—they had simply jumped out of the frying pan and into the fire.

Stretching languidly, he slipped down the empty, scorched corridors and passed curiously over the library. Unmoving figures lay curled up on the floor and sprawled among the stacks, glassy eyes staring upward into nothingness. Energy tickled at the edges of his shadowy form as his sensitivity felt the low, pulsating thrum of the coiled-up mass of wasted essence, trickling from the dead students, gathering together in one sad pool before it faded into the ground, with nowhere else to go but be reabsorbed by the earth beneath. Unusable. Elias smirked, even amid such vile tragedy.

At least this way, Elias thought smugly, *the Head can't have it.*

Thinking bitterly of the Head, his wounds still smarting, he swept effortlessly back through the hallways and paused for a moment in the Head's office. He laughed as he saw that the door had been blown off entirely and the Head was still inside, launching things around the room in a fit of fury, his voice rising to a howling scream of rage. It felt delicious to Elias, to watch the Head so riled up.

The Head turned, as if sensing Elias's mocking presence.

"This is all *your* fault, Elias! You let him get away! I *needed* him, Elias! I would not have killed him, and yet you stood in my way! *You* are responsible for what is going to come, you—"

Elias didn't stay to hear the rest, making a swift exit as a train of expletives followed him. The words made their mark on Elias, however, as he glided over the desolate grounds.

Night had drawn in, giving him the freedom of the manor as a whole, not batted back by petty rays of sunlight. He manifested himself as a man on the hillside overlooking the *Fields of Sorrow*, watching over the vast expanse with its smoking heart and still-scorched earth. He grinned coldly, teeth flashing, as he convinced himself he could already feel the tremors of something beneath the earth, rising up.

What will happen now? he wondered gleefully.

"You can't keep the evil at bay forever. A void must be filled," he whispered to the emptiness, closing his eyes in delight at the prospect of its coming.

The only wrench in Elias's plan was that the Head was still alive. He had been relying on Alex to surprise him, but had been left disappointed. Elias was certain the notebook he had given to Alex contained some mention about death magic, and yet Alex hadn't delivered the goods. All that talk of silver light and shining heroes, and Alex still hadn't called on a little death magic.

Elias felt dissatisfied, but blamed himself; he knew he had not given Alex the chance to play the martyr. He knew he had let the echo of his human feelings get the better of him. He had felt anger and gotten carried away, and now he wasn't sure what he was supposed to do. With the stolen part of his essence back within his possession, he supposed he could go after the escapees if he wanted, since he was no longer tied entirely to the manor. He could see what else he could get them to do. But they had already done so much.

Alex had proven an excellent pawn, if a bit slower than Elias had hoped. He would think about it—after all, he had plenty of time. Where they had gone, they wouldn't find much joy, Elias thought smugly as he stretched out his shadowy limbs. The magical world frowned upon fugitives.

In the meantime, he decided, he would revel in the Head's misery and the glimmer of hope for what he wished to come crashing down around the manor.

No, not just the manor. His plans were far bigger than that.

A comeuppance was long overdue, and Elias had been *so* patient.

Dear Reader,

Thank you for continuing Alex's journey with me!

I'm excited to let you know that Book 3 of the series, **The Chain**, releases **June 3rd, 2017**.

Please visit: www.bellaforrest.net for details.

Until next time,

Bella x

ALSO BY BELLA FORREST

THE SECRET OF SPELLSHADOW MANOR

The Secret of Spellshadow Manor (Book 1)

The Breaker (Book 2)

The Chain (Book 3)

THE GENDER GAME

The Gender Game (Book 1)

The Gender Secret (Book 2)

The Gender Lie (Book 3)

The Gender War (Book 4)

The Gender Fall (Book 5)

The Gender Plan (Book 6)

The Gender End (Book 7) > Final book in series, release date TBC.

A SHADE OF VAMPIRE SERIES

Series 1: Derek & Sofia's story

A Shade of Vampire (Book 1)

A Shade of Blood (Book 2)

A Castle of Sand (Book 3)

A Shadow of Light (Book 4)

A Blaze of Sun (Book 5)

A Gate of Night (Book 6)

A Break of Day (Book 7)

Series 2: Rose & Caleb's story

A Shade of Novak (Book 8)

A Bond of Blood (Book 9)

A Spell of Time (Book 10)

A Chase of Prey (Book 11)

A Shade of Doubt (Book 12)

A Turn of Tides (Book 13)

A Dawn of Strength (Book 14)

A Fall of Secrets (Book 15)

An End of Night (Book 16)

Series 3: The Shade continues with a new hero…

A Wind of Change (Book 17)

A Trail of Echoes (Book 18)

A Soldier of Shadows (Book 19)

A Hero of Realms (Book 20)

A Vial of Life (Book 21)

A Fork of Paths (Book 22)

A Flight of Souls (Book 23)

A Bridge of Stars (Book 24)

Series 4: A Clan of Novaks

A Clan of Novaks (Book 25)

A World of New (Book 26)

A Web of Lies (Book 27)

A Touch of Truth (Book 28)

An Hour of Need (Book 29)

A Game of Risk (Book 30)

A Twist of Fates (Book 31)

A Day of Glory (Book 32)

Series 5: A Dawn of Guardians

A Dawn of Guardians (Book 33)

A Sword of Chance (Book 34)

A Race of Trials (Book 35)

A King of Shadow (Book 36)

An Empire of Stones (Book 37)

A Power of Old (Book 38)

A Rip of Realms (Book 39)

A Throne of Fire (Book 40)

A Tide of War (Book 41)

Series 6: A Gift of Three

A Gift of Three (Book 42)

A House of Mysteries (Book 43)

A Tangle of Hearts (Book 44)

A SHADE OF DRAGON TRILOGY

A Shade of Dragon 1

A Shade of Dragon 2

A Shade of Dragon 3

A SHADE OF KIEV TRILOGY

A Shade of Kiev 1

A Shade of Kiev 2

A Shade of Kiev 3

DETECTIVE ERIN BOND (Adult thriller/mystery)

Lights, Camera, Gone

Write, Edit, Kill

BEAUTIFUL MONSTER DUOLOGY

Beautiful Monster 1

Beautiful Monster 2

For an updated list of Bella's books, please visit her website: www.bellaforrest.net

Join Bella's VIP email list and she'll personally send you an email reminder as soon as her next book is out: www.morebellaforrest.com

Made in the USA
San Bernardino, CA
28 April 2017